How Good Are Your Love Instincts?

Your husband tells you he needs to find closure with the high school sweetheart who dumped him. Your best option is:

a) Seduce him and make him forget all about her
b) Ask him to define "closure"
c) Send him to a psychiatrist
d) Help him search the Internet for her

You make the colossal mistake of choosing answer D on the previous question, and your husband leaves you for his high school sweetheart. You should:

a) Get a makeover
b) Follow your almost ex-husband to his new town (to show him what he threw away when he left you)
c) Romance the local serial killer (because you really don't believe he's a serial killer even though he does bring home lots of large plastic containers and bury wrapped bundles in his backyard)
d) All of the above

Bobbie's final answer was definitely D—she was in big trouble!

Dear Reader,

I believe the best thing about writing is getting to ask the "what if" question. Possibilities abound, and one of those possibilities gave birth to *Sex and the Serial Killer*. What if you thought you were doing everything right in your marriage and suddenly found that you'd done everything absolutely wrong? That "what if" begins Bobbie Jones's journey. When her husband, Warren, calls from amidst the rumpled sheets of his lover's bed to ask for a divorce, Bobbie's life turns upside down and inside out. She quits her job, gets a new haircut and a new look, then follows Warren to Cottonmouth, California, where she'll show him what a big mistake he's made. And she'll flaunt a new man in his face. Sexy as the devil himself, Nick Angel is the perfect candidate for flaunting. Except that everyone in Cottonmouth thinks Nick's a serial killer.

Bobbie will touch the sky and hit rock bottom before she finally finds everything she's looking for in Cottonmouth. I had a wonderful time exploring Bobbie's "what if." She made me laugh and made me cry, as did the people she met on her journey.

Enjoy!

Jennifer Skullestad

SEX
and the
SERIAL
KILLER

Jennifer Skully

HQN™

ISBN 0-373-77027-8

SEX AND THE SERIAL KILLER

Copyright © 2005 by Jennifer Skullestad

This edition published by arrangement with Harlequin Books S.A.

® and TM are trademarks of the publisher. Trademarks indicated with ® are registered in the United States Patent and Trademark Office, the Canadian Trade Marks Office and in other countries.

www.HQNBooks.com

Printed in U.S.A.

To my husband, Ole
For always believing in me

Acknowledgments

A writer doesn't work in a vacuum.
I'd like to thank all the people who've been there
for me (which would be a book in itself),
with special mention to:

My first critique group,
who started me on my way and have been there
ever since—Pamela Britton, Cherry Adair,
Susan Plunkett and Rose Lerma, who discovered
the meaning of "moving fast."

Moni Draper and Cheryl Clark, my buds in the
RWA Kiss of Death Chapter, for all their input.

Jenn Cummings for loving the sprinkle
in Mavis's hair, and Kathy Coatney for pushing me
on the daily page count.

The Supergirls, Liz Maverick, Cathy Yardley
and Maragold, for all their wonderful advice.

My agent, Lucienne Diver,
and my editor, Ann Leslie Tuttle.
Thank you both for everything!
And my mom, who has read everything I've ever
written and always said she loved it no matter what.
Thanks, Mom!

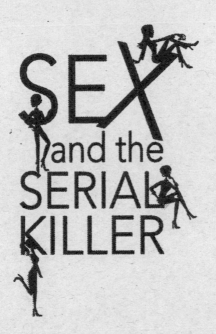

PROLOGUE

A MIXTURE OF RED DYE and sweat trickled down her forehead. It hovered on her eyebrows, poised to drizzle into her eyes. Soon to be blinded by runaway hair products, Roberta Jones Spivey could force nothing more than a mousy squeak from her throat. She was about to go deaf, too, from the hair dryer blasting her eardrums, and still she couldn't open her mouth wide enough to shriek. Any moment now her hair would spontaneously combust. They'd smell the smoke first, then the aroma of singed hair, but by the time any of the umpteen stylists scurrying about the Head Hunter's main salon came to her rescue, she'd be bald. If not charred to a briquette.

Help me before my demise becomes a fifteen-second slot on a tabloid show. Now was not the time for a panic attack.

Drip, drip, drip, from her eyebrows to her eyelashes. In a last-ditch effort to save herself, she squeezed her eyes shut. Burning tears leaked out to mingle with the caustic fluids. She clamped on to the chair's arms—a death grip—terrified that if she touched the stuff, she'd end up rubbing her flesh off, too.

Someone. Please. Notice me.

The bowl of the dryer was suddenly jerked up, cool air from the overhead fans wafting across her scalp.

"Bobbie, honey, why didn't you tell me the color was running?" Mimi Dodd was the only person who'd ever called her Bobbie.

Roberta dragged in a breath of air to explain, then collapsed in a spasm of coughing as the stench of chemicals, dyes, perm solution and her own terrified sweat swooped down into her throat.

Mimi's shoes click-clacked away, then back again. "Here, drink this."

Water had never tasted so good. All Roberta had wanted was a new look. Okay, so she needed a new life, too. Instead, she'd almost died, and her heart was still pounding like the pony express. She handed the empty paper cup back to Mimi, who crumpled it, executed a perfect free throw into the trash can, then tugged at a few squishy locks on Roberta's head and pronounced, "You're cooked."

Roberta was cooked all right. Roasted, basted, filleted, flambéed. And limp as a wet noodle to boot. Residual quivers made her knees wobble as she tried to stand up.

Mimi put a hand beneath her elbow. "Bobbie, honey, you okay?"

"I'm fine." Well, except that Warren had walked out on her three weeks, six days and seven hours ago. On April eighteenth. Three days after tax day. Two days after he'd left for his little mission up north. In Cottonmouth, California. He'd dumped her with nothing more than a phone call telling her he wasn't coming back. Ever.

Roberta blew out a breath. "Yeah, Mimi, I'm just fine."

"Good, for a minute there under the dryer you looked

a little panicky." Mimi patted her arm and led her to the rinse bowl.

"I just didn't want to bother you while you were busy." Her, panic? Just because her husband of fifteen years had left her for his long-lost, recently located-through-the-Internet high school sweetheart? The love of his life. The teenage bimbo who'd broken his heart and then disappeared off the face of the earth—at least left the San Francisco Bay area for parts unknown. Cookie. What kind of name was that, anyway? It made Roberta think of some hairy blue monster on a kids' morning show. Warren was bound to see he'd made a mistake.

Okay, so she'd made a mistake, too, by actually helping him search the Net. And mailing the hundreds of letters—because he was nervous about calling all those women looking for the right one. And letting him drive to Cottonmouth all alone that fateful weekend. She'd only wanted to help him solve his problem. Because his problem was her problem.

Mimi pushed her head back into the bowl and began rinsing with warm water. Roberta closed her eyes. The water turned off, the soothing scent of citrus conditioner replaced the stinging dye in her nostrils, and gentle fingers massaged her scalp.

"Bobbie, honey, you're tense. Is work getting to you?"

"No, it's fine." Except for those dreaded whispers of "restatement" trickling out of the audit committee, and her boss, Mr. Winkleman's, finger pointing firmly in *her* direction, as director of accounting. But she wasn't worried; she knew every balance, every detail, inside and out. Her numbers were solid.

She gave herself up to the finger pads working her scalp, relaxing the little knots at the base of her skull. Her breathing relaxed, the whir of her mind's gears slowed. Ahh.

"So, where's your husband taking you for your birthday?"

Roberta's eyes flew open, and all that lovely mellowness fled through the soles of her low-heeled pumps.

"He's picked out this new restaurant he heard about on Nob Hill." The lie just sort of slipped out. Roberta believed in little white lies to keep everyone comfortable. Except that there wasn't anything comfortable about turning forty. Or about being dumped. What was next? Menopause. Old age. Death. "It's very exclusive, very dressy and very San Francisco, he says."

She wouldn't have had a thing to wear because she'd lost ten pounds since Warren left. But if Warren was taking her out for her birthday, then she wouldn't have lost the ten pounds because he wouldn't have left, and then she would have had something to wear. Her temples throbbed. Everything was so confusing.

"You've really got yourself a prince there."

Yeah, a prince. She just hadn't realized that princes needed Prozac. Or that a good psychiatrist cost upward of two hundred dollars an hour—excuse me, fifty minutes—just to say, "Mrs. Spivey, you must realize that antidepressants will have a negative impact on your husband's sex drive."

He *had* no sex drive. That's why he went to a doctor to begin with. Well, there was that state of depression he'd been in for five years or so.

Tears suddenly pricked the corners of her eyes. "Yes, Warren's a wonderful man."

At least she'd thought so. But he'd gone off the drugs for the Cookie Monster, for God's sake. And the woman was married. Another dumpee in the making. Maybe Roberta should call *Mr.* Cookie Monster, to commiserate.

Maybe she should sue Warren's psychiatrist for putting the idea of finding "closure" with his high school sweetheart into his mind in the first place. Instead, she'd dyed her brown hair red.

"Maybe I need a new haircut, too."

Easing her to a sitting position, Mimi wrapped a white towel around Roberta's head and squeezed the water from her hair.

"Something bouncy and short?"

Her head enshrouded in terry cloth, Roberta nodded.

"Thank God, Bobbie. I've been telling you your hair is naturally curly, the length and weight just pulls it all out."

Mimi pulled Roberta to her feet and guided her to a chair. The towel came off. What she'd thought would be red was merely a darker brown. Richer maybe, but still brown.

"Don't pout. It'll look red when it dries. Now, how short shall we go?" Mimi fluffed the drying strands.

Roberta pointed to her shoulders.

Mimi grimaced in the mirror. "That'll drag your face down. As we get older, we need to make sure our faces don't drag."

Who was this we? Mimi was a pert, perpetual-twenty-nine-year-old with lively black hair, wood-nymph brown eyes and unlined skin. Without opening her mouth, Roberta skimmed the bottom of her ears with shaky fingers.

Mimi beamed. "Perfect."

And then she started snipping, clipping, drying and poofing. Roberta squeezed her eyes shut amidst the cacophony of voices, laughter, running water and blow-dryers.

"You can open them now."

A scintilla of the hysteria she'd felt under the dryer tingled along Roberta's nerve endings. Then she looked in the mirror.

"Oh, my."

Behind her, Mimi bounced with expectation. "Whad'ya think?"

Roberta didn't recognize the face framed in silky red hair just brushing the tips of her ears, hugging her nape, gently curling across her forehead. Her hazel eyes looked greener, lush, like new spring grass. Her lips looked fuller. And the tired lines pulling at her mouth seemed to have vanished.

"It makes you look like you've lost weight. I think you need to buy a new outfit to celebrate."

The woman in the mirror needed a whole new wardrobe. Business suits and tailored blouses just wouldn't go with that face. That face needed vibrant colors and short skirts. Four-inch spike heels.

The hand in the mirror touched the full lips. Lipstick. Something overstated. "Maybe I need some new makeup, too, Mimi."

"I've got just the thing." Mimi disappeared from the mirror, click-clacking across the linoleum.

Yes, she needed new makeup. Because fixing your whole life couldn't be accomplished simply by changing your hairstyle.

No, that new hair needed new makeup, new clothes,

new shoes. And a new name. Like Bobbie. Bobbie
Jones. Without the Spivey, which had always sort of
made her think of the word spineless. Spineless Spivey.
Warren? Or herself?

And director of accounting would never do for Bobbie Jones. Bobbie needed something...exciting. A job
where she'd meet new people every day. Doing something she'd shine at. Where she couldn't help but be noticed.

Where there were no Mr. Winklemans pointing their
fingers and saying, "She did it. Fire her."

God, could she really do it? Could she really quit, try
on another career like a new outfit?

What on earth was standing in her way? There was
no Warren. And there was money in the bank to tide her
over until she found just the right job.

Could she? Would she? She stared at the familiar-
yet-changed woman in the mirror. That woman could
do anything she set her mind to. That woman would find
a new goal in life.

Roberta sat straighter, squared her shoulders, put a
hand to the brand-new curls that overflowed the top of
her head. Bobbie Jones wouldn't have to worry about
negative impacts on a man's sex drive. Bobbie Jones
would have her pick.

Roberta Jones Spivey could stick with a job she
hated and grovel at the feet of the Winklemans of the
world. Roberta Jones Spivey could have panic attacks under a hair dryer because she'd decided to
change the color of her hair. Bobbie Jones had better
things to do. Important things to do. One all-important thing.

Bobbie Jones was going to Cottonmouth to show

Warren what he'd thrown away when he'd driven off into the sunset to find the Cookie Monster.

Oh, yeah, and one more really important thing. Bobbie would have sex for the first time in...much too long.

CHAPTER ONE

BOBBIE JONES—she'd tossed out Roberta along with her job, her tailored suits and her frilly blouses—tapped her brilliant crimson lip with the tip of a matching manicured nail. A new woman with a new attitude. And no ugly, painful thoughts.

"I must have that cottage." *No, no, we can't possibly do this.* Bobbie quashed another annoying little Roberta whine. She was getting so much better at doing it, since that day in the salon, a little less than a month ago, when she'd decided every page of her life story needed revising.

Top-selling real estate agent and self-proclaimed Cottonmouth maven Patsy Bell Sapp opened her mouth so wide, the wrinkles marring her tanned face vanished. Almost. "You don't want *that*."

Bobbie smiled. "Yes. I do." *No, we don't.* Buzz off, Roberta.

The house, little more than a cube tucked into a postage-stamp lot, was the antithesis of her former pristine residence on a stately San Francisco street. Warren had chosen the property over having children, a plan she'd, no, *Roberta* had gone along with because being a parent was too awesome a responsibility.

"But the serial killer lives right across the street."

Patsy hacked out a cough, her penciled-in eyebrows disappearing into the fringe of her bouffant hairdo. With a vigorous shake of her head, multiple shades of gray sparkled in the sunlight.

"Excuse me?" Was the woman serious? Probably not. If she was, why would she even bring Bobbie by this rental, the fourth they'd visited?

Still looking at her, Patsy pointed at the shaded two-story house across the street. "He's a serial killer," she mouthed.

The title had a ring to it, even if it was most likely a town joke. Serial killer. Didn't that fit her mood to a T? *Her* mood, not Roberta's. She itched with a mixture of danger, disbelief and anticipation. Heavy on the disbelief part. But still, he must be a real bad-boy type to fuel such rumors. Back home in the Head Hunter's salon, she'd sworn to herself she was going to have sex with someone. And sex with an alleged serial killer sounded risky. Edgy. Exciting.

Just the kind of thing a Bobbie Jones, not a Roberta Spivey, would do. It would tweak Warren's nose right out of joint. And that's what this whole excursion to Cottonmouth was about, right?

Her luck, the man would turn out to be a toilet paper salesman originally from Boise.

She turned back to the rental, her mind made up. "I'll take this house. I want to move in as soon as possible." Roberta muttered a few more whiny rebuttals, but Bobbie ignored her.

Patsy sputtered, "But you haven't even seen the inside yet."

"The gargoyles do it for me." Six snarling, winged creatures lined the front walk. Warren hated yard statues.

A porch swing drifted idly in the slight breeze. The cottage came fully furnished, Patsy had told her, all of it probably shabby lived-in, not shabby chic, but that wouldn't matter. Her brand-new Pippin-apple-green VW, for which she'd traded Warren's status-symbol BMW 740I, blended perfectly with the riot of multicolored flowers overrunning the small lot. Warren would hate the quaintness of it. A tiny smile quirked the corner of her mouth. She deserved this house.

Best of all, according to Patsy, danger and excitement lurked right across the street. Yeah, right. A real serial killer would be behind bars. Wouldn't he?

"What's his name?"

"Who?"

Bobbie tugged at the belt loops of her tight new jeans, pushing the waistband lower on her hips. "The serial killer."

Patsy didn't answer immediately. The sounds of splashing and children's laughter wafted over the rooftops. Someone started a lawn mower a few doors down. Sunday afternoons didn't sound like this in the city. They didn't smell like this, either, the air heavy with the scent of freshly cut grass.

And Patsy's cigarette. She stamped it out in the gravel drive. "His name is Nick."

"Nick what?"

"Nick Angel." Patsy grimaced, adding a few more wrinkles above her lip.

Great name. A lot better than Warren Spineless Spivey.

Patsy stepped closer, smoothing her knee-length, A-line skirt and tottering on her chunky high heels. Obviously seeing the excitement in Bobbie's eyes, she said, "You don't understand." Her voice lowered a note. "It's not idle gossip. Don't let his good looks fool you. He's a bad apple. We know he kills animals."

Well, that could sort of creep people out. Bobbie reached up to brush the hair back off her shoulders, then stopped midmove. She'd forgotten she'd had it cut. Warren hated short hair.

"You mean he likes to hunt?" Maybe Cottonmouth residents didn't approve of hunters.

"No," Patsy said. "I mean, he buries dead animals around his yard. No one ever catches him actually killing them. But…we know."

Bobbie shivered as if a cloud had passed over the sun. Except there wasn't a cloud to be seen. "Dead animals in your yard doesn't make you a serial killer. Maybe they died a natural death, and he's just giving them a Christian burial."

Patsy's eyes went wide, her mouth made a perfect *O* as if Bobbie had said something blasphemous.

"What I mean is, there could be other explanations," Bobbie amended.

Patsy leaned close, obviously not willing to consider any other explanation. "There are the paintings, too."

"What paintings?"

"We're sure he sells them for god-awful amounts." Her voice dropped to a whisper. "He paints like John Wayne Gacy."

John Wayne Gacy? "Sorry, but who's that?"

Patsy rolled her eyes. "He killed all those boys, oh, I forget exactly when, the seventies, I think, and buried them under his house. They executed him. But his clown paintings go for thousands now."

Clowns? "I've never read anywhere that painting

clowns was a symptom of being a serial killer." Or even an animal killer.

"It's all those things together, dear. And the worst is…" She leaned in to whisper words Bobbie could barely make out, her smoke-laden breath hot and sour in Bobbie's nostrils.

Bobbie clapped a hand to her mouth. "You mean he's a porn star?"

Patsy's eyes darted to different spots of the yard as if to make sure the gargoyles couldn't hear. "Not anymore. He's too old."

Wasn't it the women who got too old for those kind of movies, or rather too old for the men who watched them? "How old *is* he?"

"Thirty-eight, I think."

Two years younger than she was. That wasn't too bad. They said a woman's sexual peak was later than a man's. "I'm still not sure the evidence means he's a…" She allowed her voice to trail off meaningfully.

"He was a troublemaker in high school, always getting into one scrape after another. I'm surprised they never put him in juvenile hall. Maybe if they had…"

"Boy, Patsy, you've done a lot of research on your serial killer." Bobbie wondered for a minute if she'd gone too far with her skepticism.

But Patsy didn't seem to mind. The woman actually batted her had-to-be-fake eyelashes. "He's not *my* serial killer. But I've lived in Cottonmouth all my life. I knew his dear departed parents." She put a hand over her heart. "Goodness, the trials and tribulations they had to endure with that boy, racing around the county in that monstrous orange car of his, trying to corrupt his friends." Her brows vanished once more beneath her shellacked bangs. "The town had to lock up their daughters. And that poor Mary Alice Turner…" Patsy's words trailed off, her eyes suddenly misty.

"Mary Alice Turner?" Bobbie prompted.

Patsy sniffed. "It's just too terrible to talk about."

A murder victim? No. She really didn't believe this serial killer stuff. Bobbie wanted to hear that story, but, in deference to the moisture in Patsy's eyes, she decided to leave it for another time.

"So, he's lived here all his life?" she asked instead.

"Except for the twenty years he was away making those…" Patsy's lips pursed, and her eyes squinted. "Those *movies*." She rummaged in her immense handbag for her cigarette case. "The Angels passed away just over a year ago, car accident, and when does he come back to town?" She jabbed a now-lit cigarette at the house across the street.

Bobbie surreptitiously waved away the smoke. "Right after they died?" she ventured.

"Vulture," Patsy spat through a smoke plume. And that seemed to be the worst sin of all.

They turned to stare at the house in silence. A child rode his bike to the edge of the property, stopped, gaped, then turned around and furiously pedaled away.

The hot June sun beat down on the street and the homes lining it, but the serial killer's faded-blue house stood in the shadows of its tall surrounding oaks. A porch, dim beneath an overhang, ran the length of its front and disappeared around either side. Weeds had invaded the lawn still covered with a blanket of last fall's leaves. Dormer windows accented an attic room. She thought of Norman Bates in *Psycho*. And shuddered.

Bobbie shifted from one foot to the other. And Roberta, well, Roberta was shrieking at the top of her lungs, but Bobbie steadfastly refused to listen. Of course, Patsy was making all this stuff up. Wasn't she?

Dead animals in your yard, clown paintings and a porn-star reputation didn't necessarily translate to killing human beings for kicks. *Yes, it does,* Roberta insisted.

Shut up, you wimpy woman. She decided right then and there this was the *last* she'd hear from Roberta. She wouldn't be Roberta anymore. She *couldn't* be. That old life was over. Forever. No matter how much her old Roberta self sniveled about it.

But Bobbie did have to sort Patsy's rumors from fact here. "If he's a serial killer, why hasn't he been arrested?"

"It's not for lack of trying. The sheriff says there's no evidence."

"How about some dead bodies, other than animal carcasses?"

Patsy looked from the house back to Bobbie. "We think he does *those* dirty deeds out of town." The dirty deeds presumably being the real serial-killer stuff. "At least for now," Patsy added with portent.

Something, a curtain maybe, flickered in the right dormer window. Bobbie's heart fluttered. A breeze blew across her bare midriff. She tugged her shirt down.

Porn star. Painter of god-awfully expensive clown art. Grave digger of animals. High school troublemaker. She didn't really believe Patsy's melodrama, except maybe that last part.

But she was willing to risk the odds that the man actually was a serial killer in her quest for Warren's attention.

GAZING OUT THE UPPER WINDOW of his parents' home, Nick Angel smeared charcoal from his fingers onto his once-white T-shirt.

Patsy Sapp was attempting to make another convert in her war against the infidel serial killer. Actually, it was Eugenia Meade's war. Patsy was just a private. Not that their opinions irked him. Their reasons were legitimate. So screw it.

As for the woman with Patsy—now, she was a different matter. Screwing her wasn't a bad idea at all. Tight jeans displayed a slender set of thighs. A short top revealed a bit of tasty bare flesh. The total package was not the normal Cottonmouth fare. Another time, another place, he'd consider sketching her, just like this, from afar. Wearing a tiny leather thong and snake-tooth amulet hanging between her plentiful breasts.

He shook off the tantalizing image.

Another potential tenant for Mrs. Porter's place? Probably. Damn, he missed seeing the old lady putter in her garden, tending her bright flowers. Maybe he should plant a few in his own yard. Christ, his mother would roll over in her grave if she could see the weeds infesting her untended beds. He was a real prick for letting them get that way. Maybe if he wasn't so busy digging holes down there... Something caught his eye.

A dark shape crushed the weeds. A cat? Something small and furry, anyway. And mangled. Shit. He'd have to perform another burial rite. Neighborhood kids had been throwing roadkill in his front yard for months now. Why they'd started doing it, he didn't have a clue. Why they kept it up, that was easy. He was The Serial Killer, after all, and running up to his front window in the dark of night gave them a thrill. Teenagers thrived on danger and risk. He knew that better than most. He could have called Animal Control to clean up the mess, but he wasn't sure they'd come. Or that he wanted them to.

He'd bury the animal tomorrow. Today he needed to get back to the painting. His newest creation called to him like a siren; he couldn't rest until he'd brought her fully to life on the canvas.

THE MOVE INTO THE COTTAGE on Garden Street had taken the whole of Sunday evening. Once Patsy had accepted Bobbie's decision, she executed the paperwork and handed over the keys with miraculous speed. Bobbie considered the transaction's ease to be one of the beauties of small town living. Within half an hour of her arrival, Bobbie had unpacked the two suitcases of new jeans, clingy T-shirts, short skirts and several pairs of sexy little thongs—everything new and unlike anything she'd ever worn before. New clothes for her new life.

The small cottage came furnished with the bare minimum, a bed, dresser and beautifully carved cheval mirror in the bedroom, vintage rattan furniture in the living room. At least the cushions had been replaced recently on the sofa and chair, and the bathroom sported a combined shower and tub.

Bobbie took longer to deal with the kitchen, which was large enough to fit a small Formica table and two chairs by the corner window. First she carefully stowed away the items that came with the rental. Then she unloaded her own pans, bake ware, knives, sharpener and the precious tart tins her mother had left her. Utensils were sort of like pets—they grew on you. Last, she'd unpacked her pride and joy, the mocha machine with special superfoam attachment. Warren had given it to her last Christmas, and unlike the BMW, she'd rather die than part with it. If he wanted that in the divorce, he'd be in for one nasty fight.

Now that she'd settled in, Nick Angel was on her list for Monday morning. Her mother had always said the way to a man's heart was through his stomach. Though it wasn't her intention to capture his heart, she figured the same method applied for finding her way into his house. And *other* places. After all, it had worked with Warren. It just hadn't kept him. But who was talking about keeping, anyway? She was only thinking about showing Warren a thing or two about his mistakes.

COOKIES, CAKES, OR A CASSEROLE, to start? Bobby wondered the next morning. *Coffee tea or me? Me.* Ohh, wasn't she just too funny. Once upon a time, Warren had thought so. Bobbie winced at the sudden pain in her lower lip where she'd bitten down a little too hard. Bad thoughts—think only good thoughts.

She pulled on her new backpack purse, tied her perky white tennies and headed out for downtown Cottonmouth. The minimall at the junction of Highway 26 and South Main—recently built, by the look of freshly planted trees and shrubbery barely providing shade in the concrete parking lot—just wouldn't do for her shopping excursion. No, after living in the city for fifteen years, she wanted the flavor of Cottonmouth to permeate her very bones. A full morning's drive northeast of San Francisco, Cottonmouth seemed miles and miles from her former life. Remote and surrounded by lakes, it was practically in the boonies. Maybe in a past life she'd been a small-town girl. Then again, in a past life she could have been Anne Boleyn. At least Warren hadn't chopped her head off when he dumped her. He'd just cut her heart out.

But who needed a heart, with all its messy emotions? Sex for Sex's Sake, that was her new motto.

With a glance at the serial killer's house, she relished the drama all the gossip added to her life. Getting dumped counted as bad drama; contemplating serial killers—though she didn't really believe it—counted as good drama. Especially a handsome serial killer, if Patsy Sapp was to be believed. From Garden Street she turned right on Pine. Midmorning sun warmed the top of her head. She imagined her new red hair glistened. When was the last time she'd thought about glistening? Cottonmouth air must be good for her.

Besides feeling good, she looked good in the blue fitted sweater she'd worn just in case she ran into Warren. Thank God the ten pounds she'd dropped hadn't come off her chest.

With school still in session for a few more days, the only person she passed was an elderly woman pulling a wire shopping cart, the wheels crunching on the gravel. Bobbie smiled. The lady returned it with a toothy grin. In the city people didn't even meet each other's eyes, let alone smile.

Beau's Garage stood at the corner of Pine and Main Street like a battle-scarred cactus amidst a rose garden. If you wanted gas, you went to the minimall where you got a free wash with every fill-up. If you wanted your oil changed, you went there, too, because there were five lifts and ten techs. Bobbie had already figured these things out, and it was only her second day in town. By the looks of the dusty, weed-choked concrete pad, everyone else in Cottonmouth knew it, too.

Turning the corner onto Main Street, she caught her breath. Awnings, colorful if a bit faded, stretched over the sidewalks on either side of the street. A barber pole swirled with red, white and blue. A theater marquee, unlit during the daytime, reached up to the clear blue sky. The sight was something out of *Ozzie and Harriet* or *Leave It to Beaver.* People said *Ozzie and Harriet* was hopelessly unrealistic, but like an addict sneaking a fix, Bobbie still watched reruns on the TVLand channel and smelled again her mother's jam tarts cooling on wire racks on a summer afternoon. Cottonmouth was the land of *Ozzie and Harriet* come to life.

Beside her, the door of Bushman's Clothiers opened, a broom walked out and down the three steps. No, a man with a broom. Hair slicked back, neat lines pressed into his gray slacks, and an out-of-date, too-thin tie. He smiled. Gee, everyone smiled.

"You must be the little gal who moved into Mrs. Porter's place," he commented as he began sweeping the sidewalk, scouring away the dirt that had crept into the cracks in the pavement.

The little gal. Bobbie fought the urge to roll her eyes. Despite his receding hairline, he couldn't be much older than she was, maybe even a couple of years younger. But the fact that he was right about who she was and the way his eyes kept falling to bosom level warmed her the same way the sun had. Politically incorrect or not, she was one forty-year-old woman who didn't mind being ogled. Especially since she'd never *been* ogled.

"Yep, I am."

His eyes crinkled at the corners. "And your name is

Bobbie Jones. You'll have to excuse us, we're not really nosy, but Patsy's been spreading the word along. I'm Harry Bushman." He stopped sweeping and used the broom like a crutch while he waved his other hand at the seasoned brick facade. "This is my store, been in my family for…a long time. Men's and women's fashions." He brightened like a flashing advertisement. "No reason to get in your car to find what you need. We're right here."

"I'll keep that in mind. Thank you."

"Cottonmouth's also got a pharmacy, grocery store, hardware, barbershop, hair salon, whatever you need."

She picked up an edge of desperation in his pleasant voice. "Well, thanks for telling me, Harry. I'm on my way to the grocery now."

"That's great. I won't keep you, then." He shifted from one foot to the other. "Have a nice day."

The forlorn furrow on his brow urged her to ask, "Do you carry shoes?"

His shoulders pulled back as if he were a puppet reacting to the tug of her words like strings. "Of course. Just about anything you could possibly want."

She'd done all her shoe shopping before she left San Francisco. But hadn't *someone* said a woman could always use another pair of shoes? "Today I've got to get my groceries, you know, the mundane stuff, but when I've got myself settled…" She let the sentence trail off, a promise with no expiration date.

Harry Bushman smiled again. She wondered if he realized how grateful it looked, half-cocked like that.

"Bye, then." She gave him a wave over her shoulder, caught him checking out her butt in her tight jeans. She'd be back. Harry had just sold a pair of stilettos.

Any man who looked at her forty-year-old butt like that deserved a reward.

She passed Fry's Pharmacy, the gold-stenciled name chipped and worn off in spots. Johnson's Soda Fountain continued the tired, worn-out theme of downtown Cottonmouth, white wrought-iron tables, turned gray, arranged on the sidewalk in a pathetic attempt at a dapper city sidewalk cafe.

The only spots of frenetic activity along the street involved the beauty salon—the Hair Ball—which made her think of something cats puked up—and the Cooked Goose, some kind of specialty restaurant. As she passed the eatery's dirty window, a Help Wanted sign seemed to plead for a waitress, and the booths, though filled with customers, were scarred and ragged. A bit like the town itself.

Bobbie opened the door of Dillings Grocery. A waft of cool air greeted her, scented with cleaning agents, flowery perfume and the spicy tang of rotisserie chicken. A sign on the empty checkout stand commanded, "Yell when you're ready." Too trusting, but nice. Like leaving your doors unlocked at night.

Quiet surrounded her. The slap of her tennies on the battered linoleum floor and the squeaky sound made by the wheels of her wonky cart echoed off the ceilings and walls.

She reached the meat counter before finding the first signs of life. A woman, mid-thirties, butcher's apron stained with dried blood, hopefully animal, and dark frizzy hair pulled back into a hair net, beamed at Bobbie with a sweet smile. "You must be the new girl."

"Yes, Bobbie—"

"Jones. I know." Her smile was marred only by the

lipstick smear at the corner of her mouth. "I'm Janey Dillings." She stuck her hand over the high glass countertop, thought better of it and pulled back. "Better wash up before I shake your hand."

"Don't bother. I need some hamburger, anyway."

"We cut and grind our own meats. Low-fat hamburger to die for. You won't find that at the big chain stores."

The one out in the minimall, the words left unsaid but implied. The meats were as promised, a fresh red instead of the usual packaged brown. Bobbie had the woman wrap a pound of the best.

"What are you making?"

"Lasagna, I think."

"Noodles. Aisle five."

"Thanks." Bobbie pushed her cart.

"Call me when you're ready to check out. I promise I'll wash my hands."

"Do you take credit cards?"

With a finger, Janey Dillings lowered her slightly smudged glasses and gave Bobbie a look that said, "What, like I'm going to give three percent to the credit card companies?"

"How about checks?"

"Now that we can do."

Smiling, Bobbie left her for aisle five, then moved on to aisles six, seven and eight. They were as devoid of shoppers as the others.

Right there and then, Bobbie decided she wouldn't patronize that horrible new minimall. Not ever. Cottonmouth needed her. Needed her business.

And to top it off, the town even had its very own serial killer.

Did serial killers like lasagna?

BOBBIE REVOLVED in front of the cheval mirror in her new bedroom, assessing her body from every possible angle. With her push-up bra, if she stood just so, at a slight angle in relation to the object in front of her, her breasts could pass for C-cup instead of B. At least on a good day with the sunlight behind her creating a nice shadow.

Maybe she shouldn't have cut her hair. Men liked long hair, didn't they? She sighed. Warren did, as evidenced by the Cookie Monster. True, the picture he'd shown Bobbie was from high school, and the hairstyle might have long since changed. But somehow Bobbie didn't think the Cookie Monster had to worry about her face being dragged down by the length of her hair.

God, was her butt drooping? Hind end toward the mirror, Bobbie hefted the jeans, noticed a slight lift, let them fall again. A squeak escaped as she saw, indeed, that her butt had dropped. Not by much, maybe half an inch, tops. But it was no teenage rear end and hadn't been for twenty years.

The afternoon sun crept across the white eyelet bedspread. Bobbie flopped down on it, stretched her legs out. Forty years in man time didn't mean much, but in woman time it meant the need for face-lifts and butt tucks. At least it did if you weren't loved.

Bobbie turned her head on the pillow, the sweet fragrance of baby powder and gardenias fluffing out around her despite the fact that she'd put on fresh sheets. Mrs. Porter's essence lingered, smelling like a grandmother. Lying on the bed with the sun across her face, the laughter of children coming home from school and the indestructible imprint of Mrs. Porter on her pillows,

Bobbie decided there were probably worse things than butt droop. Things like dwelling on Warren and the Cookie Monster.

But where Roberta Spivey might give up, Bobbie Jones was a force to be reckoned with. *Bobbie* had a lasagna to deliver, and a serial killer to seduce. After all, a cookie was just a snack, while cereal was a whole meal. Take that, Warren.

Five minutes later, lips glossed, foil-wrapped lasagna in her arms, Bobbie crossed the street. The picket fence was no longer white, but bleached through lack of interest. Its latch broken, the gate swung open at her touch.

Stopping beneath the sheltering limbs of the first big oak, she shivered. Gee, it was colder on this side of the street, and she got the feeling it wasn't just being in the shade. She stumbled over a root that had broken through the front walk. As she climbed the steps, they creaked and squished beneath her platform shoes, the wood of the porch old and rotten.

Lifting the lion's-head knocker, she let it fall back to the door. And waited.

No one came to the door.

Anxiety washed over her in waves. Didn't he know that she'd had to work herself up to this? How could he not be home?

She knocked again. The sound echoed uselessly. No one was going to answer.

Blast him. Had he seen her from the upstairs window and deliberately ignored her? Okay, she was putting too much into it. Warren had always said she catastrophized everything, interpreting every nuance, when there really wasn't any nuance at all.

"Who cares what Warren always said," she whispered, the lasagna warming her arms. "Warren's gone."

She turned the corner of the wide wraparound porch. They didn't make houses like this anymore.

And, boy, they didn't make men like that anymore, either. All those beautiful muscles working and rippling as he dug a hole in the backyard. Her eyes went wide, her lashes fluttered and her heart kicked up the beat. The lasagna, nestled against her breasts, overheated her body.

The serial killer's naked chest gleamed in a patch of sun in the backyard. Skin bronzed and hairless—thank God, she wasn't partial to hairy chests—his pectoral muscles flexed as he stamped a shovel into the ground. He worked the base with a foot encased in black leather work boots. His jeans hung low on his hips. Bobbie licked her lips, then raised her gaze to his face.

Her heart stopped. Devil-dark hair hung in his eyes. His face was all sharp angles and strong lines. His jaw tensed as he gave the shovel one more stomp before pushing down on the handle and lifting dirt. His arms bulged.

Heck, everything bulged.

Bobbie's eyes followed a trickle of sweat running down the center of his chest.

So this was what women got out of watching construction workers. If she hadn't had an armful of lasagna, she would have fanned herself.

A door slammed next door. The serial killer looked up and over as a flurry of white fur pounded against the fence.

"Don't start with me, you little runt, or you'll be next."

Surely he wouldn't do anything to the little dog. He wasn't really a serial killer. Was he?

No, not with a voice like that. It was pure sin. Like warm syrup running along her nerve endings, it begged to be licked off.

The dog on the other side yapped, a series of high-pitched sounds that grated like nails on a chalkboard. So much for her warm, syrupy feeling.

The serial killer threw down his shovel and reached for a small wrapped bundle lying at the edge of the hole he'd been digging. He leaned down to set it in the... Oh, my God, not a hole, but a grave. And that little bundle was some poor dead animal.

She must have gasped because he looked up, right into her startled eyes. Now she knew how Jimmy Stewart must have felt in *Rear Window* when Raymond Burr caught Jimmy watching him dispose of his wife's body parts.

CHAPTER TWO

THE WOMAN FROM ACROSS the street edged along the side porch with some silver-wrapped casserole thing clutched to her chest like a shield. Nick stuck his thumb through a belt loop.

Oh yeah, she'd heard the stories about him. No doubt. So what the hell was she doing in his backyard? The good ladies of Cottonmouth wouldn't come within a hundred feet of his house, let alone venture onto his property. Maybe she was like those women who wrote letters to killers in prison, even married them. The allure of the bad boy. Or maybe she was just pure whacko.

But a hot little whacko if there ever was one. Easing down the rickety porch stairs, she stepped closer, into a scrap of sun, her red hair dancing with brilliant prisms of light. Surely that color could only be factory born and bred, but he'd never been one to scoff at man's ingenuity.

Next door, the mutant mutt's barking continued, slightly higher, slightly louder, and a whole helluva lot more irritating. "Princess, I'm warning you…"

"Don't you like dogs?"

"That's not a dog, it's a rodent." Actually, he did like dogs, even had one when he was a kid. A real dog, a malamute named Dodger, who had barked instead of yipped.

"I have to admit. But Princess—" she looked to him to verify the name "—does have a nerve barking at you in your own backyard."

Would ya listen to that? Someone in this town actually agreed with him. Call *Ripley's Believe It or Not*. Call the *Guinness Book of World Records*. "Maybe you should make sure Princess hears that."

The gutsy woman eased her death grip on the foil-covered offering and dared to take two steps closer, braving the supposed killing fields. She wasn't young, probably around his age. Tight jeans and a form-hugging sweater testified to good genes or a health club membership. Toes and nails painted to match suggested a woman out to make an impression. So again, why in the hell was she in *his* backyard? A woman like her could do better than the local bogeyman.

Nick picked up his shovel deliberately and began dumping dirt on top of the sheet-shrouded cat.

"What are you doing?"

"Burying a cat that got on my nerves."

He looked up to gauge her reaction. A step back or a step forward? Only her arms moved, balancing the casserole against her midriff and, in turn, accentuating a very nice pair of breasts. And a telltale impression on the ring finger of her left hand.

"Did it meow too loudly outside your window?"

"No, it showed up dead in my yard. I really hate that. The smell, the insects it attracts." Not to mention nosy neighbors. He'd make an exception for this one, she was far too delectable to send away with a pat on her rump. The thought of cupping that butt made his hands twitch.

"It just 'showed' up? Or did you bludgeon it to death?"

He almost smiled, then shrugged instead. Why bother to explain? He found himself doing it anyway, simply because she was only the second person to voluntarily walk into his yard in the year since he'd come home. That deserved something. "If I was inclined to *bludgeon* small animals, I'd start with Princess over there."

He tamped down the earth over the now-filled hole. Maybe he should start marking the little graves so he didn't accidentally dig one up.

"So, you don't actually kill them."

Ah, the serial-killer bit. He couldn't resist feeding the gossip just to see her reaction. "Animals or humans?"

Her eyes widened, their color a luscious green that complemented her hair. All his fantasy women had green eyes. He wondered if he could duplicate her exact shade on canvas.

"Either," she said, a hint of a quiver in her voice.

She'd make sounds like that in bed, he was sure, moans to drive a man over the edge. He leaned on his shovel, let his gaze drift over her breasts. "What do you think? Do I look like I kill cute little animals or sweet young girls? Or both?"

She chewed her lip. He almost offered to help her with the task. Her taste would be…spicy, like the color of her lipstick. Red-hot. Tongue sizzling.

The crazy woman smiled then. Like she'd just won the lottery or he'd said the secret word, whatever the hell it was. "I just moved in across the street. I'm Bobbie Jones." She thrust the foiled dish at him. "I thought it would be neighborly to bring you a lasagna."

When other people brought him things, it was usually roadkill he had to bury in the backyard. "Isn't it supposed to be the other way around, *I* bring the new neighbor the lasagna?"

She tilted her head. "Men don't cook."

"You think they live on peanut butter and jelly sandwiches?"

"Something like that." Hungry green eyes fixated on his naked chest. She licked her lips. His jeans got tighter.

The last time a woman came bearing gifts, with that same predatory look in her eye and lies on her lips, her husband had tried to pound Nick into the dirt. He didn't relish a repeat. He let the shovel fall to the ground beside him. "You divorced?"

Her full red lips clamped together. This time she chewed the inside of her cheek. Finally she murmured, "Not yet."

"Planning on making your almost-ex-husband jealous by hanging around me?"

No response, which made the answer fairly fricking obvious. Shit. You win some, you lose some.

Seconds passed. Princess stopped barking. Neighborhood noises faded into the background. The awkward silence stretched between them until something or someone had to give.

She pushed the lasagna at him. "Bake it at three-fifty for thirty minutes. And you should probably let it sit for another ten to set. That's what I always do."

He should have let her go then. It would have been the smarter thing to do. But he'd never been particularly smart when it came to women. "You left a mark on your sweater."

Her eyes followed the line of his pointing finger. "Oh." Then she looked back up to meet his gaze. "Do you have a sponge I could wipe it off with?"

If the mark had been on her skin, he'd have licked it off with his tongue. "Looks like you need to take off your sweater to really do a good job."

She gave him a wide-eyed look as if she were a mouse in a trap. "It would be polite to introduce yourself, you know."

"Before or after you take off your sweater?"

Bobbie Jones flushed like a schoolgirl and shook her head, curls bouncing softly, gleaming red and gold in the dappled sunlight. He thought again about sketching her. Naked.

He added, "Just to clean it, of course."

She shoved the dish in his hands. He had to take it or drop it. Hell, it *had* been a while since he'd had lasagna…or anything else she might be offering.

"I better run back home and take care of the mess."

And run she did, giving him a rear view that made his hands sweat. Forget sketching her, there were better things he could think of doing.

"The name's Nick," he called. "You just stop on by any time you get the itch, ya hear."

What a goddamn tragedy she had baggage he had no intention of dealing with, like an ex-husband she wanted to make jealous. Otherwise, he'd enjoy scratching her itch.

STANDING IN FRONT of the small bathroom mirror, Bobbie uncapped her lipstick. She hadn't run away from Nick Angel yesterday afternoon. After she'd decided he wasn't an animal killer, that he just buried the carcasses, she'd made a tactical retreat.

Okay, so he hadn't said he *wasn't* a killer. But the way he'd stood with his foot propped on that shovel, chitchatting, almost flirting—he wouldn't be doing that if he'd been about to bury the evidence of his crime. And he'd made sexual innuendoes about taking off her sweater. Wow, finally she'd been the object of a sexual allusion. And from a man with an extraordinarily gorgeous chest.

It was a start. And today was definitely another day.

But first, BSKFFA—before serial-killer full frontal assault—Bobbie had other plans. She needed to find Warren. And she wanted to find a job. Not that she really needed one. She had enough in savings. Then, of course, there would be the sale of the house in San Francisco and the division of assets and... Darn, she'd smeared her lipstick. That's what thinking about Warren made her do.

She wanted to fit in. In Cottonmouth that would be most easily accomplished if she was employed.

Fifteen minutes later Bobbie wheeled her shopping cart toward Dillings Grocery.

Janey Dillings, minus the bloodstained apron, washed off the concrete sidewalk. The smell of wet cement rose like perfume in the air. Water hissed from the wall opening where the hose wasn't properly attached. A fine mist cooled Bobbie after her walk.

"I brought your cart back. Thanks for letting me borrow it yesterday. I couldn't have carried all that stuff."

"Bobbie. What a sweetie." The endearment and the delighted use of her name warmed her. "How was the lasagna?"

"Great. The meat was the best." Another face-saving little white lie. She hadn't tasted the lasagna, except for those few bites of sauce she stole while making it. A cook's treat.

"Where are you off to?"

"Job hunting." Warren hunting.

Janey pushed her glasses up her nose. "Good luck in this div—I mean, town."

"Thanks." Bobbie already had a destination in mind for the first stop. A rush of cool air whooshed out of the open doors of Dillings Grocery as she passed, the store seeming as empty as it had yesterday. Was there a husband? Roberta would hate to pry. Bobbie was dying to know. She turned, sucked in a breath, then blurted it out. "Is there a Mr. Dillings I haven't met yet?"

Janey pointed up, water flashing momentarily across the faded stripes of the awning. "Upstairs." She rolled her eyes. "Has a migraine," the word stretching out to match the eye roll.

"Oh, I know all about migraines." *Not tonight, honey, I have a headache* was not a solely female refrain.

Moving on, there was a bounce to Bobbie's step despite the reminder of Warren. She'd asked a personal question. And gotten a personal answer. Without getting her head bitten off. Cool. Way cool. Warren would have called it snooping.

Unlike the rest of the street, the parking spaces in front of the Cooked Goose were filled, as was the small lot at the side. What on earth did a place called the Cooked Goose serve for breakfast that would attract so many customers? Probably some sort of specialty crepes.

The odor of grease assaulted her nostrils as she opened the door, and the noise level was eardrum-puncture loud. The blemished booths accommodated a primarily male population. Bleached red leather stools at the counter and yellow-and-gray-checkerboard lino-

leum—which once might have been white and black—
suggested a fifties motif. A young waitress with skinny
legs and taped wire-rimmed glasses sprinted between
tables, the pockets of her white apron overstuffed and
the hem of her black uniform flapping in the wind tun-
nel created by her movement.

Behind the long, Formica-topped counter, a woman,
with yet another drooping gray bouffant much like Patsy's, shoved an order in the roundabout sitting in the
opening above the grill. Stacking plates along her arm,
she headed out, the slam of stoneware echoing above
the din of voices as she made her deliveries. Her eyes
seemed to dart everywhere at once as she grabbed a coffeepot, sloshed the hot liquid into mugs with one hand
and slapped down a check with the other.

Bobbie edged toward the door. She'd come back another time, when things were slower, maybe midafter-
noon between lunch and dinner. But suddenly the
bouffant lady was right in front of her.

"Park yourself, honey." Gravel crunched in her voice.
"Counter's about the only place left, but the service is
faster there. We're kind of shorthanded today."

"Actually…" Bobbie swallowed to cover the crack at
the end of the word and almost stopped right there. But
then she forced the words out. "I saw the Help Wanted
sign in your window, and I'm here about the job."

"Why didn't you say so?" Reaching in a pocket file
by the register, she snatched a menu, shoved it, a pad
and a pencil into Bobbie's hands. "Ellie, bring me an
apron," she shouted above the racket. "Don't worry
about the uniform today. Later I'll find something in the
back that'll fit." She nipped around for a peak at Bobbie's denim-encased butt. "Olga was about your size."

"You want me to start now?" Her brain froze as if she'd just downed an entire ice-cream cone in one bite.

"Take those five tables in the corner." The woman waved to the far side of the restaurant by the ceiling-high windows. "Write the ticket up using the item number off the menu. Make sure you get your tips off the table before Billy starts bussing. That boy's got sticky fingers. And don't worry about ringing stuff up, I'll take care of it."

With that, the bouffant lady jumped behind the register to tackle the line of men who'd appeared within the space of the five seconds it had taken the woman to bark her instructions.

Bobbie took four steps toward *her* five tables and stopped. She was an accountant, not a waitress. She'd never waited tables, not even in college for extra cash. Oh, my God. The banana she'd eaten before leaving the house shot back up her throat. The fight-or-flight response drummed in her veins. Flight won. Or it would have if her limbs weren't paralyzed.

"Hey, Mavis, can I get some more coffee?" A burly guy raised his mug.

The woman with the gray bouffant called back. "Dammit, Jimbo, can't you see I'm busy? The new girl'll help you."

The new girl? Oh, my God. Jimbo was looking at *her.* She'd totally blown the opportunity to flee. Her feet throbbed in her tennis shoes, her knees started to buckle and the plastic menu fused to her sweaty palms. Where *was* the coffee? She spotted it just behind the counter.

Each step came in slow motion. She didn't want to trip in front of all…these…men. The noise had risen to such a level that all she heard was a collective roar.

God, why was she here? She was crazy. Crazy for letting Warren look for Cookie. Crazy for quitting her job, selling her car and moving to podunk Cottonmouth—which, incidentally, sounded like something you got after smoking illicit green stuff.

God, Roberta was back. Full force. And Bobbie just couldn't let her take over.

The coffeepot was a two-ton anchor weighing her arm down, not to mention the menu, pad and pencil. She knew she'd drop something, trip over a foot too far out in the aisle, make a fool of herself and die of mortification. Whose idea was this anyway? She didn't even need a job.

Roberta would have wimped out. But Bobbie would *not* be that weak woman again. Ever. She moved away from the security of the front door.

"You're a sweet young thing." The man called Jimbo beamed up at her, coffee mug now firmly on the table. Waiting. She couldn't quite remember the whole trip from the coffee machine to his table. Amnesia. Blackout. Post-traumatic stress. Whatever. She'd made it.

"I'm forty." She couldn't believe she'd said that.

"Well, you don't look a day over twenty-five. Just half a cup. My wife says too much caffeine makes me constipated, but do I look constipated to you?"

She didn't respond but instead hefted, and carefully, oh, so carefully, poured. The darn stuff had a life of its own and gushed from the spout like a geyser. It was all over the table, dripping onto the floor, spewing all over her brand-new *white* tennies and the legs of her jeans. And would have landed smack in the crotch of Jimbo's extra-large-size trousers if he hadn't sidled like a crab into the corner of his booth.

"Oh, my God. I'm so sorry. It came out so fast." *Can I just die now?*

She grabbed at his used napkins, dabbing ineffectually at the lake of coffee on the table.

"Hey, sweetie, don't cry. It's all right. It didn't get on me, and we can have this whole mess cleaned up in a jiffy." Jimbo patted her hand.

"I'm not crying." Well, if she was, they were tears of humiliation. "But I don't know where the washcloths are."

"In a bin under the counter by the coffee." He looked at the still-quavering pot in her hand. "And maybe you should put that down for now."

"Yeah." She smiled, her eyes watering just a tad because something noxious had gotten in them.

"Billy, get out here and clean up Jimbo's table," a gritty voice shrieked above the racket. Bobbie's face flamed. The room went silent, broken only by the slap of nylon shoes on the linoleum.

"Never worked tables before, have you?" The woman's voice grated in Bobbie's ear.

"No."

Mavis looked at Jimbo. "Well, at least you didn't get his family jewels."

"I didn't break the coffeepot, either." Bobbie pointed to the pot on the table.

More footsteps, softer, quicker. The skinny-legged waitress handed her something white and starched. "Here's your apron. Sorry it took so long."

Still clutching the menu and her pad to her chest, Bobbie said, "I don't think I'll be needing that now."

"You'll need it to hold your pad and the menu," Mavis snapped.

Bobbie felt as if her brain had atrophied. "But I made a mess."

"So don't go dropping coffee all over the customers again."

"Sweetheart, she's desperate. And you're cute." That was Jimbo. But Bobbie could only stare at Mavis.

"They've been leering at your rear assets. It's good for business," Mavis announced.

Bobbie's eyebrows shot up. "My butt is good for business?"

"Yeah." Mavis turned. "Where the hell is that little lackwit? Billy!"

"Having a smoke," Ellie whispered, then disappeared.

She was being hired for her butt. That was sexist. Definitely antifeminist. And absolutely perfect.

"Okay." She tied the apron round her middle, stuffed the pad in the pocket and shoved the pencil behind her ear.

"She can take my order." That from the youngish buzz cut at the next table.

And Bobbie started her new career. With lots of mistakes, of course. But when she brought a side of pancakes instead of toast, and when she took an order for Canadian bacon and brought back steak, no one cared. When she wrote slowly and carried plates only two at a time, men waited. Patiently. And smiled. And stared at her butt.

By the end of the morning, she'd developed a system; she had the customers point to the menu so she could get the right number. It worked. Now she was the one who smiled and made jokes while she swished her attention-getting hips. And she was loving it.

Things like this just didn't happen in the city. Sexual harassment was a dirty word. A man wasn't allowed to look at a woman below the neck. A woman couldn't admit she wanted to be looked at like a sex object.

At eleven o'clock, Bobbie fondled the tips in her pocket. *Her* tips for *her* butt. Her mouth quirked in a tiny grin. That sweet man Jimbo had left her five dollars, when all she'd done was almost pour coffee on him.

Mavis crooked a finger at her. "Come back into my office while there's a sane minute for us to talk."

The accountant in Bobbie kicked in. "I should ask about employee benefits."

Mavis snorted and led the way back through the kitchen. The odors of pine cleaner, grease and male sweat hung in the air like a palpable, unpleasant fog. JJ, the cook, stared at Bobbie's butt. Her stomach lurched. Was the difference merely whether you got tipped for it or not? Nah. JJ was slimy.

Mavis opened the door to an office only slightly larger than a closet. A cluttered desk crammed one corner, grease stains dripped down the back of the once-white door and a calendar featuring dragons and buffed, scantily clad women adorned a wall. The odd decoration didn't suit the Cooked Goose. Nor Mavis.

Her new boss took the only chair, continuing the conversation as if there'd been no break. "Benefits? Like what?"

Bobbie leaned against the wall. "Well, how about medical and dental?"

"Not."

O-kay. That was all right. She could stay eighteen months on the plan with her former employer.

"How about a 401K?"

Mavis laughed so hard, she had to wipe tears from her eyes.

Bobbie stiffened. "Maybe an SEP?"

"I don't even know what the hell that is."

"It's for self-employed people."

"Honey, this place doesn't even make money. Why would I worry about SEPs and 401Ks?"

Mavis seemed to live moment to moment. Not planning for retirement or any other bad thing that happened in life was an alien concept. But *Roberta* hadn't planned on Warren divorcing her.

Bobbie chewed the inside of her cheek. "Well then, I guess that just leaves the hourly wage."

"Minimum, to start. Especially because you don't know jack about being a waitress."

She certainly couldn't argue with that. "How much is minimum wage?"

Mavis just looked at her, her bouffant bubble tipping slightly to one side. "You're kidding, right?"

Okay, so maybe she'd wait to find out on her first paycheck, if she didn't want to appear stupid. Which reminded her. "Do you have auto-deposit?"

Mavis put her head down on the desk and cried, at least that's what those loud snuffling noises sounded like. Finally, she looked up. "Can I ask what your last job was?"

She wondered if Winkleman would give her a good reference after the way he'd had her escorted out, even though she did give him a two-week notice. "I was director of accounting at a firm in Silicon Valley."

And then she knew Mavis was laughing, her mascara streaking down her cheeks. Hands spread in the air, she asked, "And you want to be a waitress in my restaurant because…?"

"I wanted something less stressful." It wasn't really all that funny.

Mavis wiped her eyes. "Honey, I like you. I like you a lot. But you're really kinda dumb."

Bobbie thought about that for a moment and said, "Thank you."

"You're also a little weird. But here's the deal. You get the day shift Monday through Friday."

"But wouldn't someone more senior want that shift?"

"Besides me, Ellie's the most senior thing we've got." She grimaced. "Except that Kelly person."

Ellie and Kelly. Bobbie decided not to laugh, especially since Ellie didn't look as if she'd been out of high school more than a year. "Guess you are shorthanded."

Mavis rolled her eyes. "That's an understatement. But you're interrupting me."

"Oops, sorry."

"There. You did it again. And that's why I won't trust you not to screw up my weekend tourist trade."

"Okay." Not that Bobbie really understood what the weekend and tourists and the fact that she'd interrupted had to do with anything. "So, at this juncture, maybe I should confirm what minimum wage is." It really would be unwise to wait for her first check.

Mavis told her. Bobbie did a quick calc. She started to laugh. She'd just taken a job where she'd be making about ten times less than she'd made in Silicon Valley. Maybe Mavis was right—she was dumb.

But, oh, boy, Warren was going to have to cough up a lot of alimony. She couldn't wait till he saw her work-

ing at the Cooked Goose. He'd be in, she knew. Because
Warren couldn't even boil spaghetti. His one culinary
triumph consisted of pancakes made from a mix. Of
course, they were very good pancakes, especially when
he made them on Sunday mornings…. A hand closed
around her heart.

Mavis stuck out her hand. "Deal?"

Bobbie took it. A busy job would keep her from
thinking about pancakes and Sunday mornings. "Deal.
May I ask you a question?"

"Not if it's about benefits."

"Why do you call it the Cooked Goose? You don't
even have goose on the menu."

Mavis slapped her forehead. "It's a joke. Nobody
gets it. The Cooked Goose. Your goose is cooked?" She
threw up her hands when Bobbie didn't laugh. "We'll
see how long you last around here, honey. Here's an ap-
plication. Fill it out and bring it back tomorrow."

She'd last, all right. Even if it killed her.

Mavis mumbled to herself as she headed back
through the kitchen. Bobbie was right on her heels.

And then she saw Warren. Sitting at one of *her* tables. Oh, my God. She wasn't ready, not after the unset-
tling pancake memories. She wanted to be *looking* for
him when she saw him.

Don't panic. Remain calm.

Mavis stood at her elbow. "You know him?" she
whispered.

Bobbie didn't turn. "My ex-husband. Almost."

"Oh" was Mavis's only reply, then, intuitively, she
wandered off.

Warren's face was thin, almost gaunt. His pale hair
touched the collar at the back of his navy-blue polo

shirt, and the cotton outlined a surprisingly nice set of pecs. My God. He didn't have boobs anymore. He hadn't looked this good in ten years.

His slight paunch gone, he reminded her of the Warren she'd married, except for the increase in bare scalp that climbed back from his forehead. New laugh lines crinkled the corners of his eyes. She'd always loved the two dimples that appeared by his mouth when he laughed. Over the last few years, she'd missed those dimples. When had Warren stopped laughing with her?

He'd lost weight. He'd started laughing again. He'd stopped his Prozac. Goodbye sexual dysfunction. All for the Cookie Monster. Spineless Spivey had finally gotten it up. That...that...bastard.

Bobbie suddenly needed to sit down, before her legs gave out. But she wouldn't give Warren the satisfaction of seeing the slightest indication of distress.

Why did he want her more than me?

Bobbie immediately squashed that little Roberta whine. Thank God there wasn't an Uzi within reach or he'd be a dead man.

This called for a new plan, an extraordinarily brilliant plan.

CHAPTER THREE

THE FIRST THING Warren noticed was the new waitress's bottom as she pivoted to grab the coffeepot. A shapely bottom as bottoms went, but he was more a breast man. As she turned he detected a particularly delightful set, shown to advantage by a fitted sweater. When his gaze reached her face, he felt as if he'd been knocked upside the head with a two-by-four.

That couldn't be Roberta. This woman's hair was red. And short, with fluffy, appealing curls that softened the angles of her face and accentuated the green of her eyes. She appeared younger, though Roberta hadn't aged badly. She'd gained far fewer lines over the years than most women her age.

It *was* Roberta, he saw as she marched his way. And she looked damn good. Better than he'd remembered. Sexier. Not that she hadn't been sexy before. She had been. He'd just had trouble acting on those feelings.

But now, with Cookie, there was no problem.

"Roberta, what are you doing here?" A tense vertebra pinched his neck.

She slapped a menu down on the table. "I'm here to take your order."

He was dimly aware of the booths filling up around

them, the noise level rising and Mavis Morgan staring at him like he was a slug.

He leaned closer to Roberta. "I mean why are you *here?*"

Her painted lips curved into a wide smile. "You made Cottonmouth so attractive that I just had to see it for myself."

"But what about your job?"

"I quit."

She quit? Why? Emotional trauma over the divorce? She should have been all right when he left. He was sure she would be.

"But you loved your job."

"I hated my job, Warren." Her stare conveyed that he should have known all along, if he'd ever had the decency to ask. "So, have you decided what you want?"

What he wanted was for her to go back to San Francisco. He had…other problems to deal with right now. "Pancakes."

She let out a slow breath, then finally smiled and said in a sugary-sweet tone, "Oh, Warren, they're not as good as your pancakes. Try the waffles instead." She was practically cooing now. He'd never heard Roberta coo.

He was in really big trouble, especially when Cookie learned who she was. He'd just have to see that she didn't. "Roberta, we have to talk."

She took a small pad from her apron, her tongue stuck between her scarlet lips as she wrote. God, her fingernails dripped with red, too. "One order of waffles. With whipped cream. And the strawberries are really good."

"Roberta."

"Have you met Mavis yet? She's a doll." With a flip of her wrist, she motioned the older woman over.

"She knows me, I've been here before. Roberta, we need—"

But Roberta breezed right over his words as she grabbed Mavis's arm. "Mavis, you've just got to meet Warren. He's my ex-husband." She shook her head, red curls bouncing. "Well, not exactly ex yet, but soon. How long did you say before I'd get the papers, Warren?"

Christ, by tonight the whole town would know she was here. Cookie would know. "Could we talk about this later, Roberta?"

Mavis drilled him with a look as she spoke to Roberta. "I thought your name is Bobbie."

"Well, Roberta's my old name. Bobbie's my new name."

Bobbie? That explained it. She was suffering from multiple-identity disorder. He knew he couldn't reason with either personality. So how was he going to find out what she wanted?

"Warren's been such a sweetie during the divorce, haven't you, Warren?" She turned to Mavis. "He's letting me have all the furnishings in the house, including the big-screen TV, and all the movies. Even *A Man and a Woman,* which was always his favorite. And my car." She flashed him a devious look. "Oh, by the way, Warren, I traded it in. On a new VW Bug. Those guys at the car dealership were just so accommodating. They took the BMW in a straight trade, even though it was a different brand and everything. They figured they'd have to do a fire sale to get rid of it."

"You traded the BMW for a Volkswagen Bug? But that car's worth—"

"Oh, and I put your Austin Healey in storage. There was just this one teensy-weensy little dent I made when I was trying to back it out of the garage. You know I could never push in that clutch worth a damn. Actually, it's sort of a scratch. Along most of the driver's side. I guess you could call it a dented scratch."

"My Healey?" His voice cracked. His 1958 Austin Healey. His pride and joy. A painstaking restoration he'd spent months on, including a hunt for an exact match of Healey blue. Had Roberta said "damn"?

She flipped a hand at him. "Oh, don't look like that. I touched up the paint with that leftover stuff you had in the garage. It's as good as new. Warren, Warren, are you all right?"

Spots floated before his eyes. Her voice faded in and out. He grabbed the table, afraid he might topple over.

"Is he having a heart attack?" Was that Roberta or Mavis? He wasn't sure.

He'd never heard such a profusion of ditzy words out of Roberta's mouth. Even the tone wasn't hers. She was the most unditzy person he'd ever known. Hell, she even made lists of her lists.

His leaving must have affected her more than he'd ever imagined. He'd thought the divorce would be nothing more than a blip on her chart.

The blood vessels at his temples pulsed. Roberta fanned him with a menu. His vision blurred. Claustrophobia swept over him as people crowded round the booth.

Roberta touched his clammy forehead. "I think we better call the paramedics."

Just as he was about to say he didn't need any help,

the front door burst open. All eyes turned toward the intrusion, allowing him to regain control of his faculties.

"Mavis, why aren't the posters for the Accordion Festival up in your front window? It's less than three weeks away." Mayor Wylie Meade's voice boomed out as if he were using his bullhorn.

"The Accordion Festival?" Roberta's eyes lit up as she turned toward the mayor. Once again Warren wasn't sure he knew this woman anymore. "Are they going to play polka music?"

"And wear lederhosen," Mavis said, poking an elbow in Roberta's ribs.

"Ooh, men in lederhosen." Roberta fanned herself with the menu. "I can't wait."

If Warren had anything to say about it, Roberta wouldn't be here in two weeks, or even tomorrow. He had to get rid of her, especially now, when he had this little problem with Cookie. But all that came out of his mouth was a wheeze.

Roberta leaned toward Mavis and whispered loud enough for him to hear over the buzzing in his ears. "Who's that?"

"It's our mayor, Wylie Meade."

Roberta covered her mouth with her hand and snorted. "Wylie? Is that appropriate for a politician or what?"

Mavis rapped her elbow in Roberta's ribs once more. "Balls, I better get over there or he'll be putting those posters in the windows all crooked. Wylie always get things crooked, no pun intended." Then she hustled down the aisle to the mayor, his hand extended with a sheaf of flyers.

Wylie gave Mavis a toothy politician grin. "It's going to be a magnificent extravaganza. We've got Cookie

Beaumont heading up the decorating committee. She did a bang-up job last year."

Mavis's lip seemed to curl. Warren almost passed out at the mention of his beloved's name. Twin images of Roberta danced before his eyes. He forced her into focus. Her face had paled, then her pencil snapped. The sound echoed as if a bullet ricocheted inside his head.

"Roberta, please," Warren labored, as he managed finally to form words.

"I have to help my other customers, Warren. Are you all right now?" Her eyes glittered like hard green stones.

He wasn't, not at all. "I need to talk to you about...you know."

"You know?" She wore a singularly innocent expression, masking all emotion. This was not good.

"About..." He looked around. He'd lost the restaurant patrons' point of interest, Mavis and Wylie had stolen it. He tugged on Roberta's arm. His bowels crimped in terror. "About...Cookie."

Fatal Attraction's Glenn Close must have looked like that just before she dropped the rabbit in boiling water. "I don't think we need to discuss that issue, Warren. I'm over it."

"Yes, but, I have to tell you..." Unseen hands squeezed his throat, stopping his next words.

"Warren—my customers." She rolled the broken pieces of pencil between her fingers.

Live by the sword, die by the sword. He rushed into it. "She hasn't told...anyone...about her impending divorce...or anything else yet."

Roberta gathered a large breath, her breasts expanding against her sweater. "And why should I be interested in that?"

"I'd just rather you didn't…mention her to anyone." Sweat broke out on his upper lip, his forehead. His gut rumbled. Anxiety was an evil, insidious thing. So was waiting for her answer. Maybe he should have stayed on the Prozac until after this whole mess had been settled.

But Roberta did the most amazing thing. She zipped her lips, then broke into a brilliant smile. "Uh-huh, sure, Warren. Just between us."

It should have been reassuring. It chilled him to the marrow of his bones.

His troubles weren't nearly over. He was very much afraid they'd only just begun.

NICK HAD JUST ABOUT DECIDED a running toilet was preferable to listening to the drivel coming out of Eugenia Meade's mouth. Separated from her by an aisle of plumbing fixtures and housewares, her semiscreech carried to the far corners of Sylvestor's Hardware Emporium. The woman had a pitch that could shatter glass. No wonder Mayor Meade had ordered a pullout sofa for his office at city hall.

"Patsy did her best to warn her, but she's taken Agnes Porter's place right across from That Man."

When he'd first moved back to Cottonmouth, Nick had checked his birth certificate just to see if his real name was "That Man." He selected a ball cock and waited for more dirt on his new neighbor across the street.

"Janey Dillings and Patsy say she's just an utterly adorable little thing, sweet as the dickens. Everyone's wondering why on earth any sane man would leave her."

Christ. How was he supposed to have fantasies about an "utterly adorable little thing"?

"She's working for Mavis down at the Cooked Goose. I heard her husband came in. He's her ex-husband, actually. Well, not quite, seems they haven't gotten the divorce yet."

Eugenia Meade had better take a breath soon, or she'd faint from oxygen deprivation. A conversation with Eugenia didn't require verbal participation from her companions. Vague "Mmm-hmms" were all that was necessary or even allowed, and those were so she'd know her audience hadn't expired.

"Isn't it odd she's come to Cottonmouth, too? Well, not odd. I think it's for revenge. Not that most men don't deserve it."

Guess he'd made a sound decision when he'd tried to scare the woman off. Being part of a vengeful almost-divorcée's scheme wasn't on his list of ten favorite things. Still, there was no reason he couldn't let her sneak into a fantasy or two.

"I think she was some sort of accounting-type person down in the Silicon Valley." Eugenia's tone indicated that anything south of Cottonmouth was akin to the devil's lair. "And her husband is that new man who just set out his shingle in Bert's old office space. He's an accountant, too, a rather insipid little man in my opinion. I'm sure he's trying to run poor Mr. Crouch out of business, at least that's what Jimbo says."

Jimbo. Shit. The whole incident with Jimbo—and Jimbo's wife—had been another of Nick's regrettable errors in judgment.

"And you know the reputation accountants have these days," Eugenia went on. "Why, it's almost as bad as being a lawyer."

Finally she stopped long enough to suck in a lungful of air. Nick imagined her companion contemplating the cosmos...or how to get away from Eugenia. But to give the woman her due, Eugenia was the town's best gossip. Hell, he'd learned many an interesting tidbit about himself while lurking in store aisles right next to her moveable pulpit.

"Why she didn't listen to Patsy's words of wisdom, I'll never know. It won't be long before we find *her* body in That Man's front yard. Mark my words, he's going to move beyond cats, dogs and raccoons before long. In fact, he probably already has. You know, they say most serial killers start doing humans when they're in their teens." Eugenia gasped. "And you do remember that poor Mary Alice Turner?"

In the world according to Eugenia Meade, his sins were many. But Mary Alice wasn't one of them. She was the only thing in his past he didn't regret. But he would never atone for coming home *after* his parents died. And for that he did deserve Eugenia's wrath.

"I've tried to get Wylie to talk to the sheriff about keeping a closer eye on him. But you know Wylie, he never listens to a word I say."

Not true. Wylie had definitely been listening when he'd refused to hang Nick's donated paintings in the hallowed halls of the newly renovated city building, known around town as the Taj Ma'Wylie. Of course, all Wylie had really done was whitewash the building and replace the scrubby lawn with drought-resistant plants. As far as Nick knew, the walls were still bare.

"Then again, if something happens to Bobbie Jones, it could be the husband. I wonder if Brax has thought of that."

Nick squeezed the rubber end of the ball cock. His

old buddy, Sheriff Tyler Braxton. They hadn't spoken much since high school. Since Mary Alice had to leave town. Except when Brax threatened to arrest him over that misunderstanding with Jimbo.

"I wonder if he used to beat her," Eugenia mused. "You have to admire a woman who doesn't air her dirty laundry in public."

Right, just like Eugenia never aired her dirty laundry.

Then, with an audible wheeze, she continued. "What if *she* whacks the husband?" Eugenia's banshee wail resonated with what sounded like glee. "I mean, there's got to be something wrong when a woman is that delighted with the divorce settlement. And why is she here, anyway, if she's so ecstatic?"

And why had she been in Nick's backyard?

Unconsciously he'd walked to the end of the plumbing aisle. Eugenia's pontificating littered the air in the Rubbermaid aisle.

"Mark my words, we're going to have a murder in this town one way or another."

His naturally evil nature rising again, Nick couldn't resist.

"Excuse me, ladies, I'm looking for those containers, you know, the kind Jeffrey Dahmer had in his refrigerator for storing—" he paused, smiled and pursed his lips around the word "—parts. It has to be something really strong. Something acid won't eat through."

Eugenia dropped her basket, the contents rolling out across the floor. Her companion, Marjorie Holmes—as his high school drama teacher, she sure as hell had never been that silent—stared at him through her tortoiseshell glasses.

"Oh, sorry, maybe I should ask Sylvestor. But since I heard you over here…"

Eugenia collapsed to her knees, her mouth open, pudgy fingers grappling with the plastic goods strewn about her on the linoleum. Ms. Holmes continued to stare, as if keeping him within her sight would prevent him from slicing her head off with a scythe like the Grim Reaper.

"Let me help you clean that up." He took two steps before Eugenia threw up her hands in the sign of the cross.

"No, no, I can get it." She tugged on Marjorie's sagging nylons and hissed, "Help me down here."

"Well, if you're sure." He started to back away, wondering how the thin, frail-looking Marjorie was going to get Eugenia's plentiful body up off that floor.

"Oh, yes," Eugenia sucked in a breath, "I'm sure."

His fun over, he decided to leave before the lady hyperventilated. He smiled, gave them both a wave and headed to the checkout counter. Yep, he was a bastard. But sometimes it felt good.

The women's harsh whispers followed him.

"Did you see those eyes?"

"Inhuman. Maybe he's a vampire. He just might suck the lifeblood from this town if we're not careful." He hadn't known Ms. Holmes believed in vampires. But then again, she had staged Bram Stoker's *Dracula*—twice.

"I'll have nightmares, mark my words."

He plunked down his purchases on the counter. "Afternoon, Mr. Sylvestor."

Sylvestor ignored the greeting. Nick counted out the dollars and change. The old man's crab-like fingers, shaking with Parkinson's, grabbed and recounted. It would be easier to do his shopping at the minimall's Home Depot. But Sylvestor needed Nick's business. At least Harry Bushman's parents had retired to Florida before Cottonmouth's economy had gone down the toilet. Mr. Sylvestor, on the other hand, was stuck. Shit.

Call it a sense of loyalty to his hometown, call it atonement, whatever, with Jimbo's new minimall doing all the sucking of Cottonmouth's lifeblood, Nick would keep his commerce inside the city limits. The ball cock would suffice for today.

I JUST WANT TO DIE.

Her muscles had tightened into painful, immovable masses. It would take a team of masseurs to untangle all the knots. Her whole body seemed encased in concrete. Her hands had gone numb.

Like those lonely nights she'd lain next to Warren, silently begging, *Please, please touch me,* until the cadence of his breath roughened into sleep. But she'd never lost hope. Not until the day he told her he wasn't coming back. How could Warren do that?

Because he was…an asshole. There, she'd said it. Or at least thought it. Her stomach knots lessened a smidgen. The man was an asshole, and he didn't deserve her pain or grief.

Yet it hurt just the same. She missed the good years she and Warren had. He had wanted her in the beginning. She was sure of it. He'd surprised her with weekend getaways. Once he'd even closed the garage door and made love to her on the hood of his car. And boy, that man could make her laugh, or make her cry as they watched a sentimental movie together. When had they stopped doing those things? Had he faked it all, the laughter, the fun, the desire? Depression hadn't been part of the lexicon then. Or had she not seen it?

All her triumphs of the day—her new job, the male population's adulation of her Bobbie-self and the generous tips—were stolen by Warren's desertion.

The spineless jerk had left her for a woman who hadn't even ditched her own husband yet. What's up with that? Who did Cookie think she was? To steal Roberta's husband without taking a loss of her own? That sucked.

It wasn't fair.

She'd finally have to admit it, even if only to herself and within the four walls of Mrs. Porter's house, the Cookie Monster frightened her. She'd changed her life, changed her name, moved to Cottonmouth, all for nothing.

As she lay on the bed, concentrating on each breath and trying to ignore the butterflies wreaking havoc with her stomach, an ingenious insight flashed across her mind. Seeing Warren, she'd reverted to Roberta. *Roberta* was afraid of the Cookie Monster.

But *Bobbie* wouldn't let this minor setback get in her way. *Bobbie* had slammed Warren mercilessly. *Bobbie* had lied about the BMW and the Austin—she'd eventually tell him the truth—and given him an anxiety attack. People had noticed Bobbie and liked her. She wasn't going to let Cookie and Warren take that away from her.

For their entire married life, she'd let Warren make all the choices. What job she took, what promotion, when they made love—which meant never—whether they had children. God, she'd given up children for him. He'd kept putting it off, saying they should wait. She'd meekly agreed, then finally stopped asking. And now it was too late. She'd given up the chance to have children because *he* hadn't wanted them. *She'd* let him make that decision, too. She'd let him make all the decisions, whether she agreed in her heart of hearts or not.

Now he'd made the final choice to divorce her.

And that was the last decision she'd ever allow him to make for her. If she just lay here on this bed feeling sorry for herself, or worse yet, if she'd stayed in San Francisco and kept the job Warren thought was best for her, lived the life he thought she should, she'd be Roberta Jones Spivey for the rest of her life. *She'd* be Spineless Spivey.

She'd rather die at the hands of the serial killer.

The moment screamed for action. Something momentous, something Roberta would *never* do.

Five minutes later, teeth brushed and lips freshened with her new bubblegum gloss, Bobbie knocked on Nick's door.

It took him forever to answer. And when he did, he glowered down at her with a formidable look exactly like a...well, like a serial killer.

A lock of hair fell across his forehead. Colored smudges marred his white T-shirt. Faded black jeans hugged his thighs and outlined...other things. Very big things.

She finally found her voice. "Hi. I was wondering if you have cable TV."

Moving just his eyes, he looked from right to left, then back at her. "Yeah."

"Well, I've been twitching Mrs. Porter's rabbit ears on that old black-and-white." She hadn't even tried, but he didn't need to know that. "And I just can't get *Buffy*. I was wondering if I could watch it on your TV."

He did that left-right thing with his eyes again, as if he thought someone else might be hiding in his front porch shadows. *"Buffy?"*

"Buffy the Vampire Slayer. I've never seen it, and I know there aren't any more new episodes, but I promised myself that I'd watch all the reruns." Warren had always said it was an idiotic show and a waste of time. Well, he was a History channel addict; she could become a *Buffy* addict.

Nick pushed back that stray lock of hair. "You know, watching a show about a vampire slayer is a bad idea. Especially since just today, someone called *me* a vampire."

With his dark hair and equally dark eyes, he looked a bit vampire-like. He was also playing her game. The wonder of it made her reckless. "She doesn't slay good vampires, only bad ones." She'd figured that much out from *TV Guide.* "And you're a good one, right?"

A ghost of a smile crossed his lips. "I thought they were all bad."

"Well, that depends on your point of view."

He stared at her for a long, considering moment, his pupils contracting, while she mentally prepared the perfect answer when he asked what her point of view was.

Instead, he squashed all her fun. "Lady, I don't know what you want, and quite frankly, I don't want to know. I've got work to do, and I don't have time for divorced women on the prowl, looking for a substitute or someone to make their ex jealous."

She gulped a breath. "I told you, I'm not divorced, at least not yet. And I'm not on the prowl."

Okay, maybe she was. But only for someone who would make Warren see what he'd thrown away. There was the getting-laid thing, too. But he didn't have to make it sound so…black widowish.

She continued. "And if you want to start getting nasty, what about you being a serial killer?"

He ran a hand down his chest, the material outlining a hint of male nipple. "You shouldn't listen to gossip."

She dragged her gaze from the potent sight. Hands on her hips, she glared up at him. "Neither should you."

He cracked a smile. Her heart tripped. He had a devilish smile. "Touché."

Silence stretched between them. It gave her too much time to think about that chest without a shirt on. Bobbie eased the tip of her tongue along dry lips. "So, what did they say about me?"

He fixated on her mouth. "Who?"

"Whoever was gossiping about me." Duh.

His voice mimicked a female pitch. "She's as sweet as the dickens. How her husband could have left her, we'll never know."

She covered her mouth to keep from laughing at his antics, while she blushed to the roots of her red-dyed hair at the same time. "They did not say that."

He crossed his fingers and held them up. "Scout's honor."

"I don't think that's the correct hand signal."

"Works for me. So tell me, what do you do that's so sweet?" He eyed her up and down, as if she were an ice cream melting too quickly in the sun.

She *was* melting.

"Cat got your tongue?" He was laughing at her. He also seemed to fill his jeans a little more tightly than before.

She really should stop looking down there. "I'm not sweet. I hate sweet. Patooey." She scrunched her nose in disgust. "Sweet sucks the big one."

"Interesting choice of words."

Oh, my God. Spontaneous combustion really did exist, if the heat of her face was any indication. And the way his gaze seemed to turn to melted chocolate, oh, my goodness. "I didn't mean it that way."

"Freudian slip?"

When in doubt, huff. She crossed her arms over her chest, tapped her foot on the wooden porch and blew out a really big puff of irritated air. But the rising temperature on the porch was doing pleasant things inside her body. "I think we were originally talking about you, not me."

"We were talking about you coming over here to watch *Buffy*." He arched one brow, hot eyes lingering on her breasts. "The answer is still no."

Darn. She sought something else to keep him from closing his door on her. "We were done with *that* subject and had moved on to whether or not you're a serial killer."

"Didn't we discuss this yesterday?"

So what? "You never really answered."

"Do you think I'm actually going to tell you? What if you're my next victim? That would be like warning you."

She'd really like to be his next victim. She tapped her foot a little harder. "I don't believe it."

"You don't believe I'm a serial killer?" His lids did a slow blink, as if he scanned her body all the way down. Then up again. "Or that you're my next victim?"

Even the tops of her thighs felt steamy now. She cocked her head to one side. "I don't believe any of the gossip. I bet you're every bit as angelic as your name, and that there's not a mean, demented bone in your body. You're clearly misunderstood and misjudged. And I bet whatever happened with Mary Alice Turner wasn't even your fault."

He took an extraordinary amount of time to digest her opinion. And she knew she'd said something terribly wrong. His eyes narrowed, his jaw tensed, muscles rippled in his cheeks.

"In case you haven't noticed, Ms. Jones, I'm not a nice guy. I'm a total dickhead when it comes to manners. I can't be bothered. So, if you're wondering exactly what *that* means, let me make myself clear. I don't invite strange females over to watch *Buffy*. I don't return lasagna bake ware. And I don't give a damn what my neighbor thinks about me."

He closed the door in her face.

Okay. Maybe she shouldn't have mentioned Mary Alice Turner quite so soon in the relationship. But she'd wanted to let him know she'd give him the benefit of the doubt. And of course, she'd harbored a burning curiosity about the story since Patsy had mentioned the girl's name.

Well, there was always tomorrow. And then she'd wait until *he* mentioned Mary Alice.

THE SLAP OF HER SANDALS on the porch steps died away. Nick leaned against the door and drew in a deep breath. If he didn't know better, he'd have said he'd just finished a 10-K run.

She was one brick short of a full load, or something just this side of insane. Worse, she had that trait common to all women—she didn't take no for an answer.

Even being downright rude hadn't flashed a bright red stop sign in her face. He was going to have to bar the windows and nail the door shut to keep her out.

She wanted something. Screw *Buffy*. Screw baked lasagna. She wanted a piece of him. He could feel it, taste it, smell it. Like her bubblegum scent. Sweet. Innocent. Irresistible.

He'd wanted to touch her, feel the heat of her, skim his thumb over her peaked nipple, slide his hands beneath her short denim skirt. Like a fresh canvas, he could repaint his life through her eyes. Expunge his mistakes.

Did she even have a clue how seductive that idea was?

Probably. He'd learned the hard way to avoid women who sucked up big-time, telling you how misjudged and unappreciated you were. Sobbing women with an agenda and a finger on your Achilles' heel.

Damn, he was such a fricking idiot.

Because he'd wanted to tell her everything about Mary Alice. Closing the door in her face had been one of the hardest things he'd ever done.

CHAPTER FOUR

ANOTHER DAY, another pocketful of tips. Let's see, how many mistakes had she made today? Bobbie stared sightlessly into the front window of Bushman Clothiers and did a mental tick off. She'd dropped the pancakes in an attempt to emulate Mavis's amazing stacking ability. She'd given a trucker twenty in change instead of a dollar. He'd been so darn sweet about insisting she'd made a mistake, even when she'd argued with him.

Mavis had tapped her temple. "Now I know how those accountants *misplaced* four billion in unrecorded expenses at that telecom giant."

It certainly wasn't Bobbie's fault that someone had put a twenty in the ones slot. Or was it?

All in all, it had been a good day. She still had a job, and she'd made more in tips than she had on payroll. Maybe it was learning all her customers' names. Maybe it was the too-tight uniform or the number of times she'd bent over to rescue something she'd dropped only to feel appreciative eyes caress her rear.

Mavis had explained it thus, "Your butt's a seven-day wonder. Next week your tips'll be cut in half. I guarantee it."

Whatever. As long as they liked her.

And she liked Cottonmouth.

Just looking at the display in Bushman's front window made her yearn for long-ago, hot summer days at the beach. Bobbie plucked at the sticky material of her uniform, fanning her chest. Neither the crack in the glass nor the yellow flip-flops and the pink polka dot beach umbrella that had seen too many seasons sitting in the front window could dampen her fond memories.

Movement flashed beyond the glass. Harry had a customer. Wonderful. Bobbie shaded her eyes against the late-afternoon sun bouncing off the glass. Harry helped a chic woman with a big hat, sunglasses and an expensively cut suit. Considering the profusion of polyester on Harry's racks, it was a sure bet she hadn't purchased her ensemble from Bushman's. Harry, hands beating the air like hummingbird wings, hovered around the woman.

Poor Harry. The woman simply walked away while his hands fluttered ineffectually. Then she stopped, stared, maybe even glared at the front window, though Bobbie couldn't tell for sure with the oversize sunglasses masking her eyes. She half turned and said something to Harry over her shoulder. Probably wondered who the maniac woman in the limp waitress uniform was.

Busted. However, the last time she'd checked, looking in store windows wasn't a crime. Besides, this was *her* town now.

The door opened. The woman descended to the sidewalk, a small, neatly folded Bushman Clothiers bag tucked beneath her arm. What on earth could that woman have bought from Harry?

Bobbie did a critical once-over of Ms. Cottonmouth Society Lady. Long, lustrous blond hair flowed from beneath the hat. It looked like real blond hair, probably the texture of silk, like something out of a romance novel. Romance heroines never dyed their hair. The pink tones of the costly suit complemented her high, rouged cheekbones. Her stomach made barely a ripple against the knit skirt, and gravity didn't exist as far as her butt was concerned. That delicate skirt should have shown every flaw, every modicum of flab, every wrinkle in her skin. My God, she didn't even have VPL—the dreaded visible panty line. The best Bobbie could hope for were crow's feet behind those massive sunglasses.

The sunglasses came off. Oh, my God. Bobbie should have recognized her worst nightmare. This was Cookie Beaumont in all her absolute perfection. Far better than the picture in Warren's high school yearbook. White chocolate mousse with real whipped cream. Standing next to her in a machine-washable, nylon waitress getup, Bobbie felt like tapioca pudding past the freshness date.

The Cookie Monster even smelled good as she moved to within a foot of Bobbie. Something subtle and exotic, like passion fruit or maybe passionflowers. Definitely something with the word *passion* in it.

So much for Bobbie's hopes that Warren's love would be a greeter at a discount department store.

Bile threatened to force its way past the constriction in Bobbie's throat. If she wasn't careful, she'd throw up on the Cookie Monster's pale pink, high-heeled slippers. Not just everyday shoes, but more like slippers. Like something Cinderella would have worn. Bobbie's tennies, with their dark smudges of pancake syrup, assured that no man was going to get his nose anywhere near her feet.

I hate you, Warren. I hate you more than anyone I've ever hated in my whole life.

Not that Bobbie had ever hated anyone before.

What made the situation worse was that there was no doubt in her mind that Cookie Beaumont knew exactly who she was. And from the look on the woman's face, Warren had probably told her every revealing, humiliating detail of their lives. Even the sex stuff.

Sweat trickling down her back in the hot sun, Bobbie shuddered. Of course, the Cookie Monster's skin merely glowed through a fine sheen of perspiration. That was the essence of it. Bobbie sweated. Cookie Beaumont perspired. Delicately.

"I know who you are."

She even had dulcet tones. Chocolate probably melted in that mouth. Okay, so it melted quite well in Bobbie's mouth, too, but then it went straight to her hips. Cookie Beaumont didn't wear chocolate on her hips. She wore pink knit.

Her feet cemented to the sidewalk, Bobbie couldn't run. The most she could manage was a wrinkling of her nose, as if she smelled something bad.

"If you try to mess with my plans," Cookie trilled, "I'll make sure Warren doesn't give you a dime in the divorce."

Warren hadn't signed a single legal paper yet. He'd only made promises. But if Cookie wanted Warren to break those promises…

Say something. Anything. Tell her to go…bleep herself.

But Bobbie's lips wouldn't part. She couldn't even turn her stiff neck to give the horrible woman a menacing look as she passed. All she could do was stand there as the Cookie Monster's heels clacked down the sidewalk. In the window's reflection, a beautiful black

Jaguar XK8 enveloped the pink suit and hat, then glided out of the parking space.

From inside, mute witness to the mortifying event, Harry stared, slack-jawed, as if he'd just seen Joan Crawford bushwhack her unsuspecting cousin in *Harriet Craig*. As far as master manipulators went, the Cookie Monster ranked right up there.

It was deplorable, shameful, idiotic. She'd botched the all-important first battle with her enemy. The Cookie Monster had stormed the beach and dug in.

But it was only a minor battle, just a skirmish. The war was yet to be won.

Bobbie's tennies felt glued to the sidewalk. It took a whole five minutes to loosen her frozen, shocked muscles. It also took that long to pry her lips apart.

The first word that came out was a heartfelt "Bitch."

Oh, my God. She was developing a potty mouth. And she enjoyed it. Nothing kept her down for long, not since she'd become Bobbie rather than Roberta. The Cookie Monster might have fancy clothes and a disgustingly firm bottom, but she was also a first-class bitch. And that's where Bobbie had her beat. No one had *ever* called her a bitch.

She'd survived her first two days at the Cooked Goose, two encounters with a serial killer and her first battle with Cookie Beaumont. *Survival* was the key word.

Bobbie hopped the step down to street level and crossed the intersection devoid of traffic. Her tired feet just might make it the few blocks to Mrs. Porter's cottage.

"Hey, come here."

From amid a weed patch covering the concrete pad

of Beau's Garage, a grizzled old man waved his arm. Sweat stained the armpits of his blue work shirt. He spat tobacco juice at an offending weed. Eeuw. The darn thing shriveled like the toes of the Wicked Witch's sister after Dorothy's house fell on her.

Bobbie looked from left to right. She was the only one on the street.

She pointed to her chest and mouthed, "Me?"

"Yeah, you."

She crossed the last few feet to the weather-beaten gas pump, then stopped at a distance guaranteeing safety from any potential streams of juice.

"Yes?"

"I just wanted to warn you that woman's a viper."

Well, here was someone she could see eye-to-eye with. And on closer examination, he wasn't quite as old as she'd first thought. It was the gray, grizzly sprouts of beard that made him look somewhere in his sixties rather than his fifties. Nor did he smell as bad as the sweat stains indicated.

"You mean Cookie Beaumont?" she said to spur him on. Goodness, the people in this town loved to gossip. At this rate, she'd know who had done what to whom over the past fifty years before her first week was out.

"I'm talking about that conniving woman you work for." He rolled his eyes as if he'd encountered an imbecile.

"Mavis Morgan?"

"That's the one."

"Why?"

He scratched behind his ear. "You ask her about it."

The mangled spines of the overhang barely shaded her eyes from the sun as she looked at him and murmured with exceeding politeness, "Might I at least tell her whom I heard it from?"

"Name's Beau. I own this garage."

Duh. His much-washed blue shirt had his name emblazoned over the pocket.

"Your car need a tune-up?"

"Actually, it's new."

"One of those foreign jobs?"

Somehow a Bug seemed as American as apple pie. "It's a VW."

"Well, you gotta be sure to do an oil change every three thousand miles even on those German cars. Can't let a good engine rot, ya know."

At the rate she'd been driving, she wouldn't be reaching three thousand miles for at least three years.

"I don't sell gas anymore," Beau went on, "but I still do oil changes. Better than anyone you'll find up the highway. Those wet-behind-the-ears punks have been known to leave screwdrivers in the fan belt. They don't love cars the way a man should. It's those damned electronics, confuses the hell out of 'em."

He smiled then, a big toothy grin that showcased two rows of straight white teeth. She gaped. How on earth did he have white teeth in seemingly excellent condition when he chewed tobacco? Was that possible?

"It's that whitening crap you put in little trays and stick in your mouth for twenty minutes," he said, correctly reading her slack-jawed look. "Ex-wife makes me use it every day or she won't kiss me. And she sends me off to the dentist twice a year to get 'em cleaned. I'm on her dental plan seeing as how I don't have one of my own over here."

"Well, that's very nice of her." Being an ex-wife and all. Warren could pay for his own darn dental insurance.

And he could *dream* about kissing her again. Not in this lifetime. All she really wanted was a chance to turn her back on him when he came begging. Vindictive, yes, but oh so satisfying.

"Which reminds me, I better shave just in case she shows up for sex tonight. Hasn't been around in…oh…three or four days. Starts to get a little cranky if she doesn't get it often enough. But you're a woman, you know all about that kind of thing."

She did know all about a woman's needs, about not having them met on a consistent basis. But this did not seem like a proper discussion to be having at the corner of Main and Pine Streets with a stranger, and after Beau had just called her boss a viper.

"Well, thanks for warning me about Mavis. I'll be sure to ask her about it."

"You watch out for her, else she'll stab your eyes right out of your head. Just like she did me."

Oh-kay. Bobbie sidled two steps toward Pine Street. "I better be going now."

He raised a finger at her. "And come to think of it, better watch out for that bitch Cookie, too. Mavis'll stab you, but at least you'll see it coming. Cookie, she'll turn your own family against you and make you think you deserved what you got."

Now that was the Cookie Monster *she* knew. What did the woman want from Warren? Certainly not money, if her expensive suit meant anything. And it most definitely couldn't be the sex.

Could it? Eeuw.

HE SHOULD STOP answering the doorbell. She was the only one who ever rang it. Yesterday, he hadn't quite recognized the sound. This time, however, he knew. He opened the door anyway. Today she was carrying a stainless steel bowl of…pasta salad.

Shit. He liked pasta salad. And if it was anything like her lasagna, he didn't stand a chance.

"I've already had dinner," Nick told her, while enumerating to himself all the reasons he shouldn't invite her in. She'd just been dumped. She was needy. She was no spring chicken, had probably gotten ousted for a younger model. She was also excessively chipper. He didn't trust chipper.

Bobbie held out the bowl like a religious offering. "You can eat it tomorrow."

He held on to the door with one hand, ready for the slam. She was pushy, and he didn't trust pushy, either. "Lady, what does it take to get rid of you? Permanently."

He expected a serial-killer comment. Instead she seemed to take him seriously, pulling her lower lip between her teeth and chewing, giving the matter her considerable brain power. Christ, the idea was for *him* to chew the lipstick off her mouth. And damn, he wanted to. Badly.

"Well, I'll get off your porch this time. If you promise to go to the Accordion Festival with me in a couple of weeks."

He laughed. Lasagna, *Buffy the Vampire Slayer,* pasta salad and now the Right Honorable Mayor Wylie Meade's Accordion Festival, which was supposed to cover the budget shortfall caused by his erection—of the Taj Ma'Wylie, that is.

Damn, a Freudian slip. He shouldn't be considering erections and Bobbie Jones in the same thought. "Don't think so."

"But they'll be having polka dances and stuff. Don't you love watching the polka? Haven't you ever seen Lawrence Welk do it on PBS? He was the most marvelous dancer."

She gave him a dreamy, half-lidded look reserved for *NSYNC band members, if you were under the age of fifteen, or the prospect of sultry Southern nights spent on satin sheets if you were over the age of consent. The bulge in his pants indicated they both clearly met his age requirement.

Bad idea, really bad idea. *Repeat after me, you learned your lesson when Cookie Beaumont came sniffing around.*

Bobbie licked her lips, and his dick twitched. Apparently, he hadn't learned his lesson.

"Stop that."

Her eyes widened. "Stop what?"

She stared at him, all innocence and sweet green eyes. And the funny thing was, he wasn't sure she had a clue what she was doing to him. "I'm not going to the Accordion Festival."

"Aw, come on. You might find everyone will start liking you when they figure out you're just a normal kinda guy."

He ignored the insult of being considered normal. "Do I look like I care if any of them like me?"

She pursed her lips, considered him a moment, as if she couldn't believe he didn't give a damn. He was about to reiterate when she conceded. "All right, then settle for surprising people. They'd never expect it. You'd drive them crazy."

Especially Eugenia Meade, who'd planned the whole thing right down to headlining the Linz Minyon Band from Milwaukee and snookering Cookie Beaumont into decorating. Bobbie's eyes sparkled with excitement at the prospect. Suddenly Nick saw exactly what Janey Dillings and Patsy Bell Sapp saw. The man who'd left her had to be freaking insane to kick the brilliance of that smile out of his life forever. Not to mention his bed.

"When is your divorce final?"

She clutched the bowl of pasta to her stomach as if he'd punched her. "Warren is working on all that stuff."

He squashed the rumble of remorse over wounding her. He needed to know. "You don't really want a divorce, do you?"

She took a deep breath, her chest straining the stretchy sweater material, then said, "It's the height of bad manners to stay where you're plainly not wanted." Her eyes opened wide as she made the connection between divorce and standing on his porch. "So, I guess my coming over here is the height of bad manners after you've plainly told me to go away." Then she shrugged, smiled and held out the bowl one last time. "You can have it, anyway. No strings attached. From one outcast to another."

God, the woman had an uncanny sense of word use, picking just the right ones to reach up inside and twist a man's heart. Nick didn't take the dish from her hands. Instead, he found himself giving her, what was for him, an apology. "Actually, the first time I told you to come over whenever you got the itch. Bad manners on my part to take back the invitation the next day."

He could have gotten rid of her if he'd just taken the dish and closed the door. What the hell was wrong with him? His gaze fell to her firm breasts beneath the sweater. And he knew damn well what was wrong with him.

Bobbie arched a pretty brow. "I totally agree."

He could only hope she'd agree to anything. "You aren't an outcast by any means. Cottonmouth loves you, if the gossip I've heard is reliable." *Shut your mouth before you actually beg her to come inside.* What was he trying to do, make her feel better or something?

"Let me put it another way. You're the outcast. I was cast out." Then, smiling, she shook her fist in the air. "And darn proud of it, too."

Only an optimist could smile like that after getting the heave-ho. Or a psychotic. Since he was pretty sure optimists were a figment of someone's imagination, he opted for psychotic.

And there was that old proverb, better to keep the psychotics out of your house. Hadn't Jung or someone said that? He pushed the door fully open. "Wanna come in and wash out your lasagna dish so you can take it back home?"

Idiot. He felt like banging his head against the door as she took him up on the invitation.

BOBBIE DIDN'T FIND any frying pans with human livers on the stove. Not that she would have known a human liver from any other kind of liver. Nick had washed out the lasagna dish despite what he'd said. And he shared the pasta salad with her. He was even a sort of accomplished host. He provided napkins in the form of folded paper towels, and sat her at the kitchen table instead of making her eat over the sink.

His skill at conversation, though, could use some help.

"Do you know Beau down at the garage?"

"Yeah."

Bobbie waited for more, but nothing was forthcoming. She probed further. "Why doesn't he sell out that place and start somewhere else?"

"It's his home."

Daintily spearing and chewing two more bits of curly pasta and an artichoke heart, she waited. Again, nothing. Air drifting in through the open back door caressed her cheeks like warm fingers. She imagined that's how his touch would feel. The spicy tang of the dressing exploded in her mouth. And that's how he'd taste. Swallowing, she pushed on. "Is Beau a little...off?"

Nick spooned more pasta into his bowl. "No. He's right on."

What did that mean? "So, is there anything else you want to tell me about him?"

He put down his fork and gave her the full benefit of a dark-eyed stare. "No."

"Don't you want to gossip?"

"I don't gossip. I am merely the subject of gossip." Said like a king, with a diabolic grin that made her pulse rat-a-tat.

"So I guess that means you don't want to tell me anything about the mayor either?"

He raised a brow, and she knew there were all sorts of juicy things he could reveal. But he wouldn't.

She tried another route. Compliments. "I love your kitchen."

He looked down at the linoleum. Probably once a rusty redbrick simulation, it was now faded and peeling back in the corners where it met the cabinets. Bleach stains spotted the Formica countertops, and paint blotches ornamented the porcelain sink. The harvest gold stove and refrigerator, entering the house sometime in the early seventies, were probably here unto death.

He gave her a you've-got-to-be-kidding look.

"It reminds me of when I was a kid." Her mouth watered with the memory of jam tarts and chocolate chip cookies baked in her mother's harvest gold oven. She'd been a jubilant eater, licking the last of the chocolate smears from the corners of her mouth in a last-ditch effort to keep the flavor on her tongue as long as possible. Heaven was a man tasting of chocolate.

He looked at what she saw. "Yeah, well this *is* the kitchen from when I was a kid."

"You're not thinking of remodeling it, are you?" A shiver of regret swept through her.

"How could I replace it? They don't make harvest gold anymore."

Her initial intent for invading the serial killer's home had been merely a reward for enduring the Cookie Monster. But here was an added bonus she'd never even dreamed of. If she wanted to remember her mother before Alzheimer's claimed her life, all she had to do was bask in Nick's kitchen.

There was so much she wanted to know about him. But she wouldn't make the mistake of asking about Mary Alice Turner. Not after yesterday's negative reaction. "Can I see your paintings?"

He choked on his last pasta swirl, then coughed. "No."

"Oh." She chewed on her bottom lip. His gaze dropped. "Why not?"

"Because."

Jeez, he was a tough nut to crack. Their bowls were empty, as was the dish she'd brought the pasta in. The polite thing to do, as her mother always told her, was not to overstay her welcome. But Roberta had been the mannerly child. Bobbie would stay as long as Nick let her.

He drummed his fingers on the table. Long elegant fingers, much as she imagined an artist's to be. He probably did lots of things well with those dexterous fingers. Her face heated with all the possibilities.

"I don't paint clowns," he said finally, almost as if the prolonged silence had drawn the admission from him. "I never have painted clowns. And I never will paint clowns."

Bobbie soaked up the fact. She'd decided days ago that Cottonmouth was wrong about him, but it was nice to confirm he was no John Wayne Gacy. Now, though, she longed for more information. "What do you paint then?"

"Sci-fi fantasy." He shrugged, maybe a little too carelessly. "For book covers and calendars. Posters."

"Like Conan the Barbarian type stuff?" With near-naked women battling dragons and taming warriors with rippling, muscled thighs the size of tree trunks.

Where had she seen something like that? Recently, too.

"That's part of it," he said.

Bobbie shivered. Some of that stuff could be quite…erotic.

She pushed her bowl to the side, crossed her forearms on the table, the notion of Nick's erotic art luring her closer.

His gaze buried itself in her cleavage. Her nipples tingled against her lacy bra.

"Can I see your book covers?" He would keep copies of them, wouldn't he?

"No."

Darn it. She'd never been forward, couldn't have imagined it would be this difficult. But being Bobbie, rather than Roberta, she persisted. "Can I see the rest of the house?"

She mentally crossed her fingers and hoped for something other than another no.

"Why?"

Well, that was better. Sort of. "Because."

He snorted and leaned over his bowl, then raised his hands in defeat. "Just the living room. Not upstairs."

Which was probably where he did his painting and kept all his book covers. Hidden away from prying eyes.

"Great." She grabbed their bowls, skipped over to the sink and rinsed them. She'd work her way upstairs later.

"Has anyone ever told you you're a pain in the ass?" The slight curve of his mouth kept the insult out of the question.

"Just you." She dried her hands on the towel hanging from the refrigerator door. The fabric was surprisingly clean. "I've learned if you don't ask for what you want, you don't get it."

Though sometimes when you did ask, ad nauseum, you didn't get it, either. So, she would *not* ask for sex. She'd maneuver him into asking for it, pleading for it. Yeah.

When she turned, he stood in her way. Her nose almost bumped his shoulder. His voice rumbled over her. "And what is it you really want?"

Gosh, he was tall. And he smelled good, an indefinable "something" there. A spicy, tingly aftershave maybe? Shampoo? Definitely eau de male of the good variety, not the bad.

"And the answer is?"

She'd been sniffing him and forgetting his question. Which, now that he reminded her, made her face burn with a mixture of embarrassment and overactive sexual imagination. *Go ahead, Bobbie, ask for what you want.* Not yet. She had to make him realize how badly he wanted her first. "To make a new friend."

Didn't *that* sound totally lame. The best she could do on the spur of the moment when what she really wanted to do was climb his body until she could wrap her legs around his waist.

He looked down at her. His eyes narrowed, then he shook his head. He didn't believe the "friends" thing, either. He took her hand in his big, hot and pleasantly rough one—which raised her temperature at least two degrees—then dragged her across the front hall and into his living room.

The drawn drapes turned the contents of the room into hideous shapes. He flipped a light, banishing the monsters. In their place stood a plaid couch, its fabric looking scratchy to the touch, and a vinyl recliner still imprinted with the shape of a man's bottom. A very big bottom.

"Was your dad a big guy?"

Following the direction of her gaze, he dropped her hand, leaving her suddenly cold. "Yeah, a big guy. And he liked baseball. Never missed a game—" he pointed to the impression "—from that chair. In front of that TV."

Impossible to tell what he felt from either his tone or his shuttered eyes. The TV wasn't much newer than Mrs. Porter's, but at least the screen was larger than a postage stamp. The beaten-down shag carpet might have been brown, then again, it might have been a dirty gold to match the kitchen appliances. Behind the TV, bookshelves lined the wall, filled with hardbacks, paperbacks, DVDs and videos.

A dazzling idea lit up her brain. "Do you have any of your own movies?"

"My own movies?"

"You know, the *P-O-R-N* stuff."

He dropped his head in his hands and proceeded to run his fingers through his hair. He groaned in disgust. But the sound tripped along her spine like lust.

"It was *not* a porn film."

"But I heard—"

He lifted his head. "You heard wrong. It started out as a regular movie with some hot sex scenes. But the director cut most of the dialogue and added someone else's private parts in my scenes—" He snapped his mouth closed. Red tinged his cheeks.

Gosh, he was embarrassed. "It's okay," she said, as her mind flooded with images of *his* privates. "You can tell me."

"There's nothing to tell. Are you done in here?" He pointed. "The front door's that way."

Oooh, touchy subject. Hands clenched at his sides, jaw working, he was clearly pissed with himself for offering even *that* minuscule explanation.

"And there's only one?"

He kept his lips firmly together, probably to avoid risking any further juicy tidbits slipping out.

"Well, I knew there was more to the story than just the gossip. But why does everyone think you made a career out of it?"

His lips turned white with the effort at silence.

"Oh, yeah, you don't care what everyone thinks." She angled her head and chewed her lower lip, giving the matter great thought. "I could tell them for you."

Words finally burst out. "Keep your mouth shut."

"You're really determined to make sure they don't like you."

"They can all go fu—" He stopped and glared at her, his pupils dilated. "Screw them all."

Why did he pretend he didn't care when it was obvious he did? A great deal. Maybe she could spread the word unobtrusively, like telling Mavis and letting the news sift through Cottonmouth. By tomorrow, he'd have a whole new reputation.

"Don't even think it."

She raised innocent brows. "Think what?"

"Whatever. You're scary when you think."

It was kind of nice that he thought he knew her so well. She turned and gazed at the rows of movies. He'd told her to get out, but...he didn't mean it.

With the dim lighting, she shouldn't have been able to pick out the box. But the name was short, in white letters, and printed right side up instead of sideways.

"Oh, my God, you have *Laura*." She rushed to the shelf, fell to her knees beside the video of her most favorite movie in the whole world. She turned to him. "1944. Best picture. Gene Tierney, Dana Andrews."

He was silent a beat or two. "It's amateurish."

She gaped at him. "Amateurish? It's Otto Preminger's masterpiece. The dialogue is superb. Clifton Webb is sublimely urbane and sarcastic."

She traced the name with her finger, but restrained herself from hugging the movie to her chest. "It's so utterly romantic."

His gaze moved from her face to her finger stroking the box. His eyes seemed to get darker. "My dad must have bought it."

Liar, liar pants on fire. "What's your favorite part?"

He held a breath, and she just knew he was going to lie to her. She put her hand behind her back and crossed her fingers for real this time.

He shifted uncomfortably. "The part where he's getting drunk and looking at her portrait."

Oh, my God. "And he knows she's dead, and he's falling in love with a fantasy he can never have."

She could still remember the first time she'd seen the movie, on late night TV when she was sixteen. She'd been right up there on that precipice with Dana Andrews. Not knowing the truth yet. It was a sensation you could never recapture, only remember and savor.

Nick stared at her as if he'd fallen off the cliff, too.

His Adam's apple slid along his throat. Three steps closer, he towered over her. She was still on her knees. She couldn't breathe. She couldn't speak.

Beneath the porn star/serial killer facade lurked a closet sentimentalist.

She would have thrown herself at him.

If the darn doorbell hadn't rung right at that very moment.

CHAPTER FIVE

HIS EARS WERE RINGING. Nick slapped his hand to the side of his head to make it stop. It didn't work.

"Aren't you going to answer the door?"

Bobbie was still on her knees in front of him. His head reeled with images of the things she could do to him in that position. The last thing on his mind was answering the door.

All he said was, "No one ever comes to my door."

"I did."

Shell-shocked, light-headed, he could barely recall the movie she was so entranced with. Celluloid figures flavored scenes with a hint of mystery, of the impossible, the unattainable. But Bobbie herself had made the hairs along his arms rise to attention. The zealous light in her eyes beguiled him. Her unquenchable faith in him, despite all the stories, seduced him.

He could tell her anything; she would believe. It was a heady power he held in his hands. Beyond sex. Beyond mere physical desire. Beyond the feel of her skin, the firmness of her breasts and the gasp of her breath.

She was the fantasy portrait he could fall headlong for.

Shit. He didn't indulge in romantic fantasies. He preferred wet dreams, down and dirty, totally emotionless. With none of the mystical, idyllic stuff of her favorite movie. Or his own paintings.

What he wanted from her was sex. Plain and simple.

The ringing started in his ears again. It *was* the doorbell.

"You want me to get it?"

"I'll get it." Probably a Jehovah's Witness. Mind-blowing, body-morphing, sinful thoughts scrambling his brain, his only desire was to get rid of whoever it was as fast as possible. One glance at the too-snug fit of his jeans, they'd be running for the nearest sanctuary before he even told them to get lost.

He yanked the door open, putting a screw-you-and-the-horse-you-rode-in-on scowl on his face.

Kent English took a big step back, holding his hands up in surrender. Then his gaze swept past Nick's shoulder.

Damn. Bobbie hadn't stayed where he'd told her to.

Kent was all-American. With good looks, short brown hair and smooth, even features, he was the kind of guy a mama wanted her daughter to bring home. And he was giving Bobbie a twice-over perusal.

"What do you want?" His statement sounded like a growl even to Nick.

Kent shook his head. "Just a friendly call, buddy. Why don't you introduce me to your friend back there?"

He spoke without turning. "Bobbie Jones, Kent English." *Now get the hell out of here.*

Like a predator, he scented her beside him. A hint of cinnamon and mocha. The mouthwatering zest of something citrus. Edible smells surrounded her as if she were a man's sustenance.

With a wolfish grin, Kent extended his hand. Nick

had known Kent since grade school, buddied around with him during high school, and since the prodigal's return, Kent was one of the few who didn't cross to the other side of the street when Nick sauntered down the boulevard.

But right now Nick resented the hell out of him.

"I'm just on my way out," Bobbie said as she dropped Kent's hand, then slipped past Nick through the doorway, her fingers skimming his arm above the elbow. Sparks set his skin alight.

"Don't let me interrupt," Kent said.

"Gotta run," she answered over her shoulder as she skipped down the porch steps, sprinted across the road and through the tangle of flowers in Mrs. Porter's yard.

"Hot," Kent said, watching her backside. "She the new girl?"

Nick cracked his knuckles. He didn't trust himself to speak.

"Sorry I ran her off." Kent turned, his brown eyes saved from a whipped-puppy look by a lascivious glint.

"I was trying to get rid of her anyway." Liar. "She keeps turning up uninvited on my doorstep."

Where had his brain been, telling her all that crap about his art, his dad, his kitchen, his one big movie? Oh yeah, in the middle of her cleavage. A second more and he would have told her he'd been doing a favor for a friend, only to have the director dupe him. There's a sucker born every minute, and that had definitely been his minute. Still, he'd thought the video would die a natural death. He'd never expected his mother to find out about it. Christ.

"Bobbie Jones doesn't waste time," Kent mused.

Nick shrugged off the memories. "Grass will never grow under that woman's feet."

"So. You doing her?"

Nick snorted as he moved back inside, Kent following. "She's in a messy divorce. I don't like messes."

"She trailed her husband here. You know that?" Kent crossed the living room and plopped down in his father's old recliner, the springs protesting. Nick hadn't used it since he'd been back.

"So I've heard. All over town."

"How is it I never get to scoop you, Nick, when no one else even talks to you? Got a beer?"

Nick returned, two beers in hand. Slouching down into the ancient plaid sofa, he propped his feet on the coffee table and popped his can. Christ, that made him imagine Bobbie, on her knees, making *him* pop.

Kent knocked back a slug, then wiped his lips. "You betting she'll whack him first or he'll whack her?"

He didn't want to think about Bobbie and her husband in any respect. The man had to be a loser to let her get away. God, he needed to stop thinking about her entirely.

Nick's lack of conversational participation didn't faze Kent. "I'm betting the husband'll whack her. Heard he showed up at the Cooked Goose—you know she's working there?—and the man's eyes damn near bulged out. He was practically hyperventilating. Something tells me she didn't used to wear short skirts and tight little sweaters back home." His lips curved in a leer. "So spill, does she like thigh-high stockings and crotchless panties?"

"How the hell should I know? I told you, I'm not doing her." But his blood surged southward just contemplating it.

Kent gargled his beer, at odds with his Mr. *GQ*

image, swallowed, then laughed. "You will be soon, dude. She's got 'fuck me' written all over her."

Nick's neck muscles tensed. Kent's description pissed him off. Bobbie wasn't some cheap bar pickup. But saying that would only keep Kent going down the same path.

"If you swear you're not doing her—"

"I'm not doing her."

"Then I'm sure *he'll* whack *her.* Brax is gonna crap in his pants. He hates that murder shit in his town."

Nick's scalp itched at the mention of Sheriff Tyler Braxton.

A grimace must have creased his face, Kent answering it with, "It's not his fault that Jimbo's money got him elected. Roles being reversed, you'd have made the same choice he did when it came down to that fight."

Nick grunted. Brax had come close to hauling Nick in, but…something had changed his mind. Probably Cookie calming her hapless husband before anyone got wind of the truth.

James "Jimbo" Beaumont should learn to keep his wife at home. Prowling the bars in Red Cliff was no place for a so-called lady. Not that Cookie was by any means a lady. A bitch in heat was more like it.

"Lucky for you I didn't have to choose, huh, buddy? Without me, Jimbo's whole damn business would go under while he's keeping both eyes on Cookie. And he knows it." Going on fifteen years now, Kent had managed Jimbo's chain of lube and oil changers.

"Screw Jimbo." But definitely don't screw his wife.

"You know, Angel, if I didn't know better, I'd swear you sounded bitter and self-pitying."

He did. Legacy of Bobbie Jones walking out his door

before he got to indulge himself in any mind-bending, sinful stuff. "You're right. Screw self-pity. Why'd you come over?"

"Just wanted a gander at your new neighbor."

He should have expected that. Kent had never come over before, usually they went up to Red Cliff.

"Harry said she was a hot little number. If he didn't have a wife and three kids, he'd give her a run for her money." Kent smirked. "Brax gave the idea a resounding second."

Jesus H. Christ. Nick couldn't seem to help himself, asking, despite the obvious answer, "How the hell would Brax know?"

"He's seen her around, everyone's seen her around. Can't miss those tits and that tight ass."

"She's old." But then who wanted some sweet little ingénue? Not him.

"The older they are, the more they know. There's something to be said for experience."

Nick's sentiments exactly.

"I saw the way she was looking at you. Do her and put her out of her misery."

A sneer rose to Nick's lips. He crushed it. "Not a chance."

Kent chugged his beer, then shot another volley. "Brax is thinking about hitting the diner tomorrow morning and getting himself a proper introduction. Why don't you join him?"

The idea almost choked him. "I don't do the Cooked Goose. And, as you can see, I've already made her acquaintance."

And why did Kent care one way or the other? Most likely because he loved a good bet with even odds. And maybe the bets weren't just on who would kill whom first, but also on who'd be the first to get her out of her panties.

He didn't like anyone betting on Bobbie's sex life.

"You're afraid of competing with Brax. He came out on top in high school, you think he'll come out on top here, too."

On top of Mary Alice Turner, that is, without appropriate protection and without taking appropriate responsibility for the consequences. Ancient history, though. But Bobbie and Brax? Nick shuddered.

Damn. He felt…jealous. Bobbie was a pain in the ass. She was in the middle of a divorce. Rebound. Transference. Replacement. No way did he want to get a piece of that. Luckily, he'd been saved from that folly by Kent ringing his bell.

"Brax can have her. I don't give a damn."

"Sure you don't." Kent slugged his beer, then smacked his lips. "That can only be because you've already done her."

Nick merely rolled his eyes.

"And if you haven't, then you better get cracking, old boy. Unless you want Brax to win."

He hadn't, he wouldn't. He was too old to compete.

But he still had the urge to beat Sheriff Tyler Braxton to a bloody pulp. Damn, that woman was getting to him.

BOBBIE WOKE in the early morning, stretching with the seductive aftereffects of a tantalizing dream where Nick the Barbarian had tossed her over his shoulder. Maybe she should have waited out his visitor last night. Just to see what interesting things developed. Maybe a mock battle with a couple of dragons, then…

She sat bolt upright in the bed, suddenly knowing where she'd seen a sci-fi-fantasy calendar, presumably one of Nick's. In Mavis's office. At the time she'd thought it oddly unlike Mavis's style. Maybe Mavis had a secret hankering for the serial killer. No. Oh, no, no, no.

She tackled Mavis before her shift started. "Is that Nick Angel's calendar in your office?"

Mavis raised one brow. "Maybe. Why?"

"Curiosity."

"Killed the cat," Mavis finished.

She had a curiosity about a great many things, one of them being why Mavis had his calendar. But first, she wanted to see what he drew. "Can I take a look?"

Mavis glanced at the huge digital watch on her bony wrist. "You've got less than ten minutes."

Bobbie darted through the swing doors, ignored JJ's leer and threw herself over Mavis's desk to grab the calendar from the wall. She huddled in the chair, feet balanced on a rung, open pages spread across her thighs.

Not a single clown on those pages. Instead, his paintbrush caressed full feminine lips. Light, shadow, color harmonized into sleek limbs, soulful eyes and lush curves. He lavished attention on the subtle outline of a peaked nipple, the swell of a toned calf muscle, the hue of windswept hair.

Nick Angel loved women. His art worshipped them. He portrayed them as mythical, revered creatures. Powerful, fearless, invincible.

Bobbie wanted to climb into his canvas and become one of his women with a desperation that stole her breath.

Patsy was wrong. Not that Bobbie had ever believed all that serial-killer stuff. But the evidence of Nick's innocence was right here in his reverent depictions. Not to mention the fact that he'd "gotten" the romanticism of *Laura*. The man who painted women with such... worship could never be capable of killing the very objects of his desire.

"Bobbie." A shriek ripped through her blissful thoughts.

Bobbie hung the calendar in its place on the wall and scuttled back through the kitchen.

"Hustle your butt out there," Mavis hissed. "Here, take the sheriff his breakfast."

Mavis dumped the plates in Bobbie's hands. Panic set in, not as bad as the hair dryer business, but on a par with the time she'd been stuck in a malfunctioning car wash that wouldn't turn off. A tall glass of orange juice in her right hand, superdeluxe eggs, home fries and steak balanced with a separate small plate of toast along her left arm.

Bobbie maneuvered down the aisle, bent to slide the superdeluxe onto the sheriff's table and almost lost the toast. A massive male paw reached out at the last moment to save it. And her.

"Thanks."

"Welcome, ma'am. So. You're the new girl," said the big, blond...brute. He could crush beer cans against his forehead without getting a headache.

"I'm not quite a girl anymore." She might have told sweetheart Jimbo about the big four-oh, but she certainly wasn't telling this brute. Not that brute was bad, in his case. In fact, it was sort of appetizing.

"Girl or woman, you look just about perfect to me, ma'am."

His blue eyes flashed over her, head to toe, so fast she almost thought she'd hallucinated it. Except for the lingering tingle. That was very real, leaving her speechless for a moment. The short, tight skirt of her uniform suddenly seemed a tad shorter and a tad tighter.

"Why don't you sit a minute?" He indicated the seat opposite with one of those big mitts of his.

She glanced over her shoulder for rescue or confirmation.

"Mavis said it was okay."

The breakfast crowd was thinning out, all Bobbie's tables were empty except for a little snub-faced guy over in the corner. Mavis gave her the thumbs-up. She sat while the sheriff drank his coffee, staring at her over the rim of his mug.

His short hair frizzed with the promise of uncontrollable curls if he didn't keep an eye on its length. Being a guy, he probably hated that. He blinked with long, gold-tipped lashes.

"Now, why would a pretty lady like you want to leave the big city? For Cottonmouth." He dug into his eggs, splitting them, letting the yolks leak out, then spread the yolk all over his home fries. Her stomach rumbled daintily.

"Want some?"

Oh, yes, please. The sheriff was as delicious as the serial killer. Both ends of the law. "No, thanks, I had a bagel earlier."

"Wimp food." He took a healthy mouthful of his *manly* food, swallowed, then struck up more conversation. "Now, you were saying about why you left the big city."

She hadn't been. She'd been avoiding it. "Midlife crisis." Premenopausal.

He nodded, tucked into his yolk-slathered home fries with gusto.

"Incidentally, does everybody know everything around here?"

"People around here don't have much else to do but gossip." He pinned her with that blue gaze. "Don't let it get on your nerves. They don't mean anything by it."

"Actually, it's kind of nice. I didn't know my neighbors' names in San Francisco. Here, I don't even have to introduce myself. I always thought small towns would be like that."

"Can be a pain in the…patoote if you've got something to hide." Cutting into his steak, he raised just his eyes to her face.

"Thank God I don't."

He scanned her features a moment longer than necessary. "Got any kids?"

"No." She swallowed, then leaned her elbows on the table, palms flat against the scarred Formica. "I'm not the mothering type." She might have been. A long time ago. If Warren had wanted to… The backs of her eyes ached suddenly. She felt too old to begin a family now. And beyond any regrets except the one about having let Warren make the decision.

"Doubt that. All women have the instinct."

She smiled brightly, blinking away those bad thoughts. And if her eyes were moist, it was only because she'd gotten some dust in them. "Not me."

He mopped up vestiges of yolk with a piece of toast. She hadn't even noticed him eating the steak, but it was almost gone. "What about other family?"

"My parents are dead. And I'm an only child."

He didn't offer condolences or apologies. Instead he reached out to trace the pale band of flesh on her left hand. "What about a husband?"

She pulled her hand from beneath his, ignoring the tingle, and tapped her chin with her index finger. "Now, Sheriff, you and I are both aware that you know all about my husband. You know he has an office just down the street, and you know we aren't divorced yet."

He polished off the remainder of his orange juice in one big swallow, then grinned at her. "Busted."

"Are you this obvious when interrogating suspects?"

"Way better at it. I was just checking availability."

Availability for what? The suspense raised her pulse rate. "I have to get back to work."

"Name's Tyler Braxton," he said as she rose. "But you can call me Brax. Everyone does."

"Nice to meet you, Brax."

"And you can call on me, Bobbie, any time you'd like."

Hmm, big, blond, blue-eyed sheriff or dark-eyed, dark-haired, devilish serial killer. A veritable smorgasbord for such a small town. She'd be willing to bet, though, that the sheriff wasn't a sentimental guy. He'd probably never even heard of *Laura*, let alone watched the movie.

"One more thing, Bobbie."

She tipped her head.

"Just make sure you don't murder your ex in my county. I'd really hate to put you in jail."

BOBBIE HADN'T COME to his house last night. Three nights in a row, she'd bellied up to his porch, but last night not so much as a boo. And yesterday she'd served the sheriff his breakfast and sat with him while he ate— that info gleaned from a trip to Sylvestor's to get the rest of the items he needed for the toilet-restoration project.

Not that Nick gave a flying freaking rat's ass. It was merely curiosity. In fact, it'd be a good thing if Brax took her off his hands and his porch.

And that's the only reason he'd ventured down to the Cooked Goose. Curiosity.

Shit. Why bother denying the truth? She'd left her pasta bowl behind, and he felt obligated to return it.

Double shit. All right, already, the real truth. He couldn't stand the idea of Bobbie being anyone's quarry. He should probably warn her about Kent's bet.

So here *he* was, the one bellying up to the Cooked Goose, choosing the middle of the afternoon in order to make the least spectacle of himself. Truly pathetic.

He opened the door. Silence descended like the curtain going down on the first act of a bad play, *The Life of Nick Angel*.

"Well, well, well, if it isn't Nick Angel. I think I'm going to have a heart attack." Mavis Morgan grabbed her scrawny chest.

He should have known she wouldn't let him in without a scene. Only four or five tables were occupied at this hour, late for lunch, early for dinner, no Brax, no Jimbo.

The diner was Jimbo's territory. Cookie might be a Venus's-flytrap, but a man had to take responsibility for letting himself get trapped. So, Nick solicitously avoided Jimbo's favorite joint. Until Bobbie came to town.

All eyes—except the big guy at the counter slurping his soup—focused on him, some avid, some terrified, as if they expected him to whip out an Uzi right then and there.

Behind the counter, Bobbie started a new pot of coffee brewing. God, she looked hot in that uniform. He couldn't take his eyes off her.

"Must be something new on the menu you've heard about." Mavis's sly gaze moved from him to Bobbie.

He mentally shook himself. "Just a hankering for that sludge you call coffee, Mavis."

"Have a seat over…let's see, over there." She pointed to a spot in the back, isolated from the rest by empty booths and vacant tables. "Bobbie, why don't you get him his sludge?"

His shoes pounded the linoleum in the relative silence. Sliding into the booth, he watched Bobbie's progress.

Armed with a white mug, wearing black tennis shoes and black nylons, she made his mouth water. What was it about her? She wasn't pretty in any standard way. Her red hair was a tad too short. Yet…something in her green eyes reeled him in, a twinkle. And her mouth, that was real pretty, lusciously red.

And that hint of a smile made him distinctly uneasy. As if she could see right inside him to find secrets no one else did.

She set the mug of steaming coffee on the table along with a couple of tubs of cream, then stuck out her pelvis to facilitate pulling a pad from her apron.

"You sure know how to make an entrance," she said, pencil poised.

"All I did was walk in."

"That's what I'm talking about."

Whispers and low voices began to fill the room again. Ceramic plates clattered from the kitchen. A basket of French fries hissed in hot grease.

Pointing at his closed menu, she asked, "You want something to eat?"

Just her. "No."

"You only came in for the coffee?"

He dumped two creams in before answering. "No." Unable to raise his eyes beyond the level of her plump, perfect breasts, he stirred. And stirred. "I just dropped by about your pasta bowl. You forgot it the other night."

She doodled on the pad. "You could have left it on my porch."

"Someone might have stolen it."

"Yeah. Right." She licked her lips, drawing his gaze from her breasts.

He thought about asking why she hadn't come over last night. Why was he here, like a nerdy teenager wanting to ask the head cheerleader for a date?

She stopped doodling and stuck pencil and pad back in her apron pocket, jutting her pelvis again. Did she do that in front of everyone? "Well, I should get to work then, if you have everything you want."

He didn't. But revealing that was out of the question. His mind swirled around the things he could say to get her to stay.

"Shit, lady, what the hell are you doing?"

Bobbie jumped as the big guy at the counter bellowed. The crash of glass and a yelp followed.

Little Ellie Brooks backed up against the stainless steel drainboard. "I'm sorry, mister, I'm really sorry."

"You burned me, Godammit."

"It wa-was an accident."

"Where's Mavis?" Bobbie whispered beside Nick.

The big oaf at the counter had come off his stool, shaking his finger at a terrified Ellie. "You stupid cow."

"Hey, that's not very nice." Bobbie's voice couldn't have carried beyond Nick's hearing. "I should do something."

Nick started to push himself out of the booth. The bastard needed to learn some manners. "I'll take care of it." Bobbie blocked his way. "So move."

"I can't just stand here," she muttered to herself, not even hearing him. Then she pursed her lips, snagged a deep breath and surged forward, her black tennies stomping the floor.

Dammit, didn't she see how big that guy was?

"Hey, leave her alone. She told you it was an accident."

Burly Ass turned on Bobbie when Nick was still several feet away. Shit.

"Butt out, bitch. I'm gonna get her fired."

Bobbie stared, long enough for Nick to make it another three feet, then suddenly she stabbed her finger in the big man's chest. "Don't threaten her. Get. Out."

The guy's arm pulled back, and his fist bunched. Nick started to dive for him. Only, someone grabbed his arm.

"Let her handle it." Mavis, her voice like steel wool in his ear, her grip a vise.

Nick almost leaped anyway, but then Bobbie's pencil was suddenly in her hand, dagger-style. "You punch me, and I'll poke your eye out."

Something in her tone, in that narrow-eyed look, stopped the man's arm midswing. The big guy crouched, and Bobbie's nose was right up in his face. "Now, you apologize to Ellie for calling her a cow."

The man's Adam's apple bobbed. He didn't take his eyes off the pencil in Bobbie's hand as he muttered out of the corner of his mouth. "Sorry I called you a cow."

"And accept her apology for spilling the coffee on you."

"I accept your apology."

"Good." Bobbie lowered the pencil dagger. "Now,

the meal's on me, but you get out of here, and don't come back."

Burly Ass sidled around her and pushed through the door, the bell tinkling overhead.

Nick let out the breath he hadn't realized he was holding. The sound of a clap beat against his eardrum. Mavis. Others joined in, until everyone was standing, the clapping deafening despite the relatively few patrons. Or was that his heart pounding right out of his chest?

Ellie, somehow having scampered from behind the counter, hugged Bobbie, throwing her whole bony frame into it.

Not a part of this, Nick took a step back, then two. He might have made it out the door if Bobbie hadn't turned then. Flushed with excitement, her eyes the brightest of greens, almost a shade not duplicated in nature, she called out, "Fresh coffee for everyone."

Mavis held on to his arm like an anchor. "Don't you dare leave now. Take your seat." Then louder, so that Bobbie could hear, "Don't forget you owe $8.32 for the jerk's meal."

"I won't." High on adrenaline, Bobbie bounced around the restaurant, wielding the pot she'd started when Nick first walked in.

She topped off his cup. "Did you see that? I beat him."

"He could have broken your jaw." Not that Nick would have let the guy that close, with or without Mavis hanging on his arm.

She snorted. "But he didn't. He backed down."

Nick still wasn't sure why the man had. "Give me the look you gave him. I couldn't see it well enough."

She narrowed her eyes. But he knew that wasn't the

look; it didn't scare him one damn bit. In fact, it made him hot. "You can't do it again."

"I can, too." She brought her light brows together.

"It's still not menacing."

"It was the heat of the moment then."

"You should have let me take care of him."

"I—" She stopped. "I had to do it."

"Why?" It was suddenly the most pressing of issues.

Avoiding his eyes, she looked toward Mavis helping Ellie clean up the broken glass and spewed coffee. "Because."

What didn't she want to say? "Because why? I'm not going to let go of this until you tell me."

She poured a trickle of coffee into his mug, though he hadn't touched it, bit her lip, then set the pot down. She put her hands flat on the table and leaned in, giving him an impressive view down the front of her uniform. He almost forgot the question.

"Because Mr. Winkleman almost made me…tried to intimidate me when I turned in my resignation."

Who was Mr. Winkleman and what had he almost made Bobbie do? He waited, as if he had infinite patience.

"He called me some awful names, none of which I can repeat because I'm a lady." She gave Nick a look, daring him to say otherwise. "But I knew he was only angry because he didn't want to have to deal with the auditors himself. He thought if he humiliated me enough, I'd stay. And *then* he could fire me, when he didn't need me anymore."

She took a deep breath. "I should have told him…to…stick it where the sun don't shine. But I didn't want to get fired. And then I thought, I'm quitting anyway so he can't fire me." She smiled at that notion. "Still, I didn't want to burn any bridges if I ever needed a reference…"

Nick remembered the way she'd talked to herself as the Ellie scene played out. As if she'd needed coaching to step in. She hadn't kept quiet with Winkleman merely to get a good reference.

Bobbie rolled her eyes and went on as if she hadn't just turned on the proverbial lightbulb above his head. "You know, it's the old male authority figure thing." She stood straight, puffed up her chest, which didn't need an iota of puffing to rivet his attention. "Bluster, bluster, blather, blather. On and on. You never know what they're going to do when they're cornered."

She'd been scared, maybe even irrationally so. And she hadn't told Winkleman where to get off. Nick had the suspicion that wasn't the first time she'd let a man intimidate her. She wasn't the woman-on-top, go-for-what-you-want type she pretended to be. Which was why she'd gone on the offensive for Ellie.

She might have gotten decked for her trouble, but she'd proven something to herself. And to Nick. "You handled him. That was good."

She flexed an arm muscle. "John Wayne, the Duke, fearless protector of women and small animals, at your service."

The twinkle in her eyes captivated him.

Sometimes it was doing the things you were afraid of that made you really brave. Wasn't that the definition of courage?

He had an absurd urge to kiss her. Shit. That was scary, almost as frightening as the realization that he was starting to like her for more than her magnificent breasts and squeezable tush.

CHAPTER SIX

"SO, WHAT'S GOING ON between you and the serial killer?"

Though she'd guessed this conversation was coming after Nick had dropped by the Cooked Goose that afternoon, Bobbie almost choked on the banana split she was sharing with Mavis.

It was seven-thirty on a hot Friday evening, and Johnson's Ice Cream Soda Fountain swelled with screaming children, sweating, harried parents and teenagers on dates. No sign of a failing Cottonmouth economy here. Thank God the Little League team had just left, or even Mavis's voice wouldn't have penetrated the din.

Bobbie managed to swallow the bit of banana, then dabbed at the chocolate sauce on her lips and ventured, "Serial killer? Have there been murders around Cottonmouth?"

God, she couldn't believe she'd almost told Nick her boss had been close to making her cry. She'd only been that close because of the whole Warren business at the time, of course. But gosh, she'd been so proud of herself, standing up to that horrible lout, that she'd almost revealed far too much to Nick.

"Do not give me any crap about not having heard all

the stories about Nick Angel," Mavis muttered around a mouthful of chocolate ice cream, then abruptly reverted to their earlier argument. "I don't know how I let you talk me into coming. That Kelly person is probably robbing me blind."

It had taken Bobbie over half an hour to talk Mavis into the short outing. And she was sure there was nothing wrong with Kelly that a little higher education wouldn't fix. Except if you listened to Mavis, who was still going on about her. "Or she'll burn the place to the ground, and if she does, it's coming out of *your* paycheck."

Mavis punctuated the threat with another stab at her ice cream. "What was I saying? Oh, yeah. Nick Angel."

Did Mavis see the same things in his art that Bobbie did? "Why do you have his calendar, Mavis?"

Mavis shrugged, a stray candy sprinkle falling out of her hair. How it got there, only God knew. "I like him," she said simply.

Shock of shocks. Bobbie thought everyone in Cottonmouth hated the serial killer. "Do you know him very well?"

"Used to. But that boy hasn't been into my place since Jimbo tried to knock his block off."

Which was, presumably, a long time. But now he'd made an exception. Because Bobbie was working there? What a nice thought. She hid the secret pleasure. "Why would that sweet man beat up Nick?"

"I said 'tried.' And you'll have to ask the serial killer. Or Jimbo."

And hadn't it been the most perfect time for Nick to show up, when she'd flawlessly played warrior princess, like a model for his artwork? Maybe she should have said something about the calendar. No, she wanted him to show her first. "I'm certainly not going to ask Jimbo something that's none of my business."

What would Warren have done if he'd ever seen the warrior princess? It occurred to her that he might have chosen the Cookie Monster, anyway. Chocolate sauce curdled in her stomach. Ohh, bad thought, conquer it.

Mavis's next comment helped Bobbie do just that.

"So, ask the serial killer."

Ask Nick? That would be a conversation starter. "I think you should stop calling him the serial killer."

Mavis spread her hands. "And I should do that...because?"

Because Bobbie's Cottonmouth reputation probably couldn't withstand the impropriety of sleeping with the local serial killer. If she did manage to get him into her bed, no sleep intended. "Because he's actually a very nice man. And he didn't mean to make that porno-graphic film. It was a mistake."

Mavis leaned forward, an avid light glittering in her eyes. "How do you know?"

"He told me."

The older woman gaped. "He told you a thing like that?"

"Well, yes. He said they tricked him into it."

Mavis drummed her fingers on the table. "Honey, a man can't dip his wick into something hot without him knowing that's what he's doing. I should know."

"It wasn't *his*...wick."

It started as a guffaw, then turned into tears. Mavis almost fell off her chair. The shop quieted around them. Bobbie's truck-stop mentor had the grace to lower her voice. "Yeah, right. That's why his poor mama went ballistic in the middle of her little 'my son's big movie' party. You'd think she'd know her own son's *wick* since she used to bathe him when he was a baby."

Hopefully, his wick had changed considerably since then. "She had a party to show people his movie?"

Mavis wiped her eyes. "They had to call the paramedics for Eugenia Meade. She said she was having a heart attack, but knowing the mayor's wife, all she needed was some attention. Marjorie Holmes, his high school drama teacher, went into the bathroom and used a pair of his mother's nail scissors to cut off her hair."

No wonder Patsy and everyone else in Cottonmouth had a bad taste in their mouths. And maybe that's why Nick's face had reddened last night in his living room's gloom. Because of the embarrassment he'd caused his mother. He must have felt awful.

"I'm sure it was terrible for his mother."

Mavis snorted. "It was hilarious. Of course, I was the only one who ever thought so."

Bobbie herself struggled to keep the smile from her lips.

Mavis tapped her spoon against her teeth. "You know, I think he'd rather everybody believe he intentionally made that movie. For his sake, don't spread it around that he was tricked."

The somewhat melted ice cream froze in Bobbie's mouth. "I would have thought he'd want to clear his name."

"Not if it means showing how stupid he was. Take it from me, he'll thank you for letting him remain a fallen man."

"Oh." She could understand that. She'd rather everyone believe she and Warren had the most amicable of divorces than tell them he left her for a hairy blue Sesame Street character. See, Warren needn't have worried that she'd spill the beans about Cookie, even if the woman hadn't asked for her divorce yet.

"But he must want in your pants real bad if he's revealing his big bad mistakes to get there."

And it just might work.

"Women are such suckers for a tale of woe," Mavis muttered.

A tale. Which reminded her. "What's the scoop on Mary Alice Turner?"

"Mary Alice? Where did you hear that name?" Mavis quickly held up a hand. "Don't tell me, it was Eugenia or Patsy. I, for one, never believed he did it."

"Believed he did what?"

"Got her pregnant when they were in high school, refused to marry her and instead handed her money for an abortion."

Oh, my. That was bad. But at least Mary Alice hadn't been anyone's murder victim. Cottonmouth did seem to have such a long memory, if the mistiness in Patsy's eyes had meant anything.

"He forced her to get an abortion?" Bobbie didn't want to believe it of him.

Mavis spread her hands. "That's what they say. But in my opinion, he seemed more protective of her than anything else. He wouldn't let a bad word be said about her, even after her parents moved her away. His attitude just didn't have the feel of a boy shirking his responsibilities."

Bobbie let her shoulders relax. Mavis was right. No man sentimental enough to appreciate the romanticism of *Laura* would force his girlfriend to get an abortion.

"In fact, I recall him having a little out with the sheriff at the time," Mavis went on. "Of course, he wasn't sheriff then. Captain of the football team."

Oh, my God. Mary Alice wasn't to Nick what Cookie was to Warren, was she? Near panic made her tamp the idea down. Please, not again. She focused on another thought. "The sheriff grew up here, too?"

"Yeah, his daddy owned the dry cleaners. When Brax's old man died, his mama wanted to move to Palm Springs and his sister went off and married the fruitcake. So Brax sold out."

Somehow she couldn't imagine Sheriff Braxton working in a dry cleaners. Or "selling out." He looked as if he was born to be a cop. But with an odd family.

"His sister married a what?"

"A fruitcake." Mavis rolled her eyes. "A nut. She met him in Las Vegas and married him the same weekend if I recall. Then he dragged her off to some hole-in-the-wall Nevada town called Goldstone. Brax's mama says the man's never had a job. But that's a whole other story, and I know you're avoiding the real topic."

Darn. Mavis had figured her out. "I forgot what we were talking about."

"That boy is hot for you, Bobbie dear."

Bobbie felt herself blush, but thanked God the subject of Mary Alice Turner was over for now. "He just wanted to make sure I wasn't going to kill Warren in his county." She tapped her chin. "I wonder if it's okay to do it in the next county?"

"Don't waste your time on the nimrod."

"Warren's not a nimrod," she automatically defended, then wondered why, except that it was such a reflex.

"Answer me this. When was the last time you had sex?"

Oh, my God, was the truth written all over her flaming face?

"I thought so. Now, the question is, the sheriff or the serial killer. The choice is yours. 'Cause they both have the hots for you."

It was such a wonderfully delicious thought. Two men interested.

"I'm partial to the sheriff myself," Mavis stated, "only because you wouldn't have to fight the whole damn town to do it. You choose the serial killer, and you won't be able to walk down the street in daylight without being stoned."

"Oh, come on. They just need to see him as a human being." And maybe if she helped bring him out in the light.

"He *isn't* a human being. He's an icon. Now the sheriff, they'll trip all over themselves trying to set you up with him."

But Bobbie didn't need anyone's help. She could do it on her own. She scooped melted ice cream, nuts and whipped cream from the bottom of the dish. On the one hand, she liked the idea of Cottonmouth rooting for her. But on the other, she just plain old liked Nick. Maybe it was because she'd known him three more days than she'd known the sheriff, but still…she figured it was time for another subject change. Which, after all, was the real reason she'd invited Mavis out for ice cream in the first place.

"Why does Beau hate you?"

Mavis threw down her spoon with enough force to knock a chink out of the glass dish. "What's that weasel been saying about me?"

"He called you a viper." Bobbie justified tattling on two counts. First, Mavis should know what the man was saying about her, and second, Beau had told her to ask Mavis.

"Creep."

Mavis squinted her eyes together and pressed her lips into a white line.

"So, why does he think you're a viper?"

"Probably because I threw him out of the house ten years ago for sleeping with that tramp married to his brother."

Her ears burning, Bobbie wasn't sure what to ask first. "*You're* the woman who pays for his teeth?"

"You don't think I'd have sex with him if his teeth were falling out from that disgusting tobacco problem he has?"

Eyes wide with wonder, Bobbie pressed the obvious. "You threw him out of the house, but you still have sex with him?"

Mavis tossed her head, threatening to topple her bouffant hair. "A woman has needs, you know."

Yes, Bobbie knew, all right, but she couldn't see herself sneaking over to Warren's office in the middle of the night. "But your ex-husband?"

"He's not my ex-husband. We never got divorced. Medical and dental rates would have been higher if we had. I just make him live down at his damn garage."

"But…he slept with his brother's wife?"

And that was pretty horrible. At least Warren had…what? Waited until he left her? She didn't know that. She couldn't ask him that. She shouldn't have cared anymore.

"I'll grant him one thing," Mavis went on. "He's been pretty damn consistent about denying he did it with her."

"So you think maybe he's telling the truth?"

Mavis shrugged. "Could be. I wouldn't put it past her to lie about it. Bitch never did like him."

"Why did you kick him out if you weren't sure it was true?"

"That old man's a frigging sex addict. He might not have been with *her,* but there was that old biddy English teacher at the high school. I would have caught them at it, too, if she hadn't made him crawl under her desk. I'll tell you this, I wasn't about to stoop to looking under her drawers, if you know what I mean."

Bobbie put her hand under her chin to keep her mouth from falling open. "So what happened to your sister-in-law?"

"Nothing. Yet. But I'm not done with her, you can sure as hell bet on that."

Bobbie wondered if big cities had as many intrigues as small towns. Probably. It was simply that she'd never known her neighbors well enough to ask. "So, is she someone I've met?"

"I haven't said her name in ten years. I'm not going to start now. Ask the weasel. I'm sure he'd bend over backward to tell you."

And Bobbie was equally sure she wouldn't walk over to Beau and say, "So, who was the woman you were having an affair with when Mavis kicked you out?" Maybe she could finagle the answer out of him without being obvious.

"You ladies didn't leave any for me?"

The bass voice wasn't loud, but Bobbie jumped as if it had boomed in her ear. She'd been hanging on Mavis's every word.

Mavis recovered first, batting her lashes. "Oh, Sheriff, you can lick my ice-cream cone any time." Then she pointed across the table. "Or maybe you'd rather have Bobbie's."

Oh. My. God. Flame, flame, foam, foam. Bobbie sputtered but nothing came out. She started coughing, then her eyes watered, and she was sure her mascara streaked down her cheeks.

"You shouldn't embarrass her like that, Mavis. She's not used to you."

The sheriff gave her a surprisingly gentle pat on the back that helped stop the coughing fit. It didn't do anything, however, for the smudged cheeks. She'd die for a compact mirror.

"It's all right," she managed, surreptitiously wiping under her eyes. "I'm starting to understand Mavis perfectly."

Why was everything suddenly so quiet? She peered around the sheriff's big body to find every single pair of eyes in Johnson's Soda Fountain right on her. Oh, except the baby, who was happily smearing ice cream over his, or her, entire body.

"I have to go." Mavis scraped back her chair.

"So do I." Bobbie executed a matching scrape.

"No, you don't." Mavis pushed her back down. "Keep the sheriff company while he eats his ice cream."

The sheriff himself settled it, thank God. "Sorry, ladies, but as much as I'd like to, I can't stay. Just stopped in to say hi." Bobbie realized his hand was still on her back. Warm. Did it feel better than Nick's? Hmm, had Nick ever even put his hand on her anywhere?

The sheriff was looking at her with a very blue, very knowing gaze—had she said that aloud? "I'll take a rain check, okay?"

"Shall I put that in writing?" Mavis offered.

"I think we can both remember, Mavis." He put a hand to his cute sheriff's hat, did a mock bow and left.

"What'd I tell you?" Mavis whispered. "He's got a cucumber in his pants for you."

Bobbie stared through the window as he climbed into his green-and-white car. "I think that's cool as a cucumber. You're mixing metaphors."

"No, I'm not. He gets a cucumber when he looks at you, and there ain't nothing cool about it."

"WE'RE OPEN seven days a week, my dear." Mr. Fry cleared his throat with a great rumble. "Won't find a pharmacy at the minimall that responsive to the everyday consumer's needs."

This had to be the absolute dumbest idea Bobbie'd ever had. No, not coming to Cottonmouth—although at the moment that ranked second. Second only to coming to Fry's Pharmacy on a hot Saturday afternoon for…a prescription.

Mr. Fry stared at the paper in his hand, first at arm's length, then close to his bifocals. "Oh," he finally cried out, tapping at his hearing aid. "Birth control pills." Bobbie tried to sink into the floor. "I wish these damn doctors would work on their damn handwriting." Then he smiled at her.

Bobbie could only thank the Lord there were few shoppers in Fry's Pharmacy. And they were in other aisles at the moment. She should have purchased her darn pills back in San Francisco. But how could she know how dramatically her life would change in the space of just one week?

"When do you need them by, my dear?" Mr. Fry peered over the top of his half-glasses.

Nothing more than a puddle of mush on his nice clean floor, she pasted on a dazzling smile. Oh, God, were those footsteps behind her? Biologically, the timing would be perfect for effectiveness if she got them tomorrow, but she couldn't say *that*. "No hurry."

The change was subtle. Mr. Fry's gaze shifted to somewhere over her shoulder. His already thin lips flattened slightly. Fine hairs stood up on her neck. She would not turn around, she just would not.

The pharmacist's voice rose to a level just below a shout. "So, about the sheriff." Had they been talking about the sheriff? "You won't find a nicer, more stable character in the whole town."

"Uh, that's good to know." Was that a whiff of manly-man soap behind her? No, it couldn't be. *Please*.

Mr. Fry's white eyebrows came together in a glower, directed over her left shoulder. "One might even say he's Cottonmouth's most eligible bachelor."

"You don't say," she mumbled. The scent was definitely a *familiar* manly-man soap.

"Hear you two have a date tomorrow night."

That was news to her. The tips of her ears started to burn. "The sheriff and me?"

"Yeah. Heard it from…" He tapped his hearing aid as if the information was stored somewhere in there.

"Eugenia Meade, perhaps."

Nick's voice trickled over her like maple syrup. No, oh no, no, no.

"No, it most certainly was not Eugenia." Mr. Fry

sniffed like an irritated old woman. Even if Nick hadn't spoken, the old man's tone revealed exactly who loitered at her elbow. Not to mention the manly-man scent.

"How about Patsy Bell Sapp?"

Nick's body heat settled next to her left arm, sending a wave of warmth over her back. Why did he have to stand so close? She didn't dare turn around.

"I don't like your implications, young man."

And why did he have to be here today, of all days?

"I was just trying to be helpful, Mr. Fry."

"Well, you're not. It's making me forget things."

"Sorry about that." Nick didn't sound in the least bit sorry—amused was more like it.

Mr. Fry thought the amusement was at his expense. "What do you want?"

Nick stepped forward to look at Bobbie, very slowly, up and down, like a touch. She squirmed with the need to cover her chest. Goodness, her nipples had peaked against her thin cotton tank top, and goose bumps peppered her bare legs.

"Well, let me see…" Staring at her breasts, Nick tapped his ear in imitation of the elderly pharmacist.

Please don't say it. This was all Warren's fault. If she'd needed birth control pills with him, she wouldn't have had to buy them here. She wouldn't be in this mortifying position. She'd be back in San Francisco.

And she wouldn't be getting a divorce.

"I'll come back tomorrow, Mr. Fry," she yelped, like Princess, the irritating pooch.

"Oh, my dear, I'm so sorry. This…person made me forget what I was doing."

She hoped he didn't accidentally make her prescription up with cyanide. On second thought, maybe that wasn't a bad idea. She could crawl over to the serial kill-er's backyard and die there. Then Nick would have something else to bury.

"Tomorrow's fine. Really. Just fine." She started backing away, hoping she wouldn't accidentally touch Nick.

"Wait, wait. Let me get you something." As fast as his creaky knees would let him, Mr. Fry scurried from behind the counter and down an aisle.

Nick took one step to her two. "Got a date with the sheriff, huh, Bobbie?"

He should have been laughing at her total humilia-tion and embarrassment. But his eyes, much darker than their normal brown, were not amused.

"Ahh, not that I know of."

He wasn't listening. "Extremely fast work there."

Another step. She resisted the urge to feel if anything stood in the way behind her.

"Stop bothering my customers." Mr. Fry, at her elbow, rustled a paper bag.

"Am I bothering you, Bobbie?"

Yes. "I'm fine, gotta go, though, you know." Another unnaturally high, dog-like yip.

"Here, dear, take these." Mr. Fry shoved the bag in her hand, then leaned in for a faux whisper Nick was sure to hear. "Something to tide you over, on the house, just in case you and the sheriff can't wait."

He wouldn't have. Couldn't have. He was close to seventy years old. He probably had to look up *S-E-X* in the dictionary. So he couldn't possibly have just given her a bag of…freebie condoms to use on the sheriff.

She wouldn't wait around to find out. "Thanks. Bye. Tomorrow." She only hoped the overly helpful pharma-cist would understand her code.

She shot down the open aisle, Mr. Fry's voice carrying like a foghorn. "Now you just get out of my store." Pause. "Unless you want to buy something."

Stepping out in the afternoon heat was like getting in a hot shower with a bad sunburn. The sidewalk was on fire, and she still had to walk home. The few blocks would drench her in sweat. Everything was so close in Cottonmouth, Bobbie didn't like to use the car, but with the heat, she now wished she'd driven.

Behind her the door whooshed open. A wave of cool air washed over her scorched back.

"Need a ride, Bobbie?"

Why did he keep saying her name like that, with a sultry puff of air that sent a tingle from her ear, down her spine, to the insides of her thighs?

"No, thanks." She looked up and down the street, avoiding him. Then, almost involuntarily, she drew in a deep breath that seared her lungs. She held it until she felt dizzy. Tension drained out with the exhale. She only had to feel humiliated if she wanted to.

"You did that on purpose to embarrass me, didn't you?"

Nick slipped on a pair of mirrored sunglasses. "I think it was more for the druggist's benefit."

She didn't doubt it was for hers, as well. "At least you're not lying about playing a game in there."

"I've never thought you were an idiot." Which didn't mean he wouldn't toy with her. "What's in the bag?" He tickled it with the tip of his finger.

"Stop it." She really hated sunglasses on a man when you wanted to see what he was thinking. Except that, with men, it wasn't easy to tell, even when they weren't hiding behind shades.

"What exactly is it you want me to stop, Bobbie?"

A strangely numb feeling edged down her arms to her fingertips. Despite her momentary embarrassment inside Fry's, she didn't want Nick to stop anything. Because everything he said or did was new and exciting and made her feel alive.

NICK SLAPPED SOAPY WATER on the already clean surface of his orange-and-black 1970 Charger. He'd bought it used during his junior year of high school, and he'd washed it every Saturday since, whether it needed it or not.

The sun settled down over the detached garage as he squatted, scrubbing the wheels viciously. His gut roiled. That's what he got for thinking about her date tomorrow with Brax and the condoms Fry had stuffed in that damn bag she'd clutched tightly beneath her arm. That's what he got for following her in there in the first place.

Get out unless you want to buy something. The old man's usual down-his-nose look had never bothered Nick before. So why now? Because Bobbie had witnessed the antagonism? What did that matter?

He'd scrub off the chrome if he wasn't careful. He stood, slammed the sponge into the bucket, spraying soapy water over his legs up to his cutoffs.

That's when she came out on her porch. He had to admit, washing the car had been an excuse to wait for her. Christ, he'd morphed back to high school.

She stopped, waved at him, then scampered down her steps to her car, legs wobbling as if she wasn't quite used to the height of those heels. The skirt of her flippy black dress swished around her thighs. Sequins glinted in the early evening sunlight. Two thin straps holding the dress up bared her shoulders. Nick held his breath waiting for a glimpse of the neckline. Plunging, he was sure. His heart plunged with it. She beeped her car open and climbed in.

Where the hell was she going dressed for a party?

And worse, who was she going with?

THE CHALET. Five miles out of town along Highway 26, the restaurant nestled in pine and oak. She'd wanted expensive and fancy, and Mavis had said she wouldn't find more expensive or fancy unless she drove fifty miles into Red Cliff.

Fans hung from the high, raftered ceiling, circulating the warm air comfortably. A four-foot wall topped with potted flowers separated the two halves of the large room while the tables were spaced far enough to discourage eavesdropping. A candle burned on the white tablecloth, a sweet-smelling rose in a bud vase next to it.

The purpose for her dinner out? She'd never in her life had a fancy dinner all by herself. Even on her infrequent business trips, she'd ordered room service. In her view, people didn't go out by themselves, as if dressing up and treating yourself was something you only did with someone else. As if it lost its taste when done alone.

Only a confident, self-assured woman would dress up in a skimpy cocktail dress and ask for a table for one. And that same woman would buy birth control without embarrassment because it was her God-given right as a woman.

And a serial killer would not be thinking about some girl he may or may not have gotten pregnant years ago when he was looking at Bobbie today. And Nick *had* been looking at her as she bopped out to her car tonight. Oh, yes, he had. A mutant tingle still lingered in her midsection.

Her champagne cocktail arrived, the sugar cube still fizzling at the bottom of the glass.

"We have some wonderful specials tonight, ma'am..." Her waiter proceeded to enumerate them all.

She didn't listen. In her head she played eenie, meenie, minie, mo. She wanted the most expensive thing on the menu, which was lobster, because she never ordered the most expensive. Warren had always gotten that *look* on his face when he got the bill, even if she'd ordered chicken.

Lobster? Or braised chicken livers? She adored chicken livers, but she'd only ever had them when Warren had a late meeting because he hated the aroma of cooked chicken livers. He said it smelled like...piss. She could hear him now. *You want to order something that smells like piss in a five star restaurant?*

"I'll take the chicken livers."

"Wonderful choice, ma'am."

"It is, isn't it." Not a question at all, a powerful statement. Her waiter went on his merry way, to the next table.

Chicken livers or lobster. The concept could actually be applied to the idea of the sheriff or the serial killer. Lobster was flashy and showy and best when dipped in hot butter, sort of like Nick. Chicken livers were less exotic, more of a staple, but they melted deliciously on your tongue when done just right. Sort of like the sheriff. Except for the piss part.

Eenie, meenie, minie, mo. The sheriff or the serial killer. They were both interested. Weren't they? Yes, they were. Be confident.

The sparkling wine sizzled down her throat.

And suddenly stopped halfway down when she saw the Cookie Monster. Bobbie wheezed, swallowed. Cookie Beaumont had ordered the lobster. She laughed, Bobbie imagined it was the off-key tinkle of an out-of-tune piano. Only it wasn't. It was pretty and sweet. Freaking melodious. And her hair was long and blond.

And jeez, that wasn't Warren with her.

Cookie Beaumont was holding Jimbo-from-the-diner's hand. A bottle of champagne—probably Dom Perignon—cooled in a bucket beside him. A small jewelry case sat on one corner of the table. Cookie flashed an enormous ring under her companion's nose.

Bobbie's waiter brought her chicken livers. They smelled like piss.

"By the way, who is that happy couple over there?"

"Why that's Jim Beaumont and his wife. They come here every year for their wedding anniversary. I think it's fifteen this time."

Jimbo? Jim Beaumont? His *wife?* A *happy* couple?

The Cookie Monster didn't look like she was getting ready to ask for a divorce. Not if she wanted to keep eating lobster, drinking Dom Perignon and wearing rocks the size of Kansas.

What on earth was Warren thinking?

WARREN PARKED his BMW in front of the house next to Roberta's. He wasn't sure why the clandestine action, but he felt better doing it. She'd called him half an hour ago, at nine o'clock on a Saturday, asking him to come over immediately.

She pulled into her driveway only minutes later, slammed her car door, then tottered over on those ridiculously high heels of hers. Roberta hadn't owned a pair of heels over a sensible two inches. Nor a dress that short or low cut. And she was gorgeous in both. He'd never thought of her as gorgeous, not since...well, never. He'd married her for her practical steadfast nature, but that nature didn't seem to be in evidence tonight. Usually, Roberta was down to earth, solid. She'd never been demanding, always supportive.

She signaled him to roll down his window.

"You really should leave your porch light on when you go out at night."

"My porch is my business, Warren. I want to talk to you."

He unlatched his door, started to open it. "Why don't we talk inside your place?"

Again, that niggling fear that someone was watching, that someone wouldn't want him talking to Roberta.

"You're not coming into my house."

Her eyes widened with something like horror, but there was just the slightest curl to her upper lip, a sharp edge to her tone that sliced him cleanly like a freshly sharpened knife. He'd put it there, anger barely veiled with sarcasm. And when Roberta got angry, she was either hurt or afraid. Maybe both this time, hurt for the past, fear of the future. Because of him.

"In my car, then?" A question, but he expected her to fall in line. Roberta always fell in line with whatever he said. At least she had once upon a time.

He closed his own door. She slammed the passenger side as she climbed in. She started in before the sound of it died away.

"She isn't getting a divorce, is she?"

He didn't have to ask who. "Roberta, you—"

"Don't call me Roberta. My name is Bobbie."

"Bobbie..." She didn't sound like the same woman he'd been married to for fifteen years. Shit. If she wasn't, it was his own fault. "Bobbie, it's very complicated."

And all the while, his mind worked furiously at what was the best way to protect Cookie.

"*You* didn't find it too complicated to say 'I want a divorce.' Why does *she?*"

He winced. Is that how he'd said it? That cold and callous? No, it was just her interpretation.

"Her situation is different." Maybe the truth would make Roberta feel empathy. Right. But it was all he had.

"I'm sure it is. She didn't have an adoring partner sitting in front of the computer for six months, night after night, addressing envelopes, licking stamps, taking the letters down to the post office instead of trusting the mail lady, thinking this would solve all the problems." She took a deep breath as if there was so much more inside that had yet to burst out. Held it seconds longer than he could have held his own. Then she finally let it wheeze out like the air from a balloon.

She had done all that for him. Roberta had always been a good hand-holder. But...why hadn't she fought for him?

The reason no longer mattered, hadn't from the moment he'd found Cookie again. "Will you please let me explain?"

Her jaw flexed, her lips thinned, then finally, "What does she want from you, Warren?"

Not that it was really any of Roberta's business. Yes, he'd done what he'd done to her, but once done, the rest of it had nothing to do with her.

"As I was saying, her situation's very complicated. Her husband—"

"Jimbo. At least call him by his name while you steal his wife."

God, she was angry. Roberta would never boil over, but she was on a slow simmer that could eventually sear his ass if he wasn't careful. Even if he deserved it.

"Jimbo has a temper," he told her.

"That sweet old guy?"

"It's just a facade, Rober—" She gave him the eye, and he cut himself off. "Everybody loves Jimbo, but at home he's not such a sweet guy."

"You're saying he beats her?"

"Yes."

"Warren, I don't mean to be cruel." She gave him a long look. "But you're stupid. I saw them at The Chalet tonight, and she—" said like something the cat dragged in "—was the furthest thing from unhappy I've ever seen. He'd given her this huge diamond rock, and she was holding it to the light, this way and that way, looking at all the different refractions. It was pathetic."

"It's an act she has to put on. He gets…upset if she doesn't show the proper respect for the things he gives her." Cocooned in the dark car, he felt safe telling her these things.

"She's got you snowed. Did she tell you how she threatened me the other day?"

Warren sighed. He didn't want to fight. He didn't

want to have to defend Cookie or his decision. "She told me *you* threatened *her.*"

"That bitch." There wasn't the slightest hesitation in the use of the word. Nor a hint of apology since she was talking about the woman he intended to marry as soon as he could.

Good politics not to mention her new penchant for bad language, though. "I'm sure she didn't mean it the way you think."

"She told me to quit messing with her plans or she would make sure you didn't give me a dime."

Roberta just didn't understand that Cookie was afraid. It wasn't really a threat. "You know you get fifty percent."

"I should get the one hundred thousand off the top of the house sale because we used *my* inheritance from *my* mother to pay off the mortgage." Another deep breath, then she cleared her throat. "But I'm sure you'll be fair, Warren."

She was right about the money. He'd already taken it into account. But it wasn't like Roberta to harp on it. Two months ago, she'd have trusted him.

"About Cookie. She needs me, Rob—Bobbie."

Roberta's nostrils flared. Maybe she was closer to the boil than he'd thought.

Warren stoically persevered. "Her husband's erratic. She says he's impotent and he beats her up when he can't…" He waved his hands in the air ineffectually.

"Can't get it up?"

"Yes." Her tone made bile rise in Warren's throat. He hadn't exactly been impotent, not like Jim Beaumont. It was the drugs. His psychiatrist said so. But there was always that little voice in the back of his head—one that sounded like Roberta—saying, yeah, but what about before the drugs?

He'd never meant to hurt her. How had things gotten so complicated? All he'd wanted to do was find himself, rid himself of the anxiety. Instead he'd created a mess.

"Go on." It was a go-on-if-you-dare tone.

He did go on. He had to keep his original goal in mind, to protect Cookie. "He takes his failings out on her physically."

"Warren, this is the biggest load of—"

He put his hand on her arm. He had one last card to play. He could only hope it worked.

"She can't ask for a divorce, Roberta. He'll kill her before he'll let her go."

CHAPTER SEVEN

BOBBIE'S STOMACH HURT so badly, she just wanted to lie down among the flowers and shrivel like last season's blooms. Maybe the chicken livers had been bad. Okay, okay, it wasn't the chicken livers. Organ meat didn't make you want to cry. It didn't wrap itself around your chest and squeeze like a python. It didn't sit on your head and pound like a woodpecker. Not unless it was that good old human heart organ.

The Cookie Monster needed Warren to protect her from her husband. Hah. Total doo-doo. Didn't the way Bobbie had needed him count for anything? Godammit! She stamped her foot on the gravel, a sharp pain shooting from her heel straight to her offending heart organ. Now Warren had her cussing like a sailor and hurting herself in the process.

What did the woman want from Warren? Bobbie was sure she had some nefarious plan in mind. Why else had the husband stealer threatened the dumped wife who'd suddenly shown up to throw a proverbial monkey wrench in the works?

"I'm going to find out what she really wants if it's the last thing I do," Bobbie whispered. Gosh, didn't that sound like an embittered, abandoned wife. Maybe. Regardless, the Cookie Monster had an ulterior motive, and she *would* discover what it was.

"Buck up." Another whispered encouragement as she climbed her porch steps, heels tapping on the wood. The porch swing creaked in the breeze. Except there was no breeze, the air hanging inert and hot in the night. Suffocating.

"Who you talking to, Bobbie?"

She almost screamed, as if Nick really was a serial killer. "What are you doing skulking in the dark?"

"I'm not skulking. I'm waiting for you."

Warren was right, she should have left a light on. Nick waited on the porch, a hulk in the shadows surrounded by the flowered trellis. She had the urge to hightail it back to her car and drive away. She didn't have the energy to face him now.

Okay, focus on the plan. Jeez, she'd forgotten the plan. Oh, yeah, show Warren exactly what he threw away, through osmosis, i.e., other men making love to her. And here was this prime candidate "waiting" for *her*.

Warren was five minutes ago, Nick was now. She clutched her purse to her chest, took a deep calming breath. It succeeded only in elevating her heart rate.

She pasted on a smile, wondering about her lipstick. "So, what brings you here?"

There, that was better, nice and bright.

"I taped a couple of *Buffy* episodes off cable for you."

She finally noticed the box in his hands. "Well, how sweet. But I don't have a VCR." Instead, she'd brought the all-important espresso machine and a DVD player.

"I have a VCR." Obviously.

Interesting. A semi-invitation. Enough to make her forget all about Warren and the Cookie Monster? Almost. "I'd love to watch them sometime." Now?

"Nice dress you're wearing."

Okay, not now. "Oh, this old rag." She'd almost forgotten how she was dressed, except for the pinch of her shoes and the ache they caused in her ankles. "I haven't worn it in ages."

It was new, at least to her, bought at a consignment store. Part of the plan to make Warren *see* her. He hadn't even noticed. Emotion rose up and grabbed her by the throat. Bad thoughts getting away with her again. She concentrated on Nick's voice, a pleasant growl she felt along her bare arms.

"Why not?"

Why hadn't Warren noticed her dress? Because he was too busy being *needed* by the Cookie Monster. "He really isn't into what a woman wears."

Nick tipped his head, his brows together in one long line. "Who?"

God. He hadn't been asking about Warren. He'd been asking why she hadn't worn the dress in ages. Stupid. "Uh, sorry, nobody."

His eyes were dark pools without benefit of light. "Out with your husband?"

His words resurrected the anger, at her idiocy for mistaking Nick's question, at Warren…for just being alive. "Ex. He's my ex. And I wasn't out with him." Nick must have been watching the whole time. How had he known it was Warren? Duh, he'd probably heard the yelling. "We were discussing…property rights."

Nick raised his hands in mock surrender. "Sorry for asking."

Breathe, Bobbie, just breathe. Listen to the crickets. Aren't they sweet? "Oh, it doesn't bother me. We've still got a few things to settle."

"I can see that." A neutral comment, but said with a hint of sarcasm.

Now what was that supposed to mean? She was spinning out of control again. "Warren's not important."

"Yeah. I can see that, too." He made for the edge of the porch. "Gotta go."

Go? Just like that? She stepped in his path. "What about the tape?"

He shoved it into her hands. "I'm sure your ex must have a VCR you can borrow."

She felt the slam in her chest. Warren was stealing even this, *her* serial killer. It wasn't right. "I'd rather watch it on your machine."

"I taped it for you, what more do you want?"

What more? She wanted him to notice her, that's what she wanted. She wanted him to stop looking across the street at his house as if it was a refuge. From her. She wanted to stomp her feet, jump up and down, scream and scream and scream until someone paid attention.

She grabbed his T-shirt, ready to shake him, to rattle his brains in his head. Instead she rose on her toes and fastened her lips firmly to his.

Mint tingled against her lips, then sparkled in her mouth. Her body quivered from the tips of her breasts to her thighs, everywhere she touched him. She abandoned his shirt to push her hands through his hair, soft, curling around her fingers.

He put his arms around her, locking her to him, opening his mouth to her assault. Where a moment ago he was merely stiff, now he turned hard, took over what she'd started. His hand flexed in the material of her dress. His tongue skimmed her lips, then dove in, driving her head back. It was like being devoured by a hungry animal. Warren had never kissed her as if he savored her taste, as if he couldn't get enough. She hadn't a lot of experience, but no man had kissed her with Nick's whole-body potency. A zing shot down between her legs when his touch dropped to her bottom and pulled her snug against him, the tape box still in his hands nestled beneath her cheeks. Oh, my God, he had a hard-on. For her. She felt warm and creamy on the inside, like chocolate chip cookie dough. Knead me, need me. Now.

She was absolutely sure he was not thinking about some high school sweetheart named Mary Alice while he was kissing her.

She pulled her lips away, just enough to ask, "You want to come in?"

Big mistake. His hardness fled and the stiffness came back. His hands fell away, and he pulled her arms from his neck.

"No."

She sucked her bottom lip between her teeth and bit down. God, there was just something totally debilitating about begging to be touched, to be wanted. A lump in her throat, an ache at the back of her eyes, and a tight band squeezing her chest. With Warren, she'd begged more times than she cared to remember, more times than she *could* remember. And it made her sick to her stomach. She wouldn't do it this time. "All right."

NICK HANDED HER the tape. She dropped it, the clatter coming back to them in a harsh echo. Neither of them bent to pick it up. Across the street a door banged. Princess started barking.

Nick wasn't stupid. She'd kissed him because something her husband did or said in that fifteen minutes they'd sat in his car pissed her off royally. Maybe just being with the guy pissed her off. Women were like that, you couldn't say or do the right thing. Nick had just made the mistake of being on her porch to take the brunt of it.

He was no stand-in, even if her lips did have the sizzle of champagne and her body fit his like a hot summer night.

She made a motion to pick up the tape, and he grabbed her arm. "I'll get it." He didn't want her head anywhere down there. He bent, keeping his eyes on her, fished for the tape, found it.

She hadn't moved. To get off the porch, he'd have to push her out of the way. He felt one of those difficult, woman-type questions coming on.

"So, I take it you didn't like kissing me."

Hell, yes, he liked it. She'd spoken just in time, broken the spell, before he'd put his hands up her dress. Might have been no going back then. "I'm only interested in sex. Recently divorced women are usually interested in more than that."

She blinked, looked at the tape in his hand, then took a deep breath. Her breasts rose and fell, snagging his attention. "I'm not divorced yet. So 'just sex' is fine with me."

Not. Though she probably didn't know that. "I'm saving us from the messy stuff by not getting started in the first place."

"You're a chicken."

He laughed, reminiscent of a disgusted snort. "You got that right, lady. You've scared me since the day you showed up in my backyard. So, I think it's the better part of valor to just get off your porch right now."

She let him go, then got off a final shot before he made it down the path. "Why were you even here in the first place?"

Because she was funny and said the unexpected. Because she didn't seem to care about the mistakes he'd made. Because she was a little damaged, a little vulnerable, and something about that called to him.

"Hell if I know," was all he said.

If it really had been just sex he wanted, he'd have been the one begging her to let him in her house. There was only one sensible choice here, run for cover.

A SLEEPLESS NIGHT and morning light made Nick realize he had to prove himself strong, even if only in his own eyes. That was the reason he opened the door to her at just shy of nine o'clock on Sunday. To prove he could resist temptation.

"I take it you're here for 'just sex.'" He was sure she wouldn't pick up the challenge, not after last night.

Bobbie smiled, lips an invitingly hot shade of dark cherry. "I'm here to invite you to church."

"Church?" He let his gaze roam over her from head to toe. Her black dress two inches too short for Sunday-best and her heels two inches too tall, she'd tried to minimize the cocktail-evening-out effect with a pink cardigan sweater. Because the sweater was too small to button over her breasts, one could easily see the bodice of the dress was nipple tight. And she did have a pair of succulent nipples. Tempting, but resistible.

"It's the only dress I have besides the one I wore last night." She tugged at the hem, barely bending to do so.

"Very nice. But the earrings are a bit much." A turquoise Indian pattern, they dangled to just below her ears.

She grabbed her ears, making him want to slick his tongue along the sensitive shell. "Should I take them off?"

"No. It's a big no-no to have bare ears at church." As if he'd know a damn thing about it.

"You think so?"

She'd scandalize the congregation. But Brax would like the ensemble, and Brax was a churchgoer, even if only because he thought it was expected of a sheriff. The thought irritated him enough for Nick to say, "You better run along or you'll be late."

"Come with me."

"No."

She put her hands on her hips, causing the dress to rise an inch up her thigh. "It isn't polite to give an unequivocal no. You're supposed to make an excuse I can beat down."

He stroked his unshaven chin, looked down at his paint-splattered shirt and jeans. He had plenty of excuses, none she could beat down. "Did we not have that conversation last night about how I'm only interested in sex and I'm not interested in women on the divorce rebound?"

The MacAffees pulled out of their drive, staring as their car rolled past. Bobbie didn't notice. "I slept on it, and now I only remember that you kissed me."

"*You* kissed me."

"All right, I started it, but you kissed me back."

"Then I pushed you away."

She puffed out a little breath of air, tapped the fingers of one hand on her hip. "Eenie, meenie, minie, mo."

Now what part of that did not make a single bit of sense? "What?"

"I was just wondering how many times a girl should let herself get turned down before she considers option two."

That made him think of Brax, irritating him again. "Is that a rhetorical question or do you expect an answer?"

"Rhetorical. I've already made up my mind." She held up her hand, lifting fingers as she counted. "One, two, three, four, five." The hand dropped to her hip once more. "We've hit five already. That's enough. Option two, here I come."

Option two. Brax. Whom she had a date with tonight, if Mr. Fry was right. "Wait a minute."

She waved. "As you said, I'm going to be late."

He grabbed her arm before she could take a second step away from his doorway. "So be a little late."

Annoyance that she would turn to Brax was the only reason he pulled her through the door, into his hallway and into his arms.

She gave a muffled little "oh" as he planted one right on her kisser. She tasted of her usual cinnamon and mocha. He parted her lips with his tongue and sank in. Ah. The scent of her, spice, sweet apple shampoo and hungry woman, went right to his gut, and all of sudden, he had to have his hands on her. He found her breasts, her nipples tight in his palm. With a slight little answering "Ooh," she tangled her fingers in his hair.

So nice, the idea of just laying her down on the cool hardwood floor. His hands left her breasts, drifting south to her hem with the idea of finding her thighs. When he did, he stroked, the feel of firm flesh stoking his boiler. He moved from her lips to her throat, tasting her like candy. He maneuvered beneath her skirt to squeeze her butt before his fingers touched the elastic waist of her nylons.

"You're not getting paint on my dress, are you?"

Her hands were no longer in his hair, but on his shoulders.

His mind was still on getting to her panties. "Huh?"

"I don't have anything else to wear to church. And I *am* going to church."

Cold rushed down his back. He pulled away. "Is this some sort of payback for last night? Turn me on, then turn me down?"

She blinked. "You started it. And if you want to know the truth, I'm not sure what just happened." She pulled her lip between her teeth a moment. "I think I got scared."

He pushed a hand through his hair. Christ, neither of them knew what they wanted. One minute he told himself to run, the next he was kissing her. And Brax had nothing to do with it. He'd forgotten about the sheriff the moment he put his mouth on hers.

"Well then, you better run along, little girl, or else the MacAffees will tell everyone you missed church because you were in bed with the serial killer."

What the hell, did it matter who was doing the running as long as one of them was?

GOODNESS, HER CHEEKS burned. Through the hymns, the prayers and the sermon, both sets of cheeks flamed. Now her bottom hurt on the hard bench, and she wondered when Reverend Elliot would stop threatening the congregation with the hand of God smiting them down for the horrible sins they'd committed in their hearts this past week.

Bobbie didn't even want to think about the sins of *her* heart.

She'd woken this morning only with the intention of going to church to see if Cookie was there with her husband. After all, everyone in small towns went to church on Sunday. Bobbie just wanted to scope things out, see how Cookie was with the rest of Cottonmouth's citizens, catch her out in some really big sin. One besides adultery with Warren. She'd gotten carried away then by the idea of killing two birds with one stone, showing up the Cookie Monster for what she really was and showing Nick for what he really was, too. A gentleman.

After all, last night he could have dragged her by her hair into the house and had his wicked way with her. He hadn't, because she was going through a slightly difficult time with the divorce and all. Wasn't that considerate?

That's where her sin came into it. She'd let him put his hands up her skirt, and she really hadn't wanted him to stop. The worst was, it hadn't a thing to do with proving anything to Warren. It wasn't about feeling desired and attractive at the ripe old age of forty. It was, plainly and simply, about wanting Nick's hands up her skirt, taking off her nylons and her panties, then... That must be some sort of sin. Especially right before going to church.

"Let us bow our heads and pray."

The sermon was over. Thank God. That was one prayer answered.

Maybe she just had cold feet. Warren always did say she had feet like a corpse. But somehow, *planning* to jump in bed with the serial killer was entirely different than actually making the jump. She had a queasy he-wants-me-but-what-do-I-do-with-him-now feeling.

The service was over, the parishioners filing out. Bobbie joined the line beside Patsy Bell Sapp.

"My dear, it's so nice to see you here." The words mere politeness, Patsy stared at her dress.

Bobbie smoothed her hands over the front of the skirt. "I'm sorry. I didn't have anything else to wear."

Patsy brightened at the news that Bobbie's attire wasn't an intentional affront. "We can fix you right up at the church thrift store. We've got some wonderful used clothing."

Did she look impoverished? "That's very nice."

"We're open Mondays, Wednesdays and Fridays from one till four."

Bobbie put a hand to her mouth. "Gosh, I'll be working."

"Down at the Cooked Goose." Patsy said it with her nose tilted in the air. "I've heard. Well, I'll be glad to pick something out for you. What's your size?"

The line inched forward. Bobbie's stomach plunged. Her size? She didn't want to think about her size, even if she had lost a little weight since Warren left. And that thought made her stomach fall right down to her toes.

Now Patsy wanted to pick out clothes for her. Gee, did everyone think she dressed like a tramp?

"Don't worry. I'm sure I'll find the perfect thing."

The thought struck terror into her heart. Bobbie had visions of red blazers and A-line skirts like Patsy favored. She'd actually be expected to wear whatever the real estate agent picked out. "Thank you."

The queue for shaking the minister's hand was now only five deep. All through the sermon, Nick had occupied her thoughts. Patsy's presence beside her served to remind her that her original intention for going to his house this morning had been to gain him acceptance via the church route. Maybe she could still do it even without him at her side.

"Patsy, I went over to—" What, the serial killer's house? That would only inflame Patsy. "To Mr. Angel's house." Though that seemed too formal. "He's really not as bad—"

Patsy latched on to her arm with a talon-like grip. "And you're still alive. Oh, thank God," she breathed, as if God had performed another miracle.

"Yes. He was actually sort of civilized."

"They say his kind can fit in anywhere. Like Ted Bundy. The boy next door." Parishioners pressed at their backs; Patsy had failed to move the line forward.

Bobbie closed the space in front of them, pulling Patsy with her. "I really think you ought to reevaluate this whole serial killer thing. Maybe he's not—"

Patsy's eyes blazed. "Promise you won't go there again."

"He's not going to kill me," Bobbie whispered, aware of how voices carried in a chapel. "He's not going to kill anyone."

"You just ask Eugenia. She knows things that'll raise your hair. She'll tell you he killed his poor mother with his horrible ways."

Wasn't Eugenia the mayor's wife? "I thought his mother died in a car accident."

Patsy's wrinkles hardened to an implacable mask. "She suffered a broken heart long before that. The accident merely ended her pain."

Bobbie knew then that Nick wasn't battling a ridiculous, serial killer reputation. He faced the very real sentiment that he'd irreparably damaged his mother. Bobbie didn't have a quick fix for that.

Then Reverend Elliot grasped her hand in both of his and shattered her chance to change Patsy's mind, if a chance even existed. "Bobbie Jones. It's so nice to finally meet you."

And everyone had heard about her, too. Good or bad? Couldn't be too bad since the minister didn't raise an eyebrow to her hastily thrown-together outfit. "You, too, Reverend. It was a moving sermon."

Over the minister's shoulder, she spotted the Cookie Monster wearing a brilliant sky-blue hat that shaded her eyes. A very bad word came to mind, worse than… bitch. Much worse.

Bobbie murmured something suitable and unmemorable to the minister, then progressed to the lawn surrounding the steepled church. Moments later, Patsy veered in the opposite direction. Perhaps that was for the best. Nick's battle would have to wait. Right now she had her own to face. With the Cookie Monster.

People milled, the chatter of voices and laughter filling the morning sunshine. A short woman on the pretty side with the expanded hips of a good cook held Harry Bushman's coat sleeve between thumb and forefinger. Three small children, all under the age of eight, clung to various hands and skirts. The oldest, a girl, bore the oddest likeness to the singer Art Garfunkel. She'd inherited her mother's curly hair. Harry, forehead wrinkled, was deep in conversation with Mayor Meade. The pretty wife listened, head tipped to one side, while her hands and gaze constantly marshaled her children and/or Harry. How did mothers do that, all-knowing, all-seeing, as if they had eyes in the back of their heads? Her own mother had been blessed with the uncanny knack.

On the other side of the lawn, Janey Dillings waved frantically. The stout man beside her, presumably her headachy husband, resembled a bulldog: short legs, droopy jowls and no neck. Following the line of his wife's gaze, his eyes widened at the sight of Bobbie's overexposed legs. Janey tugged his fleshy arm. He remained planted to the spot like a shrub. Eyes narrowing, Janey ping-ponged between his salacious stare and Bobbie a few yards away. The corner of her mouth lifted. She shook her finger at Bobbie, then uprooted her husband, dragging him to the parking lot.

Even at that distance, Bobbie had seen the twinkle in Janey's eye and assumed no hard feelings. Still, Bobbie tugged at her dress just above the hips as if that would somehow make it grow longer. Then she glued on a sparkling smile and circulated.

She stopped for a chat with Mr. Fry, who reminded her about the prescription she had to pick up, then introduced his wife. Both white-haired and thin, the two could have been made with the same cookie cutter. She met the mayor's wife, Eugenia, whose nonstop chatter caused Bobbie to ponder how the woman could manage to be thirty pounds overweight. Maybe meals were the only time she quit talking. But the one-way conversation was a good thing, it didn't give Bobbie a chance to ask any more about the serial killer's reputation. She wasn't sure she wanted to know. Besides, Mrs. Meade's exclamation of "I've heard so many wonderful things about you" warmed away the chill lingering from Bobbie's Cookie Monster sighting.

Mavis was a conspicuous absence; probably down at the Cooked Goose, which was open every day from 6:00 a.m. till 10:00 p.m. Beau was a no-show, too. He probably didn't own a suit. And, of course, Warren had never been a churchgoer. He should have had the sense to realize church was the perfect place to get to know people, especially when he'd just started his business in town.

Then again, he probably hadn't wanted to see the Cookie Monster with Jimbo in tow. Which forced Bobbie's gaze once again to that patch of lawn near the rhododendrons.

Her breath stuck in her throat as if she'd swallowed a chicken bone. Cookie's hand rested on Sheriff Braxton's arm, her French-manicured nails elegant against his dark suit, the great rock of a ring shimmering in a rainbow of color. Her laughter rose above the chatter like wind chimes tinkling in the wind. Her long blond hair glittered in the sunlight. The full hem of her chiffon dress fluttered about her perfect calves. Jimbo slapped the sheriff's back, Cookie squeezed the beefcake biceps, and Sheriff Braxton broke into a smile at something the lovely Cookie had said.

Yuck. Something burst inside Bobbie's head—a blood vessel, the biggest one. Red tinged her vision. Her world narrowed to those nails on the sheriff's arm. A proprietary grip. Confident in her ownership, in her power.

How dare that woman put her hands on the sheriff? She was married. She had Warren. It wasn't right; it wasn't fair. She had everything: a rich husband, gorgeous clothes, long hair, a flat stomach, a butt that hadn't dropped and probably never would.

Cookie was the enemy. And this was war.

Bobbie stalked, her heels sinking into the deep grass like quicksand. She bounced up on her toes, feeling her dress ride higher on her thighs. She didn't care. She had good thighs. Nick had liked her thighs. And Mr. Fry thought she had a date tonight with Brax.

Cookie tossed her head, her hair gleaming. Smile, beam, laugh. Bobbie wanted to rip those shining locks out by the roots. At that moment her feelings for Cookie had nothing to do with Warren. This was about woman power.

"Hi, Jimbo, Brax." Perfect voice, light, airy, a hint of delight. Though Bobbie did have a uniform thing, the sheriff looked scrumptious in a charcoal suit.

Like the parting of the Red Sea, the two men moved to include her, forcing Cookie to drop her hand from Brax's arm. Good, very good.

Brax gave her a "hey" and a crooked smile, coming to rest closer to Bobbie than Cookie. The woman's contact-lens-enhanced blue eyes narrowed, crow's feet clawing at the corners.

Bobbie stuck out her hand. "I don't think we've met before. I'm Roberta Jones Spivey." She said it for the dig, not caring if Jimbo or the sheriff wanted to call her on it. Neither did. "Everyone calls me Bobbie, though."

Cookie looked at the extended hand, then at the way Brax's eyes shifted down to Bobbie's chest. Her lips compressed into two thin lines. She took Bobbie's hand only because she had to. Double points to Bobbie Jones, one for Cookie's capitulation and one for Brax's scrutiny of her legs and breasts.

"This is my wife Cookie," Jimbo announced, since Cookie hadn't introduced herself. Maybe her lips were frozen together.

Bobbie gave Jimbo a beam that included everyone in the small, cozy little group. "Your wife. How lovely. Jimbo and I met down at the Cooked Goose."

Cookie finally had to answer or appear rude. Another point to Bobbie. "I've told Jimbo how bad all that cholesterol is for him, but he just keeps on going down to that…place." A point to Cookie for the diminishing pause.

"Ah, honey, you know Mavis needs me down there every day. It's good for business." Jimbo put his big arm around Cookie's fragile-looking frame and almost yanked her off her high heels.

"You aren't responsible for helping that woman's business."

Hmm, something there in the tone. Cookie didn't like Jimbo seeing Mavis, or maybe she just didn't like Mavis. Bobbie poked whatever little wound festered there. "Mavis has been so sweet and welcoming since I came to town. Don't you just love her?"

Beam for Jimbo, beam for Brax. They both nodded agreement, though Brax did take a step back, assessing. Cookie's nostrils flared, then settled. She couldn't argue unless she wanted to appear churlish.

Peripherally, movement caught Bobbie's eye. The mayor and his wife, marching to the Beaumonts' group like ants to a picnic.

"Cookie, you darling woman, Wylie just wanted to check how the decorations for the festival were coming." Eugenia didn't wait for her husband, leaving him several steps behind. "You did such a wonderful job last year, we just know it's going to be even better. When's the committee meeting?" Cookie's mouth worked like a fish, but Mrs. Meade didn't take a breath. "Not that we're checking up on you, dear. But Patsy said she hadn't heard from you."

Another of Bobbie's brilliant plans sprouted fully formed. "I'd be glad to help out, Mrs. Meade."

Cookie sputtered, her blue eyes flinty. "We have quite enough helpers."

Eugenia squeezed the Cookie Monster's arm. "Oh, dear, we can always use another hand."

Bobbie tucked a lock of hair behind her ear. "Oh, yes, Mrs. Beaumont, I'd love to help. It would be so much... fun."

Eugenia waved a hand. "Oh, you can call her Cookie, Bobbie, everyone does."

Cookie slapped the mayor's wife with a cold look, then hit Bobbie with the same. "I thought you worked down at that diner," she snapped.

"I do, but for such a momentous event, I'm sure Mavis will let me go for whatever time you need." Mavis would have a fit, but Bobbie would deal with that later.

"Well, that's all settled." Eugenia clapped her hands. "Now, Cookie dear, you just let us all know when the meeting is, and we'll be there with rings on our fingers and bells on our toes." The mayor's wife was off, pulling her husband with her like a tornado sweeping away everything in its path.

Perhaps sensing the Cookie Monster's ire, Jimbo soothed his hand down her back. "Isn't that great, hon? Less work for you."

Cookie merely growled low in her throat.

Bobbie gave her a truly magnificent smile. "Won't

this be great, Cookie?" She'd make the woman's life hell for the two weeks before the Accordion Festival.

The Cookie Monster shrugged off her husband's touch, then, with a malignant glower for Bobbie, she said, "Sweetie—" all saccharine and yucky "—we better leave if we don't want to be late for brunch. Brax, are you coming?"

Bobbie was clearly not invited.

So she put her hand on Brax's arm and held him. Cookie's turn to glare at *her* fingers clutching the lawman's biceps. "Oh, Brax, before you go, I have to ask about a rumor I've heard."

He raised a sandy brow.

"Mr. Fry said you and I had a date tonight. But, gee," she mocked, putting a finger to her nonexistent dimple, "I haven't heard a thing about it."

Big gambit here. Sheriff Braxton could shoot her down out of the sky, and the Cookie Monster would win a jillion points. Bobbie didn't care. In battle, you had to take major risks.

Brax moved only his eyes, to Cookie and back to Bobbie. "Seems I do recall mentioning to someone, can't remember who, that I thought you'd like the steaks out at the Rowdy Tavern."

Jimbo tucked Cookie under his arm and whispered in her ear, causing the horse-like nostril flare again. Wonder if she knows how bad that looks? Not. Another point to Bobbie.

"Well, isn't that sweet of you." Bobbie batted her lashes. "The Rowdy Tavern. You people really do have a way with restaurant names around here."

"Brax, we're going to be late. They won't hold our reservation, you know." Cookie clutched his other arm, and Bobbie immediately let go of the sheriff, not wanting the tug-of-war over him to get physical. She'd lose all her points with that.

"Honey, they'll hold our reservation until I call and tell 'em not to. Brax can meet us there. Bobbie, how about you? There's always room for one more. Brax can drive you."

Bobbie smiled at Jimbo and his wonderful little invitation. She could hang all over Brax and send Cookie into orbit. Cookie, however, was shooting acid-tipped bullets, if that look meant anything. And the longer she spent under that glare, the greater the chance Bobbie could lose her momentum.

"Thanks, but no, thanks." She spread her hands in the air. "Tons of errands, you know."

"Too bad." Jimbo started guiding his wife around the rhododendron bush. "Honey, sweetie pie, let's leave them to work out this rumor thing."

"Nice to meet you," Bobbie called. Ooh, bonus points for getting the last word. Her mind was a jumble of points. Had she won? She needed her calculator badly.

"What the hell was that all about?"

Oh, yes, the sheriff. "I don't think she likes me."

"I don't think *you* like *her*. Question is why?"

Uh-oh. The only way out of this was to bait him with something else. Besides, she really wouldn't win the skirmish if she didn't get the sheriff to confirm a date. Even if Cookie wasn't there to bear witness, she'd hear about it. This wasn't about a contest between the sheriff and the serial killer. It was about riling the Cookie Monster.

"Actually the question is whether *you* want to take me to the Rowdy Tavern for steaks or if you just thought I should try them on my own."

He gave a soft almost-snort, then smiled. "You know I'm going to figure out what you're up to one way or the other."

Suddenly she didn't care. Cookie was Warren's secret to keep. If Brax figured it out, so be it. And she liked being bold, even if it did scare the bejeesus out of her. "Over dinner?"

He shook his head at her, still smiling. He had a nice smile, not overly toothy, just a little cheeky. "I'll pick you up at seven."

Hmm, there was the matter of juggling the sheriff and the serial killer. She didn't want to pit them one against the other. Bold she could be for a few minutes at a time, but confident for the long haul? She wasn't so sure about that. "I'll meet you at the tavern at seven."

One brow quirked, then he backed away, turned and finally shot back over his shoulder with, "You will tell all."

"Sounds like a challenge, Sheriff. Don't take any bets against me." She was flirting, so was he. A little ooh-la-la quiver jumbled her tummy. "Don't be late for brunch."

He gave her a thumbs-up, then, still shaking his head, crossed the parking lot to a big black SUV.

Ah, woman power. She'd won, yes, she had. And she'd confirmed something extremely valuable, too, in the process.

Cookie lied to Warren about Jimbo. That lovable guy didn't punch her around, not with all those honeys and sweeties flying out of his mouth. Cookie Beaumont was no frightened, battered wife. She was a woman who had her husband wrapped around her little finger like a big red bow. Bobbie would bet a lifetime supply of the best mochas on that.

Cookie had secrets. And Bobbie was going to expose every one of them for the whole town to see. No matter what Warren wanted.

CHAPTER EIGHT

"WARREN, YOU'VE got to stop her."

Cookie shivered in his arms even as he stroked her shoulders soothingly. She shouldn't have risked coming to his office. She should have met him at the fishing lodge like usual. Damn Roberta for scaring Cookie this much. "I'll take care of it."

"That's what you said before. But she—" Cookie sucked in a breath, then hiccuped after her recent tears.

"I won't let anything bad happen to you, I swear it." He raised her face, her makeup still flawless despite her weeping. Kissing her cheeks dry, he couldn't help himself from moving on to her lips. Just a taste, one taste.

"What if someone comes?" she whispered.

He should have worried, but with her in his arms, nothing else mattered. "The door's locked. I've closed the blinds. And no one's coming to my office on a Sunday afternoon."

He didn't follow that up with the fact that he didn't have any clients yet. His lack of clientele would only scare Cookie more. Security was important to her. She'd already been frightened enough to sneak in through his back door. Instead, he coaxed her lips open with his tongue.

She sighed, moaned, squirmed against him, her fingers flexing on his shoulders. God, how she wanted him, needed him. It had never been like this with Roberta. He'd never felt consumed, on fire, uncontrollable. He'd only ever felt that with Cookie, now, so much more than a mere high school attraction.

He'd thrown her hat to the floor minutes before, when he'd pulled her onto the new leather sofa. Cookie devoured him with her mouth. Sensation shot straight down to his crotch. Wrapping her arms around his neck, she pulled herself astride, her full skirt flowing over them. Then her hands were everywhere, working the buttons of his shirt, tugging at his nipples, then reaching down for his belt. Shoving his hands up beneath her dress, he caressed until he found the top of her thigh-high stockings, then the edge of her silk panties. She lifted, and he stroked his fingers across her dampness. She was hot and wet for him. Roberta had never been so quick with a response.

"Warren, oh, Warren." She hummed against his mouth, her fingers dipping into his slacks and around his swollen penis. He rocked into her grasp.

Sliding down his body, she pulled on his zipper, the harsh rasp of it competing with the groan rising in his throat. And then her mouth was on him. She drew him deep, all the way, until he touched the back of her throat. Ah, God, so good. He buried his hands in her thick hair, winding it around his wrists, trapping her to him.

Roberta had always hesitated. Cookie gave without his asking. His hips pumped as she sucked on him, using her tongue, her lips, her teeth.

"Oh, God, Cookie." She moved faster now, taking him in, sliding him out, burning him up. Stars burst behind closed lids. And then he was erupting. She drained him, swallowed him. Roberta would have cringed if he'd ever asked her for that.

Cookie kissed his limp, spent flesh, suckled him, rubbed her cheek against him.

"Oh, Warren, I love doing that."

And he loved the way she did it. "I can't get enough of you, baby."

Kneeling between his legs, she stared up at him. "I'm sorry, I couldn't help myself. I just had to feel close to you." She hiccuped, tears close to the surface once again. "I'm so scared. Jimbo's face, after she came over. He suspects something, I know he does."

"He can't know. We've been so careful. Roberta can't hurt us, I won't let her."

"What does she want, Warren?"

He hesitated. Had he told Roberta too much last night? Was she trying to verify what he'd said?

A single drop of moisture slipped from the corner of Cookie's eye. "Are you going back to her?"

"Of course not." Never. Cookie needed him. "But you have to leave him. I'll protect you, I swear, with everything that's in me."

"I can't. You know I can't. He'll kill me." She heaved away from him, threw herself across the end of the sofa, the tears now coming in a torrent. After zipping his pants, he curled over her, taking her shoulders in his hands.

"Don't you trust me, sweetheart?" he whispered against her nape.

"You don't know what he's like. But I don't know what I'd do without you, Warren. If it weren't for you, I think I'd commit suicide. I'm not sure how much more I can take." Her body shook with the force of her sobs.

"Baby, please, never say anything like that. I've got money. Leave him and we'll run away together."

She shoved at him, looked up with stricken eyes. "It's not about the money."

"I know that," he soothed.

"He'll never let me go. He's possessive, jealous. Look at what he did to me after she came over at church." She jerked the top two buttons of her dress free and bared her shoulder. She'd shown him bruises before, but this... He almost gagged. The skin was mottled, red and blue, vessels ruptured, but he could make out clearly what it was. A bite mark. Jimbo had bitten her. He shuddered at the pain she must have felt, the terror.

"He can't make love to me, but he's still got to put his mark on me." She closed her eyes, threw her head over the arm of the sofa, a hand across her face, her suffering evident in the tense lines of her body.

"I'm so sorry, baby, I'm so sorry." His helplessness choked him. He held her, kissed the mark, put her dress to rights. "I can't do anything if you don't trust me enough to leave him."

She drew in a breath, slid down enough so that he could once again see her eyes. This time her mascara had not sustained itself, and lay in murky puddles beneath her lashes.

"He'll hunt me down if I leave him. And nothing you can do will save me."

He was so afraid she was right. "We can go to the sheriff."

"Brax won't lift a finger. He'll never believe Jimbo is violent."

"Show him the bite."

"Jimbo will find an excuse. He'll say I like sex that way. Or he'll say he didn't do it. He'll find a way to discredit me."

"I'll tell the sheriff, then."

She looked at him for a long time, just looked at him, and he saw the futility of that gesture. It would play right into her husband's hands. Outside, a car passed, a child shouted, another shrieked with laughter, then silence.

Her voice dropped to a whisper in the quiet room. "You have to do it."

He swallowed past the lump in his throat. "Do what?"

"Help me."

"How?" He could only mouth the word.

"Before Jimbo can get rid of me for good—" she blinked back another tear "—you have to get rid of him."

Jesus H. Christ, she wasn't talking about murder, was she?

He saw by her wide-eyed terror that she was.

THERE WERE SEVERAL PLACES Bobbie would rather be, like over at Nick's house watching *Buffy* reruns, eating popcorn and figuring out just exactly how far the serial killer wanted to go. And how far she was willing to let him go.

But Warren had left a garbled message on her machine, most of which she hadn't understood. Was he having an anxiety attack? She'd have to convince him to start his Prozac again. And that was the only reason she walked over to his office and knocked loudly on his door.

He didn't answer. A minute ticked by. She had the sudden vivid fantasy of breaking in to find him hanging from his ceiling fan. That had always been one of her greatest fears, coming home from work to find Warren dead. She'd told his psychiatrist that. The woman had sniffed and said Warren wasn't suicidal, his was a chemical imbalance that drugs would reverse.

But Warren wasn't on the drugs anymore.

She pounded the wood and called his name. Just when she was ready to run to the sheriff's office, he yanked the door open, eyes sunken, chin drooping and stubbled, which was kind of hard for a man who was incapable of growing a real beard. It ended up looking like dirt.

"You rang, I came," she said brightly, to dispel the dark and frightening ceiling-fan image.

"I told you to leave Cookie alone."

If she wasn't such a lady, she'd have punched him for scaring her, then for having the Cookie Monster's name first thing on his lips. But she was a lady, so instead she said, "Did she come running to you with some tale about the big bad ex-wife?"

"Rob—Bobbie, you just don't know how badly this is—" He stopped, looked at her, a brow-wrinkling perusal. "What on earth are you wearing?"

She looked at her crop top and blue leather skirt. She hadn't worn it for him, it was for her date tonight with the sheriff. "What's wrong with what I'm wearing?"

He looked up and down the street, then grabbed her arm and pulled her inside his waiting room. "Nothing's wrong with it." Hah. "I've just never seen it before."

"I threw out everything I had from when we were married and bought all new." Just like he'd thrown her out and gotten something new. No, Cookie was old, old news.

Nothing moved but his throat muscles as he swallowed and his eyes as his gaze fell to her bare legs. "We're still married."

"On paper only." There, that was nice and calm. And her heart wasn't racing because he'd made her angry, or jealous, or evoked any other silly emotion at all. It was just the fear about finding him dead. That was only natural, anyone would feel that. "Aren't you going to show me your new place?"

Her pleasantness seemed to throw him even further off balance. "Ah, sure, I mean…well…if you're interested."

"Of course, I am, Warren." Sugar and spice and everything nice, she marched through the only other door in the small anteroom.

He'd done well for himself, as he always did. The desk was big and made of some expensive dark wood, a cushy black leather chair pushed beneath it. Oak bookcases and filing cabinets lined the back wall, with his collection of GAAPs and FASBs and tax codes. She'd always hated reading that stuff, hated researching and interpreting. Accounting principles were at least as bad as legalese. Which was probably why he needed that big leather sofa, to find a relaxing position for all the research on clients' behalves. She would have fallen asleep.

It was a damn sight better working at Mavis's Cooked Goose. See, there was another advantage.

She flopped down on his leather couch, kicked off her sandals and pulled her legs beneath her. He watched every move.

She fingered the bottom of her midriff-baring shirt. "You didn't say if you liked my new clothes." Testing, testing.

"Ah, sure, yes." He cleared his throat, then he started to pace, running a hand through his short hair. Yes, he liked them.

His polo shirt was buttoned up to the neck, and once or twice his hand fell from his hair to his collar as if he wanted to loosen it. He hadn't looked at her like that in God knew how long, and the knowledge that her new attire unnerved him now settled like a balm right where her ribs met.

Take that, Cookie Monster. "So, you called to admonish me for introducing myself to Cookie at Church this morning."

He looked from her to the sofa to the closed blinds of his window fronting Main Street. He moved to open them, then sat in his chair, effectively making the desk a barrier between them. "I thought we had an understanding last night." Pulling a stack of folders close, he shuffled through them, then shoved them aside, going for the pen holder next. "She's got enough problems with Jimbo without—"

"Warren, she doesn't have any problems with Jimbo. If you observed her with him every once in a while, you'd see she's playing you for a fool. She's Kathleen Turner in *Body Heat* and you're a poor sap like William Hurt who doesn't figure out until it's too late that he's being used."

"Stop it." He slammed his fist on the desk at the same time he shouted. Bobbie jumped half off the sofa.

Hmm, this wasn't like Warren. "Do you think you should start taking your Prozac again?"

"Dammit, my drugs aren't your business. In fact, nothing I do is your business. I don't know why I bothered to explain in the first place."

He stood, moved back and forth in front of the window, then came out from behind the desk to pace. Usually a man with an economy of movement, this wasn't like him either.

Must be what getting involved with the Cookie Monster did. Made him antsy, out of character. "You're right. And the same goes for you. If I want to go to church and talk to Jimbo and the sheriff, I will. No matter what your little Cookie says."

"The sheriff was there, too?"

She smiled, and not twisting the knife never entered her mind. "Cookie was very insistent he not be late for brunch. Do you think something's going on between her and the sheriff behind your back? Oops, excuse me, behind her husband's back."

He stopped, stared at her, then began the pacing again. "What are you trying to do, Roberta?"

To hurt him, to annihilate him, to… Oh, my goodness, when had she become so vindictive? Wasn't she the little dumped wife who didn't have a spiteful bone in her body? She suddenly and desperately wanted to believe her own rhetoric. Vengeful wives scared her. "I'm sorry, Warren. It won't happen again."

But it would. She wouldn't be able to help herself, no matter how much she'd never wanted to hate Warren. But sometimes, she did.

And darn it, she relished the thought of the next encounter with Cookie. At the Decorating Committee. She deserved it. She deserved to be spiteful. *Vindictive, here I come.* It felt so wonderful, she didn't even bother to remind Warren her name was Bobbie.

Back and forth he went, back and forth. She felt like she was watching a tennis match. "We've both been under a lot of stress lately, Roberta."

Deep breath. *Pretend you're not ready to spit nails.* "I suppose I'm just nervous about my date with the sheriff tonight."

She was quite pleased with her ability to slip that one in. After all, hadn't showing Warren that other men found her attractive been her original and primary goal? Vindictive and vengeful aside.

He stopped just short of wearing a hole in the carpet. "You have a date with the sheriff?"

"Yes. Dinner at The Rowdy Tavern."

"Why did he ask you?"

She pushed out a huff of air, and something started to boil inside of her, something a bit like the passion that had sent her across the lawn into Cookie's quagmire. "Why shouldn't he?"

"I didn't mean it like that." He waved his hands in the air. "Of course he'd want to. You're a very beautiful woman."

"Don't patronize me, Warren." *Woman power, watch out, Warren, or it just might crush you.*

He rushed back behind the desk and settled in his chair once more, as if he knew how telling his pacing had been. Leaning forward, he put his elbows on the desk and his head in his hands. For just a moment. Then, "I just wanted to ask for your help with—" He stopped abruptly.

And she knew he was thinking exactly the same thing as she was. She'd already given him as much help with Cookie as he was ever going to get from her.

"This is your problem, Warren, you're going to have to work it out yourself."

It was a measure of his desperation that he tried one last time. "I'm thinking about the whole town here, Roberta."

She pondered what new and potentially juicy item the Cookie Monster had fed him. "I'm all ears."

"I'm sure you haven't learned all of this yet, but Jimbo built a mall out—"

"At the junction off Highway 26 and Main. Of course I know about it." But she hadn't known Jimbo had built it.

"Yes, well…" He couldn't stand it, and rose to do his pacing before going on. "It's put a lot of the merchants in town in a pinch. They've lost a lot of their business. And Jimbo owns most everything around here…"

"He's their landlord?"

He flung himself down on the opposite end of the sofa, gave her a beseeching look. "For most of them. And Cookie, well, she's been trying to get him to be a little more lenient if anyone gets behind on the rents."

"Cookie?" Yeah, right.

He was up again, three seconds more than he could bear to be still. "Most of the people in this town are her friends. She doesn't want him taking his anger out on them."

And if you don't get your head out of that place where the sun don't shine, you're going to suffocate.

But she didn't say it, because she was willing to bet yet another lifetime mocha supply, with whipped cream no less, that greedy little Cookie had wanted the mini-mall and Jimbo was the one being lenient with his tenants. Or maybe she was extorting money from everyone to make sure Jimbo didn't kick them out. There had been that day she'd seen Cookie in Bushman's Clothiers. Hmm, what had really been going on in there?

"Can you see how important it is that you…just leave things alone?" That pitiable gaze again. Tinged with anxiety. Was he terrified of losing Cookie, the way he had twenty years ago?

Time to go before she let herself get really angry. Bobbie unfurled her legs from beneath her and slipped into her sandals. "Yes, Warren, I can see how important this is to you."

And a big so what.

Maybe she'd been fooling herself this last month. Maybe she really had come here not just to show what he was missing, but to break up Warren and his little Cookie.

Not that she'd want him back or anything.

"So you'll be a little more…circumspect?"

Not on your life, Warren. "Of course. Bye-bye."

Now, how to use the information he'd just given her?

She reflected on that as she stepped onto the sidewalk, the afternoon still hot despite the fact that it was almost five-thirty. Down the street, the parking spaces in front of Johnson's Soda Fountain were full, dribs and drabs of ice-cream buyers flowing out onto the sidewalk. Hmm, ice cream on a hot day after a face-down with Warren sounded just right.

"Is that what you're wearing tonight?"

She squealed and turned to find Sheriff Braxton hovering over her. He'd changed from the charcoal suit into a black button-down shirt and black jeans. Black went well with that blond hair. Though the same honey-wheat, Warren's was thin where the sheriff's was thick and beckoning. He'd masked his beautiful blues with a pair of dark shades.

With a hand to her chest, she said, "I still have time to go home and change. If you think I should."

"Don't bother on my account." He pulled the glasses off and shoved them in his shirt pocket, his eyes roving from her shirt to her skirt to her bare legs much the same way Warren's had. She liked this better. "In fact, I like you just the way you are."

He really was quite cute with that soon-to-grow-out-of-control hair and big wide shoulders. Serial killer or sheriff? Eenie, meenie, minie, mo. While the sheriff's appreciative perusal gave her a tingle, it was nothing to the visceral punch of Nick's gaze on her. Or his tongue in her mouth and his hands up her skirt. Still, one should always have a backup plan in case the first one didn't work out. Hadn't she told Nick that this very morning?

Something flashed behind the sheriff's head. Warren at the blinds. He'd flipped them closed. But he'd looked, she knew he'd looked. And she hoped he was jealous. Or something. Some emotion that didn't involve the Cookie Monster.

Okay, she had to do something about that hint of residual anger festering just beneath her breastbone. It might soon get the better of her, and maybe right in front of the sheriff.

Rescue came from the sound of a voice behind her. "Oh, Bobbie." This time she didn't jump.

Brax looked over her shoulder. "Mr. Fry's calling you."

Mr. Fry. Warren's call had made her forget about that prescription. The elderly man shouldn't run like that. He was out of breath as he slid in between her and the sheriff.

"Hi, Sheriff. Bobbie, I didn't want you to forget—" he forced the bag into her hand "—theeeese." Dragging the word, making eye contact, letting his gaze slide surreptitiously in Brax's direction. "But don't forget that little something extra I gave you. In case." Nudge, nudge, wink, wink.

Oh, my God. Her face flushed, though she knew Brax wouldn't understand. And maybe a tiny bit of the flush wasn't just embarrassment, but a tinge of warmth at the idea that Mr. Fry, and maybe others in Cottonmouth, thought she was a perfect match for the big sheriff. It was enough to make her sort of halfway forget about Warren telling her to lay off Cookie. Almost, but not quite. She shoved the bag into her purse. "Thanks so much, Mr. Fry. I'll take care, I promise."

A date with the sheriff, a kiss from a serial killer, and now birth control pills. What more could a girl ask for?

Well, there was that little thing about lightning striking the Cookie Monster.

NICK NURSED HIS BEER. It wasn't that he had a thing against getting drunk, he just had a thing against getting drunk when he had to keep an eye on Bobbie and Brax.

Which had been Kent's idea when he'd dragged Nick and Harry Bushman, another old buddy from high school, out to the Rowdy Tavern. Kent claimed it was all over town that Brax was taking Bobbie to dinner there.

The Rowdy Tavern, as deafening as its name proclaimed, was a long warehouse, bar in one half, restaurant in the other. Country music pounded out over the bar, and the tantalizing scent of grilling steaks hung like a fog in the air. Kent had found them a table on the edge of the floor with a clear view into the restaurant. With a clear view of Bobbie seated next to Brax, not across, the way she should have been. Dammit.

"She's had a migraine for a week." Harry was on a rant, which was the only reason he'd ventured out of the house on a Sunday night against his wife's wishes.

Christ, Bobbie was laughing at something Brax had said, leaning close so that, if he was clever, the bastard could see right down her shirt. Nick yanked his gaze away and concentrated on Harry's tale of marital woe.

Kent threw a handful of nuts in his mouth, crunching them. "Maybe that has something to do with you impregnating her like clockwork every two years."

Harry's bushy brows rose in an attempt to meet his receding hairline. His ever-growing bald spot seemed to have the equal but opposite effect on the growth of his eyebrows. "She likes having babies."

Kent snorted. "I saw the video of that last one making its appearance. And I don't think she was screaming in ecstasy."

Nick had been relatively silent on the subject up to now. But Jesus. "You took a video of Sarah having the baby?"

Harry shrugged. "Yeah. I took one of each of the kids. You know, so they'll have a keepsake when they grow up."

Even Kent couldn't handle that, his mouth twisting. "You're giving your kids a video of their mother's twat? That's sick."

"Childbirth is the most natural thing in the world."

Right. What was not natural was the way Bobbie kept touching Brax's hand, patting it, like it was part of whatever story she was telling.

Dammit, concentrate on something else, anything else, Harry's video even.

"Well, I gotta say, a porno, it wasn't." Kent drew his hand down his face, pulling at his lower lids in parody of his disgust.

Nick elbowed his arm. "I can't believe you watched it."

"Neither can I." He elbowed Nick back. "But that," indicating Bobbie with a nudge of his chin, "I could watch that in a video any time."

Dammit, he'd been doing real good at pretending they weren't there until Kent pointed them out again.

He couldn't remember if she'd ever laughed with him like she was laughing with Brax.

"I can't believe you're letting Brax have a go at her first."

Shit. "He can have her. She's a pain in the butt." But she tasted damn good.

Kent leaned back and gave him a disbelieving smirk. "I've never seen you cave this easily."

"You know, you're getting goddamn pushy about her." Nick shoved the bowl of peanuts closer to Harry. "What difference does it make to you?"

Kent spread his hands in surrender. "None, buddy, just thinking about your lack of sex life. Doesn't your dick fall off after a certain amount of time?"

"Yeah, and maybe you should know. When was the last time you got it?"

The man smiled the serpent's smile. "I like to take my pleasures elsewhere. Say at least fifty miles away so they don't try following you home."

When Nick had gone hunting fifty miles from home, he'd ended up with Cookie Beaumont, the she-wolf and her pack of lies. And she had followed him back.

"So that's why you're not going for Bobbie yourself, too close to home?" Thank God Harry was the one to ask the question that had been on Nick's mind.

Kent buffed his fingernails on his flannel shirt. "I happen to have the hottest little filly over in Red Cliff, so I'm not in the market right now."

Kent, for all his blustering, hadn't dated anyone in town in the entire year that Nick had been home. They'd done their share of making the rounds of the Red Cliff hot spots, but Kent had never picked up a girl. Maybe this filly was a little more to him than he claimed she was.

"But don't wait too long or I'll give you a run for your money with Ms. Bobbie Jones."

The threat struck Nick as entirely empty.

And dammit, he didn't care if she was laughing way too much with Brax. He looked to Harry to break the mood, since Kent had a one-track mind. Old Harry seemed to be sinking down into his beer. Nick nudged him under the table. "Don't go getting sloppy on us, you haven't even finished your first one."

"Sorry, just thinking."

"She'll come round. She always does." Nick felt a little sorry for Harry. He wasn't hen-pecked, just married with three kids.

"It's not just Sarah. It's the store. I don't know how we're going to make the rent the first of the month. And if things don't pick up soon…" He let the thought trail off.

Shit. Poor Harry. "Ask Jimbo to cut you a little slack."

Harry snorted. "Yeah, right, Magnanimous Jimbo." He cut himself off, looking around as if someone might have overheard the sarcasm laced with anger. "Been there, done that. The last two months. Next step is borrowing money from Sarah's parents."

Kent punched Harry's arm. "That's really why she's cut off your rations, isn't it?"

"Her dad can be a…"

"A peckerwood." Kent had just the right word for the occasion.

"Yeah. But that store's been in my family for sixty years." Harry didn't want to be the one who failed at it. Nor, Nick knew, did he want to ask his father, happily settled into Florida retirement, to bail him out. "It's that damn minimall. We were doing fine until they opened that department store. Who pays thirty-five bucks for a nice white shirt when you can buy it down there for $9.95? Even if it does fall apart after the first wash."

Jimbo and his damn minimall. It wasn't just Harry and his clothing store. If you didn't have a liquor license like the Rowdy Tavern or sell greasy home-style food like Mavis's Cooked Goose or make the best damn milkshakes for fifty miles like Johnson's, you didn't stand a chance in Cottonmouth. Jimbo owned them all, and the minimall sucked them dry.

Still, what Harry didn't seem to get was that no one was buying white shirts at all, unless it was a T-shirt. "Maybe you need to reevaluate what you're stocking, Harry."

"You don't understand. I'm over-inventoried. I can't change the stock until I sell what I've got so that I can have enough money to pay off the old. I'm maxed out with my suppliers as it is." In his misery, Harry guzzled half his beer. "I fucked up royally, I know that, but Jimbo didn't have to turn the screws."

"God, you're making me want to cry here, Harry. Next beer's on me. And will you get a look at that?" Kent pointed none too covertly across the dining room, changing the subject abruptly, to Harry's relief and Nick's chagrin.

Brax was pulling back Bobbie's chair, like an ever-loving goddamn gentleman. As she rose, damn near half her naked thighs were visible in that leather mini-skirt. And four inches of bare midriff. Nick salivated as if she were a juicy bit of steak. She tucked her tiny matching blue purse under her arm and headed off to the ladies' room with a sashay that jumbled Nick's insides.

And Brax had not been looking anywhere close to eye level as he watched her. Christ, the bastard really did want her.

Nick sure as hell didn't want him to get there first. He didn't want Brax to get there at all. Not that he'd admit it to Kent, but yeah, he had one helluva jealous streak regarding Bobbie Jones.

CHAPTER NINE

"YOU STILL HAVEN'T told me why you're so interested in Cookie Beaumont."

Could it be because Bobbie'd been dumped by her husband even though Cookie wasn't getting a divorce? Sure, the Cookie Monster said she was afraid of Jimbo. Bobbie didn't believe a word out of that woman's mouth. "I'm not interested in her."

"And you haven't been grilling me about her for the last hour?" Sheriff Braxton was no dummy.

"Of course not. *You* started talking about her."

Brax's mouth quirked, and he shook his head. "Right. Forgot about that. I guess you didn't ask me out to dinner just so you could ask me the *A* to *Z* on Cookie."

"Absolutely not." She'd asked him because seeing Cookie's talons in Brax's arm had driven Bobbie insane for a moment.

He really was a good-looking specimen, a very nice table decoration. And he had a sense of humor. She couldn't remember everything he'd said, but she did remember laughing a lot during dinner. The steak had been as delicious as he'd claimed.

The man had been a fountain of information. Cookie had arrived in Cottonmouth some fifteen years ago—

what had she been doing in the ensuing five after she'd left Warren? She'd latched on to Jimbo right away, the rich, older man, and married him in less than a year. Then, with sufficient time, she'd severed Jimbo's relationship with Beau.

Unbelievable as it was, Beau, of Beau's Garage, was Jimbo's brother, which meant that Cookie was the woman who'd ruined Mavis's marriage and broken her heart. And, Bobbie was sure, had lied to her husband about what had happened with Beau in the first place. What was it Beau had said about Cookie, that she'd stab you in the back and you wouldn't even know she'd been holding a knife? Bobbie believed it with all her heart and animosity.

"Let's talk about Jimbo. Do you think he beats his wife?" She lowered her voice despite the noise being at the totally rowdy level the tavern's name advertised. She'd sat next to him instead of across so she didn't have to yell.

Brax almost choked on his last bite of barely-beyond-raw steak. "Jimbo, a wife beater?" He shook his head. "He's a pussycat. Why?"

Why indeed? *Why* seemed to be Sheriff Braxton's favorite word. Why do you want to know? Why do you think that? Why is that important? By the end of the evening he was going to want those *whys* answered. Maybe she ought to start throwing him offtrack right now. "I want to make sure he hasn't got any hidden vices I should know about before I steal him away from his wife." She leaned forward, lowered her voice once more. "See, I've got the secret hots for Jimbo."

He laughed until his eyes watered and heads had turned in his direction. His face turned a dangerous shade.

"Are you all right?"

He gulped at his water, then his beer. "I'm fine. I have never met anyone like you. Why'd your husband leave you?"

Why, why, why. Her neck chilled as if he'd dumped his mug of beer down the back of it. Her fingers numbed. The question was such a surprise that the truth almost overwhelmed her.

Because Warren had never loved her in the first place. He'd never stopped loving Cookie. Cookie, no matter how many lies Bobbie had told herself for fifteen years, had been a specter in their marriage bed since the day they first inhabited it. She was the reason nothing had worked between them. She was probably the reason Warren had never wanted children with Bobbie. Cookie was the reason everything had gone wrong in her life.

"I'm sorry," Brax said. "That wasn't fair."

She sipped her chardonnay, then gave him a bright smile she knew was minutes too late. "Not a problem."

"Let's be honest here. I like you. I think you're an attractive woman. But you've got some weird agenda going. I won't rest until I figure it out."

She studiously scooped up the last of her mashed potatoes, avoiding his eyes. "You're the sheriff. You must see hidden agendas everywhere."

"No, I don't."

She waited for him to go on. He didn't. That seemed to make her talk to avoid the silence. Good interrogation tactic he had there, but she had questions, too. "Why'd you tell me so much about the Beaumonts?"

"I didn't tell you anything you couldn't find out by asking anyone in town."

Figures. "I guess I was supposed to just naturally tell you what you wanted to know in return."

He nodded. "Didn't work, though. You're more of a clam when it counts than I thought."

All the diversionary tactics suddenly exhausted her. The last week had exhausted her. And in that moment of weakness, another truth slipped in through the chink in her armor. All she really had to do was go home. To San Francisco. End the game. Give up "Bobbie" and the misery would stop.

Except that without Warren, San Francisco was just another place to live. Cottonmouth was beginning to seem more like home, despite the Cookie Monster's presence.

And she'd die reverting back to her Roberta self. Roberta had been well on the way to doing that even before Warren left. She'd just never known it.

"I used to go to high school with Cookie," she lied, not sure whether she was covering for Warren or herself. "As you can see, she didn't recognize me."

He tipped his head, his blue eyes blank. "I suppose it was a shock to see her here in Cottonmouth."

"Yes, it was." How many lies was he going to believe?

Brax leaned back in his chair and laced his fingers. "What'd she do to you in high school, steal your boyfriend?"

She grimaced at how close he came to the truth. "How did you guess?"

His index fingers came up, tapped together. "The comment about stealing her husband."

"Oh, yeah, I forgot about that."

A smart man, he knew right when to change the subject. Before she started blubbering. "Want dessert?"

"No, thanks. I'm full."

"I've got just one more question."

She hoped she could come up with just one more lie. "Shoot."

"How well do you know Nick?"

"Nick?" Her stomach jumped into her throat, and her face heated.

"Nick Angel? Lives across the street from you?"

"Oh." Oh, my God. "Oh, not well. Why?"

"Because he's been staring at you for the past hour, and he looks like he could shoot me right between the eyes."

BOBBIE HAD ARGUED out in the parking lot with Brax for five minutes about why she didn't want him to follow her home to make sure she was safe. His infernal *why* again.

The thing that did it was her declaration, "Because I'm not going home."

He stopped asking why. Something hard and implacable passed over his face. And then she saw what he saw, Nick standing on the wooden front porch of the tavern. Watching.

Brax hightailed it to his SUV and would have burned rubber if the parking lot hadn't been dirt. She wondered if he would have kissed her if Nick hadn't been there. She wondered if she would have let him follow her home.

"You know," she whispered, "you're a mixed-up fruitcake." Never had truer words been spoken.

She was also a coward. Brax could have been a fountain of information about Nick and Mary Alice. Bobbie had plain chickened out of asking the sheriff. She kept telling herself Nick's past was nothing like Warren's with Cookie. Besides, she wasn't looking for a lasting relationship with Nick, so what he felt about his high school sweetheart didn't matter a whit.

So why had she been afraid of Brax's answer?

She unlocked her car door, climbed in and gave the tavern one last look. Nick was gone.

Figures. She started the engine, punched the accelerator and fishtailed across the lot. She stopped at the access to let a car pass, a BMW just like Warren's.

My God, it *was* Warren, hunched over the wheel like an old man. Or someone with way too much on his mind. He was headed out of town. In the opposite direction of the house he'd rented in Cottonmouth. Didn't Cookie live out that way somewhere?

The decision was split second. She didn't give herself a chance to think about it. Following smacked of obsession. She didn't want to be obsessive. But then again, she'd already followed him to Cottonmouth. What could be more obsessive?

She stayed several car lengths behind him, almost a block, though she didn't think he would have noticed her, anyway. He'd had that faraway look on his intent face. He could very well have an accident in that state of mind. See, she was only looking out for him, trailing to make sure he was safe. Yeah, right.

Five miles, ten. Wasn't Lake Beaumonde out here somewhere? Man-made, County Parks stocked it with fish during the season. Just as she'd thought, he turned to the left, his headlights flashing across tree trunks, then dipping down as he hit a rut.

By the time she turned, his taillights had disappeared around a bend in the small dirt lane. Through the trees, moonlight glistened on water. She took the same bend, and once again his lights disappeared around the next. Getting closer to the water, she didn't dare follow and find herself right up his tailpipe. After the next turn, the road forked. He'd gone right. She went left, pulling to the side a hundred yards later, shutting off her engine and lights and climbing from the VW.

What was he doing here? She already knew the answer. The rumble of another engine, out by the road, carried in the quiet night. Bobbie scampered off into the trees, heading to the lake at a right angle, in the direction she assumed she'd find Warren.

The moon dipped behind the clouds, the dark closing in around her. Silence. The car she'd heard must have moved on. Or had stopped somewhere along the dirt road to the lake. What kind of car did Cookie drive? Oh yeah, a Jaguar, low and sporty. With an animal snarl like the growl she'd heard? Maybe. Probably. Damn Warren. He was meeting her. And Bobbie didn't want to see. So why was she still creeping through the woods?

She might not *want* to see, but she *had* to. She had to find out what Cookie was up to. The lake opened up before her, but she kept to the line of trees. A dark shadow close to the edge of the water, Warren leaned against the hood of his car, staring out at the lake. Then his head dropped to his chest. Where was Cookie? She should have reached the spot already, if that sound *had* been her car.

Bobbie slipped from tree to tree, closing in. An owl hooted in the forest. In the lake something splashed. She didn't dare get closer. She stood in the silhouette of a tall tree and rested her hand against its trunk.

Warren hadn't moved.

A twig crackled behind her.

Then an arm snaked around her waist, yanking her back against a hard body, and a hand clamped over her mouth.

HER ASS WAS WARM and soft against him. Nick's erection was immediate. She twisted in his arms, then bit his palm.

He groaned. Leaning down next to her ear, he whispered, "You don't want him to hear us, do you?" But part of him wanted the man to know.

Her body relaxed against his like a gentle wave lapping over him. First her torso, then her butt, until she was flush up against his flaming hard-on. She felt so good, smelled so good. He stuck his tongue in her ear. She drew in an audible breath.

He wasn't sorry he'd followed her. Nick caressed the shell of her ear with his tongue. Her hands gripped his wrist where he held her at the waist. He breathed hot against her, her shiver worming beneath his skin.

He whispered, "Why'd you follow him?" His gut clenched waiting for her answer.

Her asshole husband stared at the barely rippling water. Dammit, here she stood in the dark mooning over a man who had dumped her. She hadn't let go. Maybe she'd never let go. Nick had correctly surmised that she'd been showing up on his front porch simply to make her husband jealous. Dammit to hell. He was no stand-in.

And he'd damn well prove it to her.

Nick let go of Bobbie to shove both hands up beneath the short shirt she'd worn for Brax. Damn her for that, too, for choosing Brax to be seen in public with, for dressing sexy as all get-out for another man. She could have pulled away then. She didn't. Nor when he nudged aside the lace cup, either. Her nipple had already peaked and when he flicked it, she burrowed her bottom harder against him and teased him with the tiniest of moans. He hushed her once more with his tongue in her ear.

He undid the bra's front clasp and held the weight of her in both hands. The scent of damp earth against the tang of her fruity shampoo made him dizzy. He squeezed her breasts and rocked against her bottom.

"When was the last time he made you moan like that?"

He found both nipples at once and pinched lightly. She turned and bit his neck, stifling her gasp.

Then, "Never."

Christ, he wanted her. Now. Right here, with her husband only yards away. He wanted his stamp on her, his claim. He wanted to beat the crap out of the bloody careless bastard for trampling her. He wanted to show her how hot she was.

He wanted to wipe any desire for her husband or Brax from her mind.

His fingers slid down her abdomen to trace her skirt's waistband. He dipped inside, far enough to caress the edge of her panties. He'd been there this morning; she'd stopped him. Leather creaked, like a breath of wind, as he inched up her skirt. She reached up, pulled his head down to the hollow between her shoulder and throat. He licked, bit, sucked and pulled her skirt to her waist. She squirmed against him, nothing between them now but a thin scrap of lace and his jeans. Too much, way too much. He had to touch her.

When he stroked beneath the elastic at each leg opening, fine curls brushed his fingers. He insinuated his leg between hers, opening her more fully to his touch. Shuddering as she swallowed, she let her head fall back against his shoulder.

"Did he ever make you this hot?"

"No."

Her soft admission reached up inside him and filled a spot that ached. "Did he ever try?"

"No."

The man was a fucking idiot. "Do you want me to touch you?"

"God, please."

He looked up at her husband, still leaning on the hood of his expensive import, still oblivious. Nick knew he was crazy for touching her now, in this way, but he was past caring about right or wrong.

He slid one finger inside the man's ex-wife and claimed her for himself.

She was wet. Hot. His. This time she spread her legs, then went up on her toes to grind back against him. He leaned into the tree to bear their combined weight. She bit down on her lips, holding in the cry, as he buried a second finger in her. Out again, along the fold, finding her clitoris. She started to shake as he rubbed, in circles, up and down, soft, then hard. Her hips rotated against his hand, her butt hugged his cock. He wanted to ram it inside her, but first there was this.

Eyes squeezed tightly shut, fingers digging into his thighs, her shudders consumed her whole body. He could think only of making her come, over and over. He moved inside her again, pressed his palm down hard on her clitoris, then slid back out to start all over again, in small tight circles. She mewled like a cat, and he pulled her face to his, covered her lips and devoured her cries. She blew apart in his arms. And he almost came with her from the glory of her response alone.

HEADLIGHTS SPLIT THE NIGHT, flashing within inches of where they stood. Nick froze. Bobbie gasped, breathing hard with the afterglow of orgasm.

Nick locked his arm around her waist and pulled her farther into the shadow of the trees.

Bobbie's skirt still ringed her waist. Her damp panties chafed. But, oh, for a moment there, she hadn't cared about anything but Nick's touch. She'd forgotten about Warren, about Cookie, about Brax. All she'd wanted was that orgasm, stretching, striving, finally falling into it the way she fell into his kiss, with everything that had been living in a vacuum all this time. Screaming, kicking, crying, wrenching, if only in her mind. Nick wanted her, desired her. Nothing had been more important. Given another minute she would have had him flat on the ground with his pants around his ankles and his penis buried deep inside her.

His breath beat harshly against her ear, echoing the strain of hers. His erection pulsed in the cleft of her behind.

"Who is that?"

The car pulled to a stop behind Warren's. A silhouette rose from the open door. Sickly sweet perfume wafted on the air.

"Christ. Is that Cookie Beaumont?"

She bit her lip before answering. "Yes."

Nick pulled back from her, physically and metaphorically. "What the fuck is she doing here?"

She scrabbled her skirt down. "Shh. They'll hear you."

But even as she said it, she knew they wouldn't hear anything. Cookie had reached the front of Warren's car. Their lips didn't meet, but their bodies did, melding as if they were one. Then Cookie slid to her knees in front of him.

Oh, God. Oh, God, no. This was too much. She'd throw up, she'd—

She ran. She would have fallen, but Nick grabbed her hand, hauling her up. Minutes later she collapsed against the passenger side door of the orange Charger he'd parked behind her VW. That was the car she'd heard, the low rumble. Cookie's expensive engine hadn't even broken her orgasmic stupor.

"Your husband's fucking Cookie Beaumont?"

"Actually, it looked to me like she was about to give him a blow job." Right hook, left jab, straight into the guts. Her own. Better for her to say it than him.

"How long has this been going on?"

She smiled, her lips curling back over her teeth. "Since he left me."

"Shit." He turned, ran his hand through his hair. "What does she want?"

"Him. I guess."

He massaged his neck, staring off toward the lake as if he could still see them. "That bitch. She's up to her old tricks. You can be damn sure she wants more than just a roll in the hay with your husband."

"I know that. I'm not stupid." She stopped, stared at him. "How do you know?"

"How do you think I know? Because I fucked her when I first came back to town."

All the oxygen flushed out of her brain. "You had an affair with her?"

"It wasn't an affair. It was fucking. Then she started telling me—" He cut himself off with a clamp of his lips.

"Telling you what?"

He didn't say. "She's a user and a manipulator."

"And you…fucked her?" She never used that word before in her life. But then, there really wasn't another word that carried quite the same meaning. And she'd never wanted to die the way she wanted to right now, not even when Warren had called at three-thirty in the morning to tell her he was never coming back.

Nick had given her the most momentous orgasm of her life, because it wasn't self-induced, because he'd *wanted* to touch her. She'd felt desire in his body's tension, in the timbre of his voice, so needy she could have wept for the sound of it. It had been so long since she'd heard anything like it, if ever, and she'd felt it deep inside her. There was something so utterly overpowering about an orgasm gifted from someone else. It couldn't be duplicated, couldn't be simulated, couldn't be…

But Cookie had been there first. As with everything else.

Cookie Beaumont had the serial killer. Cookie Beaumont had Warren. Cookie Beaumont had it all. Bobbie wanted to lie down in front of Nick's car and let him run over her until her head squashed like a pumpkin.

"Are you in love with her?"

He grabbed her by the shoulders, shook her. "Are you listening to me? I fucked her. That's all there was. I didn't know she was married. When I found out, I dumped her. She told Jimbo I came on to her, then stood back while he tried to bash my face in with his fists."

She plucked his fingers off one by one. He let her. It

didn't matter how it had ended or who had ended it. Cookie had still had him. Mary Alice who? That's what he'd think about her silly question now. Men never got over Cookie. Nick was tainted. Bobbie still hadn't gotten to the finish line first.

And she never would.

"Move your car."

"Talk to me, Bobbie."

She wouldn't. She couldn't. Warren had made her lose faith in marriage. Nick had just made her lose faith in herself. Her serial-killer days were over.

Yanking the car door open, she found her keys still in the ignition where she'd left them. "Move. Your. Car. Or I'll ram it out of my way."

NICK WAS A CLASS-A JERK, and he knew it. He had moved his car, and now he was following her to make sure she got home okay. Especially in her state.

Christ. What an idiot he'd been. She told him Cookie had stolen her husband, then he went on and on about how he fucked the woman. Mr. Insensitive.

And what was all that shit about doing her with her husband standing only a few yards away? He would have gone all the way, too, if Cookie Beaumont hadn't driven up and almost caught them in flagrante delicto in her headlights.

Jealousy. It turned the best of men into jerks. And he hadn't been the best of men in the first place.

He wanted to beat his head against the steering wheel. He couldn't have screwed up more.

He remembered Bobbie's face in the dome light as she threw herself into her car. Pale cheeks, shimmering eyes, trembling lips. He'd known from the beginning she was on the rebound from a really big hurt. He just didn't know how bad it was. But that was no damn excuse for making her come up against a tree while her husband waited for his lover in the moonlight.

Shit. She'd known Warren the Ass had been waiting for someone. And she hadn't been surprised it was Cookie. What had she really been looking for when she'd driven out there? The orgasm was incidental.

Women. He'd never figure them out. But one thing was sure. Cookie Beaumont was working another patsy.

He wondered how long it would be before she told Warren Spivey the old sob story about Jimbo beating her.

WARREN COULDN'T COME. In fact, he couldn't even get a full erection no matter how hard Cookie sucked him. Damn.

She'd called him two hours ago, said they had to meet, but not at the fishing lodge and not at his office. Out by the lake.

He knew why. She wanted an answer. He couldn't pretend she didn't want him to rescue her from her husband in the most final way possible.

"What's the matter, Warren?"

"Long day." Bad day. Tired. Have a headache. How many excuses had he used with Roberta for just this same lack of performance?

"Don't you love me anymore?"

Why did women think sex and love were synonymous? How many times had Roberta said the same thing? He didn't make love to her, i.e. he didn't love her. Hell, things were miles different with Roberta. This had nothing to do with his feelings for Cookie. It had to do with her husband.

"Of course I love you."

Cookie rose from her knees, stepping back while he zipped and buckled. "Something's wrong. I know it is."

"Nothing's wrong." Except his whole entire life.

Suddenly she flung herself against him. "He hit me again, Warren. That's why I called you. I know I shouldn't have. But I just wanted to taste something good in my life."

Had she heard her own pun? He should have been in the moment with her, but somehow it was as if he stood several feet away, watching. And not caring.

"Leave him. I'll protect you." His voice lacked vehemence.

Her tears didn't. She rocked, sobbed, clutched. "It's no use, Warren. I'll never be free of him." She pulled back, tears streaking her cheeks. "You have to help me, Warren, you have to."

"You want me to kill him, don't you?"

"It's the only way I'll be free." Her fingernails pierced his arm. "It's the only way we can be together."

He'd always felt as if he wore a heavy mantle. Roberta hadn't been the one to put it there, though for years he'd tried to tell himself she had. He'd donned it the day Cookie left him when he was eighteen.

Her departure had crushed his self-esteem. He'd believed she dumped him because there was something terribly wrong with him, exactly what, he'd never figured out. Roberta came along and just seemed to accept him. Maybe she'd had low expectations. But in all the years, he'd never been able to dispel the cloud Cookie cast over him.

He'd searched for her because he'd hoped, he'd prayed that she would help lift the weight from his shoulders, his heart.

And she would. If he killed her husband for her.

"I love you. I always have, since we were fourteen, since the first time we made love." He said the words, but it was as if he stood back from them, apart from her. Except for one thing. "I can't stand him hurting you."

For a moment the hatred threatened to swamp him, choke him, overwhelm him. When he thought about Jimbo's fists smashing into her beautiful, delicate body, he actually believed himself capable of murder. He stroked the tears dry as best he could, and she leaned her face into his palm, kissing it. Then he locked his arms around her to prevent her from pulling away when she heard what he had to say.

"I'll help you leave him. I'll go to the sheriff for you. And I'll take care of you forever." He let out a breath, her hair ruffling against his chin. "But I won't kill him. I can't do that."

She stilled. Then her muscles bunched. She pushed with amazing strength. He simply couldn't hold on to her.

Watching her hand rise, he had plenty of time to duck. Instead, he took the full force of her slap without a flinch.

"I'll be sure to leave a note that says *you* should be the one to identify my body after he's beaten me to death."

CHAPTER TEN

NICK HAD TAKEN what women believed was the typical male approach and stewed in his own thoughts instead of telling Bobbie he'd been a total shit. What women didn't understand was that these things couldn't be rushed. If you didn't think it through first, the whole scenario went to hell.

Of course, by the time he *was* ready to face Bobbie, she'd already left for her Monday-morning shift at the Cooked Goose. But Nick had never considered himself a coward, and he owed her that apology, and thus he found himself down at the diner. On the outside looking in.

You had to plan what to say to a woman. And he had. He would tell her he was wrong for touching her, but he couldn't regret it. Women liked that, knowing a man had gotten carried away. He'd tell her Cookie hadn't meant a thing to him, probably didn't mean a thing to Warren, either. That might be false, as far as her husband was concerned, but worth Nick's effort.

The parking spaces in front and the lot beside were full. He'd have an audience, so he'd have to be careful with his phrasing. She'd have to know what he was talking about while everyone else would only wonder. But women liked a little groveling in front of witnesses. It filled that void they were always thinking they had.

He found her through the plate glass. Smiling. As if nothing important had happened last night. Smiling at *Brax* as she poured him coffee. Shit.

Nick yanked open the front door with more force than necessary, the rush of voices and clinking cutlery streaming past him. And then silence. The way heads turned and conversations came to an abrupt halt, you'd think he was a mega celebrity. Or the serial killer they all seemed to believe he was.

Bobbie kept pouring coffee for the sheriff. Any minute that mug would overflow.

Every booth and every table was filled to capacity. One seat remained at the counter. Nick took it, wedging himself in between two extra larges. Voices once again roared to life around him.

Mavis slapped a mug down in front of him and shot hot coffee into it from a foot above. "My, my, twice you grace us with your presence in less than a week. What can it be that you find so interesting down our way?"

He swiveled in his seat to watch Bobbie. She was still laughing with Brax, as if she hadn't noticed his entrance. "Eggs, sunny-side up. Bacon, extra crispy."

Mavis followed the line of his gaze. "I don't think you came here for my eggs, sport."

"On second thought, make 'em over easy. I hate runny eggs."

Mavis huffed. "Men. They can never make up their minds."

She plopped the coffeepot back on the burner, shoved his order at the cook, then stacked four waiting plates along her arms. Mavis had steady, beefy arms despite her otherwise scrawny frame.

He was alone again in a sea of unfriendly faces,

some familiar, some not. The guy on his right chewed with his mouth open, sopped his toast in his eggs and slurped his coffee. The left guy wielded elbows that kept finding their way into Nick's ribs. And Bobbie didn't serve the counter.

He'd had worse ideas than this, like the time he'd convinced Kent, Brax and Harry to take a joyride in Harry's dad's Corvette when they were fifteen. That cherry-red beauty had never been the same. Neither had his reputation in Cottonmouth. He'd been down his bad road even before Mary Alice.

His eggs arrived, and the sound of Bobbie's and Brax's combined laughter was beginning to make his head ache. Christ, how many times had she been over to the sheriff's table?

She'd ignored Nick, though she'd been behind the counter to gather orders, fresh pots of coffee and throw a dirty dishrag in the bin.

The next trip, when she was forced within two feet of him to fill a cream pitcher, he said, "I have to talk to you."

She looked at him as if she'd only just realized he was there. Fumbling in his pocket for his wallet, the guy with unruly elbows did a staccato jab into Nick's side. Two seats down, a face leaned forward, then another, and silence fell like dominoes down the counter.

"About what?" Bobbie's lips creased in a pretty smile, but her eyes remained flat. No endearing twinkle.

Putting his elbows on the counter, he leaned in, dropping his voice, though he knew it wouldn't do a damn bit of good. "About last night."

She rolled her eyes and left with the pitcher of cream.

Christ. He was trying to apologize here. And she was playing difficult.

Back again for another order, she picked up a tray to load. Then she looked at him, and though she didn't have to pass by him, she did, saying, "It wasn't important. Just forget about it. I have."

What the hell did that mean? She'd forgotten how good it was? Right. He could still feel the press of her sweet tush against his erection.

But hell, the timing was all wrong. He should have waited until she'd gotten home tonight. Then he could have *shown* her how he felt, instead of just telling her. Yeah, much better idea. Women liked physical demonstration as well as words.

He reached into his pocket for ten bucks, threw it on the table. She was back with her tray and her sweet sashay. He started imagining all the ways he'd show her. She turned, her mouth open for another volley, then looked right past him. Her eyes widened as the bell over the front door tinkled.

What now? Her prick husband? He'd beat the guy to a pulp for what he'd done to her. Nick turned. Shit. Jimbo.

Wasn't this a perfect twist to a hellish mistake?

"Save me a booth, Mavis?" Jimbo's voice boomed. He didn't pick up on the silence that had fallen or the eyes that flashed between him and Nick's position at the counter.

But Nick sensed the moment he realized something was different. Jimbo's head tilted like the fox hearing the hare rustle a bush. With a look first at Mavis, then Bobbie, his gaze finally settled on Nick.

"What the hell are you doing here?"

Jimbo had big arms and even bigger fists. Arms akimbo, he marched the four stool lengths to Nick's seat.

Man, he did not need this. But after his frustrating nonconversation with Bobbie, Jimbo's tone raked his nerves.

"What does it look like? I'm having a nice, healthy breakfast." He smiled, baring his teeth.

Jimbo's eyes bulged, and his face flamed an unhealthy shade of red. "You're not wanted here."

All Jimbo had to do was open his eyes, and he'd see what a bitch he'd married. He'd dump her, and everyone would be the better for it. But no, he couldn't admit the truth to himself and acted like a blowhard instead. It was as sadly pathetic as watching Cookie go down on her knees in front of Bobbie's husband.

Nick looked at Bobbie then, standing behind the counter, tray clutched to her chest, eyes the size of saucers, as they'd been last night when Cookie drove up. In ways, she was as bad as Jimbo, running after her past, unwilling to let go, even when the truth stared her in the fricking face.

Maybe she needed somebody to show her.

He turned back to Jimbo. "By the way, how's your wife these days? Keeping good tabs on her?"

Jimbo's jaw tensed. Bull's-eye.

HOLDING THE TRAY against her breasts like a shield, Bobbie sidled out the counter opening. Customers, primarily male, rose from their seats and closed in for the fight. Mavis waved frantically at Brax in his booth at the back.

What on earth did Nick think he was doing, baiting Jimbo that way? Didn't he remember how much that whole Cookie scene had hurt Bobbie last night? Didn't he care?

Run away, little girl. You've lost. Big-time.

Jimbo snarled, and an avid light flashed in the spectators' eyes as if they were at a cockfight. Jimbo put his fists up, his legs settling into fighting stance. "I ever hear you mention my wife again, I'll knock your block off."

Nick rose, taller but less brawny. "You think you can take me, old man?"

Oh, my God. Bobbie made a mad dash to Brax's aisle. He was just watching, like all the others. She grabbed his arm. "Do something."

"Like what?"

"Pull your gun or something."

He put a hand to the butt of his pistol or revolver or whatever it was called. "That's a little drastic for this situation, don't you think?"

Meanwhile, Jimbo went on about how he could take down Nick any day, anyplace.

"Mavis will shoot you, if you let them break so much as a saltshaker," Bobbie warned.

"Now *that* frightens me." Brax pushed through the throng.

The sheriff looked first at Jimbo, then leveled a laser-blue look at Nick. "I told you to stop stirring things up."

"I didn't do the stirring. His fists are raised, not mine."

Jimbo's arms flexed, but he didn't throw the punch.

"Go home." Brax's voice, though not raised, carried through the entire diner. "Cool off."

Nick's lip curled. "Fuck you." And then he stabbed a finger in Jimbo's direction. "And fuck him, too."

Brax put a hand on Nick's chest. For a moment Bobbie thought Nick might actually belt the sheriff. He looked down at the big splayed hand, then up at Brax, at the crowd gathered round him, and finally at Bobbie.

Something spoke in that fierce gaze. Something he'd come to say, something she hadn't been willing to listen to. Maybe if she had...too late for maybes now. And Brax had pointed to Nick as the cause of the altercation, not Jimbo, the way he should have. Her hand went up, almost on its own, one cast out to an outcast. Empathy, sympathy rolled off her fingertips.

Watching her, Nick's face hardened. He stepped back from Brax, then pushed through the crowd, headed for the door. He passed less than a foot from Jimbo and his fists.

"Stay away from my wife."

Nick stopped, but didn't bother to turn. "Or what?"

Suddenly Brax was there between them. "One threat out of either of your mouths, and you're both going to jail."

Nick shot him a fuck-you glance—there was really no other possible way to describe it—then slammed through the door.

BOBBIE FILLED the first suitcase. It was time to leave. Past time. She couldn't fight Cookie Beaumont. She didn't even want to try anymore.

A fist pounded on the front door. Her heart jumped into her throat. Nick.

Racing across Mrs. Porter's pink-and-white living room, she threw the door open, a please-want-me-need-me-beg-me-not-to-go-even-if-I-don't-know-what-on-earth-I-really-want knot tying her stomach.

Brax stood on her doorstep, gun at his belt, tan uniform crisp despite a full day's use.

"Oh."

He waited a beat for anything sensible that might come out of her mouth, then leaned one hand on the doorjamb, blue eyes frigid. "Now you're going to answer last night's question."

"What's that?" She really couldn't remember what he'd asked.

"What's going on between you and Nick Angel?"

Her stomach plunged to her toes. "Nothing."

Really, nothing. Or instead of the sheriff on her front porch, it would have been Nick.

Brax didn't bother with a coaxing smile. He didn't bother with a smile at all. "You're not a good liar."

Actually, she was. And the best lies were the ones she told herself. Like how she'd only come to Cottonmouth to show Warren that other men still found her sexy. She'd come to find her self-worth again, she'd come so that Warren could give it back to her. How utterly stupid. She closed her eyes a brief moment, just long enough to squeeze the pain back into its cubbyhole.

Successful for the moment, she crossed her arms over her chest and gave him the bare facts. "I made him lasagna and a pasta salad. He still refused to let me watch *Buffy* on his cable."

Brax accepted that as if it actually made sense. "And you asked me out to dinner." He spread a hand. "Why?"

Because she hated the Cookie Monster. "I wanted to make my husband jealous. He didn't seem to notice, though."

For the first time, Brax's face softened. "At least you're being honest."

Was she? She waited him out.

He went on. "Good thing I didn't kiss you out there at the tavern the way I wanted to."

She should have felt a quick thrill instead of this hollowness. She tried the eenie, meenie, minie, mo thing, but even that didn't work. "Why?"

"I follow one good rule. Never get involved with a woman on the rebound," Brax philosophized.

Gee, was that some sort of male rule? Nick had said virtually the same thing.

"Learned that with my first wife," he added.

Okay, not philosophy, just firsthand experience. Somehow, that said more about him than anything else. Or maybe it was just her *own* experience coloring everything. "How many have you had?"

"Wives? Just that one."

She drew a breath, let it out. "It's a good rule."

And it should also apply to her—translated to—never get involved with a man right after you've been dumped. Her arms found their way around her stomach in a tight hug.

He glanced at the gesture, then back to her face. Sympathy, empathy, pity? Too close to the things she'd felt for Nick this morning.

"I came to give you a word of advice."

"I'm all ears." If she didn't start sobbing first.

"Stay away from Nick."

Oh. She'd been expecting something like her mother would say, something like, there's plenty of other fish in the sea. "Because he's a serial killer?"

He laughed, mostly a humorless grunt. "No. Because he's got 'Fuck you and the horse you rode in on' written all over him." Pause, assess reaction, continue. "If you'll excuse the language. Maybe you saw that this morning."

She'd seen Nick's facade, among other things. "Maybe I saw you blaming him instead of Jimbo."

He wagged his finger at her. "You really don't know anything about it. There's history."

She pursed her lips. "I think I've heard all the history."

"Maybe you have, maybe you haven't. One thing's for sure, whatever you're looking for, he won't give it to you. Nick doesn't need anyone, Bobbie. He's not going to ever need anyone."

"I'm not one of those women who needs to be needed." But Roberta was. And Roberta lurked just beneath Bobbie's skin.

Brax's mouth creased in a half smile, and he shook his head without telling her she was full of baloney. He was too much of a gentleman to say it. "He's actually a pretty good guy. But he's had some lousy breaks, and he's not handling them well. Makes him sort of testy even with his friends. Nick's not a guy who trusts easily anymore."

Somehow she didn't think Nick would like the description. "Is this the history lesson?"

Brax smiled, for real this time. "Guilty."

She flipped a hand and covered up every emotion that might have shown on her face. "It doesn't matter. I'm leaving Cottonmouth, packing up my stuff tonight."

He raised a brow. "What about Mavis and the Cooked Goose?"

A twinge prodded her heart. "I'll give her notice tomorrow."

He stared at her for a long time, as if he could see every sharp shard piercing her body. "You know, Bobbie, though we're gonna hate to see you go, maybe it's the best thing for everyone."

There was no maybe about it. She'd definitely over-stayed her welcome.

THE SIGHT OF BRAX on Bobbie's front stoop still stuck in his craw hours later. But Nick had to admit, he'd acted like an ass. Last night. This morning. Who the hell was he, anyway, thinking he was some sort of truth messenger? He didn't have the right. He'd regretted the words, all of them, to Jimbo, to Bobbie, to Brax, the minute he'd left the dinner.

And that pitying look she'd sent him still curled around his gut.

At this point the best thing he could do for Bobbie Jones was to leave her alone.

Damn, it was hot in the bedroom. He shoved the sheet down to his waist. Princess was going ballistic over there. Why couldn't Reggie get out of bed and shut her up? It was twelve-thirty in the morning.

Actually, Reggie wasn't a bad neighbor. He'd helped rebuild the section of fence between their yards. And he didn't usually let Princess bark her fool head off in the middle of the night. Reggie was probably in the middle of getting some, that's all.

Which brought him back to Bobbie. Yeah, go figure that thought pattern. Think sex, automatically think Bobbie.

Bottom line. Truth. Being that he wasn't going to get a wink of sleep with Princess hopping around in her backyard, he ought to at least be honest with himself.

One, he had been a bastard to touch her last night. Two, he had been a bastard to throw his certifiably insane mistake with Cookie in her face. Three, he'd compounded everything by acting like a jealous jerk down at the Cooked Goose instead of letting her in on number one and number two as already mentioned.

Reggie's back door opened, there was a thud, a curse, then a hissed, "Shut the hell up or I'm taking you to the pound."

Princess stopped barking.

And who was he kidding? He'd used the idea of showing Bobbie "the truth" as an excuse to take out his frustration on Jimbo. But none of it was Jimbo's fault, either. Nick had poached on his territory. The man was within his rights to knock Nick's block off and throw around a few combative comments. So who else was Brax going to tell to shut up first?

There, everything all out in the open. Conclusion?

He hadn't handled himself decently since the day Bobbie Jones moved in across the street.

On the other side of the fence outside his window, Princess went ballistic again, the high-pitched yelps beating on the inside of his skull. He pulled the pillow over his head.

Where was he? Oh, yeah. Indecent handling of himself, nothing to do with whacking off. Conclusion?

Leave her alone. He didn't have anything to offer. And anything else he tried to say would probably only make what he'd already done worse.

Of the two of them, Brax was the better choice.

Shit.

The only good thing to come of all his musing was Reggie yanking Princess inside the house and slamming the door. The barking stopped, this time for good.

WAS ONE SUPPOSED to hand over a typed resignation letter when one quit being a waitress?

Bobbie pondered the question throughout the breakfast rush. She'd told Brax she was leaving, but she still hadn't packed the mocha machine. Or the kitchen stuff. Tonight, she'd tackle that.

Leaning over the Formica table, she sloshed the damp cloth back and forth. Wiping tables was Billy the busboy's job, but she'd needed something mindless to do. Especially before the lunch hour started.

Gosh, she would miss Mavis. And Ellie. And Mr. Fry, Janey Dillings, the banana splits at Johnson's, even Beau, who waved and spat tobacco every time she walked by. So many people and things she'd hate to leave behind.

She hadn't felt like that about San Francisco or Mr. Winkleman or the job she'd had for seven years.

She pushed the salt and pepper shakers back against the window ledge, made sure the sugar was filled. She hated to let Mavis down this way.

As if a thought could conjure, Mavis's shriek burst forth from the kitchen. "How may times do I have to tell you—" The rest was lost in the clatter of pots and pans. The swing doors flew open.

Maybe now wasn't the time to tell Mavis.

The doors had barely stopped swinging when the front door slammed open, the overhead bell giving a frenzied peel. Patsy Bell Sapp grabbed her chest to calm her breathing, her bouffant listing precariously to the left.

"Have you heard?"

Mavis put the coffeepot on the counter. Ellie stopped fiddling with the cutlery bins. Bobbie took two steps forward, forgetting the cloth on the table.

"You're not going to believe it."

"The suspense is killing me," Mavis quipped, with a roll of her eyes.

"Mavis Morgan, you're going to be sorry you said that when you hear."

"Then, for God's sake, tell us."

Patsy drew a shaky breath. "Jimbo's been murdered."

A beat of silence followed, so profound you could hear the cars turning into the minimall parking lot all the way out on Highway 26.

Then Mavis started laughing. "I swear, Patsy, you had me going for a minute there."

"It's true. They found him out at the lake with his head bashed in."

Bobbie suddenly felt sick. "What lake?"

Patsy turned, her crinkly eyes misty. And sort of scary. "Lake Beaumonde, of course. Out at the picnic area."

She was very much afraid she knew the exact spot.

"And you know what else, Bobbie Jones?"

Bobbie couldn't drag in a breath if her life depended on it.

"Your ex-husband just confessed to killing him."

CHAPTER ELEVEN

NICK BALANCED THE flat of purple, yellow and pink pansies on his palm. Investigating the pickings in Sylvestor's greenhouse out back of the store, he'd found the choices few and what remained after the spring, near death. In all good conscience, he couldn't plant expired flowers in his mother's beds. He'd planted enough dead things in her backyard already.

The green-and-white cruiser pulled up beside him just as he walked out the front door of the Home Depot. Caught shopping at the minimall. Damn.

"Hey, Nick, how's it hanging?"

He wondered what the sheriff had been telling Bobbie last night. "Just the way it ought to, Brax. What do you want?"

Do-it-yourselfers stopped for a gander at the proceedings, then, when no guns or cuffs appeared, moved on. Being at the highway junction, the minimall served not only Cottonmouth, but the surrounding towns of Sterling, Hooker Creek and Hedston—not to be confused with Headstone. The parking lot was full, the gawkers plenty, not that Brax's cruiser was an unusual sight. The man liked to make his department's presence known, part of his campaign for keeping the peace before it was broken.

Brax stared for ten seconds from behind a pair of mirrored shades. "Just wondering if you'd heard the news about Jimbo."

Brax was not your typical gossip. Something was up. "Don't tell me. He finally kicked Cookie out on her ass."

"Nope." Brax hung his hand out the side of his cruiser, hot afternoon sun beating down on his arm in his short-sleeved uniform. "Afraid the poor old man's going to have to forgo that pleasure. Permanently. Since he got his head smashed down at Lake Beaumonde last night, sometime between midnight and 3:00 a.m. Least, that's the time the doc's going with before autopsy."

Holy shit. Jimbo murdered? Brax was looking for the slightest reaction. Nick didn't give it to him. "I suppose you're wondering where I was last night, since Jimbo and I had that argument yesterday."

Brax adjusted his glasses. "Alibis are always good in a situation like this."

Nick shifted, setting his feet apart. Hooking a thumb in his belt loop, he held the pansies with one hand. "Sorry, I don't have one. I was sleeping in my own bed all by myself."

A teenager peeled out at the stop sign. Brax ignored the car. "That's a shame, Nick, a damn shame. You could be in a speck of trouble. Be a lot easier if you'd had someone with you."

Like Bobbie? He wouldn't have used her name even if she had been there in anything other than his fantasies. "Shall I drop by the Sheriff's Department so you can arrest me?"

A woman coming up on his left gasped, stopped, then fled to her car.

Brax pushed up his glasses as if they'd slid down. "No hurry. I know where you live. There's a little matter of evidence."

"Haven't got any against me, then, I presume."

"'Cepting that fight. But that doesn't even qualify as circumstantial at this point."

What the hell was with the yokel dialect? Brax was baiting him. No sense in falling for that, either. "It wasn't exactly a fight, Brax, neither of us threw a punch."

"That's just what I'm saying. Unless, of course, you went after him later to finish it off."

Nick didn't bother answering the question in that statement. "I really appreciate you thinking of me first, Brax. Warms my heart."

"No problem." Brax draped his right hand over the steering wheel and waited for a mother and her two wide-eyed children to pass between them. "Seems the murder weapon is missing, too. M.E. says blunt instrument, some sort of flat-edged thing."

"Thought *you* were the medical examiner, Brax."

"Nah, I'm just the coroner. Around here, it's nothing more than a title." He gave a negligent wave. "Now, about that murder weapon. Hyram speculates it could be a shovel. Course, he'll get real specific once he does the autopsy. Mind if I stop by to look at your collection of gardening tools?" Brax didn't miss a beat.

Bastard. But Nick played the word game. "Collection?"

"Heard you do a lot of digging around your place."

Yeah, roadkill burial duty. And Brax knew it. "Don't you need a warrant for something like that?"

"Not if you voluntarily let me look."

"You really think you're going to find a bloody shovel in my shed?"

Brax shrugged. "Never can tell. Criminals can be real dumb. Some of them think it's better to keep the evidence where they can get to it quick, if need be."

"And if I refuse to let you in?"

The hand hanging over the door flipped up. "Well, refusing makes it look like you've got something to hide. Tends to create a bias against you."

Nick considered Brax's good-ol'-boy routine. In high school some would have called them best friends. Twenty years and Mary Alice's abortion stood between them now. "Get a warrant."

A muscle flexed in Brax's jaw, then he tapped his fingers against the side of the car, just above the big gold county star. "If that's the way you want to play it. While I'm at it, guess I'll add your shoes to the warrant, too."

His shoes? Shit. "So, you found a footprint."

"Can't be divulging information crucial to the case. What size you wear?"

Instead of answering, Nick said, "I don't scare easily, Brax. You should know that." Especially since he hadn't beaten Jimbo's head in, nor would his shoe print match the one Brax had found.

If he'd actually found one. Could be Brax was playing a baiting game.

Except that Nick had been out at Lake Beaumonde on Sunday night. Hell. Where exactly had they found Jimbo?

"One other thing. Tire tracks don't need a warrant if we find 'em in a public place. It'd be real polite if you drove down one of my nice county dirt roads when I'm around to see it. Or, driving through oil leaves a good test impression."

"Fuck you, Brax." Where the hell had they found Jimbo's body? Shit, shit.

"Now why did I expect that to come out of your mouth at one point or another?"

"Because you've known me for thirty-eight years." And because it was his usual greeting for his old pal since he'd come home. He knew it was stupid to ask, but he had to know. "Where exactly did they find his body, just out of curiosity?"

Brax smiled, all feral teeth, like he knew he had Nick by the short hairs now. "Down at that little picnic area just off Delton Road."

Holy Christ. Glad for his sunglasses masking his eyes, Nick kept the rest of his expression clean. "The whole thing seems like a run of bad luck for Jimbo. Good for Cookie, though, wouldn't you say?"

"Trying to make sure I consider her as a suspect?"

"You know what they say about the spouse having the biggest motive." Not to mention Bobbie's almost-but-not-quite ex-husband, who, last time Nick had seen him, was getting head from the freshly minted widow.

"Gee, Nick, you'da made a good cop."

"Thanks."

The sheriff took off his glasses. His expression remained as unreadable as if he'd left them on. Then he reached in his left breast pocket and pulled out a card.

"You're giving me your business card?"

Brax held it out between two fingers. "Take it. Never know when you're going to need it."

"I'm not going to need it, Brax."

"Well, just in case you think of something vital, then."

Nick looked from the card to Brax's impassive face. "You think I'm going to call you up in the middle of the night to confess?"

Brax squinted against the sun. "Let's just say I figure you probably lost my number somewhere along the way. And I wanna make sure ya got it in case of emergency." He waggled the card.

Nick finally took it. Just to get rid of him.

"Be seeing you around, Nick." Brax shifted into gear.

"Is that the proverbial 'I've got my eye on you, boy'?"

Brax shoved his shades back on. "One of these days you're going to need a friend, Nick."

Yeah, well, it sure as hell wasn't going to be Sheriff Tyler Braxton. His buddy obviously had it out for him. Was this about Bobbie? Or something more ancient? Like payback for accusing Brax of porking Mary Alice and then leaving her high and dry when she got in trouble?

"Fine, Brax. I consider myself warned."

The corner of Brax's mouth lifted, then he saluted and hit the accelerator.

The Charger baked in the sun. Nick stuck the pansies in the trunk, hoping they didn't die in the heat. Inside the car, sweat trickled down his neck as he leaned over to throw Brax's card into the glove box. It landed on top of the freshly charged but barely used cell phone he kept in the car for emergencies.

Calling a tow truck, he could handle. God forbid he should ever need to call Tyler Braxton.

So why didn't he just throw the damn card out?

Maybe it was the noose he felt tightening around his neck and the need to feed Brax any bit of exculpatory evidence that might come his way. If any did come his way.

"WHY ON EARTH did you confess, Warren?"

He slammed his hand down on the table between them. "Why do you think, Roberta?"

He was two years younger than her, but today he looked ten years older, Bobbie thought. His eyes were sunken in his head. Wrinkles littered his white shirt. Warren hated wrinkles as much as she hated ironing.

"I don't know why, Warren. You tell me." She would try to be understanding.

He didn't meet her gaze. "Because I'm guilty."

He was lying. It simply wasn't true. Warren wouldn't have the courage to murder anyone. Under the circumstances, maybe that wasn't the best thing to say.

If only she could get that image of poor Jimbo out her mind. He'd been such a sweet guy. She couldn't believe he was dead. No one at the diner could.

She'd heard the whole story in bits and pieces throughout the afternoon. Cookie called the sheriff at 3:00 a.m.—maybe an hour before, maybe an hour after, depending on the storyteller—saying Jimbo never came home. His car was found at the lake around six by a maintenance worker, and Jimbo was half in, half out of the water, like he'd been fishing and a big one dragged him in where he'd smashed his head on a rock. Of course, the sheriff pulled him out and said it was murder. His head had been bashed in. Oh, my God. Warren couldn't do that, he hated blood.

At five, Bobbie left the diner and saw the sheriff's police car parked down at Beau's Garage. Why would the sheriff be talking to Beau if he already had the suspect in custody? Maybe he was just gathering evidence that would corroborate Warren's admission. Better yet, maybe he didn't believe Warren. Whatever, it was fortuitous for her. She ran all the way to the Sheriff's Department where they were holding Warren. With Brax gone, she would have an easier time getting in to see him.

And she had. The desk sergeant gave her a private conference room with Warren. No cameras mounted in the corners and no one-way mirror/window thing like they had in all the cop TV shows.

"Did you do it for *her?*"

"No," he snapped, then shut his mouth. "I mean, I don't know what you're talking about."

"Oh, yes, you do. She told you he beat her, that she was afraid he'd kill her." His gaze fixed on the wall over her head was telling. He knew exactly who Bobbie was talking about. Her heart beat faster with anger, fear, helplessness. The same emotions she'd felt when Warren left her.

"Roberta, they might be recording us."

She ground her teeth, then leaned down and looked under the table. "No hidden devices here," she called up. Next, she turned over her chair. "Nothing here, either." She sat back down. "All right, let's talk in code."

"You shouldn't have come here. There's nothing to talk about. I killed him. I confessed. End of story."

He'd done this for Cookie. And she wouldn't let that…that bitch get away with it. "What motive did you give them for killing him?"

His head swayed from side to side. "Jimbo didn't like me starting up another accounting firm. He said it would put Dennis Crouch out of business. He asked me to meet him out at the lake so we could talk."

She let her hand fall loudly to the table. "That is so

lame. No one's going to believe it. Especially not Brax. He's not stupid."

Warren's brows pinched together. "It doesn't matter what anyone believes. I confessed."

She leaned forward. "Retract it."

His fist opened and closed on the table. "I can't. I won't."

Damn that Cookie, yes, damn her. She'd woven a web around Warren so thick he couldn't see through it. The only thing to do was poke holes in his story until he caved. "The murder weapon's missing. What did you do with it?"

"I threw it in the lake."

She stared at his bowed head, something he seemed to do every time she asked for a detail. For the first time, she noticed a small patch of bald sprouting on his crown. Cookie had done that to him, made him lose his hair. "I don't believe for one minute that you could smash a man's skull in."

He raised his head, looked at her, grimaced. "Believe it."

Pushing at him was the only option she had. "What did it sound like? A squishy whomp, you know, with all that brain gook? Or more like a crack?"

He winced. "Roberta, please."

"I'm just curious what the sound effect was. Did you hit him more than once? I guess you probably had to, just to make sure he was dead."

His skin turned a tad green. "Roberta."

"Did the shovel get stuck or anything? I suppose that would depend on how deeply you embedded it in his skull."

"Roberta, shut up."

"You can't even talk about it, so how do you expect me to believe you actually did it?"

His jaw flexed. He ground his teeth. "Some things are easier done than said."

"I think the trite little phrase is 'easier said than done.' You've got it backward." He had everything backward, especially his loyalties. "She did it, didn't she? And you're just covering for her."

His usually mild blue eyes filled with a reptilian darkness. "Shut. Up. Or get out."

He wasn't in his right mind. He couldn't be. It was because he'd stopped the drugs. He wasn't thinking rationally. Not considering the consequences of this monumental lie. He was only thinking about how the Cookie Monster needed him.

Or maybe this was just fulfillment of his death wish.

How much of this was because she'd come to town and put the screws to his relationship with Cookie? The things she might have put in motion because she was worried about her own...what, desirability, usefulness, worthiness?

No. This wasn't her fault. It was Cookie's. And she would not let Cookie Beaumont have this final triumph, not at Warren's expense.

"I'm not going to let you do this. Do you realize they could give you the death penalty?" She didn't know whether they could or not; wasn't there something about special circumstances? "Do you want to die for her? She isn't worth it."

He jumped to his feet, the chair clattering to the floor behind him. "I'm not saying another word."

Bobbie rose more slowly. "No one in this town believes he was beating her up."

"Don't you see that was the whole problem? No one would believe her at all."

"That's why she needed you. Someone from out of town who didn't know him like everyone else did. She suckered you, Warren, don't you get that?"

He kicked the chair out of his way, rounded the table, towering even though he had a mere three inches on her. Something icy slithered down her spine. This was a Warren she'd never seen before.

Could this Warren actually—

No. Not now, not ever. It was time for desperate measures under the heading Tough Love. "I know you," she whispered. "You wouldn't have the courage to kill a man even for the woman you love, Warren. You don't even have the courage to tell the truth."

He raised a fist in the air, and for just the briefest moment, she wondered if he was going to hit her. Instead he pounded on the door and yelled for the guard.

"Don't come back again, Roberta. I don't need your help."

They led him away, but she stayed in the room, walking to the other side of the table and putting the chair back to rights. Her hands shook. When she turned, Brax leaned against the doorjamb.

"Guess you didn't leave town."

"Stuff happened. I didn't turn in my resignation."

"Waitresses don't resign, they quit. That's all you had to do."

She tipped her nose in the air. "Things have changed. I'm not leaving just yet."

He smiled, knowingly, irritatingly, then punched his chin in the direction of the conference table where she'd sat with Warren. "How'd it go?"

She went for nonchalant. "Weren't you taping us?"

"Maybe, maybe not." He walked in, turned the chair she'd been sitting in and straddled it. "Did you tell him he better get himself a damn good criminal attorney?"

"I forgot that part. I'm sure he's already figured it out."

"Well, he hasn't asked for one, hasn't even made a phone call. I thought you might be able to convince him that leaving it up to the court to appoint one might be the difference between life and death." He paused. "Literally."

"So that's why you made it so easy for me to get in to see him." She should have known something was up.

"The man needs some sense knocked into him."

She took Warren's vacated chair and leaned her elbows on the table. Maybe nonchalant wasn't the right approach. How about beseeching? "You know he didn't do it."

"All I've got is his confession on record. Anything *you* want to add?"

She sat back, suddenly wary of the blankness in his gaze. "Like what?"

"Like why you've been so interested in the deceased's wife. Or do you want me to draw my own conclusion?"

Her and her big mouth. Right now Warren didn't have a real honest-to-God motive, as far as Brax was concerned. But if he found out about Cookie and the affair... "Can he really get the death penalty for this?"

Brax didn't answer. God, she'd have to scour the Internet to find out. She didn't have time to scour the Internet. God, what was she going to do? How could she save Warren this time if he didn't even want her to?

"Since you don't want to tell me about Cookie, mind

telling me where you were between midnight and three this morning?"

The world suddenly tilted. "Do you think *I* did it?"

He merely raised one eyebrow.

"I was at home. Alone. I don't have an alibi." She chewed on her cheek. "But then again, I don't think I have a motive, either. Jimbo was a nice man."

He blinked. Slowly. "Yeah. He was a good guy." Something flickered in his blue eyes. Regret? Sadness? The emotion was gone in the next instant. "Obviously not everyone thought so." He leaned forward, a strange smile growing on his face. "Good to know you were alone, though."

Holy moly. What an idiot. She should have seen the trap before she fell into it. He wasn't asking for *her* alibi. He was asking for Nick's.

Nick had a feud going with Jimbo. Nick had had an affair with Cookie. If Bobbie did manage to get Warren to admit he hadn't killed Jimbo, the next suspect in line was Nick.

That said it all. Thank God she hadn't packed up the mocha machine last night. Because Bobbie wasn't leaving Cottonmouth. She had a new mission—to prove Cookie Beaumont killed her husband.

NICK DIDN'T NEED to check his shed for anything incriminating. Because he hadn't killed Jimbo.

But Brax's voice kept playing in his mind like an old forty-five stuck in a groove.

Nick succumbed after a dinner consisting of two pieces of cold meat-lovers' pizza. Princess rushed up to the other side of the fence when he crossed the porch, starting her usual loud yipping as he neared the shed.

He yanked open the metal door almost in protest against Brax's voice. And stared inside.

"What are you doing out here?"

Bobbie. He turned to look at her. "I could ask you the same thing."

She still wore her uniform, the apron stiffly starched, but the white collar drooped around her neck. The top three buttons lay open, affording him a view of creamy cleavage.

"I rang your doorbell. You didn't answer."

"I was busy."

"Looking for more roadkill?"

"Not today." He stepped inside the darkened shed.

"Did you hear about Jimbo?"

He couldn't tell a thing from the question or her tone. "Yep. Got whacked with a shovel out by the lake in the middle of the night." He waited.

She stepped right into the hole his silence left. "Why are you looking in your shed?"

"I just want to make sure I didn't leave any tell-tale bloodstains on my supplies out here. Or brain matter."

He turned to find her with arms crossed over her chest and a step back from where she'd been before. "That's not funny."

"I didn't mean it to be." Now was the time for her to say she knew he couldn't possibly have done it.

She didn't. "Brax asked where I was last night."

He moved a few of the tools, clippers, hedger, examined them, put them back. "Guess that means you weren't with him."

She gasped. "Of course I wasn't."

He hefted the big shovel away from the metal wall,

let it fall back with a clank. "Good," he said, letting relief show only in the word, not the tone.

"That's what Brax said."

Nick looked over his shoulder. "Good what?"

She put a hand on her hip. "Good that I was alone."

He let a beat of silence last between them. "Not much of an alibi for either of us, then." But did she think he needed one?

"I don't think that's what he wanted to know."

"He already knew you weren't with me." So why was Brax testing Bobbie, too?

"How?"

"Followed me out to the minimall for a little tête-à-tête."

She cocked her head and stepped up to the edge of the doorway, one foot in, one foot out. He wanted her all the way in. Firmly beside him.

"Why would he do that, Nick?"

"Because I'm a suspect. He wanted to know if he could come over and inspect my shovel collection."

She didn't pick up on the sarcasm, or if she did, she passed on commenting. "What time did you talk to him?"

"Afternoon." She was jumpy, something on her mind. "Why?"

"Because sometime this *morning,* Warren confessed to killing Jimbo."

"Your husband confessed?" What the hell was Brax playing at? What was *she* playing at?

"At least, Warren *says* he did it."

Christ. Why all Brax's questions about alibis, footprints, shovels, tire tracks? He'd even brought Bobbie into it. After he already had the killer in custody. Then something in Bobbie's words, stance, whatever, struck him. "But you don't think your husband did it."

"He really isn't capable of murder."

Nick moved the post-hole digger and the pitchfork he used for loosening dirt. "Everyone's capable, given the right set of circumstances." He waited for some sort of reaction, but she only went back to the question of her husband's guilt.

"Not Warren. He's the original Spineless Spivey. If he did it, it could only have been an accident. I didn't get the impression that Jimbo came by his injuries accidentally."

"Nice sentiment you've got about your husband."

She ignored the little jab. "You know, it happened by the lake, where *we* were the other night."

What did that mean to her? "Yeah. Off Delton Road."

It suddenly occurred to him that Bobbie was his alibi, at least for how his prints and tire tracks got there *that* night. Reasonable doubt or something. Yep, Bobbie was his alibi. His only alibi. So, just how far would she be willing to go to prove her husband innocent?

Would she be willing to lie?

Maybe Bobbie was the reason behind Brax's little fishing expedition out at the minimall. Maybe she'd gotten him to doubt his suspect's confession.

Christ. Nick really didn't want to think about that.

Instead, he turned back to his job of turning the shed upside down.

"You still haven't told me what you're really doing," Bobbie prodded.

He leaned on the pitchfork and stared her down. "Actually, I'm trying to figure out why the spade I was using that day you first turned up seems to be missing now."

CHAPTER TWELVE

WARREN ACHED WITH the need to sleep. It had been a helluva day, starting with that life-altering call from Cookie at a little after three o'clock this morning. And he still couldn't get Roberta's words out of his mind.

You wouldn't have the courage to kill a man even for the woman you love.

She was right. His inaction had forced Cookie's action. And now his only choice was to protect her.

"Let's go over it one more time, Mr. Spivey."

"There's nothing else to tell."

Sheriff Braxton pushed back in his chair, wheels squeaking, and spread his hands over his stomach. He was a big man, well over six feet, and his feet stretched out past his desk. The lamp he'd turned on, tilted to the right, shone in Warren's eyes. He squinted.

"Sorry about that." The sheriff leaned forward and snapped the light down to gleam on the desk.

It didn't help. Warren still felt spotlighted.

Braxton slid his fingers through his hair, curls springing back up in the wake, then returned to his original position, legs crossed at ankles, hands on stomach. Relaxed. In control.

Warren's belly jerked.

"Now, where were we? Oh, yeah, clearing up a few details."

"Shouldn't we be in some sort of interrogation room?" The sheriff's informality made him nervous. "With witnesses and maybe a videotape."

"That's not necessary. Unless you think I'm going to beat the information out of you." The sheriff smiled, lots of teeth, predatory.

"No. Of course not." Warren's own teeth threatened to chatter. He clamped his lips over them.

Braxton picked up a pencil, tapping it on a small pad. "Now, why don't you tell me what kind of shovel you used."

What kind? God almighty. He hadn't even thought to ask Cookie that. "Isn't that in my statement?"

"Nope."

His thoughts whirling, Warren stalled. "Why is that important?"

"Well, since we don't have the murder weapon…" Tap, tap went the pencil, and Warren winced at the word murder. "We've got to make sure the wound pattern matches your description."

Think of something. "Well, I can't really remember. I just bought it. I was going to do a little gardening…" He let his words trail off, hands held aloft in a helpless gesture. Christ, he was helpless, all right.

"That should be easy to trace. Where'd you buy it? Sylvestor's in town?"

"No, out at the Home Depot in the minimall." They must have tons of different kinds of shovels there.

"Even easier." The sheriff wrote something on his pad. "Those places have computer tracking these days."

Warren's heart stuttered. "I paid cash."

"They track that, too. Piece of cake." The sheriff flashed him another smile, this one friendly, two guys shooting the breeze. "What day did you buy it?"

"I'm not exactly sure."

"The weekend? Last week? Week before?"

The tapping pencil had begun to feel like a drum beating inside Warren's skull. He wanted to scream. "I couldn't say for sure." He wouldn't say for sure.

The sheriff nodded, wrote on his pad. "Well, my boys'll have no problem tracing it, anyway." He looked up, met Warren's gaze. "They're good. Now, you said you threw it in the lake."

"Yes." Cookie told him she'd buried the shovel in the woods, she couldn't remember where, but she'd walked a long way. Would her fingerprints still be detectable after the thing had lain beneath all that dirt? He prayed to God not, but he wasn't taking any chances. "It was a spur of the moment thing."

The sheriff looked pointedly at Warren's arms in his short-sleeved shirt. "How far did you throw it and in what direction?"

Goose bumps rose on Warren's skin, despite the day's heat still trapped in the room. "As far as I could. I'm not sure what direction. I did a sort of whirling motion, then let go."

The man wrote something else. "Couldn't have gone too far. And it's pretty shallow right there. Funny my men can't find it."

"Maybe they're not as good as you think." The sheriff's eyes hardened, and Warren corrected his mistake. "Maybe it got buried in some silt."

Braxton smiled. But the harshness never left his eyes. "That's a good thought. I'll have them dig down a little."

Warren gulped air. "Yes, I think you should do that." When would this end?

"Did you get any blood spatter on your clothes? Stands to reason there would be since you gave Jimbo one helluva whack or two." Braxton paused. "Or three."

The man was good. Warren's stomach now threatened to turn upside down. He cleared his throat. "I can't remember about any blood. I really don't think there was any...on me, I mean. But I went home and changed before I called...you."

"Then the clothes should still be there. I'll have someone pick them up." Another neat note on the pad.

"Thank you." What the hell else was he supposed to say under the circumstances? Suddenly a ray of hope bloomed. Cookie hadn't had blood on her. Maybe she'd told him at least the partial truth. Maybe she really was just a victim of circumstance and bad judgment. If only she hadn't picked up that shovel...

"What shoes were you wearing?"

"Shoes?"

"We need to match prints at the scene."

Christ. Another thing he hadn't thought of. What if Cookie's prints were visible? What had she been wearing? He should have wiped the area clean of any footprints. "I...well, not these ones. I guess they must be with my clothes."

The sheriff jotted. "You're being very helpful, Mr. Spivey. Thank you. Now, about your car."

Blood rushed to his face. What else had he forgotten? He should have watched all those detective shows Roberta was so fond of.

"There was a whole mess of tire tracks out there. We'll need to match at least one set to yours."

He could breathe again. Cookie had parked her car on the road and walked in. Her tire tracks wouldn't be down at the lake.

"My car is at your disposal." His tire tracks, they would find. "Are we done, Sheriff? I have to admit I'm a bit tired."

And he needed time to think. Right now the only thing he was sure of was that if Cookie had murdered Jimbo, it was only because he, Warren, had failed to protect her.

He wouldn't fail her again. No matter what he had to do, he'd make sure Cookie did not go to jail for her husband's murder.

Reviewing the notes on his pad, Braxton said, "Just a few more questions." He looked up, his gaze laser sharp. "I'd like to go over why you were meeting Jimbo out at the lake again."

Roberta had told him the Dennis Crouch thing was lame. She was right. He worked furiously on how to jazz it up, make it believable. Without truly altering it. "Well, he was angry about the fact that I might be stealing business from Dennis Crouch." He took a deep breath, then rushed on. "And he was really angry about my treatment of my wife, too."

The sheriff raised a brow.

"You see, he really liked Roberta. Thought she was sweet. Which she is. And he felt that I'd done her a great disservice. Which I had." Did this sound any less lame? He didn't have a choice now that he'd started. Too many deep breaths were making him light-headed. "And he was very angry."

"But Jimbo had only known Bobbie a week."

"Yes, well…" Well, what? *Come on, man, think.*

Cookie's life is at stake. If he didn't come up with something good, Cookie was right, they'd start looking straight at her. "You know, I'm really getting tired. Could we continue this tomorrow?"

"Just a little more, Mr. Spivey. You're on a roll here."

He had that right. A roll that would lead right to Cookie if he didn't shut up.

"Why don't you tell me why you think Jimbo would call you in the middle of the night and ask you to meet him out at the lake when he could have come to your office the next morning?"

He didn't believe him. The man did not believe him. "I can't tell you why he called me in the middle of the night. I wasn't inside his mind."

"Oh, wait a minute. I forgot." The sheriff pulled a document close, flipped the pages, read. "Yep, it's right there." He glanced up, pinning Warren with a look. "I got it wrong, Mr. Spivey. In your statement, you said *you* called Jimbo."

Shit. "I've had enough, Sheriff. I've decided you're right. I need a lawyer. I'm not saying another thing until I get one."

The sheriff raised his hands in surrender. "Whatever, Mr. Spivey. That's your right. I'm sure he'll help you get your story straight."

He'd fucked up. Badly. First he hadn't known the answers to stuff he should have known if he was guilty. And now he'd contradicted himself. *Cookie, forgive me, but I'll still protect you with my life.*

He just might have to.

"One last thing, if you don't mind. Feel free not to answer, of course."

Warren closed his eyes and nodded.

"We found some awfully big prints out there, ten to one says they're from a man's shoe. Didn't match Jimbo, we checked. What's your size?" He leaned out over the desk and looked at Warren's feet, then grunted. "Way too big to be yours." His gaze shot to Warren's face. "Know anyone else who could have made them?"

BOBBIE PURSUED NICK to the house. "What do you mean your shovel is missing?"

He turned on the porch. She almost ran into his hard chest. "I used a spade to bury the cat last Monday. Today that spade is gone." He stared down at her, his eyes as hard as his chest. "And Jimbo had his head beaten in with a shovel. So, what do you think I'm saying?"

"Well, you're certainly not saying you had anything to do with it." She bit her lip. "Are you?"

He opened his mouth. She snapped her hand up to cover it. "I didn't mean it the way it sounded. I don't think you did it."

His eyes were chunks of black ice. He shoved her hand away. "You don't *think?*"

She put her hands on her hips. "I *know* you didn't do it." But God, this was bad, really bad. If Warren took back his confession, Nick was next in line for the gas chamber. She drew her lip between her teeth, bit down until it hurt. "But I'm wondering what Brax is really thinking."

He stared at her a long time. She couldn't be sure which part of what she said was taking him so long to digest.

"So, why is your shovel missing, that's the question."

He quirked a brow. "Brax is trying to frame me?"

She huffed. "Don't be ridiculous. He thinks you're one of the good guys, even if you two seem to be at odds."

Nick laughed outright. "At odds? Bobbie, I figured you for an eternal optimist, and I was absolutely effing right. Brax hates my guts, and he'd love nothing better than to pin Jimbo's murder on me." He ran a hand through his thick hair. "But he wouldn't plant evidence to do it. He's by the book."

"He's one of the good guys, too."

His gaze skimmed her face, looking for something she wasn't sure he found. "I hate to agree. But he's still an ass. Guess that leaves you."

"Me?" She barely avoided letting her voice squeak.

"Yeah. You. Your husband. And what you'll do to save him."

He might as well have reached inside her chest and ripped her heart out. "I wouldn't do anything that hurts you."

He looked at her, eyes dark, simmering with some hot emotion. Rage. Or hope.

She'd have put her hand on his arm, except that she was afraid he'd tear it off like some savage animal. "Not even for Warren."

He didn't answer with words, muscle movement was enough. Some of the anger leached from his gaze. The tight jaw eased.

"So what are we going to do about the shovel?" she asked, hoping he'd hear the "we."

"Nothing we can do since it's already gone." He looked down at her empty hands. "Didn't you bring something good to eat?"

She unclenched her fists. Emergency over, at least for

now. "I've been with Warren. I didn't have time." She licked her lips. "He didn't do this, you know."

Nick turned and banged the back door open with the flat of his hand. Moving swiftly through the kitchen, he bounded up the stairs two at a time. By the time she located him, he was in his bedroom staring into his closet, a bare bulb lit above his head.

"What are you doing?"

"Just wondering if I've got a pair of missing shoes, too."

"Why?"

He didn't answer, clicked the light off instead and closed the door. "Guess they're all there."

"You can't tell if you're missing a pair of shoes?"

"I've got a big yard. With a lot of dog shit. Neighborhood dogs. I throw out a lot of shoes."

Settling her hands on her hips, she peered at him. "Is Brax looking for shoes as well as a shovel?"

"Yep."

"And if I prove Warren didn't kill Jimbo, then Brax is going to come after you."

"Yep."

"And you think someone's got your shovel to trot it out just at the right time. To make it look like you killed Jimbo."

"Yep."

"Would you stop saying yep?" She was almost shouting. It was worse than she'd thought. "I can't let him go to jail for something he didn't do."

Nick took a step forward and dropped his voice to a seductive, frightening whisper. "Do you want to know what I really think, Bobbie?"

No. "What?"

"I think Cookie Beaumont asked your husband to kill Jimbo in order to get her out of her marriage."

Her insides crimped. "She did tell him that Jimbo beat her. But to actually ask Warren to kill him?" She shook her head. "I don't know."

"She fed me the same sob story about Jimbo being abusive. You have to ask yourself why, now that Jimbo's dead."

He stood in the shadows cast by the blinds. Strips of light slashed his chest and face but covered the slits of his eyes. And he waited.

What was she supposed to say? Or even feel? Too much had happened too quickly, and now each new bit of information only brought a numbness to her bones. Cookie had tried to coerce Nick. Which meant Cookie had planned her husband's murder long before Warren came to town. *Warren, you fool.* She could almost feel sorry for him. "We have to tell Brax."

"It's too late. And it wouldn't matter anyway. Brax'll just think I'm saying it to cover my own butt."

"It will at least get him looking at Cookie."

"He'll already be looking at Cookie because she was having an affair with your husband."

Paralysis crawled down her arms to her fingers. "Warren didn't tell him about Cookie. He said Jimbo was mad at him because he was stealing clients from someone named Dennis Grouch."

"Crouch?" Nick snorted. "Didn't *you* tell Brax then?"

"No." The word didn't make much of a sound in the quiet room. Princess had long since stopped barking. The streets were devoid of children, mothers having called them in for the night. Silence reigned except for the echo of that word between them.

"Why not?"

"Because…" She licked her lips. "Because if Brax knows Warren was having an affair with Cookie, then he'll also have a motive. Nothing would save Warren after that."

"He confessed, Bobbie. Whether he did the deed or she did it, he's covering for her. He's already made his choice about what he wants to do."

"But I can't let him—"

He spread his hands. "Is he asking for your help?"

"No."

"Then tell Brax the truth and let what happens happen."

It would be the easiest thing. No struggle. No saying horrible things to Warren to get him to cave in. And Brax wouldn't look at Nick as suspect number two.

She put her hands to her cheeks, covering her lips with her pinkies. "I can't."

"Because you're still in love with him?"

The very idea made her sink onto the edge of Nick's bed. "I…"

What? She didn't know? Worse. She simply hadn't given her love for Warren thought for so many years, she couldn't even begin to count. Despite what Warren had done, that had been her crime against him.

"It's not his fault, you know. He's a good man. He always tried to do his best."

But he'd stopped wanting her. All she'd wanted was to make him start again. At some point, love had ceased to be the issue. "He's trying to prove to Cookie that he's worthy. But I won't let him sacrifice himself." She swiped a tear before it overflowed her eye. "It isn't because I hate Cookie. This is about Warren."

Nick towered above her, expression implacable. "He isn't a child, Bobbie. You can't wave a magic wand and make all his troubles go away. He's the only one who can solve his problems."

"Don't you see?" She stared up at him, needing him to understand for some inexplicable reason. "That's how this whole thing got started. Because I *did* let him solve his own problems. Because I let him make all the decisions whether I thought they were the right ones or not." And because she'd been afraid to make the decisions herself. She'd been a coward. They hadn't had kids, not solely because of Warren, but because *she* was afraid to have another human being depend on her. She'd never taken responsibility for anything.

"And look what happened," she whispered. "He's in jail for a murder he didn't do."

"Maybe he did it. Maybe this was important enough for him."

"No." Her vehemence clogged her throat. She swallowed. "I know him. He wouldn't." She bit her lip. "He couldn't."

Nick was unrelenting. "Because it would mean he loved her more than he ever loved you?"

She squeezed her eyes shut. Warren had never loved her the way he'd loved Cookie. His high school sweetheart had lived in his dreams, his midnight fantasies. Roberta had been a substitute. Always. To chase away the chill in her fingers, she tucked her hands between her knees. The mattress sagged beside her. She tilted toward Nick, her shoulder brushing the warmth of his. She wanted to crawl into his arms.

But nothing could warm her insides.

"Let him do it his own way." Nick's gentle murmur wafted against her ear.

"I always let him do it his way." If the wall had been within striking distance, she'd have smashed her fist through it. Instead, she glared at Nick, aiming her fifteen years of rage straight at him. "He was in love with Cookie in high school. She left him. I helped him find her. So that he could get over it."

There was so much more to it, but Nick didn't ask. He simply took her wrath unblinkingly. She looked down at her hands, avoiding the pity in his eyes.

"We subscribed to a search service and wrote every woman who fit the age range." And she'd pathetically kissed Warren every time a letter came back unopened. "I never told him how much it hurt to help him look for her." She clutched her stomach, the ache fresh.

Nick's hand twitched, as if he wanted to touch her but decided against it. "So, you helped your husband look for his old lover?"

God, this was like admitting to ax-murdering your family. Then going into all the gory details just so they'd know how really really evil you were. Or stupid.

"I know how bad that sounds." Roberta hadn't been just your garden variety stupid, she'd been colossally stupid. Brain-damaged. "The psychiatrist who was treating Warren said that if he faced Cookie again and found out she wasn't this big monster—" She laughed then, feeling on the edge of hysteria. The Cookie Monster. Oh, that was rich. "What I mean is, if he faced that Cookie's dumping him didn't mean he was this awful person who deserved to be abandoned, he'd be able to get over her." Deep down, Warren was afraid she'd be a rich woman with a wonderful husband and that she really had done so much better than she could have with him.

Nick moved, hunkering down in front of her. Pulling her hands from her knees, he engulfed them with his own. "So you helped him find his old girlfriend. That doesn't make everything your fault, Bobbie."

"You don't understand. I was desperate. I would have done anything. He was on those drugs, and he hadn't made love to me in—" She cut herself off, digging her teeth into her lip as if the physical pain could outweigh the emotional. "The psychiatrist said it was the drugs. Decreased sexual desire, side effects and all. But—"

Oh God, she couldn't even bear to think about it, yet she couldn't stem the tide of words pouring out of her mouth. "But I never told him how much it hurt. How abandoned *I* felt. I let it go on and on until I just sort of convinced myself I didn't need sex anymore. I'm one of those terrible people who lives with the status quo because they're afraid that whatever is out there has to be worse." She let the tears flow freely down her cheeks. "Do you know how long it's been since a man has made love to me?"

Had a man *ever* made love to her? She wasn't sure what she and Warren had done even qualified. At least not after the first years of their marriage.

And other men in her life? She'd been a late bloomer, hadn't dated much, and before Warren, she'd had only one serious but not very memorable lover.

Nick shook his head, put his hands on her shoulders and stroked.

"Five years," she whispered. "Five *years*. What kind of woman lets her husband avoid making love to her for

five years? And never even does anything about it?"
Begging didn't count.

She should have made him go to marriage counseling with her. Something, anything. Instead she patted him on the back when he got depressed, made him a cup of tea and handed him more pills.

"I was afraid he'd leave me if I made a fuss. But he went off the damn drugs for her and left me, anyway." A tear dribbled past the corner of her mouth. Nick whisked it away with the pad of his thumb.

She drew a shaky breath and risked looking at him. "Isn't that the most pathetic thing you've ever heard?"

His hands dropped to her legs, rubbing her from knee to thigh while her hands twisted in her lap. "Not the most. A few of my own stories would sound worse."

Nick didn't get it. Nothing could be worse. She set out to show him, as if revealing every pathetic thing she'd done, thought or felt would somehow release her. "He kept this box of mementos. One of those little Hallmark books that talks about loving and never leaving. Cards she gave him. She even made him this jean shirt that had a big tiger embroidered on the back. He asked me to wash it, and I made all the colors run." Talk about passive-aggressive. "But he didn't throw it out. I think he took it with him when he left. Maybe he thought she could fix it. Or make another one."

Nick gripped her fingers again. "Your hands are cold."

Her hands had been cold for fifteen years, as if all the feelings turning her insides to ice spewed out her fingers. "I just wanted him to stop talking about her," she whispered. "I was so sick of hearing about her and the things they used to do togeth—" She sliced through the word. God, there were some things that should *never* see the light of day.

Nick's grasp tightened almost to the point of pain. "Why didn't you just leave him?"

"Because." She stopped for a big sigh and a little sniffle. More pathetic truth she hadn't wanted to face. She told Nick anyway, just to get it all out. "I didn't want to be alone."

He chafed her hands. "Did you ever think that you wouldn't be alone for long?"

Now that was a thought. It had never occurred to her. "No."

"Maybe you were wrong about that." He tucked loose strands of hair behind her ear.

She tried not to compare him to Warren, to compare Mary Alice Turner to Cookie. She concentrated on confessing.

"I'll never know. All I do know is that I let him make some very bad choices for our marriage. *I* let him. He was a crazy person on drugs. And he's still crazy. I've got nothing left to lose but my self-respect." God, had any self-respect even survived? "If I let him go to prison or—" She shut her eyes. "Or die, because I don't think I can make a difference, or I'm afraid of the consequences, or because I want to make him pay for hurting me, then I'll just keep on being pathetic Roberta Jones Spivey for the rest of my life." She opened her eyes to look at Nick. "I can't do that."

His irises had softened to warm brown. Dark hair fell across his forehead. His gaze rose from her lips to her eyes. "You call yourself pathetic. But I don't think I've ever known a more loyal woman."

Kind words. Her fingers trailed his jaw, then his

lower lip. For now she'd let him believe what he wanted to. "I don't intend to sacrifice you, either. I'm going to prove Cookie masterminded it all. She's the one who killed Jimbo, then she told Warren some big lie to get him to confess. She's the one setting you up, too. I'm going to prove it even if it kills me."

Which it might very well do. But then, she'd only been half alive for the last fifteen years.

CHAPTER THIRTEEN

HER HUSBAND was a freaking bastard. Five years? Nick found it hard to believe. Bobbie must be damn near ready to explode. But now wasn't the time to think about it.

Or maybe it was. Tears stained her cheeks. Confession, while good for the soul, had left her eyes bleak and a tremble on her lips.

Roberta Jones Spivey hadn't had a man make love to her in five years. He might not be good for a helluva lot else, but that, Nick could give her.

Maybe even restore a little of the self-respect she was looking for. Damn Warren Spineless Spivey for taking it away from her in the first place. The asshole should rot in jail for what he'd done to his wife. Or hadn't done.

Nick framed Bobbie's face with his hands. "I want to make love with you." He could have called it any number of things, but there was only one she really needed to hear.

"You do?" The tone of a nonbeliever desperate to be convinced.

"Yeah. Real bad." He kissed the corner of her mouth. "Couldn't you tell Sunday night?"

She thought she was weak, a failure. He knew better. She was devoted, tough enough to stick it out, optimistic. There was nothing he could do to make her see that. He could, however, show her what an idiot her husband was.

He started with her shoes, the slip-ons plopping to the carpet when he tugged on the toes.

Still hunkered before her, he spread his legs along the outside of hers and dropped his hands to her knees. Stroking up her thighs, he reached under her to squeeze. "You've got a gorgeous butt."

She blinked, then let her gaze fall to his thumbs tucked in the crease at the tops of her thighs. He knew she wanted more.

He lifted a finger to trail from the hollow of her throat to the vee between her breasts. Then he toyed with the fourth button of her uniform, the one she'd kept buttoned. "Your breasts are perfect."

She took what he gave, no more questions asked, no more doubts raised. Her hands sank into the bedspread.

He slipped the button loose, found the front clasp of her bra, then bypassed it for the next button. The starchy material spread to reveal the edges of lacy white. She stared at him, eyes wide, a deep bottomless green he could lose himself in.

He slipped another button, then another, until the top half of her uniform sprang open. She sat up straighter, sucking her stomach in self-consciously. He bent his head and kissed her abdomen just above the apron, giving her flesh a lingering trace with his tongue. "You smell good."

"It's mango." Her voice, barely a whisper, shivered down his spine.

Her fingers clutched his mother's ancient spread, her

knuckles almost white. She waited. He wanted her an active participant. "Undo your bra."

Watching him, her hands unfurled, rising slowly to farther push aside the material. His gaze greedily followed her progress. The clasp undone, the bra eased, but didn't reveal her breasts. "Let me see you."

He leaned in to prod the lace with his tongue, then retreated. Her nipples peaked. His mouth watered. One ripe bud beckoned. He teased with the tip of his tongue, encircled with his lips, nipped. Not quite a moan, her intake of breath became a gasp as he sucked hard. Then let go.

"Take it off."

She did, arching back to push the sleeves of her uniform and bra straps down both arms. As the scrap of lace fell to the bed, he swatted it to the floor. "What do you want me to do to you?"

Her glance flashed over his face. Uncertainty. Trepidation.

"Tell me." He'd do anything, everything she asked.

Her pupils dilated to fill her eyes as she drank in the rough demand, his quaking voice. "Kiss me."

"Oh, that'll be so easy, sweetheart. For as long as you want."

The squat started an ache in his knees. He planted one on either side of her feet and rose above her. Taking her face in his hands, he covered her lips. First a taste, then a lick along the seam, then he slanted over her mouth, forcing her to open.

Tongue to hers, he sucked, licked, cajoled until she put her hands to his shoulders and leaned against him. He rubbed his cotton T-shirt across her breasts, the nipples pebbling. She moaned and tugged at the shirt still tucked in his waistband. He pulled back enough for her to raise it to his armpits, then dragged her close for skin-to-skin contact.

He took his tongue out of her mouth long enough to say, "That feels too damn good."

It wasn't as if he had to lie, either. All he had to do was make sure she knew what she was doing to him. Words were as important as action. Maybe even more.

"Is it better than with Cookie?" she murmured against his lips.

"Shit." He pushed back, tucked a lock of hair behind her ear, cupped her face. "She was just a lay."

"What am I?"

He could lie, tell her he loved her. But lies weren't what she needed. "I don't know what you are, Bobbie. But you keep me awake at night. And I'm not going to let you walk out that door before I finish what we started Sunday night."

In the heat of the moment, sometimes being wanted, desired, was more important, more powerful than love. She drank it in.

"Kiss me again."

He did, willing to give her anything. The kiss was voracious, an attack, a bonding, their lips sealing his desire.

He reached back and pulled his T-shirt over his head, flinging it across the room. Then, kissing her again, he went for the tie of her apron and two more buttons of her uniform. She had to help him pull the tight material down over her hips, lifting for him. Her panties came off, as well, though he would have liked to linger over their removal.

The curls didn't match her hair. Dark, damp, inviting, he smoothed his hand over them. She held her breath as he spread her legs scant inches. Wanting to draw out the pleasure, his, hers, he slid a finger along the pink slit, not entering, merely testing.

"You're pretty down here, too."

She laughed, muffled it against his shoulder.

And then he did enter, just the tip of his finger, first gliding over the bud of her clitoris. She tugged her lip between her teeth.

"Did you like the orgasm I gave you the other night?"

"Yes." Her eyes darted from his to his hand between her legs.

He grinned. "I can do better."

An answering smile curved her lips. Her body heated, clamped his finger. "You can?"

"Much better. And more than once."

She parted her lips and leaned back on her hands as he eased farther inside. "That would be okay."

He spread her legs for a fuller touch, then put two fingers inside her.

"You're so wet. And warm." He'd never talked much during sex, but the words seemed to turn him inside out, the way he wanted to do to her.

He buried his fingers, then slid back out, easing over a sweet spot that made her breath rush out. "Do you like it?"

"Mmm. Yes." She licked her lips, panted, then took one deep breath and settled.

He put his thumb to her clitoris as he worked her with his fingers. She fell back on her elbows, her legs splaying farther. He leaned over her, manipulating her, savoring the change in her breath, the slow fall of her eyelids. Then she arched her back and let out a long, low moan.

"Come on, sweetheart, come for me. Scream. I want to hear you scream."

He quickened his fingers and thumb, not realizing how close she was until her back bowed off the bed, and she cried out. Her hands went to her face, ran through her hair, and her hips bucked at his fingers. He didn't let her go, didn't let her throw him off, just kept sliding through the slick folds, holding her at the peak as long as he could.

"You make me hot. I could watch you do that all night."

She finally wrenched away, one knee caught at his waist, her hands pushing at his. He bent forward to kiss her, his belly at the juncture of her thighs, her body slippery against his.

"That's just the first one," he promised against her lips.

"Your pants are still on."

"You can take them off when we're ready." Hell, he was ready, his cock a hard rock against the zipper of his jeans. But she'd come only once. "I'll keep them on until you've reached the fifth orgasm. At least."

"I'll die before then." She laughed. She believed. Thank heaven.

He'd kept his finger on her button, now he flicked it. Her body jerked in response. "Ready?"

"Yes, please."

He got her off twice more with his fingers. He wanted to use his tongue for the fourth, craving the taste of her. Coaxing her farther up the mattress, he shoved a pillow beneath her hips.

"What are you doing?"

"Making sure I taste every bit of you. It's a very delicate process."

"You don't have to do that." Something wavered beneath the surface, a tinge of fear. She pushed at his shoulders between her legs.

"I'm going to die if I don't do it." He put his hand on her chest, tweaked one tight nipple. "But I won't if you don't want me to."

She bit her lip, brows drawing together. That fucking husband, excuse me, nonfucking husband. He'd never done this for her. She'd wanted him to, but he wouldn't. Or if he had, he'd made her feel his distaste. If the bastard hadn't been under lock and key, Nick would have beat him to a bloody pulp.

"Let me do it," he whispered. "Let me kiss your pretty pink lips."

She stared at him a moment longer, almost wild-eyed. Then her head fell back to the mattress, her hips rising to him. "Oh God, please. I do want you to."

He didn't give her a millisecond to change her mind.

His tongue delved to her clitoris. Lips smothering her, he suckled. She moaned, writhed. He pulled her legs over his shoulders and held her hips to the pillow.

BOBBIE HADN'T THOUGHT he could wring another orgasm from her, her body spent, replete, beyond satisfied. But he did. It built deep inside, sucked up through her body, into his mouth. He used his tongue on her and his fingers inside her, and she prayed the windows were closed because when she came the fourth time, the fifth close on its heels, almost as if they were one, she did scream the way he'd told her to. An ahh and an ooh. Long and loud. She tossed her head, hair flinging across her eyes.

"Oh, my God, please don't stop, please never stop."

A voice echoed in the room, hers but not hers. So different, almost guttural. Wanton. She'd always dreamed of being a raving sex lunatic, and Nick turned her into one with his clever tongue and skillful fingers.

His enjoyment couldn't be faked. The way his fingers dug into her bottom couldn't be mistaken for casual involvement. He'd said all the right words, done all the right things. She didn't want to doubt him, didn't want to doubt herself. Not now, when she felt *this* wonderful, marvelous, stupendous. Damn, she was good. So was he. He held her to his mouth until the last of her shudders faded away, his tongue massaging, gentling.

He raised his head, dark eyes gleaming in moonlight. "Okay, that was five."

He didn't have to ask, he knew the one had quickly followed the other.

"Now what?"

"Now you take off my jeans like you promised, and you let me bury my cock deep inside you."

His mixture of compliments and dirty talk made Bobbie's heart flip. She'd give him anything he wanted. Except that he was actually giving it to her.

She pulled the pillow from beneath her hips and sat up. Hand to the front of his pants, she palmed the bulge. It was huge. And hard. Was she imagining the pulse of it?

Amazingly, this was actually mutual. He wasn't thinking about any other woman, not Cookie, not Mary Alice. Just her. It was all that counted.

Her breasts now level with his face, he pulled her close and latched on to a nipple. He tugged with his teeth, then sucked. She'd never had sensitive nipples, but a jolt of electricity suddenly shot down between her legs. She held his head to her, absorbed the new sensation.

"Do me now, Bobbie, don't make me wait. I'm ready to explode here."

She could feel that. He wanted her. He really did.

She tugged at his buckle, then reached for his zipper. He pulled her hand away. "Better let me do that. Don't want any accidents as this stage of the game."

He eased the zipper down over that rock-hard bulge. He toed off his shoes, then rose, stomped jeans and cotton briefs to his ankles. He kicked everything to one side and stood before her.

She stared at him in awe. "You're beautiful."

His penis jumped. She laughed. When had she ever had fun while making...having sex? For much of her marriage to Warren, sex had always been an obstacle to overcome, crushing all the life out of it.

"Touch it." A harsh whisper, pleading.

She wrapped her hand around its girth, just the tip peeking out from her fist. She leaned forward to run her tongue over the smooth, taut skin. He groaned, and a droplet oozed from the head. She licked it, salty, tangy.

She'd never done that to Warren, just the perfunctory seeming almost more than they could mutually handle. Maybe she'd been scared, too, that it wouldn't work, that she couldn't bring him to orgasm with just her mouth. It had been hard enough to do that the regular way. Before they'd stopped trying altogether.

Nick buried his hands in her hair and pushed her head down. She opened her mouth, slid her hand to the base and took him inside until he touched the back of her throat.

Goodness. Could she rival Linda Lovelace?

Nick pumped, once, twice, then pulled out of her mouth.

Why did he stop? Doubt twisted her stomach. Maybe she wasn't good enough to...

"I don't think I can take too much of that, baby."

Maybe she turned him on too much. She'd have given anything for it to be true. And she'd never been any man's baby.

She looked up at him, his hands still in her hair, his face and eyes dark with...yes, oh yes, passion. For her.

"I started my pills on Sunday. They should work right away." Her cheeks heated with the need to get the technical stuff out of the way.

He put his thumbs beneath her chin and tilted her head up. "Did you get them for me?"

She got them for herself. "Yes."

"Then lie down and let me in. God, I need to be inside you."

That was the same as saying he needed her. No one had ever *needed* to be inside her.

Pulling the pillow beneath her head, she fell back against it. He slid her across the covers, then came down with one knee between her legs and spread her with one of those clever hands. Pleasure jolted through her as he swept a finger over the sensitive bud, then slid down and inside.

"Are you ready for me?"

"Maybe you should give me another five orgasms, just to make sure."

"Once I'm inside," he promised, and then he put his hips between hers, pulled her knees up to his waist and thrust.

She screamed. And it wasn't with the same pleasure as before.

"I'm sorry."

She drew in a slow breath, tried to relax. "It's been…well, a long time."

"I thought you'd be ready." He brushed his mouth across hers, a hint of her own essence still on his lips. "I'm sorry, baby."

"It'll be okay. Just go a little slower."

"You know slow is gonna kill me." But he braced himself on his elbows and eased in, bare centimeters at a time. "Is that better?"

She did relax, tilting her hips to his. He began to slide, her body accepting, slowly expanding around him.

"You are so tight. Almost like a virgin."

Yes, well, she wasn't actually far from that after fifteen years of marriage to Warren and only one lover, briefly, before that.

Nick closed his eyes, arched his neck and thrust deeper. "You don't know how good this feels."

Actually, she did. She felt it in him and was beginning to feel it in herself. She'd come so many times, her juices eased the passage.

"Oh, baby, I want you." He buried his face in her neck. "Are you okay now?"

She was. Better than okay. He was all the way in. And she wanted him to move.

"Please."

"Yeah, you please me all right." Instead of pulling out, though, he gathered her hips in his hands, lifted her and plunged another inch. "Like that?"

"More," she begged. And more.

He drew out, keeping her hips angled, sliding sharply against a delicious little spot deep inside. He'd found something new.

The pillow fell off the other side of the bed, and somehow, the lack of it gave him better access to that very special spot.

He plunged back in, finding it again. She arched her back to keep the contact. Ooh, she'd never felt anything quite this nice. Not even his tongue. What *was* that spot?

He picked up speed, a quick rhythm. She panted, straining to keep up. She pulled her knees higher, gripping his waist.

She was going to come again. She couldn't believe it. Sensation crashed over her as she dug her nails into his shoulders. She screamed again, this time, his name.

"That's it, baby, again, do it again. I can feel it."

Then he was taking her hand, forcing it between their pumping hips. "Here, touch yourself here."

He put her fingers to her clitoris, and she was too far gone to stop him. Building, crashing, rising, screaming.

He came at her like a battering ram, her head hanging off the side of the bed. She jerked in a breath and with each thrust his body forced her finger against herself, feeling bursting within and without.

He threw himself into her again, then she felt him seize, tossing his head back. Orgasm rolled her over like a wave, tumbling her about, stealing her breath. Then he spurted deep inside, pulsing, pumping, beating against her.

How long it had been since a man had come inside her? Longer even than the five years. Maybe never. She couldn't even remember how it felt to have a man lie on her. He shifted, pulling up and away from her.

"Don't move."

"But I'm crushing you," he whispered in her hair.

"I like it." She tugged on his shoulders until he sagged against her once more. His delicious weight squeezed the air from her lungs. She couldn't breathe. She didn't care.

Nick might not realize it, but she'd just died and gone to heaven. And he'd been the only one, ever, to send her there.

"So, HOW ARE WE going to save Warren?"

He woke from a blissful sleep to find her sitting on the end of the bed, dressed and in the final process of buttoning her wrinkled uniform. He glanced at the clock—5:14 a.m. "What the hell are you doing up already?"

"Places to go, people to question," she quipped.

He didn't laugh, not even a smile. He wanted to make love again. For the fourth time. She'd only had nine orgasms; he wanted to make it ten before the sun came up.

"Get back in bed."

She bounced to her feet. "I need a mocha before I go to work."

"You don't have to be at work until seven-thirty. How long does it take to make a mocha?"

"Seven minutes if you want it really frothy, and that's including letting the machine work up a steam."

He looked at her tight butt and thought of how tightly her body had gripped him. How tight *she* was. "I've worked up a head of steam. I think you need to bleed it off."

She tipped her head to one side. "Somehow that seems like a sort of disgusting metaphor for what you really mean."

She was right; it was. But she'd scrambled his brains last night, and his powers of intellect might never be the same. "I want you."

She came to sit down on the bed beside him, stroked a hand through his hair, her fingers tangling. "Thank you."

"It was my pleasure." He smiled, tried to tug her closer.

She resisted. "I know. That's why I'm saying thank you."

"You drive me crazy, you know." It was true. He didn't have to fake a damn thing for her. When he came inside her last night for the third time, the feeling had been so intense he'd almost lost consciousness. Swear to God. He wanted to lose his wits all over again. And he was past caring if he lost himself as well. "Come back to bed."

She rose, stepped back out of his reach. "I can't. I have to ask around about Warren and stuff before work."

"What stuff?"

"Cookie and Jimbo stuff. Stuff that'll show she did it."

He reached for her once more, missed again. "Let Brax prove it. That's his job."

"I can't sit idly by."

Well, *he* could. She might think she'd done nothing to help Warren solve his own problems all these years, but her perception and reality were two different things. He didn't believe Bobbie Jones would ever sit idly by.

She leaned in to kiss his forehead, then jumped back before he could haul her into his arms where she belonged. At least for now.

"Someone's trying to frame you, Nick. If I leave it to Brax to solve, he's going to come looking for you. I told you last night, I wouldn't let that happen."

He hadn't believed her. Actually he hadn't given it a thought. All he'd wanted to do was show her how beautiful, how desirable she was.

But she was also like a mama bear looking out for her cub. If it were in her power, she wouldn't let anything happen to him.

He just wished he didn't resent it so damn much that she had to do the same thing for her fricking husband.

SHERIFF BRAXTON didn't believe him. That much was certain.

Warren lay on his two-foot-wide bed, hands stacked beneath his head, mattress thin enough to let the springs gouge. At least it was clean. So was the cell. Six by twelve, there was enough room for bed, toilet and sink. Concrete walls made sure he didn't mingle with the rest of the jail's occupants. If there were any. Cottonmouth didn't sport too many criminal types. Just Beau Beaumont, the town drunk and eighty-three-year-old Bertha Swurtz, whom Braxton pulled in regularly for driving without a license.

The clock tower in the square struck the five-o'clock hour. Warren had slept, off and on. But he'd been awake since the last strike a half hour before.

Cookie had begged him to help her on Sunday night. He'd flatly refused. He hadn't suspected she'd take matters into her own hands.

Pretty stupid assumption on his part. He'd left her no choice. What he'd done was to leave her totally defenseless.

She'd called him that morning, sobbing so hard it had taken long minutes just to get the story out of her. With some crazy notion that Jimbo was out there hiring a hit man to kill her, she'd followed him down to the lake. But Jimbo was already dead. She'd picked up the shovel because she was afraid the murderer still lurked in the vicinity. Of course, the killer hadn't been, as it turned out, but her fingerprints were all over the shovel. She'd panicked, buried it, driven home and called Warren.

The only person with more holes in her story than he had was Cookie.

He'd known she'd done it herself. Probably after another fight. Hell, maybe Jimbo had even followed them out there on Sunday. He'd thought he'd heard something out in the woods. Maybe he'd been angry, dragged Cookie back to the scene of her sins, maybe he'd even planned to bash *her* head in with the shovel.

It didn't matter how or why she'd done it, Warren was honor bound to save her. She'd warned him, he hadn't heeded the call, hence it was his duty to protect her.

Telling her to report Jimbo missing, he'd driven down to the lake. James Beaumont had lain half in, half out of the water, five feet from the bumper of his silver Cadillac. Unmoving, his head in the lake, he'd definitely been dead.

An owl hooted. A full moon lit the sky, creating a shimmering path across the water that led straight to the spot where Jimbo lay. Like a beacon.

Later that morning, showered and shaved, Warren confessed to the sheriff. But he'd had to confess to *himself* that saving the damsel in distress had been one massive power rush. He'd lived off it even through Roberta's interrogation, managed to hold his own with the sheriff only because of it.

But that was before he knew about the shoe print. The shoe print of a big man. Obviously not Cookie's foot.

That thought had woken Warren every hour, sometimes more.

Had Cookie been telling him the truth about a shadowy killer?

Or had an accomplice helped her murder Jimbo?

Warren had wanted her to accept him back into her life so badly he hadn't even questioned the miracle when she did. But, as Roberta accused, had Cookie pumped him full of sex and lies, looking all along for a stooge to take the rap for her husband's murder?

No, that couldn't be. He wouldn't let it be. He'd rather face the gas chamber.

CHAPTER FOURTEEN

BOBBIE WAS A NEW WOMAN. Totally. She could save Warren. She could save Nick. She could save the world.

And all because of an orgasm. Nine of them. Or was that ten? Who needed to count, anyway? Maybe she should have made Nick a mocha for all his hard work on her behalf.

That sounded a little glib for something so momentous. Bobbie secured the last three buttons on her uniform, then assessed herself in the mirror. Glib was easy, the truth harder. For the first time in God knew how long, she felt like a woman. Warren never understood how sex made a woman feel…feminine. It was integral to the gender. Oh, she could hear all the naysayers, the feminists, the careerists. Bottom line was, sex with Nick had made her feel special again. Finally. After years of drought. Today she had a new and powerful attitude. She'd use it to get Warren out of jail. And to keep Nick safe, once she'd accomplished step one.

The nice thing about feeling different on the inside was that people saw it on the outside, they just couldn't figure out what it was. That made it easier to slip a few things by them.

Before work, she had a few things to slip by Beau. First of all, Brax had been down there. She wanted to know what Brax wanted. Second, Beau was Jimbo's brother.

She tugged on a white cardigan, then marched resolutely to the corner of Pine and Main. Cars passed, starting early for the trek into Red Cliff to the north or Chico to the south, mostly men on their way to work, ties knotted, suit jackets on a hook in the back. Or trucks filled with gadgets and utensils and blue-collar workers getting a jump on the heat of the day. Nick was somewhere in between blue- and white-collar, a category all his own.

When would he show her his paintings? She felt a bit of a cheat for looking at the calendar in Mavis's office, especially after last night. She wanted the real thing—Nick's trust.

Mavis had told her Beau lived at the garage. She banged on the door. And waited. The glare of the morning sun off the corrugated metal made her squint and produced a sheen of perspiration on her upper lip. She banged again.

Had Mavis said Beau drank, as well as spitting tobacco juice? Just as she'd started to sniff for the odor of alcohol, the door was wrenched open.

"What do you want?" Beau's grizzled cheeks had sunk, and his pupils, the size of saucers, shrank in contact with bright sunlight. "Oh, Miss Bobbie, sorry, I didn't know it was you." He looked around as if someone else might be lurking. "Thought it might be those damn kids getting their kicks. You know, leaving a burning bag with a pile of crap in it, so you get it all over your shoes when you try to stamp it out."

"Isn't that just an urban legend?"

He rolled his eyes. "Around here, nothing's an urban

legend. You know that one about the hook on the car door, well, that was old Dieter Rumple—" He stopped midstory and peered at her with penetrating gray eyes. "But you didn't come here for any old stories, you came about new ones."

Bobbie, wanting to appear reticent, toyed with the strap of her purse. "I want to extend my condolences about your brother."

"Bastard. Got what he deserved." Gruff, uncompromising words, but Beau turned away quickly. Bobbie knew his eyes were hiding something, maybe sorrow. Or glee?

"Is that what you told the sheriff?"

"Sheriff already knows it." Then, before she could ask another question, he held the door wide, his gaze now clear of any mistiness that might have been there. "You want some coffee? I just made a pot."

As if the words conjured the smell, the rich scent of freshly brewed coffee drifted through the open doorway. She lifted her nose to sniff. Tanzanian. Expensive stuff. She followed Beau to the aroma as if he were the Pied Piper.

"Here, let me clear the chair."

The only chair had six holes and sixteen grease spots. He covered it with a towel that wasn't much better. The sun struggled through grimed windows, sparkling in the floating dust motes. Shiny clamps of all sizes hung from hooks along the wall over a workbench. A two-burner stove and small microwave decorated the bench opposite, above which hung a rack containing two plates, two bowls and two mugs. Two sets of eating utensils sprouted from a coffee can. The working area of the garage, or nonworking if you considered the number of customers she'd seen stopping at Beau's, lay in cool shadow through a door to the left, lift, compressor, toolboxes, monstrous yet silent.

There was a neatness to everything, an order, and a chivalry to the way Beau dusted off her seat, placed the towel, then handed her coffee. He poured milk and sugar into small paper cups so that she could fix the brew the way she liked. With Tanzanian, she opted for black so as not to dilute the flavor.

Beau hoisted himself up on the tool bench opposite. "I don't think you're here for my charming company. So let's talk turkey."

She pursed her lips. How to be subtle? "Well…"

"You're trying to get your husband out of jail, and you want to know if I've got any idea who killed Jimbo."

Subtlety wasn't necessary. "Yes." Then she went for broke. "What about his wife?"

Beau laughed, phlegm rattling through the sound. "Jimbo was Cookie's cash cow. Why do you think she got rid of me? She wanted it all. She'd never kill him."

"But that's exactly why she would kill him, isn't it, to have it all?"

"She wouldn't know what the hell to do with it minus him. She hasn't got a worthwhile brain between her ears. Jimbo managed everything. The only way she'd get rid of him is if there was someone who could manage it better."

Bobbie sipped the delicious drink, considering. The problem was, Warren was darn good at managing money. Another nail in his coffin if anyone found out about the affair.

"I could manage it better," Beau ventured.

She looked around at the austere surroundings.

"I know what you're thinking. I live in a goddamn garage, and my wife comes over a couple of times a week for sex. What do I know about managing?" He wagged a finger. "A helluva lot. If Jimbo hadn't undercut me at every turn and used dirty tactics, I'd be up in that big house instead of him."

Beau glared at her from beneath craggy, bushy brows and took another sip.

"So, you're telling me you're a suspect, too."

He laughed, phlegm starting a truly horrible cough that had her searching for the phone in case she needed 911. "You really should have that checked, you know," she said when he recovered.

He waved the comment aside. "If I was going to kill the bastard, I'd have done it ten years ago."

"And the sheriff buys that?"

"Don't know what that damn sheriff thinks. He's cagey, never letting on what's perking behind those sneaky eyes."

Sneaky eyes, she wasn't sure, but she agreed one could never really tell what was going on in Brax's head. Did he or did he not believe Warren had done it? That was the question.

Beau continued on without her one-hundred-percent attention. "I was really pissed *then,* when he ripped the business right out from under me, stole my livelihood, all on that bitch of a wife's word. Now I'm just bitter."

Well, that caught her ears. Bitterness sometimes translated to action. "Maybe it was some sort of festering thing."

"That would require my investing emotion in the

whole thing. I don't give a flying fu—excuse me, flying elephant's behind what Jimbo does anymore."

"Right, it's Mavis who really pissed you off." Bobbie remembered that from their first conversation.

He harrumphed. "She should have stuck by me, believed in me."

"Hmm, somehow I think she did. She pays for your teeth, doesn't she?"

"Screw my teeth, screw Jimbo and screw Mavis. Maybe you should be looking at that damn minimall as motive."

"The minimall?"

"Yeah. It's killing this whole damn town. Squeezing the life from it. And you know who owns all these buildings, who everybody but me and Mavis pays their goddamn rent to?"

"Jimbo." Warren had imparted that information days ago.

"Right." He graced her with a satisfied smile.

Bobbie didn't get it. "Well, he certainly didn't bash in his own head."

Beau snorted. "He wanted to tear down all these old stores and build cutesy boutiques. Turn it into a goddamn Mendocino or something. Tourist town."

Sacrilege, even Bobbie knew that. Then she focused on something he'd just revealed. "Why don't you and Mavis pay?"

"I got the garage and the Cooked Goose for Mavis—" he bared his perfect, white, dentalized teeth "—when Jimbo cut me out of the partnership."

"You own the Cooked Goose?"

He smiled. "Yup."

Ooh, Mavis must hate that.

Beau went on with his musings. "So, James Beaumont, scion and dickhead of Cottonmouth, could have thrown anyone out on their ear at any moment."

"Ahh. Yes?" Sort of a statement, sort of a question, another way of egging him on, because she still didn't really get his point.

"Which gives them all a motive for murder." The eye roll added "you idiot."

She thought about how it must be to run a business that had been in your family for years, like Bushman's or Dillings' or Johnson's, any of them up and down Main Street, only to see it all slipping away. To know one man was responsible.

Beau stared at her, an avid spark in his eye. "You like that one, don't ya?"

That the list of suspects included just about the whole town of Cottonmouth? Her newly adopted town? "No. I don't. And I bet the sheriff doesn't, either."

Beau picked his teeth with his tongue—could Mavis really have sex with this man? Bobbie shuddered.

"The sheriff's already got his confession," Beau went on after a moment's thoughtfulness. "He doesn't give a rat's patootie about what I say." He stroked his grizzled beard, shooting her with that penetrating gaze he'd used when he'd first answered the door. "Think about it a minute. Everybody had something to lose."

Bobbie felt like she was being mesmerized by a wizard.

He dropped his voice a note. "Maybe they all got together and did it."

"Now I know you're crazy."

A laugh hissed out. "Maybe yes, maybe no. But *someone* did it."

Yes, someone had killed Jimbo. And did she really know these people well enough to say that *one* of them hadn't done it?

Out in the bright morning sunlight again after leaving Beau, Main Street suddenly seemed filled with shadows she'd never noticed before.

LUNCHTIME IN DOWNTOWN Cottonmouth. Nick was doing exactly what Bobbie had wanted, scouting the town for gossip. It was the middle of June, it was noon, it was hot, that was all to be expected. What wasn't ordinary, at least since the advent of Jimbo's minimall, was the number of cars lining the sidewalks. And the crowded nature of the sidewalks themselves. Women with strollers, grannies with walkers, old men with hats who usually stayed out of the sun, preferably on their own front porches. Little kids and dogs and Patsy and Eugenia, and every blinking store owner out there sweeping down his front walk. All of them gathering or contributing to the latest scandal.

Murder in a small town brought every rat out of its hole.

Bertha Swurtz laid on her horn, though how she could tell anyone was in her way, he didn't know. Politely put, Bertha couldn't see very well. A screech of tires ripped through the air as she fumbled over the yellow line, then back again. Down the street lights flashed and a siren blared. Bertha didn't actually make it to the side of the road, but, thanks to the grace of God, she did miss the mayor's parked car. The old lady hadn't hit a single man, woman, child, or object, stationary or otherwise, in the five years since the DMV yanked her license, but Brax usually hauled her in for a few hours when he caught her, just to make the point.

The deputy climbing from the patrol car, however, was not Brax.

Nick made an about-face, almost sideswiping Mrs. Burtleson's wheelie cart. He righted her, she grumbled and backed up into one of the mayor's newly refurbished light poles bearing an advertisement for the upcoming Accordion Festival. Nick almost made a face like a gargoyle, but that was going too far. He didn't want to give the poor old woman a heart attack.

He'd heard quite enough gossip about himself this morning. In five different conversations, he'd learned that if Warren Spivey hadn't killed Jimbo, Nick Angel certainly had. Nothing new there, he already knew that, right from the horse's mouth, Sheriff Tyler Braxton.

But what other juicy stuff would Bobbie want to hear? He almost rubbed his hands in anticipation. He couldn't drop by to see her later at the Cooked Goose without something to report. Christ, he actually felt jaunty.

As he headed back to Harry Bushman's place, a hand anchored his shoulder. Shit. The sheriff. But when he turned, it was Kent English.

"Just the person I wanted to see." Now why hadn't he thought of Kent first? Working for Jimbo probably gave him all sorts of information access.

Kent cocked a brow. "Why so, buddy?"

"Tell me everything you know about Jimbo's murder."

"That's a tall order. But hell, don't make me say it twice. Harry's damn near ready to shit in his pants there."

Harry leaned his broom against the wall of the shop, the scrap of dirt he'd been sweeping back and forth small enough to disappear into a crack.

Cocky and sure of himself, Kent crossed his arms and leaned against the brick wall of Harry's store. He'd always craved the center of attention.

"I can't believe the old goat's dead."

Kent slashed Harry a look. "Christ, don't let anyone hear you say that. They'll be looking at you next."

Harry smoothed his pomaded hair. "It was a term of endearment."

The hell with all that—Nick wanted some specifics. "So, did the grieving widow show up at Oil Changers asking to see the books so she could check out the full extent of her new holdings?"

"Haven't seen her." Kent's jaw tightened. He'd never liked Cookie. "Yet."

"I'm amazed." Nick stroked his chin. "If you kill someone, do you still get to inherit?"

Harry harrumphed. "That law's only about writing a book or selling your story about the crime."

"No, I distinctly remember it saying you can't profit from your crime. That includes inheriting, too," Nick said.

"Hey, do you guys want to hear or don't you?" Kent seemed peeved he'd lost center stage.

"Yeah, tell us." It didn't really matter which of them begged.

"Brax was sniffing around."

Harry grabbed his broom, as if he suddenly needed something to keep his hands busy. "He's been sniffing all around town."

Nick snorted. "Like a hound dog."

"Doesn't he believe that Spivey guy did it?"

Kent looked down at Harry's twisting hands, back up, then spoke without speculating on the action. "What choice has he got since the guy confessed? He said they found footprints, fingerprints and tire tracks down there. The only thing he hasn't got is the murder weapon."

Here was something of interest to Nick. "Did he say exactly what the murder weapon was?"

"Yeah. A shovel."

"What kind of shovel?" he asked, hoping Brax had gotten more specific than he had outside the Home Depot.

"Let's see, I think he said a spade. A flat edge."

Shit. Just what was missing out of his shed. So that his interest wouldn't be noticed, he changed the subject. "Did he want to look at the books or anything?"

Kent eyed him. "Yeah. But the lawyers told me not to give him anything unless he came back with a search warrant."

"That's odd, isn't it? Why not just cooperate?"

Kent put up his hands. "Hell, I don't know. I just do what the lawyers tell me."

"Why's Brax interested in all of that stuff when he's got the killer in jail?" Both Nick and Kent looked at Harry. Harry shrugged. "Well, I think it's a legitimate question. And it's what everybody else is asking, too."

Kent answered that one. "You know how thorough Brax is. No stone unturned, etcetera, etcetera. And this has gotta be a helluva lot more pressure than usual."

"Well, people are mighty shook up about the whole thing." Harry turned to Nick. "And they don't like the fact that your girlfriend's been asking questions all over town, either."

Nick put a finger to his chest. "My girlfriend?"

"Bobbie Jones. The accused's wife." A trace of something almost bitter crept into Harry's voice. "Everyone knows it had to be an outsider."

And no one wanted it to be themselves at whom Brax started looking, that much was clear.

"I think you better get her to shut up."

Kent nudged him in the ribs. "Yeah, I'm sure you can get her to shut up real quick."

Well, he did know one or two ways...but nothing was going to shut Bobbie up about Warren's innocence.

"Since when do I look like a guy who can control women?" Or that he even cared to try? Sometimes they were better just the way they were. Sometimes, in the case of Bobbie. *Not,* in the case of Cookie.

Still, if folks were starting to feel a little irked with Bobbie, maybe now wasn't the time to shove their affair under anyone's nose. Dropping by the Cooked Goose suddenly wasn't the great idea he'd first thought it to be. Tonight. At home. He'd tell her everything then. Christ, when she was in his arms, he'd tell her anything she wanted to hear.

Kent slapped him on the shoulder. "You know, bud, you got worse problems than your girlfriend's big mouth—" then he smacked the back of his hand against Nick's chest "—not that big mouths aren't good for some things, if you catch my drift."

Nick narrowed his eyes. "Shut up, Kent."

"Hit a nerve, huh?" Then he looked down at Nick's suddenly bunched fists. "Shit, get a life, bud. I'm trying to tell you Brax seems damn interested in you, specifically. Like, if I've ever seen what kind of shovels you own."

Kent made a what-the-hell gesture with his hands.

Harry scratched his head.

"What's the guy got against you these days, Nick?" Kent looked at him. "You didn't screw *his* ex-wife or something, did ya?"

He shot Kent a fuck-you look. "He won't find anything on me." And it still didn't make sense why Brax had given him his card.

Kent folded his arms over his chest. "Right now I'd say Brax is looking for something to nail you to the wall. Leastwise, if he doesn't have Warren Spivey to throw the book at."

Nick snorted and shook his head. "Yeah. And Bobbie's not going to rest until she proves Warren didn't do it."

Both men raised their eyebrows at him. Maybe his mouth was bigger than Bobbie's.

"The mayor's given Brax two more days to figure it all out." Harry jumped in with that juicy tidbit.

They all stood silent a moment. Kent shoved his hands in his pockets. "Well, hell, bud, looks like you may be the one who gets screwed, then."

In more ways than one, and not all of them good.

BOBBIE HAD BEEN LOCKED in information-gathering mode all day. Between rounds of heavenly reminiscing about last night's nine orgasms.

Of course, some people hadn't liked her questions. Horace Finegold had walked out before he'd finished his eggs. The mayor's wife arrived just after lunch, glared at Bobbie, whispered in Mavis's ear and left. Patsy Sapp called on the phone, her screeching tones enveloping the far ends of the diner.

Mavis motioned Bobbie over, between the toaster and the blender, which hadn't gotten used since Mavis had stopped serving cheap margaritas at Happy Hour. The sheer volume had threatened to put her under, and she'd given up on Happy Hour altogether.

"This has got to stop."

"I'm just making conversation."

Mavis raised one brow and pouffed at her cockeyed bouffant. "Is that why you asked Ron Johnson how far behind he was on his rent?"

"I was worried about what might happen to his business before Jimbo's estate gets resolved."

"So, you asked Bruce Migglethorpe why he'd upped the price of a haircut in April and how he felt about having to do that."

"I wanted to make sure he hadn't lost any customers."

"Well, *I'm* losing customers, Bobbie." She stabbed her finger at the front door as it whooshed shut. "See that, Arnold just left without even ordering. What did you say to him?"

Bobbie scrubbed the toe of her shoe across the floor.

"You have to stop, Bobbie. People are getting upset."

"I'm sorry about that, honest." Especially since she hadn't heard one negative thing about Cookie all day. She'd tried, really she had, but she'd been met with a sea of blank stares. So she'd turned her attention to what Beau had said. After all, his accusations required due diligence in her questioning.

She'd learned only one useful but alarming thing. "They all believe Warren did it. But I know better." She crossed her arms over her chest. "Maybe they were all afraid Jimbo was going to throw them out of their stores because he wanted to turn Main Street into Boutique Row."

Mavis snorted. "You mean Boutique Hell."

Bobbie took a step back. Bitterness had crept into Mavis's voice.

Mavis stared her down. "I'm not saying we liked the idea. I am saying the people of this town wouldn't kill to keep things the way they were. So get that idea out of your head."

Beau had been the one to put it there. Maybe for a reason, perhaps as a smoke screen. "Is Beau capable of murder?"

Mavis threw her hands in the air. "Girl, you're going to be the death of me."

Bobbie tapped her foot. "Well? Is he?"

Mavis tipped her head in the direction opposite the fall of her hair. "Sure he is." She eyed Bobbie. "So am I. I was pissed as hell at Jimbo for believing that little witch he married and screwing Beau out of everything he'd worked so hard for. Remember how I told you I wasn't done with that woman yet?" She narrowed her eyes. "If it was *her* that was dead, you can bet your bottom dollar Brax better come looking for me."

Bobbie blew out a puff of air. "Yes, but we were talking about Beau and Jimbo."

"Do I think he's capable of killing someone, or do I think he killed Jimbo? Those are two totally different things, you know."

"Mavis."

"I can't think of a single reason why he'd kill Jimbo now, but then I'm biased because I'm sleeping with the guy. And I'm married to him."

Bobbie raised a brow. "And because he owns the Cooked Goose?"

Mavis met her glare for stare. "He owns the building. I own the business."

"But you pay him rent."

"In a manner of speaking." And Bobbie suddenly

knew just what manner that was. "A mutually satisfying agreement."

Bobbie didn't want to know about Mavis's sex life. "You're not being very helpful."

"All right. You want helpful? I'll give you helpful. I think he and Jimbo might have patched things up before long."

"What?" Oh, now *that* was very interesting.

"I saw Jimbo go down there a couple of times. And Beau hasn't called him a dickhead asshole in a few weeks."

"He called him a dickhead today."

"But did he call him a dickhead asshole?"

"No."

"That's what I'm saying, he's dropped the number of epithets strung together."

Bobbie slowly smiled. "So if Jimbo and Beau were patching things up, maybe Cookie—"

Mavis jammed her hands over her ears. "Don't say that name."

"Then maybe the witch was worried about Jimbo cutting his brother back in after she'd cut him out."

"I never did like her," Mavis tacitly agreed.

"Did you tell Brax this?"

"No. And I'm not going to. I'm not getting involved." She shook her finger at Bobbie. "And you ought to heed the same warning. People don't like outsiders stirring stuff up."

"But I'm not an outsider. I work at the Cooked Goose."

"You only think you aren't an outsider."

Oh. Well. That couldn't be true, could it? No. Maybe? She'd better be careful.

CHAPTER FIFTEEN

"LET'S GO to the Rowdy Tavern for dinner," Bobbie said later in Nick's kitchen.

"Together?"

"Well, of course. Isn't that what 'let's' means? As in us, plural." Something about the panicked flash of Nick's eyebrows almost to the top of his forehead set Bobbie off.

He took the mocha she'd brought him, wrapping his long fingers around the mug. "Forget it."

Bobbie stared openmouthed. "But—"

"No."

She put her hands on her hips, snagging his attention. The man was so easy. "I want to listen to gossip at the Rowdy Tavern. I've heard everything I'm going to hear at the Cooked Goose. The Chalet is too expensive. That leaves the Rowdy Tavern."

"All right, you go. I'll wait here. You can bring me back a steak sandwich." He sipped the coffee, watching her over the rim and trying to keep his expression neutral. But she knew her mochas were to die for.

"You want a steak sandwich, you have to come with me."

He put the drained mug on the kitchen table. "You really don't get it, do you?"

"Get what?"

"No one's going to tell you a thing with me around. They're not even going to stop at the table. And if there's any gossiping going on, it will be about the fact that you're with me."

"Why shouldn't I be with you?" She crossed her eyes. "Oh, you mean that whole ridiculous serial-killer thing. You need to get over that. It sort of leaves you with a chip on your shoulder. Nobody thinks you're a serial killer. Not really."

Nick crossed his arms over his chest and leaned back against the counter, regarding her until the scrutiny became just a little irritating. Heat crept up her neck.

"All right, we'll go. But they won't like your questions, and they won't approve of your being with me. So don't say I didn't warn you."

Half an hour later a buxom waitress encased in too-tight jeans led them to a wooden booth back by the bathrooms. Bobbie glanced at Nick to see if he was watching the waitress's rear end, then sighed with relief to discover he wasn't.

She took the side facing the room, and Nick ordered them both a beer. He didn't ask her permission. Bobbie was of a dual mind about that. She liked proprietary but hated controlling. She decided Nick was just trying to make some sort of weird guy point since she'd twisted his arm to get him here.

"See, there wasn't any great hush when you walked in."

He cocked his head over his beer. "How can you tell over the music?"

He had a point. And it did make eavesdropping a tad difficult. Maybe this hadn't been such a good idea. Besides, she didn't even know anyone here. Except…

Though he'd eaten lunch at Mavis's, Mr. Johnson had also masterminded a dinner break from the soda fountain. Mr. Migglethorpe had vacated his barber pole for the evening. If the pseudo woman with him was his wife, he'd robbed the cradle. Would anyone be dumb enough to take their little nymphet mistress out to dinner where everyone could see them? Had to be the wife. Or, of course, it could be his daughter.

On the far side of the bank of tables, Mr. Fry from the drugstore stared at Bobbie over the top of his menu. His wife, his white-haired clone except for gender, mimed his over-the-menu gawk. Bobbie fluttered her fingers at them both. The man's eyes dropped immediately, and the menu rose four inches to cover his eyebrows. That was odd.

"Okay, so you want to know what I learned today?"

"Nothing?" Nick ventured.

Bobbie smirked. "Very funny." She remained undeterred. She leaned closer, as if the blare of the too-loud music couldn't effectively cover her salacious comments. "Jimbo cut his brother, Beau, out of their business and left him living in that garage."

"I could have told you that."

She compressed her lips. "So, why didn't you?"

He shrugged and dug into the steak sandwich their waitress had just dumped on the table, *dumped* being the operative word. Bobbie had to ask for ketchup twice.

"There also may have been quite a few people in town who felt their family-owned businesses were in jeopardy."

Nick just kept chewing.

Tangy barbecue sauce twanged in Bobbie's mouth. She answered for him, voice deep in imitation. "I guess,

Bobbie, that means an awful lot of people actually had a motive to kill Jimbo."

He swallowed. "That isn't motive. It's business. Harry was pissed, doesn't mean he'd have taken a shovel to Jimbo's cranium."

"Harry Bushman?"

Mouth filled with another bite of sandwich, he nodded. A smear of steak sauce daubed the side of his mouth. After swallowing, he gave it a man-size lick. Oh, my God. She almost forgot what they'd been talking about. She almost forgot her own name.

Oh, yeah, Harry Bushman. "That was the first time I actually saw her, in Harry's store."

"Her?"

"Cookie."

"You're wrong. She wouldn't be caught dead in Harry's. Too much polyester."

Well, that *is* what Bobbie had first thought. "No, it was her. And she did buy something because she was carrying a little bag. Afterward, she came out and gave me a...talking-to about leaving Warren alone."

Nick lifted his beer, took a long pull. "Did you hear the slightest rumor about Cookie herself today?"

Bobbie drew a pattern on the tabletop with her finger. "No."

"If your husband confessed to killing Jimbo, he damn sure didn't do it to cover up for someone's rent problem. He came to town for Cookie, and she's the only one he'd confess for. If he did kill Jimbo—hear me out." Nick held up a hand when she would have jumped in. "If he did kill him, the only person he'd have done it for is Cookie. Anything else is bullshit. So, the only thing we really know is that your husband thinks Cookie did it, and he's willing to risk his life to protect her."

Bobbie sat back, half her barbecue sandwich untouched. Nick's argument left her feeling helpless. No one was talking about Cookie. She couldn't seem to get a straight answer, couldn't even unobtrusively overhear one.

But he was right, Warren wouldn't have confessed for anyone but Cookie. So where on earth was Bobbie going to get the evidence when no one was talking?

Nick threw some bills on the table and stood. "Are you ready?"

The whole thing had been a bust. In fact, the whole day had been a bust. "Thanks for dinner."

She smiled at everyone as she passed. Mr. Johnson. Mr. Migglethorpe with the young…whatever. Mr. Fry and his wife.

Bobbie stopped. It was impolite to move on without saying a few words, especially since the druggist had tried to be so helpful. "Mr. Fry, I really want to thank you again for—"

His wife's face faded to a sickly shade. Oh, my God, she wasn't choking on a chicken bone, was she?

"Where's the sheriff?" Mr. Fry barked.

Oh, my God, Mrs. Fry *was* choking. "Should we call the paramedics?"

The man's white eyebrows rose to meld with his hair. "What are you talking about, young lady?"

"Your wife. Is she all right?"

"She's fine. And I'd like to know if the sheriff knows that you're out with…him." He said the three-letter word as if it were made up of four, the bad four. The look he shot Nick would have flayed animal flesh.

Nick merely gave her a smug I-told-you-so smile.

"No, I don't think the sheriff does know." A touch of bewilderment haunted her words. Mr. Fry couldn't really be upset that she'd had dinner with Nick.

His next words showed that for a lie. Or wishful thinking. "Well, you can be sure he'll hear about it soon." He sniffed with disapproval. "And from several sources."

"Oh." Was he angry enough to want his condoms back? She tried to reach him once more. "Well, I'm sure he's got his hands full right now with what happened to Jimbo and all."

Mr. Fry's lips curled in a snarl. "He's got his killer, Ms. Jones. And he doesn't need anyone running around town asking a bunch of silly questions and stirring people up."

"No, he certainly doesn't," his clone echoed.

Bobbie looked at Nick with a do-you-think-they're-talking-about-me question in her eye.

Nick, in answer, tugged hard on her hand. *Exit stage left, if you want to keep your dignity.*

"Well, it was nice talking to you, Mr. Fry."

Mr. Fry merely harrumphed, as did his wife.

Bobbie let Nick lead her away. She turned back for one last survey of the crowded, overheated, too-loud room. A multitude of beady black eyes scoured her.

Gosh. They really were looking at her as if she'd slept with a serial killer.

"I TOLD YOU that's how they'd react."

"Do not dare tell me 'I told you so.'"

"I wouldn't think of it." Women liked to meddle, that's just what they did. But God forbid they should admit to it. Nick had managed to keep his mouth shut the entire drive home. He would have been safe, too, if he hadn't invited her inside his house. Big mistake. "All I'm saying is that you should leave it alone."

Bobbie opened her mouth. Nick shushed her with a finger to her lips. "I know you can't leave Warren to his fate. I'm just saying you need to be more discreet in your inquiries. It's all over town that you're stirring things up. People don't like it."

Hands on her hips, she backed him up against his living room sofa. "That wasn't because of the questions I asked about Jimbo. It was because I was with you."

"What did you expect them to do? Suddenly decide I'm a good guy? They've hated me far longer than you've been around. And you aren't going to get them to change their minds." Because she was right in his face, he put his nose within an inch of hers. "Besides, Fry thinks you're two-timing the sheriff."

She eased back a foot, giving him the full glint of her gaze. "Nobody chooses for me."

"So, this is about telling Cottonmouth to go to hell." Shit, he knew this wasn't really over him, had known that from the moment she'd stepped onto his porch bearing lasagna. He'd hoped, though, that they'd moved beyond her original intention for seeking him out.

"It's about what *I* want." She stabbed a rigid finger to her chest.

He couldn't help noting the swell of her breast where she'd touched herself, then he pulled his gaze front and center. "What exactly is it you want, Bobbie?"

She didn't hesitate or look away. "You."

"Why? Because of the ten orgasms?" Because it would piss her husband off?

"It was only nine."

"But you're itching to make it ten, aren't you?"

He was suddenly hard in his jeans. Maybe it was her sweet perfume swirling in the hot air. Or maybe it was the way she was willing to go to battle for him, no matter the underlying reason.

She licked her lips deliberately. It got to him the way she knew it would. "Are you?"

Christ, yes. He'd kill to make it ten and more. "I don't like being used as a weapon in your little war with the mavens of Cottonmouth. Or your husband."

She took back the foot of space she'd given. The tips of her fingers sank beneath the waistband of his jeans and pulled him closer still. The scent of her lip gloss filled his head. He ached to kiss it off.

"I'll admit I wanted to show Warren that other men would find me desirable." Her breath puffed against his lips. "I'll admit I thought you'd be the perfect candidate."

Hell, he didn't want *this* confession. He wanted what he'd had last night, a woman who needed him. "So, you wanted to get laid and shove it in your husband's face?"

She didn't balk at his crudeness. Instead, her tongue slicked along the seam of his lips. "I thought that's all you'd be willing to give."

"That's all I did give you."

She shook her head, and her lips caressed his. "No. It was more."

Way more. For the first time, he'd made love to a woman because *she* needed it. Last night had been all about her. And he wanted her again, just that way.

"No one's ever made me feel that desirable, Nick," she whispered. "That beautiful. That special."

He'd never really tried to make a woman feel that

way. Had never cared enough to. And feeling that way with her was dangerous.

Hands on her shoulders, he pushed her away. But he couldn't let go. "Don't go making it more than it was."

His harsh breathing, that damn bulge in his pants and the way his hands trembled now that he'd touched her put the lie to his words.

"I'm not giving you up," she whispered, "just because Mr. Fry, or anyone else, didn't like seeing us together."

He closed his eyes. God, this woman knew how to use words to get to him. Did she ever.

"Nick, will you do one more thing for me?"

"What?" He made it sound as bad tempered as possible.

"Let me make love to you this time."

He couldn't help it, he opened his eyes and licked her gloss from his lips, savored it. She took that as a yes and put her fingers to task at his belt. All trace of fight went out of him. He wanted her to make love to him more than he'd ever wanted anything. "What are you going to do?"

Her hand stilled on his zipper. She looked at him, and for the first time since they'd walked through his front door, uncertainty dulled her eyes. Filled her voice. "I want to…umm…you know."

"No. I don't. Tell me." He wanted to hear her say it.

"I want to make you…umm…" She bit her lip, then gulped a breath. "I want to make you come in my mouth."

Holy shit. "Ah, well, gee, okay." He helped her ease the zipper over his cock.

She switched off the lamp on the side table, plunging them into darkness, hiding them from prying eyes.

Then she shoved his jeans over his hips and down his legs. He still had his boots on. She bent to unlace them.

OH, MY GOODNESS, WHAT AM I DOING? Bobbie asked herself. What if she couldn't? What if she wasn't good enough? She'd never been good enough for Warren. This was the dumbest idea she'd ever had. Of course, she'd been saying that for days now, but each time she told herself it was the last time, she'd come up with another even more stupid idea.

But, oh, she wanted him. Wanted to feel him in her mouth, wanted to taste him, wanted his hands in her hair, wanted him totally out of control. To heck with Cottonmouth.

"You okay down there?"

She looked up. His hands hovered near her head, his penis bobbed in front of her face. She wanted to cry. Or laugh. "I accidentally made a knot in your lace."

He reached down, his hair brushing the side of her face, yanked, and the lace broke loose. "All fixed. Need any more help?"

She tugged off one boot and almost fell on her butt. Then she did start laughing, a bit of her tension easing.

"I think you're trying too hard. Relax, baby." He finished her task, toeing off the other shoe and kicking aside his jeans. Then he flopped back on the sofa. Putting one hand on his enormous erection, he stroked, his eyes dark, his teeth white with a smile. "Now, what was that about making me come in your mouth?"

She parted his legs and wriggled between them. "Aren't you afraid I might just be saying that so I can bite it off?"

"No, baby, I can tell you're way too hot for me to

want to ruin a good thing." He took her hand in his and wrapped it around his penis, moving their fingers together, showing her how to squeeze him just right. "Here, like that." Then he let go, giving himself up to her rhythm. "That's go-o-od."

He was saying it because she needed to hear it. Just the way he'd talked to her last night, giving her words because she needed them. She believed them gratefully.

She took him in her mouth. Hands to the side of her head, he guided her. The couch creaked as he put his head back, then he groaned into the dark and the heat.

Salty, musky, male, he was hard between her lips. She pushed her hand all the way to the base, dove down to meet it. On the way back up, she grazed him with her teeth. At the tip, she circled her tongue, testing the small crevice. His hips lifted to drive into her again. She took him, swallowing the tiny droplets that emerged. When he groaned, she repeated, harder, faster, then softer, slower. Again and again.

All the while, he talked, words about how good she was, how good her mouth felt, how he thought he was going to die. Then his hands fisted in her hair, just short of pain, and he cried out her name and a litany of swearwords and spurted into her mouth.

She swallowed all of him, savoring the taste, the triumph, the vindication. He stroked her hair, the shell of her ear, let her suck and lick until the last of his tremors faded away, then he pulled her up to look at him.

"Where'd you learn to do that?" He hauled her onto his lap and kissed her. After he'd been in her mouth. Didn't seem to care. Just the way he'd kissed her last night with her taste still on his lips.

Warren had never...would never. But then he hadn't really liked any of that stuff, anyway.

"You're thinking about him. Stop it." Nick stuck his tongue in her mouth, wrapped his arms around her until she felt crushed, caressed, wanted.

I will not say it. I will not ask for validation.

"Did you like what I did?" Darn.

Nick jerked back to stare at her. As if she had Medusa's snakes snarling on her head. "Like? You drained me dry, sweetheart." His head flopped against the sofa, and he closed his eyes. "I don't think I could get it up again for a week."

Maybe some women would have been looking for something poetic. What he said was exactly what she'd hoped for. She snuggled against him. His shirt still intact, he was naked from the waist down. She was completely clothed. Gee, this was deliciously dirty and decadent.

Feeling enormously pleased with herself and totally unwilling to contemplate Warren's situation, at least right now, she licked Nick's cheek, then kissed it. "When are we going to watch *Buffy*?"

He cracked one eye open. "Definitely not now."

Something romantic then. "How about *Laura*?"

"You've gotta be kidding."

She wriggled in his lap. "You could show me your paintings?"

"How about we work on numbers ten through fifteen instead."

Hmm, that had a nice ring to it, too.

THEY FELL ASLEEP in his bed with all the windows open.

Princess started barking at two.

Nick rolled over, pulling Bobbie into the spoon of his body. Warm and smelling of hot sex and even hotter woman, he buried his nose in the hollow between her neck and shoulder. Still asleep, she muttered and burrowed her bottom into his groin.

He'd lied about not being able to get it up again. Several times.

"Hmm," she mumbled into the pillow. "What's that noise?"

The high-pitched yelping became frantic. "It's Princess. Reggie'll yell at her in a minute." Just like he had the other night when she'd gone ballistic.

The night Jimbo died.

The night the shovel went missing from his shed.

Nick bolted out of bed.

"What are you doing?"

"Someone's outside." Searching for his jeans, he remembered they were on the living room floor. He grabbed another pair from the drawer, yanked them on, then took the stairs two at a time.

Throwing the back door open just as Reggie cussed at the dog, Nick took the back steps in a leap, then slid to a halt.

No one was out there, but the metal door of the shed yawned wide. He'd left it closed. Princess yelped once more, whimpered, then shut up. Reggie slammed his back door, still cursing, "the damned noisy little mutt."

Nick sprinted through the gate to the front of the house. He'd catch the bastard, he'd write down the license plate, he'd… The road was empty, the neighborhood quiet, now that Princess had gotten her wallop.

Shit.

He returned to the backyard, dread hollowing out his gut.

Bobbie hugged the doorway, eyes wide, wearing one of his paint shirts, white tails reaching her thighs. "What is it?"

"I need the flashlight." He pushed past her to the kitchen drawer, then marched back outside, Bobbie in his wake.

Sliding the shed door all the way open, he flashed the thin beam of light around the inside.

"What's there?"

Christ. "My spade is back."

"The one that was missing?"

"Yep." He stepped fully into the shed, hunkered down beside it and ran the beam from handle to blade. "And if I'm not mistaken, there's dried blood all over it."

Dried blood and Jimbo's gray matter.

CHAPTER SIXTEEN

OH, MY GOD. He couldn't have done it.

Could he?

The beam of Nick's flashlight hit Bobbie full in the face. She shielded her eyes.

"You think I did it, don't you?"

"Don't be ridiculous." Only for the tiniest second, wiped clean so fast in the next, it didn't even count. "Take that light out of my eyes."

He did, but only dropped the beam to her chest so that she still couldn't see him behind it. Like he was interrogating her.

"I didn't do it."

She answered quickly. "I know that. What I was thinking—" she paused, wondering what she really had been thinking "—that this proves Warren couldn't have done it. He's in jail, he couldn't have put that shovel there."

And neither had Nick. She'd known in her heart he was innocent. Now she could prove it.

"No, he couldn't," Nick growled, low, almost menacing. She had no clue what he was thinking.

"But then again," she went on, "somehow, I just can't imagine Cookie driving around with a bloody shovel in her trunk and sneaking into your shed in the middle of the night."

"Right."

Those terse answers made her nerves jump, especially when she couldn't see his face or read his eyes. "So that means someone else is helping Cookie."

"Looks like it."

"Would you stop it."

"Stop what?"

"Agreeing with everything I say."

"Don't you want me to agree?"

"No." She wanted some emotion.

"All right."

That wasn't any better. She wished she had on more than just his white shirt stiff with paint spatters. "Then this shovel is…what do you call it?" He didn't help her. "Exculpatory evidence in Warren's favor."

"I suppose it is."

She bit her lip. He was agreeing again. She wanted to smack him. "We need to call Brax."

This time he didn't say anything at all, instead lifted the flashlight beam once again to her eyes. She squinted. Telling him to drop it again would be pointless. "It's got to have the real killer's fingerprints on it."

"The only fingerprints on it will be mine."

"But—"

"Do you think they'd be stupid enough to bring it back if they'd left their fingerprints on it?"

She knew she was grasping at straws. "And Brax knows you're not stupid enough to call him if you'd actually killed Jimbo."

"Brax isn't going to care one way or the other. He'll have the murder weapon with *my* prints on it."

"Well, then, we'll wipe it off before we call him."

The flashlight clicked off, completely blinding her

after the brightness of the beam in her eyes. "I'm not going to jail to free your husband."

"I know, but—"

"Choose. Now."

"This isn't about choosing—"

"Which one of us will it be, Bobbie?"

Her hands were solid blocks of ice. She stuck them in her armpits for warmth. It didn't help.

"Choose." Softly, the sound filling the small shed.

"I…" Her bare feet numbed.

"Can't."

"You don't understand."

"I understand perfectly." Moving in the darkness, he pushed past her, his silhouette filling the open shed door.

She followed, stumbled over the ledge, hand out-stretched, but long strides had taken him beyond her. Running, with a prayer that there really wasn't any dog poop out here, she caught up with him at the edge of the porch.

"Nick."

He turned under cover of the overhang, pinpoints of moonlight reflecting in his eyes. "You can't make this town like or accept me. And you can't save both your husband and me."

Epiphany ran its fingers across her scalp, shuddered in her stomach. She wanted Cottonmouth to love her, to accept her, to make her one of its own. But to do it, she had to play by their rules. She couldn't just be herself. She'd been feeding herself lies for the last week, seeking a belonging that couldn't be hers. The need was like a sickness inside her; she hadn't quite realized how powerful until this moment.

Bobbie rolled her lips between her teeth, bit down

hard until they stung. "I don't have to choose, Nick. I can help you both." She touched his arm. "I won't sacrifice you for him."

He glanced at her clutching fingers. "You won't mean to."

"I *won't* sacrifice you."

"Fine. Whatever."

She took his words to mean acquiescence, crisis averted. But a sliver of fear still throbbed. "Let's go back to bed. We'll work this out. I won't tell the sheriff."

She sounded just the way she had with Warren for fifteen years. Placating, soothing. It was a pattern she knew well.

Nick looked beyond her to the yawn of the shed door. "I need to get a lock tomorrow. Until I figure out what to do with it."

It. The shovel. The incriminating evidence. Bobbie shivered. "Shouldn't we at least shut the door?"

"What does it matter now?"

That was sort of like closing the barn door after the cow had already gotten out. Or the shovel had gotten in.

He turned and went in the house. He didn't stop her from following, but he didn't take her hand, either.

In his room Nick shed his jeans. The mattress sagged with his weight, and he pulled the sheet to his waist. At the edge of his bed, she thought about her dirty feet. In the end all she did was shrug out of his paint-splattered shirt and climb in beside him. They lay on separate sides, not touching.

She hadn't felt this alone since…well, since the last time she'd asked Warren to make love to her. He'd pleaded a migraine. She'd never asked again. That was five years ago. Another life.

It didn't bear thinking about now. She had to come up with a really good plan about where to go from here.

Okay. Cottonmouth didn't like her questions. They didn't like her choice of lover. Well, she was good at hide-and-seek. She'd been playing it with Warren almost since the beginning of their marriage. Give them what they want, keep them happy, keep a smile on your face.

Maybe it hadn't worked completely, not in the end, but it had worked for fifteen years.

The mavens of Cottonmouth wanted her for the sheriff. Well, that's exactly what she'd give them. Date the sheriff, find out everything he knew. And save Warren and Nick in the process.

She just hoped Brax didn't think sleeping with him would be part of the plan.

"YOU'RE GOING TO DO WHAT?"

It was 2:00 a.m. Nick had been lying awake, listening for a siren. The bastard who left the damn shovel in his shed would have to call Brax, anonymously, of course. Could Brax get a warrant based on an anonymous tip?

"I'm going to go out with Brax. On a date."

Christ. He'd wanted her to choose between him and her husband. He'd known it wasn't fair, but he'd wanted it badly. As if it were a declaration, not of love, but…something.

He'd also known she wouldn't be able to do it. She'd had a marriage with her little weasel, a fifteen-year relationship. She'd only had a week with him. She couldn't abandon the old. It wasn't in her nature. If he were honest, that loyalty was one of the things he cherished about her. Not cherished, that wasn't the right word. Admired. That was better.

Brax wasn't one of her choices.

"What the hell are you going to get out of dating Brax?" His gut twisted.

"Just for the information value. Since I can't get it asking questions around town, I'll question him."

The woman wanted to have her cake and eat it, too. Date Brax because that's what people wanted, stop asking questions of everyone on the street corners. She'd let them think she was falling in line, but in the end, she wouldn't fool anyone. And he'd just bet she'd still sneak into his bed at night.

Damn if he'd let her.

"That's idiotic." He managed not to call *her* an idiot or reveal the fact that he'd rather smash his fist into Brax's face than let her "date" the man. "He's not going to tell you anything. Unless it's misinformation."

"But misinformation *is* information. You just have to decipher it."

Excitement bubbled in her voice. Never down for the full count, she was an eternal optimist. Or she was mentally challenged.

Nick was just a bug on her windshield.

He stacked his hands beneath his head. "Sounds good to me. Whatever you want to do."

The pillow rustled as she turned her head to look at him, but she didn't say anything.

All right. She'd date Brax, and Nick would make inquiries of his own. Cookie Beaumont wouldn't have driven around with a shovel in her trunk and walked into his backyard wearing her high heels, the only kind of shoe she owned as far as he knew. His mind burned with one question. Who was Cookie's accomplice?

He had one choice. Tomorrow, after he bought the lock for the shed, he'd go straight to the horse's mouth.

Cookie would love being compared to a horse.

"HOW'S THE INVESTIGATION?"

"What investigation?"

Bobbie jutted her left hip and put her hand on it, holding the coffeepot aloft in the other. Brax's cup dangled in midair, waiting for a refill. "Jimbo's murder investigation."

The sheriff looked from the pot to the hand on her hip. "The case is unofficially closed."

"Closed? It can't be closed. I told you Warren isn't capable of it."

"Are you going to fill this thing?" He waggled his mug.

She huffed out a puff of air and poured. Holding out wouldn't do much good. "We need to talk."

"The sheriff's order is up," Mavis's voice rang out sharply.

"Hold that thought, I'll be right back."

"The only thought I had was about my food," he called after her, then added, "among a couple of other things."

She stopped, looked over her shoulder. The sheriff's thoughts were obviously on her butt, if the direction of his gaze meant anything. Which wasn't a bad thing for her little plan. The one Nick had given her the go-ahead for. Sort of. As if she needed his go-ahead.

The sheriff had come in for a late breakfast. The Cooked Goose was practically empty.

"You've scared my customers away with your damn

questions," Mavis grumbled as Bobbie put down the coffee, slung a plate heavy with the works on her arm and grabbed the sheriff's toast.

"It's off-peak time, Mavis. That's why the place is empty. And I didn't ask a single question all morning."

Mavis muttered wordlessly and went back to emptying the twenties out of the cash register.

Bobbie slid Brax's breakfast in front of him, then sat opposite, on the edge of the bench seat so she could jump when Mavis noticed she was on her butt again. "Now, where were we?"

"The same place we were yesterday and the day before that, with the case closed and your husband in jail." He peppered the steak and eggs heavily.

"You said 'unofficially closed.'"

He glanced up at her, multitasking by cutting his steak at the same time. "Semantics. Mavis is going to fire you if you keep hanging around back here."

"Mavis can't fire me. She needs me. Kelly just told her she's pregnant."

The sheriff shook his head, a smile crooking the edges of his mouth.

"Has anyone ever told you how pretty your eyes are? A really nice shade of blue." She cupped her chin in her hands while she buttered him up.

"I'm a cop. Flattery doesn't work on me."

"I wasn't flattering you." She put a mortified hand to her chest. "It's the truth."

His eyes riveted to her hand against her breasts. "What is it you want to know?"

"Well, since you asked." She twirled the saltshaker between her palms. "Actually, it isn't what *I* want to know, it's what I think *you* should know."

He took a healthy bite of steak. Bobbie's mouth watered. She'd foresworn breakfast in order to get down to the Cooked Goose, just in case the sheriff came in early.

With his mouth full, all he could do was listen. "You know, I think this is all because of the minimall."

He raised a brow, his jaw still working. Maybe the steak was kind of tough.

"That minimall is ruining the town, and a lot of people were angry about it. Angry with Jimbo. Did you know that?"

He cut another piece. "Bobbie, I've lived here all my life. I know all about the minimall and the hard times."

"Well, do you know about—"

"I know about Beau hating his brother, and Mavis kicking Beau out. And I know a few things you don't."

She had him. She leaned forward avidly. "Like what?"

His knife and fork stilled. "How much are you willing to pay?"

She gasped. "You mean money?"

"No."

Whatever was the sheriff implying? Certainly not…that. Time to take control of the interrogation, oops, conversation again. "You know, on all those cop shows, they always look at the spouse first."

"And 'you know,' the little busybody always gets killed because she's sticking her nose where it doesn't belong."

Was that a warning? "Come on, Sheriff, I'm just trying to help you before you get egg on your face."

He looked down at his plate. "I haven't started my eggs."

She rolled her eyes.

Mavis's soft-soled shoes sounded like cannonballs pounding down the aisle. "You need a keeper, Bobbie Jones. Leave the sheriff alone to eat in peace."

Brax eyed her. "Maybe she already has a keeper, Mavis."

"I most certainly do not." Nick wasn't her keeper. He was just her lover. She squashed a niggling backwash of guilt for letting the sheriff ogle her breasts and butt.

Brax wiped his mouth with his napkin. "Well, if you don't already have one, maybe I should apply for the position." The word definitely sounded sexual when he said it with that blue flame in his eyes. "How about dinner tomorrow night?"

Mavis made a little hmming noise in her throat.

He'd asked her out. It was what she'd wanted. Especially since, as Nick had said, the sheriff was proving so far to be a fountain of information. She threw down the proverbial gauntlet. "How about tonight?"

He broke one of his eggs, the yolk streaming out only to be stopped by his crust of toast. "I'm busy tonight."

Most men would have at least apologized, even if they didn't mean it. "Are you working?"

"Yep." The remainder of the egg disappeared into his mouth.

Hmm, working. "Are you going to stake out Cookie's house?"

He shot her a look, then glanced at the ceiling. "Now why would I stake out Mrs. Beaumont's house?"

Bobbie shrugged. "In case she sneaks out to meet… someone. Have you got her phone tapped?" After all, Cookie would have to call Brax soon if she wanted him to find the shovel in Nick's shed.

"I'm not sure which cop shows you watch, but you might want to consider something a little more reality based."

She hated those reality shows. Bobbie glanced at Mavis, who appeared to be engrossed in the exchange and making no moves to her cash register. She backed off only when Brax stood.

"Tomorrow night, then, Bobbie?"

Mavis peered at Bobbie around the sheriff's shoulder, bobbing her head vigorously.

"I guess Friday's a good night." And maybe then he'd tell her what secretive thing he'd been doing tonight.

He threw bills on the table, patted his stomach and said, "Thank you, ladies, for another delicious meal." He let his blue gaze stroke her. "And the good company."

"What time are you picking her up?" Mavis asked when Bobbie didn't seem to have the sense to.

"Seven." Answering Mavis, he looked at Bobbie. "Tell her to wear that little blue leather thing again."

They watched until his patrol car pulled away from the curb.

"I think you better have your hair done tonight."

Bobbie ran her fingers through the still-soft curls of her red hair. "What's wrong with my hair?"

"Nothing. But Thursday night is a big 'do night at the Hair Ball. Getting ready for Friday parties and the like. Everyone will be there. And you know the old saying about a woman telling her hairdresser everything."

Bobbie gave Mavis a double take. So even her boss thought something was going on besides the obvious. "Are you suggesting I eavesdrop on them?"

Mavis examined her fingernails. "Eavesdropping is such a harsh word."

But a very good idea. Bobbie looked down at her own nails. She'd had them done just before she'd left San Francisco. The cuticles were starting to grow out. "Do they have a manicurist?"

"She even takes walk-ins. And sending you over there might put a stop to you scaring away all *my* customers."

NICK SHOVED THE CHARGER into Park and gunned the engine, just to let the lady of the house know who was in her driveway. Sort of like a battle cry.

The mission had two goals. First, Nick wanted to needle Cookie about Warren, maybe question the man's allegiance. Second, he needed to cast doubt on the effectiveness of planting the damn murder weapon in his shed.

Taking the front steps two at a time, he banged on the door. A minute later, footsteps fell on the inner tile. An elderly woman peered up at him myopically, eyes clouded by cataracts. Jimbo's hire, Cookie wouldn't have put up with a disability.

"I'm sorry, but the house is in mourning."

Not Cookie, the wife, but the house itself. "I'm here to extend my condolences to Mrs. Beaumont."

"She isn't receiving."

"Who is it, Miranda?" Cookie, voice grief-weakened, called from a room off the foyer.

"It's a man." She might as well have called him a dirty name with that tone.

"Who?" He thought he detected a sniffle or two accompanying the question. What an actress.

"Tell her it's Nick Angel," he said loud enough for Cookie to hear.

The woman's eyes went wide, as if seeing him for the first time. She opened and closed her mouth spasmodically as Cookie ordered, "Let him in, Miranda," and was forced to throw the door wide for his entrance.

His whole family room would fit in the entry hall, which was tiled in marble, the walls papered in muted gold and carved moldings around the ceiling. Jimbo sure hadn't gone the cheap route when it came to outfitting his home for Cookie.

He strolled into the Beaumont living room. Silverflecked wallpaper sparkled in the twinkling light of a chandelier. Cookie, pink negligee billowing out around her fuzzy-muled feet, lounged on a cream chaise, one hand thrown dramatically over her eyes. A table beside her held a silver pitcher and a cut-glass tumbler of iced tea. Spiked?

"I'm surprised your housekeeper isn't used to strange men at the door. After all, Jimbo's been dead two days already."

Cookie fluttered a silk handkerchief. "You're such a cad."

He flopped down on her elegant couch, heedless of the creak of the spindly wood legs. "A cad?" More on the level of an alley cat. Where had Cookie picked up the hoity-toity language? "You can do better than that. In fact, you've got a mouth like a truck driver when it suits you." She'd called him every name in the book when he'd thrown her out of his house that night almost a year ago.

"I don't know what on earth you mean." Cookie was aware that Miranda's footsteps had never sounded a retreat. "Miranda," she called, "would you make more iced tea, please?"

Personally, Nick didn't give a damn if the old lady listened in. But the slap of her shoes was followed by the shush of the kitchen swing doors. "So, when's the funeral?"

Cookie raised her arm then to reveal smudges of mascara and red-rimmed eyes. "You are so unsympathetic."

"I thought congratulations were in order. Now he can't beat you anymore."

She shot him a fiery glance, then subsided back against the cushions. "Why are you here at such a terrible time, Nick? You never liked Jimbo."

"Actually, I had no feelings about him whatsoever."

"What about that fight you two had the day he died?" Her voice rose, enough to carry through the hall archway.

"Don't worry, Brax already knows all about that. He was there. Why don't you think of something else for your housekeeper to overhear?"

Cookie swung her legs over the side of her chaise and sat up to glare at him. "Why are you badgering me at a time like this? My nerves simply can't take it." Weepiness, a sniffle, all belied by that nasty scowl she settled on him.

Time to bait the trap for real. "Warren wouldn't do it for you, would he?"

"Warren who?" She managed to meet his gaze head-on, but her fingers nervously tapped the chaise.

"The man in jail for killing your husband."

"Oh, him." Even Cookie wasn't dumb enough to ask him where he'd learned about the affair with Warren.

Instead she glossed over the how and why. "I haven't a clue why that awful man would want to kill Jimbo."

"Have you been to see Warren?"

"Why would I do that?"

"To make sure he's still wrapped around your little finger."

This time she couldn't hold his gaze, reached down to fuss with her fuzzy slipper. "I've never even met the man."

"Oh, yeah, I forgot. What are you going to do if he retracts his confession? This is a death-penalty state, after all. He might start to rethink his position." He paused long enough to let the idea sink in, though Cookie, being smart in some ways, had figured that out. Which was why she needed Nick as her alternate patsy. "When he doesn't hear from you, he might start squawking."

Her eyes flickered darkly, then she smiled, a very sure, knowing smile. "I'm sure there are other people the sheriff will want to investigate if that happens."

He'd be willing to bet she'd ensured those "other people" by getting that shovel back into his shed. He'd actually thought about tossing it somewhere in the woods, but he could imagine Brax pulling him over for some minor infraction and finding it in the trunk before he'd gotten rid of it. So, he'd bought a lock this morning. It would keep everyone out, including Brax, until his old buddy got a search warrant. By that time Nick hoped to have goaded Cookie into a major misstep.

"I know Brax will investigate, but he's not going to find what he's expecting."

Her eyes went wide with that. Message received, he'd found the shovel in a timely manner and disposed of it before Cookie and cohort could call in the cavalry.

"Whose footprint do you think that was out at the murder scene?" He went on laying his trap.

She swallowed, her pretty little neck bouncing as if someone was trying to put a noose around it. "The sheriff told me it belonged to that man in jail."

"Warren? Nope, definitely not. Brax is misinforming you." He cocked his head to look at her. "Now why would he do that, you being the grieving widow and all?"

Cookie started to play with the limp hankie.

"Well, don't worry, it couldn't have been yours. If it was a woman's, he would have come to you first, wouldn't he?"

He rose, straightened the legs of his jeans as she brought the little square of silk to her nose. "By the way, Brax says you don't have an alibi for that night."

She jumped to her feet then, her mules clacking on the tile just beyond the carpet. "He didn't tell you that. I was here all night. I even called him to report Jimbo missing. And he said that was just about the time of the murder."

He looked at her, let his lips curve in a smile. "Now, why would he be telling it around town that you don't have one then?" He shrugged. "Well, who knows with Brax? Gotta go. Nice chatting with you."

He slammed the front door on his way out.

Mission accomplished. Now all he had to do was sit back and wait for Cookie to start incriminating herself all over town. Fear of exposure would do that to a person. She might even try dropping by his house in the dead of night—or sending someone in her stead—to plant a little more evidence.

And this time he'd be waiting for her. Or them.

CHAPTER SEVENTEEN

"OH, THANK GOD, you came just in time. These things would have gone to hell in the next couple of days."

Bobbie doubted that, but she let Katie, the manicurist, fondle her nails anyway. Mavis was right—the Hair Ball was packed, obviously *the* gathering place for Cottonmouth's ladies. At least on a Thursday night. Eugenia sat enthroned before a huge mirror, her hair rolled in tiny, tight curlers. Bits of foil wreathed Patsy's head. Seated behind them both, presumably waiting her turn in the chair, Marjorie fidgeted with a hairbrush. Wasn't she the drama coach at the high school, who'd cut off all her hair after Nick's mother's movie party?

Katie tugged on her fingers. "You're tensing up, sweetie. Just relax."

"Sorry." Katie was talkative but new in town, three months old, so to speak, and therefore not high on the information quotient.

Bobbie went back to her eavesdropping, tuning out Katie's prattle about ex-boyfriends, money issues and the usual twentysomething problems. Though Bobbie did remember to give a nod every few minutes. The three dryers along the back wall roared. To their left, the faucets ran in the sinks, washing out a variety of rinses, dyes and perm solutions. Overhead fans whirred, whisking away the worst of the caustic fumes.

The cacophony, instead of masking conversation, only made the ladies talk louder. Eugenia boomed as if she had her husband's bullhorn to her mouth. The intensity might very well have been for Bobbie's benefit.

"I'd stake my life on it, I would."

"Eugenia, the sheriff has the man responsible." Her face outlined by bright foil, Patsy flung an unreadable glance at Bobbie's reflection in the mirror. She hadn't said hello when Bobbie entered, nor even nodded in her direction.

News of her date with the serial killer had obviously spread. Did that mean Patsy hadn't looked for a suitable Sunday dress at the church thrift store? Silly that Bobbie should let that bother her.

Eugenia's lips thinned mutinously. "That Nick Angel put him up to it. Why, he probably even paid him."

Bobbie stiffened, her automatic response being a desire to jump to Nick's defense. And Warren's. Still she stayed in her seat and tried not to let her hands tense.

"He was a holy terror in high school, let me tell you," Marjorie added.

"Goodness," Eugenia exclaimed, "that poor Mary Alice Turner."

"She had to leave town in disgrace." Marjorie sniffed.

Mary Alice Turner, another reason people hated Nick. And he probably had nothing to do with her leaving town. Busybodies. It was hard to keep silent while they trashed Nick's character. She nodded for Katie's sake as the girl divulged that she'd had an abortion when she was eighteen, a low point in her life.

"It's a wonder any of those boys graduated high school."

"But look what Brax has done for himself. And that Kent English, manager for all those stores," Patsy lowered her voice and mouthed, "for Jimbo," with reverence.

"He should have been sent to prison for the way he tried to lead those poor boys astray." Eugenia glowered at herself in the mirror, then tapped her stylist's hand. "Connie, dear, do you think you could pluck a few of those eyebrow hairs while I'm sitting here?"

"Thank God they had strong parents," Marjorie continued.

Bobbie tucked her tongue in her cheek as Katie expertly applied another coat of gel. This wasn't gossip, merely old news. Why couldn't these women give Nick a break?

"I always liked the Angels." Patsy tilted her head. "I think you've missed a spot there, Fanny."

"Yes, but you'd never call them strong. Why, they never attended any of my parent-teacher conferences."

"You know, I'm growing tired of making *him* the subject of every conversation. He doesn't deserve it." Eugenia wriggled in her chair, causing Connie the stylist to drop a curler. "Did you hear about that girl who disappeared over in Saskatoon County?"

"No," Marjorie gasped, popping a hard candy she'd just unwrapped in her mouth.

"Thirteen years old, I hear. Her poor, dear parents must be out of their minds with worry. Disappeared Tuesday night, I read in the *Sentinel*."

"On Sunday, I'll ask the reverend to say a prayer for her safe return." Pious Patsy. Bobbie admired the fact that the real estate agent had the thought, even if she was party to the Nick bashing.

"Odd coming on the heels of Jimbo's murder like that," Eugenia mused, but her eyes darted between the reflections of her two friends in the mirror.

"Why, I never even thought of that, Eugenia." Marjorie's brows drew together. "You don't think—"

"I've never believed in coincidence," Eugenia finished for her, sending Bobbie a sly glance. Bobbie realized she'd been doing that all along; it wasn't just a squint.

Her mouth a round *O*, Marjorie leaned forward to breathe down Eugenia's neck, forcing Connie to drop yet another curler. "Could *he* have…"

"Well, I heard he was down at Sylvestor's Hardware this morning buying a big padlock."

Oh, God, Nick again. Had the news gotten to Brax, suspicious sheriff? Bobbie's heart rate picked up.

"Whatever would he need that for?"

"What do you think a man needs a padlock for? To lock something in."

"Or some*one*. Oh, my Lord." Marjorie put a hand to her mouth. "Do you think we should tell the sheriff?"

"You will recall the other day when we were in Sylvestor's, and he asked us where the Rubbermaid was so he could buy tubs just like the ones Jeffrey Dahmer used to store body parts."

Patsy snorted. "Jeffrey Dahmer never stored body parts in Rubbermaid."

"He most certainly did," Eugenia retorted forcefully. "And if you add that to the fact that man bought a padlock…well, that poor young girl could be chained in his attic missing a few fingers and toes and God only knows what else."

Patsy smoothed her fingers over the plastic drape covering her knees. For a brief moment her gaze caught Bobbie's in the reflection. She turned, but not before Bobbie noted the wrinkle on her brow and the uncertainty clouding her eyes. Even Patsy was becoming uncomfortable with Eugenia's vicious chatter.

Katie tapped the back of Bobbie's hand. "You're tensing up again, sweetie. I can't get the gel filed properly if you keep doing that."

Bobbie's "sorry" came out with no sound. What were those women thinking? Okay, they thought Nick was a serial killer. But to think he'd torture little girls? She shifted in her seat, trying to keep her hands still. They were horrible, those women.

"Honey, I can't work with you squirming like that." A harsh note crept into Katie's voice.

"I wonder if the sheriff's checked on any other missing girls in the area in recent months?"

Bobbie's fingers twitched. Did they still lynch people in small towns and get away with it?

"Remember how I told you murder was coming our way." Eugenia shook her finger at Marjorie's reflection. "Didn't I say that just the other day, Marjorie?"

"We really must tell the sheriff. What with Jimbo's murder and all, he might not even have heard about the Saskatoon girl."

Patsy flapped a hand. "Brax knows everything. Let's not get carried away here." Finally Patsy found the voice of reason.

Eugenia was beyond hearing it. "The sheriff's busy. Perhaps we should form a citizen's committee to pay Nick Angel a call."

Bobbie's breath stuck in her throat as she had a sudden vision of Eugenia Meade carrying Nick's head on a pike. She couldn't swallow past the lump, couldn't drag in much-needed air. God, she didn't do well in hair salons. They gave her panic attacks. Listening to these crazy women, a big panic hurtled straight toward her.

"Bobbie, honey, are you all right?" Katie's voice came from far, far away.

"Connie, hand me that cell phone out of my purse, would you? I'm calling the sheriff right away to report this."

Eugenia Meade wouldn't really call the sheriff over something as ridiculous as Rubbermaid and a padlock. Oh, yes, she would, taking the little instrument from Connie's hand. And Eugenia's call might be Brax's probable cause to search Nick's house. He'd find the shovel. Oh, my God. What was Bobbie to do?

Katie filed and buffed, buffed and filed. Musical notes tinkled from Eugenia's cell phone, then, "Oh, damn, what's that number?" She punched in another number. "Celeste, I've forgotten the sheriff's number. Can you look it up for me?"

"Sweetie, are you having a heart attack or something? You don't look well."

Bobbie ignored Katie's insistent tapping on the back of her hand. Nick hadn't kidnapped any little girl. He was with *her* Tuesday night. She looked at Patsy, Marjorie and Eugenia as if through a fish-eye lens, the edges of the image all blurred. Everyone knew she'd been to the Rowdy Tavern with Nick, and they'd ostracized her in less than twenty-four hours.

They'd stone her if they knew she'd slept with him. She'd never belong. They'd never believe her claim that

Warren was innocent. The real murderer would go free. The sky would fall in. She'd have to go back to San Francisco, back to her boss, Mr. Winkleman, and beg.

But at least Brax wouldn't have a reason to go snooping around Nick's house.

She'd always played the good little wife for Warren. He'd left her, anyway. Being the good little girl for these people, denying Nick, denying their affair, pretending she was dating Brax, none of it guaranteed Cottonmouth wouldn't desert her, too. There was only one right thing to do. And doing the right thing was all she'd have to hang on to when everything was over.

"Put that phone down, Mrs. Meade."

Bobbie didn't remembering standing. The babble ceased abruptly, only the whir of mechanical devices remained. Then even the three dryers shut down as everyone leaned in to stare, and listen.

She opened her mouth. Nothing came out. Just like that other day in that other salon. Only, this time everyone was listening, everyone was noticing, everyone was waiting. Her knees started to crumple.

She blurted it out before her legs gave beneath her. "Nick Angel didn't kidnap that little girl Tuesday night."

"How do you know?" Eugenia drilled her with a look.

Who said never let them see you sweat? Like a pack of hyenas, they'd jump her if she showed the slightest weakness. "Nick was with me Tuesday night."

Eugenia smirked and started punching in numbers. "She was stolen out of her room in the dead of night."

"I said he was with me." She stared Eugenia down. "And I meant he was with me *all* night."

Someone gasped. Patsy covered her mouth in horror. Marjorie Holmes slumped in her chair as if she'd fainted. Bobbie's fate in this town was sealed.

But Eugenia Meade had to put her phone back in her purse.

THERE WAS SOMETHING WRONG with Bobbie. She wouldn't meet his eye. And she wasn't opening the cottage door wide enough to let him in.

"Just thought you'd want to hear about my conversation with Cookie today." That had been Nick's excuse for coming over.

She opened the door a full twelve inches, still not enough for him to get through unless he shoved his way in.

"You saw Cookie?" A frown creased her forehead, and her lips thinned.

For a minute he thought she'd have another go at him about his ill-fated relationship with the woman of her nightmares. Instead she hugged the door, her desire to take Cookie down winning out over jealousy.

She fired a litany of questions at him. "What'd she do? What'd she say? Where'd you see her? Did she look guilty?"

That was Bobbie, everything at once. Her enthusiasm, no matter what the subject, was another of the things that drew him to her. "Let me in, and I'll tell you."

Her eyes fell to his shirtfront. He'd put on one free of stains just for her. "I was just getting ready to go out."

Shit. She'd gone and done it, gotten herself a date with Brax. "I really think that's a bad idea. Brax is slippery, you might not even know you're telling him something he can use against you." Which was true, and better than simply saying, "I don't want you going out with him."

"I have to." She bit her lip. "There are forces conspiring against you. I have to find out what the sheriff's thinking."

"Forces conspiring against me?" He almost laughed, until he noted the tense line of her lip. "Isn't that a bit melodramatic?" But he liked the fact that she worried about him.

She tipped her head to one side and put a hand up along the door. She'd had her nails done, a spicy shade that reminded him of red-hot chili peppers. He wanted those nails scoring his back.

"When was the last time there was a lynching in this town?"

He did laugh then, but a kink ran through it. "There's never been a lynching."

She stuck her tongue between her teeth. "Let's just say I'm trying to keep it that way. Now tell me about Cookie."

He didn't. Yet. "Where are you going with Brax?"

"Umm." She looked at the scratches in the hardwood floor. "I don't know. I forgot to ask."

No woman *forgot* to ask. They had to coordinate their clothing with their destination. This could be in his favor. Then again, it might not be. Depended on if she'd forgotten because she was so excited to be out with Brax or because it didn't matter to her. "I was just curious. Cookie did the fake-grief thing with aplomb."

"You mean runny mascara, eyes and nose?"

"Yeah. Silk hankie, too. I went to her house."

"Ooh, and she let you in?"

"She didn't have the nerve to turn me away. She was scared."

"Good job. Did you push her buttons?"

Christ, the excitement in her eyes and threaded through her voice got him hot. "She was quivering with fear when I left. I wouldn't be surprised if she calls Warren to make sure he hasn't turned against her."

Her lips parted. He thought about the really nice things those lips were capable of. "You're amazing."

Yes, he certainly was. And he wanted to amaze her right now, in her bed, on the carpet, in the kitchen, anywhere. "If she doesn't incriminate herself that way, I figure she'll be back at my house trying to plant more evidence." He shined his fingernails on his shirt. "I let her think I'd found the shovel and gotten rid of it. She'll probably figure she's got to get me with something else."

The excitement buoying Bobbie up died a quick unnatural death. "I heard you were observed buying a lock."

He raised his gaze heavenward. "Can't I even take a piss around here without people noticing?"

"A pee, maybe, buying a lock, no." She chewed on a nail, risking her fresh manicure. "Do you think Brax can get a search warrant if he finds out about the lock?"

He stared down at her, looking for any telltale signs of a nervous breakdown. She really was acting weird. "No."

"You have to get rid of the shovel."

"I can't do that. First of all, I might get caught with it while I'm transporting it. And second, it's evidence. When we find out who really did it, Brax is going to need the weapon."

Emotion brimmed in her eyes, fear, pain, despair. "Do you really think we can find out who did it?"

"Of course." He sounded a helluva lot more confident than he felt. But suddenly he wanted to be the big tough hero. For her. "Let me in, Bobbie." He meant it in more ways than one.

Shit. This thing might be getting way too serious.

"I told you, I have to go out."

"With Brax." He kept the tone light, when what he really wanted was to smash something. "I don't think it's a good idea."

"I won't tell him anything I shouldn't." She zipped her lips. "In fact, I won't even open my mouth." Christ, now why'd she have to say that and bring all sorts of openmouthed images to mind? "I'll let him do all the talking, I swear."

"Fine." He didn't like it, but he couldn't stop it. And he had to admit this wasn't about Brax anymore. He would have wanted to smash things no matter who she was going out with. Brax was actually the best of a lot of bad choices. The guy might be a dickhead, but he was still a good cop. "At least I won't have to worry about your safety."

She raised a brow, a hitch in her voice. "Why on earth wouldn't *I* be safe in Cottonmouth?"

"You're right. What was I thinking?" Except that Jimbo had been murdered. And Bobbie's questions had irritated quite a few people. Not that anyone would actually think of hurting her physically just because of a few questions. "Call me when you get home and tell me what you learned."

Jesus. He was losing it. He wanted her to call him just so he could hear her voice, maybe talk her over into his bed. What the hell was up with that?

BOBBIE CLOSED THE DOOR and ran into her bedroom for black jeans and a black turtleneck. Sort of a cat burglar outfit, good for reconnaissance, or a little sneaking around. She hoped she wouldn't get hot and sticky in the high neck. She hadn't actually lied to Nick. She'd never said she was getting ready to go out with Brax *tonight*. He'd just assumed. That wasn't a lie, not really.

She had to find out what Brax was up to. The need burned in her. Especially after Eugenia's stunt in the Hair Ball. God, she still felt sick about it, the wide maniacal eyes, the curled lips, the angry mumbles. Her career in Cottonmouth was toast, but she still had Nick to worry about. Eugenia couldn't keep silent long, and if not tonight, by tomorrow, she'd be whispering in Brax's ear that Bobbie lied about being with Nick on Tuesday. She needed to know what Brax was doing, not just because he refused to take her out tonight, but because he'd been sort of...mysterious about it.

Bobbie tied the shoelaces on her black tennies, grabbed her keys and dashed out the door. Brax had given a weird laugh when she'd mentioned him staking out Cookie's house. She'd try there first.

See, the whole thing was, Nick was now her responsibility. She'd broadcast her commitment to the whole town—telling Eugenia, Marjorie and Patsy was as good as putting it in the newspaper. She couldn't let Nick down. Warren would cave sooner or later. Or the case against him would fall apart. Despite Brax's scoffing at her cop shows, she knew they didn't prosecute someone for a crime, despite a confession, unless they could corroborate the story. Warren's story had no corroboration. Come on, he killed Jimbo because Dennis Crouch didn't want Warren to steal his business? Get real.

She turned onto Cookie's lane, the VW purring slowly down the street. Lights were on in the big house, all upstairs, none downstairs. She cruised by twice, got out of her car to search in the darkness, but found sight of neither Brax nor his patrol car.

Her little Bug chugged back out onto the main road. She'd passed the sheriff's department building on the way out. Brax's lights had been off. He was up to something elsewhere, she just knew it. Where could he have gone?

To the right lay Delton Road and the lake. The scene of the crime. Maybe he was there, poring over evidence yet again. Brax was a thorough guy, wasn't everyone always saying that?

Five minutes later she pulled onto the small dirt road. Across the water, lights flickered through the trees, then disappeared as she moved on. Her headlights cut through the night. Gee, it was dark out here. Really dark.

Why did Nick have to make that comment about her being safe? All it did was make her jittery. For no good reason.

Bobbie almost turned the car around, but a flash of light cut through the forest, closer this time. It had to be Brax. Maybe he was giving the lake one more chance to cough up a shovel.

She ignored the little voice in her head telling her how stupid she was, like the teenager in the horror flick climbing those attic stairs in her bikini underwear when everyone knows the maniac is up there with his butcher knife.

It wasn't quite that bad. No serial killer lurked in the woods. But what about that girl who disappeared? That was in another county. Besides, Bobbie wasn't a nubile young thing. Serial killers always went for defiling nubile young things.

Still, she wouldn't get out of the car. And she'd only stay a minute. She'd just see if Brax was there. If he wasn't, she'd make like a banana and peel.

The last bend in the road entered the parking lot. No lights blazed, no cars idled. No Brax. Just a strip of yellow tape in her headlights, stretched between the trees, marking the scene.

Really, for the first time, she thought about Jimbo. Not Warren or Nick, but about big, sweet Jimbo. He'd died out here. She let the car roll to a stop. The little engine rumbled in the otherwise quiet night, the sound almost sacrilegious. She turned the key, killing the motor, and said a prayer into the deep silence that followed. No matter what Jimbo had done, no matter if he had built the minimall and tried to drive out his tenants, he didn't deserve what had happened to him. He deserved a prayer.

"Amen," she whispered and reached for the key.

That's when her door was yanked open. Bobbie didn't have time to scream before her head seemed to explode into a million splinters of light and pain.

WHERE THE HELL was she?

The portable phone lay on the workbench, the windows behind open so he could hear her car. Nick hadn't sketched a single line in the four hours he'd been waiting.

He wasn't jealous; he was worried. All right, so the images assailing his feeble mind were more concerned with Bobbie's limbs contorting around Brax's body than with her lying in a bloody heap somewhere. The bloody heap was definitely the worse of the two.

Christ, where was she?

An engine fired far down the street, then faded away. It didn't sound like a Volkswagen, anyway. Maybe he should call Brax. The man had given him his cell phone number for emergencies. And Bobbie's disappearance was starting to feel like an emergency.

Christ almighty, he was going crazy. Worse, he liked it in an odd way. He couldn't remember the last time he'd cared about anything, certainly not since his parents died, and maybe not for a long time before that. Worrying about Bobbie was…refreshing.

A loud crash and shattering glass sounded downstairs, then running feet pounded on concrete. Shit, another roadkill. God forbid they'd actually thrown it through his living room window. He took the two flights of stairs two steps at a time.

And skidded to a halt just inside the arch. All that remained of the front window was a gaping hole and a swinging shard of glass still attached to the top sill.

"Damn." He sniffed, expecting the smell of decomposing flesh. There was nothing. Except a brick lying in the center of his coffee table.

String secured a piece of white paper around it.

He was getting a really bad feeling.

Picking up the brick, he untied and unfolded the note. Letters cut from a magazine had been glued to the paper.

"If you want to see Bobbie Jones alive again, come to Jimbo's fishing lodge. Come alone."

Shit. They had Bobbie.

CHAPTER EIGHTEEN

DEAR GOD, I KNOW I WAS STUPID, I mean really really stupid, and I'm so sorry about that, but please help me anyway.

Bobbie wasn't Nick's warrior princess type, no matter how much she'd tried to pretend, and she didn't know kickboxing. But unlike a lot of women, she did know when to keep her mouth shut.

With her hands tied behind her back and her waist secured to a hard chair, her numb fingers swelled like cooked sausages. Her head ached like...a son of a bitch. They'd hit her with something. Where was she? The only thing she could see, without raising her head—and that she was terrified to do—was a plain plank floor covered by a braided rag rug. Her shoes were missing.

Playing possum, letting them think she was still unconscious, was the only advantage she had. Maybe she'd learn what they planned to do with her, then she'd find a way out. If she didn't start screaming in sheer terror first. Listening to the argument on the other side of the room, Bobbie didn't move a muscle.

"Why can't you just take care of it, Kent?" The Cookie Monster's whine. God, she really had played Warren for a fool. Bobbie would have liked nothing better than to punch her lights out. She choked back a whimper instead.

"I have to be outside to surprise him while you're in here keeping an eye on her," the man said. Kent. Nick's friend, the one who came to the house? Bobbie suppressed a shudder. "Get with the program, Cookie. We agreed on this already."

"Can't you just…get it over with?" Oh, my God, what was *it?* "I'll leave, then you wait for him. I don't want to be here."

"Godammit, Cookie. The timing is critical. We can't risk Nick being seen around town after *her* time of death. Everyone's got to believe he killed her, then took off. That means he's got to be *here* when we do it."

Sharp pain stabbed her temples. They were going to kill her. And they'd blame her death on Nick. How could she warn him? Stupid, stupid, what had she gotten them into? She wouldn't cry. She had to think. She had to do something.

Struggling to breathe slowly, softly, rhythmically, she wiggled her wrists in her bonds. Too tight for her to squirm out of. No wonder her hands were numb. Her brain wanted to go numb, too. These people were serious. At least, Kent was.

"I don't like this, it's getting so complicated," Cookie whined.

"It was complicated the day you decided you couldn't just divorce Jimbo, you had to kill him so you got all the money."

"I never decided that, you did."

"You're the one who claimed he was thinking about making things right with Beau."

Infighting was good. Another advantage. But how to use it when her hands were tied behind her back? With her head hanging down, her eyes began to water and her nose to run. *Please don't sneeze, please don't sneeze,* she chanted.

But oh, God, she felt it building, unstoppable. She held her breath in the sudden silence, hoping, praying the tingling in her nose would go away.

Too late.

Footsteps padded toward her across the floor, then the braided rug.

Bobbie started to shake, squeezed her eyes shut. Did a bullet in the brain hurt a lot?

Rough fingers tugged her head up. "Stop pretending. Open your eyes."

His voice curdled her stomach juices. She was too afraid not to look at him. Blazing eyes, flared nostrils, his mouth a grim line. The man ripping her hair from the roots was no friend of Nick's, not ever.

Kent gave her head a shake, then let go. Her scalp screamed.

"It's time. He'll be here any minute. Make sure you keep the gun on her every second I'm gone."

Cookie stood by an ancient sagging sofa. Strappy high-heeled sandals on her feet and a brilliant fuchsia sweater dress accentuating her slender figure, she'd dressed for a garden party. Instead of a killing. Hands pressed to her cheeks, her eyes darted from the gun on the coffee table to Kent's inflexible face.

"I can't kill her." Thank God for the Cookie Monster's lack of spine. Maybe, just maybe...

Kent tugged another gun from his waistband. "That was the deal, Cookie, I do him, you do her. We're in this together, we were from the moment we killed Jimbo."

"I didn't kill him. You did."

"I might have been holding the damn shovel, but

you sent him out there to meet me knowing exactly what I was going to do."

"Kent—"

He pointed at the gun on the table. "Pick it up and be ready when I get back." He shot Bobbie a look. "And don't talk to her."

Then she was alone with Cookie. And the gun.

NICK KNEW HE WAS WALKING into a trap. But what other choice did he have? He punched the accelerator, and the Charger leaped forward. Dark forest flashed by the windows. His life rushed past. Bobbie's life, too. *Please don't let her be dead.* He wouldn't let her be dead.

Maybe he could do a trade. He slammed a hand against the steering wheel, pain jolting up his arm. They weren't out to make a fucking trade. They wanted both Bobbie and him dead. That's what this was all about.

Who the hell was helping Cookie? The possibilities were limitless. His options weren't. Hell, he didn't have an option except to show up at the appointed place.

Then they'd kill him. Bobbie was probably already dead.

But if by some miracle she wasn't, then he needed a freaking plan. Something, anything, besides just walking in there and offering his head on a platter. He didn't even have a weapon. Except his brain, which he would have bet against Cookie's any day. Her cohort, however, was the unknown quantity.

Christ, he should have turned that bitch Cookie in the minute she started moaning her cockamamie story about Jimbo beating her. Brax might not have been able to put her away for anything, but Jimbo would have been warned. And Brax could have—

Brax.

He'd been at odds with Brax since Mary Alice aborted Brax's kid using Nick's cold hard cash. Right now, Nick didn't give a flying fuck about Mary Alice, about the animosity, about Brax's suspicions, his questions. He cared only about Bobbie.

He slammed on the brakes. The Charger fishtailed across the road, coming to rest in the gravel. Reaching into the glove box, he yanked the cell phone out. Where was the card, the goddamn card, the one Brax gave him that day at the minimall right after Jimbo got whacked? He shuffled the junk, then threw it on the floor mat, scrambling through it.

Christ, there it was.

He punched in the numbers, his hand shaking as he held the phone to his ear. The momentary delay strung out his nerves, and he could have smashed the damn thing against the wheel. Then it started to ring.

"Braxton here."

"It's Nick."

A soft chuckle, then, "Nick who?"

"Don't give me shit, Brax. I need your help. Now."

"Got a shovel you want to turn over, a pair of shoes maybe?"

Screw the fricking shoes. "Did you drop Bobbie off somewhere after your date?"

"Drop her off? She wasn't with me. Our date's for tomorrow."

Shit, she'd lied. With that weird crap she'd been spouting about lynchings, he should have known something was up. She'd probably gone killer hunting and stumbled into something. "She's missing."

Brax's voice turned businesslike. "Give me the details."

"I got a rock through my window telling me she'd die if I didn't go to Jimbo's fishing lodge ASAP."

"Shit," Brax said on a breath. "Who was it?"

"How the hell should I know? I didn't see who threw the damn rock. But that Beaumont bitch has something to do with it. Spivey was having an affair with her. She wanted him to kill Jimbo for her." He took the chance and told Brax everything. "And someone put the shovel that killed Jimbo in my shed. It's still there."

"Why are you only now telling me this?"

"It wasn't my business before."

"Shit. Shit." He could hear Brax pounding something. "What's Bobbie got to do with it?"

"She's been asking questions. Someone got scared."

"Someone?"

"Cookie's not doing this alone. I think that unidentified footprint you found is her accomplice."

Brax cleared his throat. "There was no footprint."

"What?"

"I thought I'd spread a little misinformation around and see if I got any bites."

"Fuck. You got a bite all right." They'd both screwed up. But Nick was the one who'd walked away and left her alone tonight. "Christ, Brax. They're gonna kill her if I don't get out there."

"Where are you?"

"A mile or so down the road from the lake turnoff."

"You sit tight, don't go in there without me. I can line up some guys in a matter of—"

"I'm going in now, Brax. You just make sure you back me up or I'm screwed. So's Bobbie."

Brax shouted, "Godammit, don't—"

Nick punched the end button and rammed the Charger into gear. He couldn't leave Bobbie alone for the length of time it took Brax to get there. Without him, she might not have that long.

"IT'S VERY APPARENT you didn't kill Jimbo. Kent did it." Bobbie tried to sound reasonable and nonjudgmental. But she wanted to jump out of the chair she was tied to and rip Cookie's face to shreds. *You stupid, dumb blonde.*

"I'm not listening to you." Like one of the three monkeys, Cookie covered her ears with her hands. At least she hadn't picked up the gun.

"You better listen. *You* haven't killed anyone yet. You can still get out of this. Just tell them he did it." Bobbie didn't care who'd actually killed Jimbo. She just wanted to turn Cookie against Kent.

"La-la-la," Cookie singsonged. The woman had gone crackers.

"Listen to me, Cookie." Bobbie used her most soothing voice, the one that placated irate vendors demanding immediate payment. But her stomach had sunk to her toes, and she couldn't even feel her fingers anymore. "I can help you. I can tell them he grabbed me out of my car and hit me over the head. I can tell them you said you didn't want to do it. He insisted. You don't want to go to the gas chamber, do you, when it was all his idea?"

Cookie paced, rubbed her fists against her eyes, sniffling, moaning. Then her arms slashed to her sides. "This is all your fault."

"Mine," Bobbie squeaked. She'd miscalculated, pushed too hard and lost the woman.

Cookie charged forward three steps. "Yes, all your fault. If you hadn't come to town, Warren would have done what I wanted him to. He was weakening. But then you—" she stabbed her finger at Bobbie's face "—then you started making him doubt me."

And she'd been right. But that didn't stop Bobbie's mouth from going dry. Cookie backed up, her calves hitting the coffee table where the gun lay. "Without you, Warren would have played his part the way he was supposed to."

Bobbie clamped down on the panic, fear wrenching her belly. Anger was the only emotion she couldn't hold back. Like a tidal wave, it washed over her. A litany of curses crowded her head, all she said was, "Warren's not a murderer."

"It wouldn't have been murder. He would have been protecting me. Justifiable homicide."

No one would have believed Jimbo beat her. Bobbie decided not to harp on that. How to get control? Her head ached piecing together the right words, keeping emotion out of it. Emotion was as deadly as the gun lying on the table. "It's still Kent who killed Jimbo. You shouldn't have to pay for something you didn't do, Cookie."

"But I don't have an alibi. He could say I did it." Cookie was breathing too quickly. A sign of weakening?

"But he can't say you killed me if you don't do it. You don't have to play along." She held her breath, then dove in. It was her only chance. "What's his plan, Cookie?"

"It's simple. Everyone knows Nick's a serial killer. Kent's going to make it look like Nick killed you, then disappeared. Kent'll make sure no one ever finds his body."

Please don't mean that Kent's going to kill Nick outside. If she could talk Cookie round, they had a chance. But not if Kent shot Nick before returning. Her mind worked furiously. No, no, that wouldn't work. Kent couldn't kill Nick here. The police would find *his* blood, when they were supposed to find only hers. They had to kill her first, then take Nick somewhere else. A ray of hope still shone.

"You know, two murders in a small town like this is going to look way too coincidental. The sheriff's going to know they're connected somehow. He's not stupid, you know."

"But that's why Kent put the shovel in Nick's shed, so Brax would think Nick killed Jimbo, too. If Warren, you know…" Her eyes shifted, almost as if she felt a prick of guilt. "If Warren says he didn't do it."

Bobbie forced a puff of air through her lips and rolled her eyes. "That's really a dumb plan, Cookie."

"Why?"

"First of all, Nick got rid of that shovel."

"No, he didn't. Kent says he was down buying a lock. Why else would he need one except for that shed of his? Nick tried to make me think he'd ditched it, but he was lying." She pointed to her chest proudly. "I saw right through him."

"All right. How about this?" Bobbie had to punch holes in every aspect of the plan, make Cookie doubt they could get away with it. "Everyone knows serial killers rape, mutilate and strangle. They don't use a gun."

"They don't?"

"No. Everyone will know Nick didn't do it."

"They will?"

"Yes. And there's that footprint down at the crime scene."

Cookie's brow shot up. "Footprint?" she echoed.

"It wasn't Warren's, and it wasn't Nick's. *Kent* left behind a footprint."

"He said he was careful."

"He's not God, you know. He made a mistake."

Cookie chewed off the last smudge of lipstick. "But even if he did, no one will know it's his."

"When Warren recants his confession, Brax will get a search warrant for every house in town, and he'll find those shoes." Outlandish, but Cookie probably wasn't a *Law and Order* addict.

"*If* Warren takes it back," Cookie whispered.

"*When*," Bobbie snapped. "When he hears I'm dead, he *will* start telling the truth. He'll *know* you had something to do with it." Bobbie wasn't lying. No matter how badly he'd hurt her, Warren was a good man at heart. He wouldn't simply close his eyes to her murder. He couldn't.

Cookie just stared, eyes wide, mouth open a fraction. She was primed.

"I've got a better plan," Bobbie said, weaving a seductive thread through her voice.

"What?"

Bobbie had never needed her wits and her mouth more. "I'll say you rescued me. You tell Brax you thought Kent might have killed Jimbo because he'd always hated him. Tonight, you followed him and knocked him over the head. I'll back you up."

Cookie bit her lip. She wrapped her arms around her waist, hugged herself. She chewed a fingernail. Then she said, "But what about Warren?"

"He won't say anything about the two of you if I tell him not to."

"Do you think Brax will buy it?"

Bobbie smiled. "Of course. We just have to stick together."

Cookie tugged on her quivering lip, then, in a little girl voice, asked, "Should I hide behind the door when he comes in?"

Gotcha.

THE WINDOW DOWN, Nick idled at the end of the long driveway leading to Jimbo's lodge. The Charger's engine rumbled in the night, the sound carrying for miles in all that deadly quiet. He didn't expect his arrival to be clandestine.

What he had in mind couldn't be called a plan. He would let himself be taken and hope like hell he could stall Cookie and her chump until Brax arrived with firepower. Brax was his secret weapon. Cookie, and whoever was helping the bitch, wouldn't even consider that he'd asked for Brax's aid. The ongoing feud between them was too renowned.

At least, he prayed it was.

But Christ, he was taking a big risk with Bobbie's life. If he wasn't already too late.

"Don't think like that," he whispered to the stars. "She's all right."

Foot off the brake, he let the Charger roll onto the gravel drive. Cookie wouldn't have done this on her own. That's why she'd needed him, why she then turned to Warren Spivey. Cookie wasn't a big thinker. Who the hell was helping her?

Lights shone through the trees. He wouldn't make it too easy by walking right up to the front door. That might cause suspicion that he had an ace up his sleeve. Pulling the Charger to the side of the lane, he shut off the engine and climbed out, the door snicking closed behind him.

Crickets chirped. A breeze rustled the leaves. An owl hooted over the water. No other sounds. But someone lay in wait for him. The hairs on his arms rose.

He glanced down at the lighted dial of his watch. He had ten minutes on Brax. The sheriff better put the pedal to the metal.

All right, sacrificial lamb time.

He stepped into the woods beside the drive.

Nick crouched low, pushing a branch aside to gain full view of the silent lodge. Warning came in the form of a snapped twig behind him, then cold metal nudged his temple.

"Thought you could sneak up on me, buddy?" Kent taunted.

For one blind moment, Nick's muscles refused to respond as he absorbed the sucker punch. Kent and Cookie?

"Glad you could make it, Nick."

He might have been able to get the jump on Kent, but he also might get a bullet in his brain. Where would that leave Bobbie? He reined himself in. "So, you're the one helping Cookie."

"Yeah." Kent paused, made a sound like he was sucking on a sore tooth. "Sorry about this."

Kent, the ally he'd thought he still had in Cottonmouth... Nick closed his eyes briefly. He'd think about that later, when Bobbie was safe. "Cookie isn't worth it, you know."

Kent's shrug traveled through the barrel of the gun he hadn't removed from Nick's temple. "Probably not. But the money is."

Nick sought a way to get to him. "I thought you were—"

"Your friend?" Air puffed harshly through Kent's nostrils. "That's why I'll make this as quick and painless as possible."

Nothing was painless in this whole damn mess. And the thread of excitement lacing Kent's voice said he actually relished making sure it wasn't.

Nick moved back on his haunches, easing the pressure on his knees. "I was going to say I thought you were smarter than this."

"Insults aren't going to make me mad enough to lose control so you can jump me. This isn't one of your movies, Nick."

He couldn't even summon rage over the betrayal, not now. Only one thing remained that he cared about. "Let Bobbie go, Kent. She isn't part of this."

"Afraid I can't do that, buddy."

"I'm not your fucking buddy."

Kent jabbed the muzzle of the gun hard against his temple. "That's better. For a minute there I thought you didn't care."

"About you? I don't. Let her go."

Kent chuckled. "Got a soft spot for her, huh? Thought so. Too bad. Too late."

Nick's fists bunched. He wanted nothing more than to smash Kent's face, beat him to a bloody pulp. The fury was for Bobbie, for involving her in the whole damn mess. He tilted his head against the gun, peered at Kent from the corner of his eye. "She's not as good as Cookie. Tell me, old pal, how did it feel when Cookie was fucking me so you two could have a patsy for Jimbo's murder? She's one hot little number, isn't she? And that thing she does with her tongue…"

A low growl rumbled up through Kent's throat. He pulled back, the gun now out of Nick's reach completely. Kent's lip lifted in a snarl.

Bull's-eye. Kent and Cookie had been planning for months. But Kent hadn't liked that his lover was doing someone else.

"Wonder if she was making all that noise just for show?" Nick lifted his shoulder negligently. "Nah. She was really enjoying herself."

"Get up."

Nick's eyes ached to look down at his watch. How much time had he used up? "Fuck you."

"I'll kill you right here. Crouched on your knees." Tension snapped through Kent's voice.

"If that was part of your plan, you'd have done it already. I suspect you don't want to kill me around here. You want a patsy. That's what you've wanted all along. Otherwise you would have killed Jimbo yourself right out of the chute instead of having Cookie set Warren Spivey up to do it."

He was damn sure about that part of their scheme, the failed part. But what did they now plan for Bobbie?

"I said get the fuck up." Kent stepped back, wrapping both hands around the gun and planting his feet apart.

Nick turned his head, glared into his one-time

friend's eyes. Kent's gaze glittered, his jaw flexed. Nick didn't make a move.

Kent lashed out, shoving Nick with his boot. "We're going inside. I want you to watch her die."

"You'll die first."

Kent's laugh cut across his words. "Oh, I don't think so." He waved the gun. "I've got all the advantages."

Seconds ticked by. Neither of them gave an inch. Then Kent whispered, "Guess I'll have to kill you here since you're so uncooperative."

Where the fuck was Brax? Nick put his hands on his knees, snatching a quick look at his watch, and pushed to his feet. Fifteen minutes, how much more time did the freaking sheriff need?

"You win." He leaned down to brush leaves and twigs from his jeans, then raked Kent with a look. "For now."

Kent stepped in behind him, pushed him forward with a sharp jab in the back. "Move."

He walked slowly, counting the seconds in his head. The porch steps creaked loudly beneath their combined weight, the wood of the decking groaned. With Kent's gun still gouging his back, the man behind him like a shadow, Nick eased the door open.

He almost sagged with relief. Tied to a chair, hands behind her, Bobbie was alive. Thank you, God. She cried out his name when she saw him, then snapped her attention back to Cookie.

A gun wobbled in the widow's hands.

Kent shoved him from behind, stepping over the threshold. Sliding his own weapon across Nick's ribs, he rammed it hard against bone. "Keep your goddamn hands up." Leaning in, he whispered, "Get ready for the show, buddy."

"Kent," Cookie blurted.

"What are you waiting for, baby? Do it."

Cookie looked at her lover. Her chin trembled. "Kent. I think I've changed my mind." Then she whipped the gun around and pulled it up, aiming right for Kent's head. "I think you better put yours down. Bobbie's going to tell Brax it was all you. And that I rescued her."

"YOU FUCKING BITCH."

Oh, Lord. Kent English was yelling at *her,* not Cookie. Her heart in her throat, Bobbie could only stare at Nick, at the gun in his side, and pray she hadn't made a horrible mistake.

Livid lines blanched Kent's face, Cookie's hands wavered, tears leaked from the corners of her eyes, and there were two too many guns in the small room.

Cookie hadn't followed the plan. Or rather, Kent had returned too soon, and Cookie never made it behind the door.

Nick's lips curved in a humorless smile. "Looks like she's not as stupid as you thought, huh, old pal."

"You shut the fuck up."

Nick winced at the jab to his ribs. "I'll back you up, too, Cookie."

Kent snarled, an animal-like sound that shivered over Bobbie's nerve endings. "Don't forget who's got the gun on *you,* asshole." Then the man turned his angry gaze on Bobbie. "Maybe you want to change your mind about any stories you plan to tell Brax, Bobbie. Unless you want me to shoot Nick right here."

A bubble of panic clogged her throat. She opened her mouth, ready to beg, plead, anything.

Cookie rendered entreaty unnecessary. "But I'll still be able to shoot you."

"You couldn't hit Eugenia Meade's fat ass, you stupid cow."

Cookie's eyes narrowed, her shoulders straightening. "Jimbo taught me to shoot. I'll have you know I'm an expert."

Kent's head tipped. Surprise furrowed his brow. "You never told me that."

Cookie raised her nose. "I didn't need to before."

Nick's gaze steadied on Bobbie, his jaw tilted toward Kent. Bobbie prayed he wouldn't say a word or twitch a muscle.

Something in Kent's eyes changed, a glint of craftiness. "Cookie, sweetheart, let's not fight. That bitch told you a bunch of crap. We can make this work if we stick together."

"It works better if *you* get all the blame."

The sweet talk died on his curled lip. "Who do you think Brax is going to believe? Me or you? I've known him a helluva lot longer."

"If you're dead, then he gets to hear only my side of the story." Cookie smiled. It was neither the cajoling smile she'd probably used to con Warren nor the spitfire smirk she'd blasted Bobbie with that day outside Bushman's. This was the smile of a manipulator.

The flesh of Kent's face drooped. "Cookie."

"In fact, I'm so good I can get all three of you, starting with you. Then there'll only be one story to tell. Mine."

Bobbie immediately saw the flaws in the plan. But terror tightened her belly. Cookie just might figure out a way to fix her flaws.

Kent's arm twitched.

Cookie saw everything. "Don't even think about it."

Bobbie met Nick's eyes. One corner of his mouth rose. She wanted to scream at him not to do or say anything.

He ignored the plea in her eyes. "Guess she took you in hook, line and sinker, didn't she, sucker?"

"You're dust one way or another," Kent barked.

Cookie's hand lost all trace of quiver. "Now. Which one shall I do first? Eenie, meenie, minie—" she chuckled "—mo."

Bobbie's heart stopped, the innocent rhyme wrapping around her. Her own words come back to haunt her.

"I guess that means you." Cookie aimed at Kent's forehead.

Kent's eyes darted around the room. Bobbie could see his thoughts. Turn the gun, shoot Cookie. Dive and shoot Nick. Or run like hell.

Bobbie turned back to that oh-so-steady gun in Cookie's hand and the gleam in her eyes.

"I'm so going to enjoy this, Kent."

"Not as much as I'm gonna enjoy arresting you, Mrs. Beaumont."

Sheriff Tyler Braxton's voice sliced through the thick air, and the muzzle of a gun appeared over Kent's right shoulder.

"I think you ought to set that gun down, Mrs. Beaumont, and get on the floor. Unless, of course, you prefer I drop you right where you stand."

Cookie shrieked.

"TOOK YOU LONG ENOUGH," Nick muttered, his blood roaring in his ears. Afraid of losing it completely, he couldn't look at Bobbie. One almost down, one to go. His side ached and his legs had stiffened. It wasn't over yet.

Brax busied himself watching Cookie drop her gun, kick it several feet behind, just like he told her to, and spread-eagle herself on the worn braid rug.

"Now it's your turn, English." Brax's second weapon fit neatly to the top of Kent's spine.

"Brax—"

"Don't call me Brax, asshole. Not ever again." The lazy drawl vanished, replaced by a deadly tone.

Sweat popped out along Kent's upper lip. "I can shoot Nick, even on reflex. You don't want to risk that."

Behind him, Brax shifted. "What do you think, Nick?"

Nick's gaze latched on to Bobbie. Her mouth sucked at air she couldn't seem to drag in. Her eyes bulged. Nick prayed she wouldn't have to watch him die. "Waste the fucker."

"My pleasure."

One second, two. Nick didn't breathe. Kent panted sharp bursts of air. The gun quaked against Nick's ribs. Three seconds, four.

Kent's weapon clattered to the floor, he turned, then took two steps to the right. "It was all her idea. Right from the beginning."

"Shut up, you idiot," Cookie cried, her voice muffled against the rug.

"On the floor, asshole," Brax growled.

Kent's knees hit the planks, and he went voluntarily face first into the wood.

"You moron," Cookie screamed. "You said he'd never call Brax."

"Shut up."

Brax rolled his eyes and shoved a gun in Nick's hand. "Blow her head off if she so much as moves."

Nick smiled mirthlessly. "My pleasure."

Yanking out a pair of handcuffs, Brax rammed his knee into Kent's back, and secured his wrists. The sound of sirens suddenly split the night.

"There's my team. Figured I'd get here before they could." Brax stepped over Kent's prone body to repeat the cuffing procedure with Cookie. An especially malicious glint transformed his eyes.

Nick looked at Bobbie. She stared at the gun in his hand. He set it on the nearest table. In the span of a breath, he was on his knees beside her, yanking at the ropes chafing her wrists. She'd worn her skin off, raw, bleeding flesh turning his stomach.

"You saved me," she whispered.

"It was Brax." He worked the rope off her waist.

"But you brought him."

Pulling back, still on his knees beside her, he smoothed her hair back from her forehead. Dried blood matted her hair at the back of her head. His gut twisted. "You all right?"

Her green eyes sparkled. "You rescued me. My hero."

"Jesus, I'm so sorry." Then he pulled her off the chair and into his arms, sinking his face into the crook of her neck. The beat of feet hit the wooden porch, voices and bright lights erupted around them. He shuddered in her arms. God, if he'd lost her… "You know, that was pretty stupid going out by yourself. You said you were seeing Brax."

"I had to do something," she whispered against his ear. "They were going to lynch you."

Jesus. And this woman was all his. What more could a sorry ass like himself ask for? He squeezed her until she squeaked.

He opened his eyes to the sight of boots standing two feet behind Bobbie.

"Well, Ms. Jones," Brax drawled, "we'll just have that head of yours checked out. Then, if you'd like, we can go down to the jail and release your husband."

Christ. Nick had almost forgotten about the loser. What would Bobbie do, now that her almost-ex no longer had a lover?

CHAPTER NINETEEN

SHERIFF BRAXTON SAT in his big leather chair, feet propped on the desk. Warren had faced the sheriff like this too many times in the past two days, and despite the changed circumstances, acid ate at his stomach lining. Roberta's elbows, one almost touching his, rested on the arms of her chair. The warmth of her skin arced across the small space separating them. Warren didn't reach for her. A patch of radiant red hair had been chopped away where a white bandage covered the bump on her head.

The injury was Warren's fault. Everything was. He didn't know how he'd make any of it up to her, helplessness adding to the roiling in his belly.

"They're turning on each other like women at a clearance sale." Braxton laced his fingers across his chest and settled deeper into his chair. "Neither of them wanted to get caught doing the actual deed. Which is where you came into it, Spivey."

Steel-blue eyes bored into him. Warren's gut twisted. The woman he'd spent over twenty years dreaming about had simply used him. Then and now.

"As for the original plan," the sheriff continued, "Cookie says it was all Kent's idea because he hated being under Jimbo's thumb, and he says she came slinking down to his office to seduce him. The he-said, she-said shit flying around is enough to drive a good cop to murder." Brax shot Nick Angel a look, as if to ask which one he believed.

The man lounged against a steel filing cabinet, saying nothing. Warren still wasn't sure how he fit into the picture, except that he'd been told Cookie had tried the same battered-woman routine on him almost a year ago.

Angel hadn't fallen for it. So, what did that make Warren? An idiot or a misguided fool? He'd given up everything trying to recapture the past, only to find that the past was as he'd feared. Cookie hadn't loved him then, she'd used him. Just as she'd used him this time around.

And Sheriff Braxton had known.

"You never did believe my confession, did you, Sheriff?"

"Shit, Spivey, it was the most ridiculous thing I ever heard."

Warren let the corner of his mouth rise, though he didn't feel an ounce of humor. "That's what Roberta said."

Braxton shifted his gaze to Bobbie. "And of course, there was the way your ex-wife reacted to Cookie Beaumont."

Roberta raised a brow as if to say, "Who me?" then picked at a hole in the armrest. Warren winced at the easy way she reacted to being called his ex-wife. To him, the term sounded unfamiliar. Inaccurate.

"But there wasn't a whiff of a rumor about you and Mrs. Beaumont. Still, I couldn't shake loose the feeling that you were covering for her. I did a little checking, and lo and behold, what did I find? You two went to the same high school. So I kept hammering at you."

"And told everyone there was evidence that didn't really exist." Nick Angel finally spoke, a current of anger running below the words and in the glare he pinned the sheriff with. "I didn't think cops were supposed to lie. Isn't that entrapment or something?"

"No law against feeding false information." Braxton turned once again to Warren. "The shoe print," he explained. "I had no idea what story Mrs. Beaumont told you, but I figured it probably didn't involve another man being there when Jimbo died."

"Didn't you ever think I might actually have done it?"

"Nope." He pointed a finger at Roberta and smiled. "Your wife can be very convincing. She said you weren't capable of murder."

Warren found the word wife without the ex in front of it strangely comforting.

Angel shifted, his elbow slamming down on the filing cabinet. The man breathed with a low-throated growl.

What Roberta had said was that he didn't have the courage to commit murder, even to save the woman he loved. She was right. It was the only time his lack of courage had served him well.

"But, Spivey, you're not off the hook yet. I expect you realize we could charge you with a shitload of stuff here, like hindering an investigation, lying in a sworn statement…" The sheriff waved his hand in the air, indicating several etceteras.

Warren blinked, his eyes gritty. Still wearing the same clothes he'd been arrested in, his skin itched. He hadn't slept more than a nod in over two days, and it would soon be morning. He was too damn tired to care if Braxton was yanking his chain.

"But you won't charge him, will you," Roberta answered for him, her words like a warm blanket draped across his shoulders. Until he realized she looked at Angel as she spoke.

"It's not up to me. The district attorney will decide."

Suddenly uninterested in the threat of future jail time, Warren stopped listening. Instead he watched the way Angel's eyes traveled the planes of Roberta's face. There was something in that look, something...intimate.

He recalled everything the sheriff had told him earlier. Kent English kidnapped Roberta. Unarmed, Angel braved the lion's den to rescue her. What the sheriff hadn't clarified was why Angel would bother.

Warren's blood turned to sludge in his veins. Lightheaded, his head spun. "Roberta, I have to talk to you. Outside."

"Her name's Bobbie." Voice low, harsh, Angel impaled him with a dark gaze. That look implied a host of crimes left unmentioned, as if he knew Warren had emotionally deserted Roberta years before he'd left her for Cookie.

"I don't think we're done yet, Warren," Roberta said, always the peacemaker.

Braxton regarded him with an unreadable expression. "We can finish this in the morning. You're free to go." Then, after an intentional pause, he finished, "For now." The last implication being the proverbial "Don't leave town."

Warren had no intention of leaving Cottonmouth. All he wanted was to lie down, sleep, perhaps never to wake up—after he learned what right Nick Angel had to study Roberta with that disturbingly possessive gaze and to tell him what his own wife's name was.

He stood. Roberta rose slowly beside him, steadying herself a moment on the back of the chair. Angel pushed himself off the filing cabinet, wrapped a big hand around her forearm, his fingers dark, yet protective, against her pale flesh. Over her head he flashed Warren an irritated scowl.

"You need to go home and rest, Bobbie," Angel said softly.

"I'll only be a minute."

Warren needed more than a minute. He felt frighteningly superfluous as Roberta looked up at the man. And why did her statement sound as if she intended to go home with Angel?

The room seemed to whirl around him, and he feared that with Roberta, the balance sheet lay heavily in the other man's favor.

He made it out into the hall without stumbling. Seeming as loud as the clang of his cell door, the latch clicked as Roberta closed the door behind them. The hall outside the sheriff's office was empty, though out in the main room, phones rang, computers buzzed, insults flew and the department dealt with the aftermath of Cookie's arrest.

"What do you need, Warren?"

Need? Three months ago Roberta wouldn't even have had to ask.

"I'm sorry about all this, Roberta." He winced at the inadequacy of the statement.

She crossed her arms, scuffed at the scarred floor with her shoe, then looked at him. "I know you are. I'm sorry, too. There are a lot of things I should have done differently."

"You mean when we were married?"

She blinked. "No. I mean since you left."

"I was wrong to do that, Roberta." He snorted softly. "Oh, not because Cookie turned out to be…" He glanced at her. God, her eyes were so green. And clear. Not hidden and devious like Cookie's. "Not because she was using me."

Roberta said nothing. The low murmur of indistinguishable voices drifted through the glass in the sheriff's door.

Warren dragged in a breath and plunged on. "I was searching for something. I thought seeing her again would get her out of my system, would allow me to put the past where it belonged."

"You wanted her to tell you it wasn't your fault. That she didn't leave you because you were a bad guy. You wanted her to see what a success you'd made of your life, what a great guy you were. You never wanted closure, Warren."

She spoke with the wisdom of having looked death in the face. Or maybe she'd known that all along.

His eyes roved her face, familiar yet so foreign. "I wish you'd told me that."

"I did, Warren. You just didn't hear."

She was right. "I'm sorry."

She ran a finger down his cheek. "You're tired. You need to get some rest."

He wanted to ask her to come with him. Back home. To San Francisco. To their old life. But he was looking to her for the same thing he'd looked to Cookie. A solution to his problems. Someone to tell him he hadn't fucked up as badly as he thought. He realized that he had to find the elusive cure all on his own. "I made a mistake leaving you, Roberta. You're a good woman. You gave me more than I ever deserved. And you deserved more from me than I ever gave."

She stepped forward, wrapped her arms around him and held him close. Her warmth, her sweet fragrance, the feel of her in his arms undid him. He almost begged her to come back to him.

Then she stood firmly on her feet again, and the moment passed. "Thank you, Warren. I hope someday you find what you're looking for. Are you going back to San Francisco?"

"No. I think I'll stay here."

"It's going to be hard, after everything that's happened. People might not want you to do their taxes."

"I think maybe I'm tired of doing taxes. I'd like to look for something else."

"What do you want to do?"

He sighed, tipped his head back and contemplated the fluorescent lights. Once, long ago, he'd wanted to build sports cars. And sometimes, working late into the night on his Healey, he'd dreamed about restoring cars for other people. "I'm not sure."

"We both had the same problem, Warren, living a life we didn't want. We just never knew what we really wanted."

She put them together in the same boat. A gracious thing to do under the circumstances. "What about you, Roberta?"

She smiled. And for the first time, he didn't see a cloud behind it. "You know, I've discovered it doesn't matter. Being a waitress isn't so bad. But who knows?" She touched his arm. "I'll be around if you need me."

He didn't ask about Nick Angel. He didn't want to know.

"YOU OKAY?"

"Why the hell wouldn't I be?" But Nick knew Brax was talking about Kent. Somehow, what Kent had done didn't seem to matter anymore. His significance had faded. Even the rage that had gripped him had ratcheted down to mere disgust. "Bobbie's alive. That's all that's important."

"Bobbie's alive, but a good man is dead," Brax said, then sat silent in his ancient leather chair, his expression unreadable. He recrossed his booted feet on the desktop, and when he finally spoke, Kent and Jimbo were no longer the issue. "Think she'll go back to her husband?"

Elbow on the filing cabinet, Nick shoved a hand through his hair. He didn't have an answer to Brax's question. Bobbie's shadow played on the glass door. He wanted to yank it open, pick her up and carry her home. His home.

"You can never tell with women," he said.

"So, why didn't you tell me about Cookie's little story? Might have saved us a lot of trouble if you had."

"I thought it was a bid for sympathy. I didn't think she was going to use it as an excuse to kill her husband."

"The story would have had a different ending if Warren Spivey had been another kind of man."

"You mean if he'd had more spine?" He used Bobbie's word.

"Less integrity, I was thinking."

Nick gaped. "Integrity? He dumped his wife. He was having an affair."

Brax raised one brow and left it at that.

Nick went on the defensive. "I never said I had a whole helluva lot of integrity, either."

"And that's why I took Jimbo's side." The words lay between them.

Being pissed as hell at Brax made it easier to gloss over the fact that he had done a pretty goddamn scummy thing to Jimbo. He'd had all the excuses, that Cookie came on to him, that he hadn't known she was Jimbo's wife, that he'd thrown her out as soon as he'd learned. But, just as with Bobbie that first day in his yard, when Cookie approached him in the bar, he'd seen that telltale band of white skin. And he'd decided not to ask why she'd removed the ring. He hadn't cared whether it was divorce, widowhood or poaching. He'd only wanted to get laid.

"You were always the one that was right, Brax. That's why you've always pissed me off." Brax would see it for the apology it was. They wouldn't talk about Mary Alice. That was done, too. "Thanks for backing me up tonight."

"Couldn't let you get yourself killed." Brax toyed with a pen from the desk. "You shouldn't have gone in there alone."

The only thing he'd been thinking was that Bobbie would surely die if he didn't. "What would you have done?"

Brax didn't need to answer. He'd have done exactly the same thing under equal circumstances. Instead he said, "You better treat her right, or you'll have to deal with me."

Nick would treat her better than anyone ever had. If he got the chance. She'd walked into his life a little over a week ago. He'd felt he'd known her a lifetime. Facing death together speeded up the getting-to-know-you stage. He didn't want to imagine his life without her. An inescapable truth he couldn't put into words for Brax. He hid his emotion behind banter. "I don't think she needs you to take care of her."

"Nope. Probably not. She does a damn fine job of taking care of everyone, herself included."

Nick glanced to the door. The shadows beyond it merged. Nick's head started to pound. He forced his eyes back to Brax.

"Not just him," Brax said with a nod of his head toward the door. "You, too. Heard the latest rumor?"

Nick shook his head, still trying to digest Brax's comment.

"Seems she gave you an alibi for Tuesday night."

"Tuesday night?" Jimbo had been killed on Monday. What the hell was Tuesday?

"Yeah. Tuesday. You know, that girl that disappeared up in Saskatoon County?"

"Hadn't heard a thing about it."

"Seems a few of our eloquent female citizens were looking at you as the culprit. Being the local serial killer and all."

"Jesus."

"But Bobbie got up there in front of God, Eugenia, Patsy, good old Marjorie Holmes, and the whole damn Hair Ball and told them you were with her Tuesday night. All night."

The air seemed to squeeze from his lungs.

"The story's all over town." Brax went on as if he

couldn't see the stunned effect his speech was having. "On the way back from Jimbo's autopsy up in Red Cliff this afternoon…" He glanced down at his watch. "Make that yesterday afternoon. I made a stop by the Saskatoon County Sheriff. Seems the little gal ran away from home. They found her in San Francisco."

"So, that's where you were when they took Bobbie." Nick shuddered to think what would have happened if Brax hadn't come right back.

"Yeah." Brax's eyes glittered. "So, you're off the hook in more ways than one. But mostly because of Bobbie."

Bobbie, who'd told Eugenia she'd spent the night with the serial killer.

"Why would Bobbie do that?" He could only hope it was because…

Brax just looked at him. "Maybe you have your head up your ass where Bobbie Jones is concerned." Brax stood, shook his pant legs down. "She's not going back to him, you know."

Nick didn't say a thing.

"Are you in love with her?"

Before Nick could formulate a good answer, a knock rattled the glass. Bobbie stuck her head inside. "Can we go home now?"

Her husband stood in the hall behind her.

"I'll need you in again tomorrow," Brax answered, then glanced at the calendar on his desk. "Or today. How about I drop Spivey off? And you'll have to go with Nick, since we'll need your car for a while longer. I'm sure he'll be more than happy to take you home." He flicked a glance at Nick. "Since you live across the street."

Nick found he was holding his breath waiting for her answer.

"That sounds fine." Then she looked at him and smiled.

Hell, yes, he was in love with her.

But who would she choose?

THE ENGINE RUMBLED through her for long moments after Nick shut off the car. Her body still hadn't recovered from watching Kent English hold a gun on Nick. Bobbie wasn't sure it ever would. She also didn't know how long she could keep on faking that she was okay.

Something had to give way soon.

She closed her eyes, let the warm night air and the darkness gather round her in the close confines of the car. The faint scent of Nick's remaining musky cologne teased her nostrils. She didn't want to move.

"I'm sorry about your friend."

"I'm over it."

Sure he was. "He really didn't deserve you."

"But maybe I deserved him."

She rolled her head on the seat to look at him. He was nothing more than a dark shape. Nick deserved a lot more than backstabbing, but she didn't think he'd accept that fact no matter what she said. "Thank you for coming for me."

"It was my fau—"

"Don't say it," she said, cutting through his blame. "It was them. All them."

She heard him swallow. "How are you feeling?" He spoke in a hushed tone befitting the near-dawn hour.

"Fine," she lied, hiding once more behind her closed lids. Her head still ached.

In those few moments with Warren, she knew she

could have said the word and they'd have returned to their old life. But you couldn't regain the past, whether it had been twenty years or three months.

Warren had left her searching for answers. He had yet to find them. And she had yet to find her own. She only knew she didn't want to be lonely anymore. If you were with a man, you darn well better not be lonely. Being by yourself was better.

She wondered if Nick could ease the loneliness. If he'd want to. The fear she'd experienced in Jimbo's lodge lingered. What would she have done if she'd lost him? It didn't seem possible that she could feel this way about a man she'd met a few days ago.

"Did he beg your forgiveness and ask you to go back to San Francisco?"

A tightrope of tension stretched between them. She felt Nick's eyes on her, and seethed with the need to ask if he wanted her to stay here.

"It's where you belong," he said slowly, as if searching for every word. "You were happy before all this shit went down."

She hadn't been happy in a long, long time.

She turned then and looked at him. Nick faced the faded head-high wood fence as he spoke. "He's probably regretting his midlife crisis."

"It wasn't a midlife crisis. He's always been this way." She hoped Warren could change that, but she wasn't so sure.

Nick wrapped the fingers of one hand around the wheel. His knuckles stretched, whitened, then he eased his grip and stroked the leather cover.

Bobbie was suddenly sick to death of the little white lies she told everyone to make them feel comfortable, especially the ones she'd told herself. She was tired of choosing each word to keep the peace, making decisions based on what others wanted her to do. She'd left the biggest thing out of her confession to Nick. If Warren hadn't left her, she would have gone on trying to make him want her until the day she died. Because starting over, possibly failing at anything, or everything, terrified her. That, not Warren, was the reason she'd never had children. And that's why she would have gone on with her life the way it was if Warren had never found Cookie. It was easier to stick with what she had, what she knew. Familiarity was safety, even if she'd been drowning in loneliness.

She hated that weak woman. Roberta. What she craved was Bobbie, the woman who stood up in the Hair Ball and told the truth no one wanted to hear; the woman who wouldn't tread lightly with Nick.

She sat up, her head swimming with the movement. *Swallow it, I'm busy.* The thought gave her courage. "I don't want to go back to Warren. I don't want to be an accountant. I'm staying here. In Cottonmouth. I belong *here.*"

Nick rubbed his hands on his pant legs.

"I'm going to open a coffee shop, like Starbucks, but better." The idea had always been there, but fear stood in her way. Now she let her dreams blossom. "Mine will be different. I'm going to rent out classic movies, too, just classics, so everyone can enjoy them the way I do. And I've got all sorts of ideas for how everyone in Cottonmouth can steal back all the business from that darn old minimall. We'll make Cottonmouth special again, with a hometown feel those big chains can't offer."

Her excitement mounted, and the nausea receded.

She stuck her neck out farther. "And you wanna know something else?" She didn't care if he didn't, she'd tell him anyway. "I belong with you."

"I…" His profile rigid, he put both hands on the wheel this time. "I was going to remind you that you've only known me a week." He laid his head on his hands and looked at her. "But fuck the week. I know what I want. I knew it when I got that note and thought you were going to die. You do belong with me."

"What about Mary Alice?"

"Who?" His eyes dropped. He knew exactly who.

Bobbie's stomach plunged. But she wouldn't keep her mouth shut about it. She couldn't, not after Warren and Cookie. Not after spending fifteen years feeling like she was treading on burning coals, hopping around Warren's feelings as if they had the power to scorch her soles or her very soul.

"You were in love with her in high school."

"Oh." He rolled his eyes. "*That* Mary Alice. I wasn't in love with her. I had a crush on her. That's a long time ago."

"I shouldn't have to remind you that Cookie was a long time ago, too. But that didn't matter to Warren."

"You're right." His gaze caressed her face. "I'm sorry. For me, it *was* a long time ago. And it did end."

"Did you get her pregnant and make her have an abortion?" She held her breath.

He let his breath out with a whoosh. "You're the only one I'll answer that question for. No, I didn't get her pregnant. I don't know who got her pregnant. At the time I thought it was Brax. But twenty years has shown me I was probably wrong about that. She wanted to get an abortion. I gave her the money. I didn't have any right to tell her she shouldn't do it. So I went with her."

"But everyone found out anyway. And they thought it was you. Why didn't you tell them?"

"If I'd made it clear I wasn't the one, her parents never would have left her alone about who the father was. It was just easier for her that way. And I didn't care what they thought."

But he *had* cared. And that had been the beginning of his fuck-you attitude that Brax talked about. He'd wanted them to believe he wouldn't have done that to Mary Alice.

But no one had.

She cupped his chin. "Thank you for telling me."

"You just wanted to make sure it wasn't Warren all over again."

God, he actually understood. "I don't want to live with ghosts anymore."

He turned his lips into her hand and kissed her palm. "No ghosts, I swear."

She wriggled across the seat, leaned over the gear-shift. "Do you really think it's possible to fall in love in a week?"

"Yeah. I do." He stroked a hand down her cheek to the crook of her neck and let it rest there. "I have never felt this way about any other woman. Tonight I would have done anything to save you. And when I thought I might not be able to—"

She put her fingertips to his lips, then closed her eyes until she'd stuffed down the memory of that gun at his head. "I don't want to think about that anymore."

His fingers twitched at her throat. "Marry me, Bobbie."

She thought of all the things that stood in the way.

Not the least of which was a healthy dose of fear about making a mistake. Again. She stuffed the fear down, too, and simply enumerated the problems. She refused to ignore them this time.

"I think I'm past the stage of wanting to have children."

Nick caressed her shoulder. "I'd probably end up raising serial killers, so it's better that way."

"I'm forty."

"I like older women."

"I'm not divorced yet."

"You will be." The corner of his mouth rose with a surety she knew he hadn't felt until that moment. "Any more objections?"

She'd hit all the highlights, though there must be a million more. All of them fear-based. Roberta Jones Spivey had made all her life decisions based on fear. And they hadn't turned out worth a darn. Why not, just this once, make a decision based on gut instinct?

Her gut said that Nick would never leave her lonely.

"Jump, Bobbie. I'll catch you, I promise."

Take a chance. Stop playing it safe.

"All right," she whispered, "I'll jump."

Then she clambered over the gearshift, squeezed past the steering wheel into his lap and sealed her fate with a kiss.

"So," she said, lip to lip, "now that you've asked me to marry you, can I see your paintings?" Maybe someday she'd tell him she'd already sneaked a peek.

He chuckled against her mouth. "Don't you want to watch *Buffy*?"

"No." She nibbled his bottom lip.

He grinned and pulled back to look down at her. "How about your favorite movie, *Laura*?"

She punched his arm lightly. "No."

"All right. You can see the paintings. But the price is your posing for the next one."

She tilted her head, a little thrill racing up her spine. "With or without clothes?"

He merely raised one adorably devilish eyebrow.

EPILOGUE

ACROSS THE TOWN SQUARE, Mayor Wylie Meade wound through the crowd of festival-goers, his large frame tucked into an extraordinarily flexible set of lederhosen. A long feather bobbed on the hat perched atop his head.

In the center of the square, on a makeshift stage, three accordion players squeezed out a rousing polka. On the portable dance floor in front, couples dressed in colorful national costumes flowed across the fake parquet, their heels adding another dimension to the music onstage.

Nick was sure he'd been dropped into a Lawrence Welk nightmare. Bobbie stuck her hand in his and pulled him past the row of food stands. Boiled cabbage perfumed the air, the spice of meatballs and other ethnic delights layered beneath it. Nick had never enjoyed a day more. He'd never enjoyed a woman more. And he'd go on enjoying this one for the rest of his life.

He knew he was grinning like a sap. A sap in love. He didn't give a damn as long as she was his.

"Nick," Mayor Meade called, fluttering his hand above a boisterous sea of unattended teenagers.

Nick tucked Bobbie beneath his arm, then wiped away a touch of mustard from her lip, the remains of her Polish hot dog. He kissed the tip of her nose. Life couldn't be better. Even if Wylie Meade was bearing down on him like a runaway semi.

"What do you suppose he wants?"

"Rumor around town has it he wants to ask you a favor." Bobbie stuck her ice-cream cone in front of his mouth for a lick. Lord, the things that woman could do with ice cream on her tongue.

"A favor?"

"Be nice," she whispered as the mayor waddled closer, "and I'll be very nice to you tonight."

"If you put it like that." *Happy* was not a word he'd used to describe his life, until Bobbie. The smile on his face was no phony.

"Nick, my boy, so glad you made it to our little festival."

After Brax revealed Cookie's scheme, Nick had, somehow, become the man of the hour. The mayor slapped him on the back.

"Bobbie wouldn't let me miss it. She's taking all the credit for the magnificent decorations." Nick let his eyes rove the gay square. Three-dimensional cardboard accordions and facsimiles of Lawrence Welk hung from strings anchored in the surrounding trees. Streamers of gold and green flapped in the warm June breeze. Next week they would come down to make way for the July Fourth parade, but for now Bobbie beamed.

"She's done a bang-up job, stepping in after…the Cookie calamity."

Nick almost laughed, erased the smile seconds short of disaster. Wylie Meade was totally serious. "This town will forever be grateful to the two of you."

Nick wasn't completely sure why. He'd almost gotten the two of them killed. Brax was the one who saved the day.

"Shucks, it was nothing, Mayor."

Bobbie elbowed him in the ribs, then turned a magnificent smile on the mayor. "You had something you wanted to ask Nick?"

Wylie cleared his throat and puffed out his chest, only to exhale with a grunt as Eugenia Meade's shriek cut across the music. "Wylie Meade, don't you dare start without me."

For one moment the square fell silent, the only sound being Eugenia's stertorous breathing as she picked up her skirts and careered across the tramped lawn.

Decked out in full costume, Eugenia clung to her husband's arm for support as she gulped air like a fish. The seams of her green suede dress threatened to give way, and her white blouse, buttoned to the collar and fastened with a brooch, appeared to be strangling her. Her cheeks blazed red with exertion.

Bobbie raised a brow at him. Nick drew the line at mouth-to-mouth.

"All right, I'm ready," Eugenia gasped.

Wylie did the throat clearing and chest puffing again, then said with theatrical majesty, "It would be Cottonmouth's honor, and my personal pleasure, if you would consent to supply a painting or two for the renovated city hall."

Hell. That was the last thing he'd expected. He wondered how many nights Wylie would have to go without sex for this one. Ah, that was his secret; he *wanted* to forgo Eugenia's favors.

Three weeks ago he would have told the mayor, and Eugenia, to stuff it. But that was before Bobbie came to town. Now her eyes danced with excitement, and she bounced on her open-toed sandals.

Eugenia stared at him with beady, expectant eyes. What the hell was he supposed to make of that? "Mayor, I'm really not sure my work will fit a city hall atmosphere."

"Of course they will." Wylie's voice boomed megaphone loud.

"Have you ever seen them?" Nick ventured.

Eugenia could no longer keep her mouth shut. "Wylie, you're botching the whole thing. Of course we've seen your paintings, dear. We drove up to that big Borders store they have in Red Cliff. And there were your calendars. Though why they're selling calendars in June, I'll never know. What am I going to do, for heaven's sake, put them in the drawer for six months?" She tapped Bobbie's arm. "A little secret, I always buy mine on January first, half off then, you know." She switched her attention back to Nick. "We loved what we saw, and of course, Wylie wants to put them in the big hall." Big was in the eye of the beholder. The Taj Ma'Wylie was no Taj Mahal.

"I'm thinking four paintings, at least, aren't you, dear?" Already having made her decision, Eugenia didn't wait for the mayor's agreement. She leaned forward, pursing her lips close to Nick's ear. "But do you think we can skip the bare breasts? After all, school children do tour the big hall, you know."

Nick raised a brow. "I think I could add a nice gossamer overlay without compromising my art."

"Oh, you're such a good boy. And I've been wanting to tell you what a lovely job you've done with your mother's garden. She'd be so pleased."

Not if she knew the amount of roadkill that was still buried there. Maybe it would make good fertilizer.

"Thank you, ma'am. Bobbie helped me plant the flowers this week."

Bobbie looked at him. Excessive politeness was not his thing, but with Eugenia Meade, what else could a man do?

"You've got to plant bulbs, too. Your mother adored bulbs."

"Yes, Mrs. Meade." Bobbie was now openly smiling at him. He'd get her. Tonight. Maybe this afternoon. Maybe...

Eugenia didn't even give him a chance for a decent fantasy. "But what I really wanted to talk about was that whole horrible Cookie calamity. You were so brave, my dear." Eugenia clasped Bobbie's hand in both hers, squeezing, then reached impulsively for Nick's, bringing him into the fold, so to speak.

"And you, sir. Why, you're the town hero, saving us all from that horrible Kent English and that woman. Why, I never liked her from the moment she came to town. She was...shifty. I'm sure they were planning to murder us all in our beds after they got done with poor Jimbo."

If Wylie Meade was a Mack truck, Eugenia was a locomotive. Nick felt himself slipping into the twilight zone. From local serial killer to local hero in one short week.

"And to think that English boy was the one throwing that dreadful roadkill in your yard just to make sure we all thought there was something sinister about you. Why, I hear the sheriff retched when they searched that boy's car trunk. Seems he wasn't too good at cleaning up after himself." She tittered as if she'd said something clever. "But I never believed the stories about you, of course. Why, just before poor Jimbo got whacked, I was telling Marjorie Holmes that everyone was misjudging you."

Eugenia stopped only because she'd long since run out of breath. Her eyes had started to bulge.

Bobbie squeezed his fingers painfully. "As I recall, Mrs. Meade, you were ready to tell the sheriff that Nick had kidnapped that little girl up in Saskatoon."

Eugenia gasped and put her hand to her chest. "Why, I do believe you've gotten me mixed up with someone else, dear." She patted Bobbie's arm, who jerked away from the touch. Not that Eugenia noticed. "I did my best to stop those stories, believe you me."

Bobbie's eyes fired up with that protective light Nick knew so well. She opened her mouth to do further battle on his behalf.

He laced her fingers with his and cut her off. "I appreciate your taking my side, Mrs. Meade, believe you me."

The woman didn't notice the sarcasm, but the corner of Bobbie's mouth rose in acknowledgment.

"And did you hear Kent English is spilling his guts about every nasty little thing he's done since he was a boy? He even admitted *he* got poor Mary Alice Turner pregnant. Why he allowed you to take the blame all these years, we'll never know."

Bobbie tugged, shooting him a look that said she'd believed him all along. But why the hell hadn't Brax said something?

Because it was the past. Done. They'd silently agreed on that the night Kent tried to kill him.

Intent on her gossip, Eugenia didn't notice the signals between them. "And why that boy's bothering to clear it all up is beyond me. I hear tell the sheriff can't shut him up now that he's started talking. I wonder if somehow he'll use the Mary Alice thing to go for some kind of insanity plea. You know, as if that unfortunate event mentally unhinged him and everything else he did was as a result." Not giving anyone a chance to contradict her, Eugenia launched into a new thought. "But I hear the two of you are getting married. We're all so delighted."

Bobbie raised their clasped hands. "As soon as the divorce is final."

She wasn't hiding anything anymore. She'd moved in to his house and thumbed her nose at the puritans of Cottonmouth. Eugenia liked her, anyway. Everyone did.

"Oh, and speaking of your husband, I've heard that poor Beau is renting him space in his garage."

Bobbie met Nick's glance. "He and Beau are going to do classic car restoration. Since Jimbo was so good to him in the will, Beau's starting his station up again."

"I thought your husband was an accountant."

She rolled her eyes at him. "Nobody *is* an accountant. It's just a profession. He loves old cars. He'll do fine."

Too long out of the limelight, Eugenia started her locomotive rolling again. "Well, and isn't there that law that you can't profit from your crimes. So that woman—"

"The Cookie Monster," Bobbie supplied.

Eugenia gasped and dragged Bobbie's free hand between her ample breasts. "My dear, that is absolutely perfect. Why didn't I think of that?" By noon she would have convinced herself, and the town, that she had. "Well, I don't think that woman will end up getting a thing. And what can she do with it in prison, anyway? She'll probably end up being some big mama's bitch."

"Eugenia!" Wylie roared.

Eugenia flapped a fleshy hand. "It's true, that's what happens. I see it on TV all the time. Now Beau gets everything. The man's a godsend. As poor Jimbo's executor, he's forgiving all the back rents. The Cookie Monster—" she beamed at the use of the newly claimed name "—was the one doing all the harassing anyway, not Jimbo. Why, Harry Bushman told me she was in there the week before Jimbo died, threatening Harry, no less, saying she'd make sure Jimbo kicked him out. After sixty years of Bushman's being there. Well, I never." She broke off long enough to fan herself in disgust. "Jimbo wouldn't have done it. Why, the minimall was all the Cookie Monster's idea in the first place. She pushed Jimbo into building it against his better judgment. But that Beau." Eugenia fluttered her eyelashes. "He's a fine one. He's organizing a committee to renovate Cottonmouth."

"Renovate," Bobbie squeaked. "I like it the way it is. So *Ozzie and Harriet.*" Nick had caught her sneaking a few *Ozzie and Harriet* reruns.

"It'll still be *Ozzie and Harriet,* dear, but he's got marketing plans that will help some of our businesses get back on their feet. The man's a font of ideas."

"What about a coffee house?" Nick decided to start Bobbie's ball rolling.

Eugenia tipped her head. "We already have a coffee shop."

Wylie shook her arm. "Coffee *house,* Eugenia. It's different. Like a Starbucks."

"Bobbie's already talked to Beau about that place on the corner of Main and Broadway," Nick supplied.

"Mavis is helping me with the start-up." There was

a little problem of on-hand cash. Bobbie would have had to use everything she had, with nothing left over for working capital until the cash flow improved. See, he was learning accounting terminology.

"Oh, my dear, that's wonderful. When are you two going to start having babies?" Everyone cleared their throat, looked up, down, around. Eugenia didn't get it. "Goodness, what am I saying, you're not even married yet. But did you hear that Mavis is letting Beau move back into the house? They're going to renew their vows." She clapped her hands to her cheeks. "You could have a double wedding." She grabbed Wylie's arm. "Darling, wouldn't that be wonderful?"

Nick thought about puking.

Suddenly Eugenia raised a hand, flapping vigorously. "Oh yoo-hoo, Patsy, we're over here."

Patsy had foresworn the native Accordion Festival costume. In white skirt and red blazer, she looked like…a real estate agent. Poor woman.

Ignoring Eugenia, Patsy grabbed Bobbie's arm. Her lipstick leaked into the lines fanning out around her mouth. "I have found the perfect little dress for Sunday service down at the church thrift. You must come down immediately and try it on."

Nick thought of that little number Bobbie had worn to church, oh, about two weeks ago. Personally, he thought that was perfect.

"Now?" Bobbie asked, while Eugenia huffed at losing center stage.

"It's only $4.99," Patsy rushed on, excitement adding extra wrinkles around her mouth. "It's got a blue tag, and today is fifty percent off blue tags. Someone's going to snap it up."

"But—"

"You can't beat this, Bobbie, I'm telling you. A pretty mock turtleneck. It's long." She looked at Bobbie's long legs, totally bare to midthigh where her short shorts ended. "Calf length," she whispered, as if she expected only Bobbie to hear or understand. "And since all the essentials will be covered, I don't suppose the reverend will mind the leopard print."

Nick wouldn't mind seeing Bobbie in animal print. Maybe some matching leopard panties.

But hell, they were talking about a dress, for church, with Patsy Bell Sapp's approval. Leopard print. It could mean only one thing, Bobbie had been accepted.

Eugenia pursed her lips. "Leopard won't do for Jimbo's memorial service." Which was tomorrow morning, attendance by all required.

"You're right, Eugenia." Patsy tapped her fingers to her chin, assessing Bobbie's figure as if she'd suddenly morphed from real estate agent to fashion designer. "Dear, you're going to have to come down to the church right away. Eugenia, we'll need your help." Patsy winked, her lashes sticking a moment. "Eugenia's a whiz with a sewing needle. There's a dress that might be suitable. But it's going to need taking in."

Then Patsy turned her full force on Nick. She hadn't spoken to him directly in more than twenty years. "Young man, do you have a suit?"

"Yes, ma'am." And damn, wasn't he lucky, or he'd be down at the church thrift with them.

"Then we're off." The women grabbed Bobbie's arms, forcing Nick to let go of her.

In the middle of the town square, an ancient crooner took the stage. Mayor Meade stood beside him watch-

ing Bobbie being dragged off by the Hair Ball's bouffant twins. Bobbie turned one last time, her lips round
with a silent scream. Patsy whispered in her ear.

"Well, boy," the mayor said, "how about I buy you
a beer?"

"I do feel a bit parched, Mayor. A beer would be nice,
thanks."

Nick realized he'd finally come home. Bobbie had
brought him there.

* * * * *

Be sure to watch for Brax's romance,
FOOL'S GOLD,
coming only to HQN Books in October 2005.

And now for a sneak preview, please turn the page.

CHAPTER ONE

"SHE'S A FIVE-MINUTE, man-on-top kind of woman. And I gotta say I'm not even sure if she has an orgasm."

Tyler Braxton cringed. "You know, I really don't think I should be hearing the lowdown on my sister's sex life." Especially not from his brother-in-law.

"This isn't about sex." A whine crept into Carl Felman's voice.

"Sorry." Brax spread his hands. "Must have been the word *orgasm* that gave me the impression."

"It's about our marriage."

What the hell had he gotten himself into? All Brax had wanted was a nice, uncomplicated, relaxing vacation.

Instead he entered a war zone.

Admittedly, it was a silent war, with both sides refusing to meet at the bargaining table or even talk to the other at all, for that matter. But it was war nonetheless.

Coming to Goldstone, Nevada, for his vacation was Bad Idea #1. The town's dusty streets had never been paved; the rusted hulks of dead cars outnumbered working vehicles two to one; and the only church he saw was made of corrugated steel like the Quonset huts that cropped up in the fifties.

Bad Idea #2 was staying with his sister at ground zero. He'd arrived that morning and learned one thing fast. A man couldn't win by choosing sides in a battle that wasn't his. The combatants, however, were equally determined he had to pick one. Or the other.

Being county sheriff back in the small California town of Cottonmouth was a cakewalk compared to this. He should have ignored his sister's e-mail inviting him to visit.

"I'm afraid she doesn't want me anymore." Carl's chin drooped close to the foam on his beer. "I don't ex-cite her."

Country music strained through the worn-out speak-ers, barely making it over the ka-ching of a slot machine in the back of the bar. Brax had thought going out for a friendly beer down at the Flood's End might ease the tension. Instead he'd heard more about his sister's love life than any brother should ever know.

"How long have you and Maggie been married?" The question was rhetorical; he knew exactly how long they'd been married. The Las Vegas wedding in Dr. Love's Chapel would forever live in his memory. Maybe the pink flamingos flanking the altar had something to do with that. Who in their right mind would want lawn ornaments at their wedding ceremony?

Carl took his time before replying, "Ten years."

"Well, things can get a bit...routine after ten years." A wild guess, since his own marriage hadn't lasted past five. Brax didn't know a damn thing that would help Carl. Or Maggie. He sure as hell didn't understand women on a romantic or emotional level. But then, what man truly did?

"Is that what happened to your marriage?" Carl asked.

Damn. He'd opened himself wide for that one.

The once-padded chair he sat in had long since lost its resilience beneath too many butts. The tabletop was gummy with age, elbow grease and sweaty palms. Brax sat back and crossed his arms over his chest.

Then he ducked Carl's question completely. "Not very crowded here tonight, is it?"

Carl's glance strayed over Brax's shoulder and not for the first time that evening. No small wonder when one considered the woman seated at the far end of the bar. Brax shifted in his chair for a better look.

She'd surrounded herself with three books opened flat on the bar top. She tapped a pencil against full lips, then hunched over to write furiously in a spiral notebook. Her blond hair fell forward, caressing her shoulders. Flipping a book page, she underlined something, scratched out a line in her notebook and began scribbling again.

"It's Sunday," was all Carl said.

And Sunday meant…what? Not that Carl's answer mattered, since Brax had only been trying to avoid answering any questions.

"You boys need a refresher?" the white-haired bartender called. A good salesman always asks, even when he sees half-full beers. Obviously, he considered theirs half-empty.

"We're fine, Doodle," Carl answered, once more sucking at the foam that hadn't yet dissipated.

"What about you, Whitey?" Doodle tipped his head at the lone man seated at the bar.

Whitey's garbled, scratchy answer was incomprehensible, but the bartender grabbed his mug and held it beneath the tap. Half foam, half beer, he slammed it

down on the scarred wooden bar without spilling a drop.
Whitey tucked his long white beard to his chest, sipped,
licked his mustache and sighed as he closed his eyes, savoring the brew. When he spoke once more, his words
were still indistinguishable, as though rocks filled his
mouth.

"Whitey, I swear, you have *the* most amazing way
with words," the blonde said, her answer giving no clue
as to what the man had uttered. "I really think you
should be a writer."

Whitey sat straighter, smoothed his beard and, Brax
could see in the mirror behind the bar, fairly glowed
with her compliment. The man mumbled something,
maybe a thank-you, and the blonde beamed back at
him with a heart-flipping smile. Brax had the feeling
she often paid the old man sweet, unsolicited compliments he soaked up like a sponge.

Slapping her books closed, she piled them up and
hugged the stack to her chest. Climbing down from her
stool to land on spike-heeled shoes, she pivoted and
headed straight for their table.

Brax lost his voice. Hell, he might have lost his mind.
She moved with the graceful glide of a runway model.
Gorgeous blond hair spread over her shoulders, bounc-
ing with a riot of curls.

She stopped close enough for him to draw in her light
perfume. Subtle. Intoxicating.

Sliding into the chair beside Carl, she plopped the
pile of reading material onto the table. "Did you get my
e-mail?"

Red seeped into Carl's face, spreading across his
cheeks and rising to his receding hairline.

Glancing first at Brax, she touched Carl's rigid arm.

"Oops, sorry, didn't mean to embarrass you in front of your friend."

Carl could do nothing more than nod his forgiveness. Any man would forgive her everything when she smiled like that.

She gave Carl's forearm another soothing pat. "Are you all right? You look a little flushed. Mr. Doodle," she called, "I think Carl needs a glass of water."

A mason jar filled with ice and water miraculously appeared at her elbow. She pushed it to Carl and curled his fingers around the glass.

Though his delivery was made, the bartender didn't leave the side of the table. "Did ya figure out a witty euphemism for tallywhacker, Simone?"

Simone, a very classy name.

A slight blush colored her flawless cheekbones. "Why, no, Mr. Doodle, I didn't," she said, then politely added, "but thank you for being concerned."

"I call it the doodle," the bartender continued. "I ask Mrs. Doodle if she'd like to be diddled by the doodle." He cackled. "Works every time."

Simone smiled. "Well, that's wonderful, Mr. Doodle, but I think our conversation is further embarrassing Carl and his friend. My mother would be horrified. She always says a lady never talks about..." She nipped her lower lip. "Um...about tallywhackers in mixed company." She glanced at Brax. "Especially when we haven't been formally introduced."

Lush eyelashes framed her hazel eyes, and her nose tilted endearingly, but it was her smile that damn near knocked a man's socks off. Sweet and genuine, it was the same one she'd given Whitey as she praised him.

"I'll introduce ya," Doodle announced. "This is the

brother-in-law we've all heard about." He tapped Brax's shoulder. "Sorry, son, I forgot your name."

"Tyler Braxton." He stuck out his hand. "But everyone calls me Brax."

She shook it with a firm grip of soft, warm flesh.

She leaned closer and said softly, "Mr. Doodle didn't mean to embarrass you. He's really just a sweet old pussycat."

"Ooh, she called me sweet," Doodle cooed. "I think I'm gonna faint." Then he waggled his bushy white eyebrows. "Now that you've been introduced, can we ask him what he calls *his* tallywhacker?"

Brax didn't know whether to laugh or run screaming from the bar. He was the closest he'd been to blushing since elementary school when he'd gotten caught sending Mary Alice Turner a love note.

Simone sat back and folded her arms beneath her breasts. Ogling women wasn't one of his pastimes, but Brax couldn't help himself. He looked. Briefly, very briefly. But one look was enough to make him lose his voice again.

"Mr. Doodle," she chided. "You really have to stop that." She nodded at Carl and patted his hand still curled around the water glass. "Carl is apoplectic over what *I* said, and Brax," she said with a gentle pucker of her lips, "is going to leave town thinking we have no manners here in Goldstone."

Brax wasn't sure he could think at all. The woman simply bowled him over. Beautiful? Spectacularly. Sexy? Definitely. But her smile, her sincere flattery of two old geezers, the way she said his name with that kiss-me pucker, those things held far more punch than the stunning package God had wrapped her in.

"Thank you for that delicious glass of wine, Mr. Doodle, but my mother always says a girl shouldn't overstay her welcome. So I'm off."

She stood and gathered her books in her arms before Brax could make a move to stop her. With a smile for the room at large, she sashayed out the door, leaving the bar in a vacuum.

Silence reigned in the small saloon at least a full minute before Brax found his voice. "Just who exactly was that woman?"

Carl busied himself with a slug of beer.

"Simone's our local porn queen," Doodle elucidated as he sidled back behind the bar.

Brax put his palm on the edge of the table and pushed back to look at the man over his shoulder. "Porn queen?" She was the furthest thing from sleaze he'd ever seen. And being a cop, he'd seen a lot.

The bartender nodded and beamed a toothy smile.

"She doesn't write porn," Carl muttered.

"So she's a *writer*, not an actress." Though most didn't refer to porn stars as actresses.

"Yeah. It's called *erotica*." Carl's face flushed an even deeper red.

"Isn't that just another name for housewife porn?" Brax had read the description somewhere. He couldn't imagine the beautiful Simone penning classless drivel.

"No. Her stuff is very—" Carl hesitated as if searching for the best descriptor "—tasteful."

It was Carl's reaction to Simone and the telltale stain on his face that unsettled the beer in Brax's stomach. Being a sheriff, Brax listened to what people *didn't* say in addition to what they did. He watched for more subtle nuances as he asked, "So, how do I get to read one of these 'little stories'?"

Carl slumped in his chair. Doodle answered the question. "She's got this really special Web site. You tell her your fantasy in simple terms, all the details you want her to be sure to include, then she writes a hot, hot story. The wife's always e-mailing her little snippets to work up."

Brax had never heard of anything like it. "She writes *custom* pornography?"

"It's *not* pornography," Carl snapped, still concentrating on his beer.

Why did it bother his brother-in-law so much when Brax described her "stories" as such? A man just didn't *blush* like that around a pretty woman unless his thoughts about her weren't exactly pure.

Damn. He did *not* want to believe Carl had been having impure imaginings about Simone Chandler, or worse that he'd acted on them.

Just a two-week vacation. That's all Brax had wanted. He hadn't taken one since his divorce. Things in Cottonmouth had gotten to him. A good man, a friend, had been murdered; Brax blamed himself for not reading the warning signs. He should have been able to stop it. That was his job, his obligation and his responsibility. One in which he'd failed. Miserably. He'd taken these two weeks to come to his senses so that he could get on with his duties. Two weeks would *have* to do. It was all the time he could allow himself away from Cottonmouth.

But he'd landed himself in the middle of a mess. His sister's marriage was on the rocks, he'd heard enough about her sex life to make him queasy, and he was attracted to the woman who just might be at the center of Carl and Maggie's "trouble."

Simone Chandler couldn't be more than thirty years old, and Carl was pushing fifty-five. Imagining her in bed with his brother-in-law was downright pornographic.

He had to prove it wasn't so. For his sister's sake, of course. He owed Maggie at least a minimal investigation.

He turned to Doodle. "What'd you say that Web address was?"

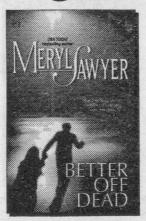